CAUGHT A VIBE

A LOVE IN THE QUARANTIMES NOVEL
BOOK ONE

EVA MOORE

For all of my online friends who got me through the Quarantimes with zoom calls, discord chats, and virtual hugs. Chapters 3, 6, 11, 13, 14, 15, and 29 are especially for you.

CHAPTER 1

PENNY

Any warrior knows the power in arming for battle, so I take my time with it. I adjust my red wig, carefully hiding any hint of my real hair, before smoothing on a bold red lip stain. Another layer of powdered armor for good measure ensures I won't be shiny for any photos or videos. In the age of cell phones and social media, there is always someone waiting to catch me off my game. Fuck the haters who try to make me feel bad for what I do. This work is important. I'm spreading love and joy to everyone. I'm practically Santa Claus, if Santa delivered orgasms.

By next year, this merry elf will be able to ship worldwide!

Tugging on the strapless bra I will regret by the end of the night, I encourage it to fight the good fight against gravity and keep my girls contained until I'm ready to set them free. Someone should really design a better strapless bra that won't try to run for my knees at the slightest encouragement. Someone who isn't already so busy. Someone who is not me. I write the idea in my planner anyway, before I set it aside. Today, I am laser-focused on my goal.

I pull the strapless body-con dress over my hips and up to my chest, carefully arranging the girls for maximum security. Straightening my hemline so it lies smooth against my thighs, I practice my lines with my reflection in the hotel mirror.

"I bet I can change your sex life forever."

"Five minutes to blow your mind."

"Best orgasms ever, I swear. Care for a demonstration?"

Nerves and excitement cycle through my body until I am tingling with anticipation. *Today, I'll share this secret part of myself with everyone, and they will love it. I will get the respect and acclaim I deserve.*

It's going to be epic.

My mental pep talk fails to calm the hornets in my stomach, so I run down my supply checklist for the day: cell phone, bump charger, wallet, repair makeup, granola bar, water bottle, extra underwear, day planner, promotional flyers and business cards.

There is something missing... Right! The lube!

Touching every item in its assigned place calms me and my chaotic thoughts. I am prepared. I can do this. Loading extra branded lube packets into my purse, I step into my killer heels on the first day of the rest of my career, ready to slay.

~

DASH

"This is ridiculous," I mutter as I show my badge at the entrance to the convention hall at the Grands Hotel. Smart home devices and wearables might be video game adjacent, but health devices? I'm just a lowly freelance writer for the gaming team at XPTech magazine. What the fuck do I know about the best step counters? I don't need another watch to yell at me to stand up more. I review video games. I sit for a living.

But the T-Con Tech Expo is the largest showcase of the year in the technology industry, in no small part due to it being hosted in Las Vegas in late January.

We all pull double or triple duty to cover the most buzzed-about devices and programming before the conference ends. Instead of getting to geek out in the gaming hall, I am literally miles away, in a sea of distraction, begging these articles to write themselves. I have ten booths to hit today, and my brain is not cooperating.

I put in my noise-canceling earbuds and look at the map, plotting my route for maximum efficiency, as if this will somehow keep me on track. Las Vegas is the absolute worst town for my ADHD on a good day. Add in all of the distractions of a technology trade show, and I'm doomed.

Diagnosed in middle school, I struggled to learn strategies to help me focus, but I've found a few that help keep me on track. Because my parents were in denial, I didn't try meds until I was grown. The side effects weren't worth the gains, so I've doubled down on systems and lists to get my work done, whether it's designing video games or writing about them.

Once upon a time, I dreamed of presenting my own game here on the biggest tech stage of the year. That dream imploded spectacularly, and I turned my job writing for my college newspaper into a freelance gig writing about other game developers' work instead. At least I get to keep my toe in the industry I love, even if I can't actually swim in that pool.

You could still be a game designer if you'd just played by the rules and tried harder. Instead you walked away from a dream job.

The voice in my head sounds remarkably like my father. Is this what they mean by gone but not forgotten? I shake my head and turn on my music to drown out my tangled emotions. This may not be my dream job, but it's a good one. And if I hustle just a little bit longer, I might get hired on full-time.

So what if I got the shittiest assignments at the con? I'll show them I can handle whatever they throw my way. I bounce on my toes, getting amped up for the day. *Stay focused and get through the list. Easier said than done when half of this list is going to bore me to tears, but I can do this.*

I round the corner to the first booth. Taking it in, the simple, clean design soothes my tired eyes. Cream curtains enclose the space, and two devices sit on elevated pedestals at the front of the booth. Simple, minimal, interesting. I check my list again, but there is no information. Just the name. MiO.

A woman at the back of the booth is deep in conversation with another woman wearing a press badge. She looks like the only person manning the display, so I settle in to explore on my own until she's free.

My fingers get curious, and I pick up the device. It's larger than a typical joystick. Is this some kind of accessibility modification? The large, round base sits heavy in my hand, and the buttons press against my palm. Why are they hidden underneath, instead of on top like other controllers?

I smooth my other hand up the wide handle. It reminds me of the old-school Atari controllers, redesigned with a curved, modern aesthetic. The light gray silicone exterior warms pleasantly against my skin, but the color choice is weird. It'll show a lot of wear and tear. One game session with Cheetos and this thing would be a mess. Maybe this was just the prototype. It would be cool to have other color options, maybe even to match favored avatars. I'd ask about it if the woman in charge would come this way.

I remove an earbud to signal I'm ready to listen. The ambient noise floods my head, and I take a deep breath and try to focus on the device in my hand.

I explore the top of the knob with my thumb, searching for the trigger button, but I find it with my index finger on the underside of the joystick. Interesting. I flick my finger back and forth over what feels like a marble underneath the silicone coating. Intriguing.

Pulling the stick back, I discover an impressive range of motion—forward, lateral, and a 360-degree swivel. Fascinating.

Maybe a new specialized controller for VR sim games? And the indent on the top of the base? Some kind of haptic feedback? Or an ergonomic thumb grip?

My list of questions grows.

It's not often a new device throws me, but this one has me stumped. I can't pin down the reasons for these design choices. With no epiphany imminent and my brain jonesing for answers, I impatiently glance over to see if the woman is free yet.

"So, what do you think?"

I spin to my right, startled, and find a different woman than the one I expected. She is stunning. The noisy hall fades as my hyperfocus kicks in, and she consumes my senses. Tall and curvy, this woman has long, bright red hair I'm pretty sure is a wig, but it's the intelligent eyes beneath the choppy bangs that fluster me. I glance down so I don't stare, and end up in troubled waters for my efforts. Her dress hugs her body, and sky-high heels tilt her hips and ankles into exaggerated curves. Won't her feet hurt after a full day on this concrete floor? And how did she manage the mile from the hotel in those?

My mind chases these questions until she clears her throat, drawing my attention back up to her stunning face. I stare. Silently. Rudely. Just as I feared.

She winks at me, and I fake a cough and struggle to shake my words free.

Come on. Get it together.

I know how this works. Companies pay a beautiful model to work the booth to attract male attention to the product, but the models rarely know any details. I can't afford to get distracted if I'm going to get the quotes and specs I need for my article. The other woman is the person I really need to talk to.

"It's, uh, interesting. I've got a few questions though, so I'll wait until she's free." I nod over her shoulder toward the woman still engaged with the other journalist. Red isn't having it. She sticks her hand out, and I reluctantly shake it. The sensation of her skin touching mine short-circuits my brain, narrowing my focus to our point of contact, and I struggle to comprehend the words coming out of her mouth.

"Well, I'm Penny Maxwell, lead engineer and CEO. I'm sure I can answer any questions you have."

I drop my gaze to her name badge to confirm her identity and get snagged by her impressive breasts that seem to defy gravity with no visible means of support. That paradox scrambles my curiosity. I catch myself staring again, and a warm flush spreads over my cheeks. Oh God, I'm *that guy*. But I don't want *her* to think I'm that guy, so I close my eyes and rally my wits.

"Oh, uh, excellent. Yeah, so first impressions... It's sleek, modern, flexible, intriguing. You've made some significant modifications to 'classic' design. Can you explain your motivation?"

That sets Ms. Maxwell back on her very sexy heels. Her expression shifts from amused to mildly approving.

"Sure. The classic design is a one-size-fits-all approach. Our goal was to make something customizable for everyone. One major change was locating the control buttons on the underside of the base, so they are easier to reach while it's in use."

I nod, though I don't understand how that could be the case. Am I looking at it from the wrong angle?

"Can you talk about the trigger location on the Me-O?" I flick my finger over the hidden marble again to demonstrate.

"We gathered extensive medical data and measurements to ensure the *My-O* would work comfortably for everyone. Here, let me demonstrate." She covers my hands with hers, cranking the joystick back until it almost lays flat. Bending it forward at different angles and lengths, combined with slight twists to either side, Ms. Maxwell explains, "See? Any angle and depth can be accommodated with one device."

I respond to her open smile and enthusiastic tone with a thoughtful nod, despite not having a clue what she is talking about. I can barely focus on what she's saying because she is touching me again and that undercurrent of electricity arcs between her skin and mine. I have no idea what my face is doing, but she chuckles.

"You're not the first guy to walk in here and be confused. How about I turn it on so you can get a feel for it?"

She pushes the round button on the front and the thing comes to life in my hands, gears and motors whirring. How the hell does this thing work as a game controller if it moves on its own?

"Go ahead. Push the control buttons."

Before I can process my confusion, she wipes my mental slate clean.

"Okay, so this," she says as she moves my hand to slide up and down the joystick, "is inserted in the vagina to align with the G-spot."

My hand clenches reflexively, the only reason I don't drop the thing from shock. She slides her fingers between mine to engage the controls.

"The buttons are completely accessible while the MiO is inserted, allowing the user to control the speed, rhythm, and range for a customized experience. The flexibility allows people with vaginas to align MiO's signature come-hither motion to their precise internal anatomy."

She moves my thumb to cover the open oval on top of the base, and it seals, creating a rhythmic pulling sensation, like someone is sucking on my fingertip. For a brief second, I imagine her mouth surrounding my thumb as I grip her chin, and I blink hard to push the image aside.

Not. That. Guy.

"This part of the base provides suction to the external clitoral gland, mimicking oral stimulation."

This image is quickly replaced by another even more dangerous.

I can feel the blush burning down to my chest. How the hell should I react to getting my thumb sucked off by a sex toy?

"The internal fingering motion combines with the external suction to create a blended orgasmic experience that can be difficult for people to achieve solo or partnered."

She pauses and looks at me, half expectant and half smirking, but what can I say? My jaw is on the floor and the blood from my brain is rushing south as I wonder what she'd look like in the throes of one of these blended orgasms.

"You should see your face right now."

I'd love to see what her face is doing as she tries to suppress her laughter, but I can't look away from the pulsing, buzzing, vibrating machine in my hands. I am trying to wrap my big head around how these movements translate to an orgasm worth dropping serious dollars on, while keeping my little head under control.

Why the hell did my zine send me here? How does this have crossover appeal for gamers?

"That's the MiO. What did you think it was?" she asks.

I shake my head. I don't want her pity on top of her mirth.

"How soon will you bring this to market?" I grasp at standard questions to get back in the game.

"These are from our first production run. We've just finished an extensive stress test, so this product will ship to preorder customers at the end of the month. We'll ramp up to full production by the end of Q2 to meet anticipated direct sales demand."

The image of her personally researching and testing

out the product screams through my brain. I snap my eyes to hers and my mouth shut until I'm sure my filter is working again.

I will not be that guy.

"What category are you showing in?"

"Health devices. Regular access to orgasms can improve pelvic floor health, manage fibroid pain, and clinically improve mood and cognition. Each climax releases dopamine, testosterone, norepinephrine, and oxytocin. I have studies—"

I hold up a hand to stop her. I am well versed in the various effects of neurotransmitters in the body, and the way she's slipped into lecture mode has my own dopamine firing hard.

"Do you anticipate high demand?" I ask.

"Have you ever given a woman a blended orgasm?" she counters.

I don't have a good answer. How would I know?

"If you don't know for sure, you probably haven't."

What, is she a mind reader now?

"Every woman who's had them wants more. And every woman who hasn't is curious. So yeah, early buzz, so to speak, is driving solid demand. We have positive movement on our second round of venture capital funding, and I get emails every week from new interested retail partners."

She has to be fucking with me. Her puns tempt me to behave badly. I hand the still-vibrating device back to its creator, determined to remain professional. "That's...impressive."

"There's nothing else like us on the market."

"And this…" My scrambled brain searches for the term she used.

"Blended orgasm?" she says, grinning.

"Yeah, that. It's worth three hundred dollars?"

"Absolutely." The tone of her voice and the look on her face are damn near orgasmic.

I was intrigued when she was just a pretty face hawking a product, but that face painted in pleasure is going to haunt me later. "Do you have any literature I can take with me?"

Ms. Maxwell pulls a folder from beneath her display, tosses a few plastic packets on top, and hands it to me. Another accidental brush of our fingers makes my hands jerk and I drop the whole thing. Bending down, I gather the materials blindly because her ankle is right there. The curve, the flare, I wonder if she…

She tucks one ankle across the other, breaking my fixation. I fight a shiver and rise, hanging on to the pamphlet like a lifeline, automatically tucking the swag packets into my pocket.

"Thanks. I've got all I need." *Lies.* I need a cold shower. "Good luck tomorrow."

"Thank you."

Her genuine smile is tempting, but I have got to get out of here before I do something really stupid like listen to my dick and ask for her number.

I'm a professional, dammit.

I am going to kill my editor though, for sending me in blind. No jury would convict.

No, I won't give him the satisfaction. I'm going to write a damn good article about an up-and-coming (pun intended) entrepreneur and prove I can handle whatever assignment they throw at me.

With a half wave and an awkward smile, I back out of the booth with the pamphlet strategically employed in front of me, but relatively unscathed. Enough information for a decent article, but hard as a rock with nine more booths to visit. For the memories alone, I still count it a win.

PENNY

I scrunch my cropped blonde hair, reviving my tired curls that have been confined all day beneath the cursed red wig. But a few hours of itchy scalp is worth every second of anonymity off the floor. Who knew making a sex toy would open the door to men who want to prove they're better than my machine?

Everyone.

Everyone could see that coming, except apparently me, who'd expected to be treated with a modicum of respect at a popular technology conference. This was cutting-edge robotics.

Maybe I was naive, but I hadn't expected men to be so brazen with their misogyny in a public setting. Male privilege was truly a thing to behold. And if I behold one more unsolicited dick pic, I will swear off men entirely.

The only one who even came close to respect was that cute e-zine reporter. He'd been flustered and stared at my chest for a beat too long, but he'd asked good questions and actually listened to my answers. His voice lingers in my mind. I wouldn't mind hearing more of it. He hadn't been hard on the eyes either, all tall and rangy. His arms showed a sinewy strength that made my lady bits take notice. *I bet he's good with his hands.*

Why am I swooning over the one guy who treated me like a professional? Ridiculous. That should have been the bare minimum of every interaction today.

He was one out of hundreds. I am disappointed in humanity.

With a heavy sigh, I release the hooks on my torture device and my breasts bounce free of their cage. I want so badly to say fuck it and let them breathe for the rest of the night, but I want a glass of wine more. I compromise with a sheer bralette TikTok convinced me to buy. It covers but doesn't confine, and the prickle of nerve pain tells me circulation is returning to the band around my rib cage.

I know some people think I've already given up. If you had access to a machine that handed out orgasms like candy on Halloween, wouldn't you give up on mere mortals?

But I like men. And women, for that matter. And everyone else along the spectrum of gender. The connection of attraction and affection between people is irreplaceable. I was never trying to get rid of human partners altogether.

But when those partners are scarce, don't I deserve a way to see to my own needs? And why not do so in spectacular fashion? And when a person is educated about their anatomy and pleasure patterns, time spent with future partners can be even better! A personalized pleasure map. Think of the possibilities!

Enough. Save the rant for the pitch sessions. Right now, work is done and there is a big glass of red wine downstairs with my name on it.

I touch my things in my purse, reassured by their orderly presence. Key, phone, ID, lip gloss, and cash. Time to find the casino bar.

I pass through hallways crowded with beautiful people, dressed to the nines for the club in my hotel, and even more people in jeans and sneakers, intently focused on gambling and drinking the night away. Thank God I changed into jeans and a T-shirt. No one notices me as I stroll and let the crowd of people flow around me. I unlock my phone and film a quick little video of "fun in Vegas" to post to my socials later, and then I tuck it into my pocket on silent. For the next few hours I don't have to be *on*, and I'm going to revel in it.

The pressure of the months of chasing funding leading up to the launch and the conference prep sits like a sandbag across my shoulders. Add in dealing with hiccups at the office from my phone while promoting and defending my brainchild to the public, and I am completely spent.

So exhausted even the MiO is barely touching it. It's a good thing I believed in my design enough to make it a reality, because I've been relying on it heavily for the last six months. I've been too busy to put the time in on a relationship, and I am feeling the lack.

A problem for another day. My wine awaits! I walk into the bar and order a bold Cabernet. The first sip flows over my tongue with a dry, peppery heat, leaving a warm trail down my throat and a looseness in my jaw. My shoulders drop a full three inches and I exhale deeply, like my meditation app tells me to, eyes closed.

When I open them, my very first employee and best friend, Nicola, is perched on the barstool next to me.

"After dealing with the males of the species all day, you deserve whatever is in that glass. The audacity..." Nic waves down the bartender and orders her trademark rosé. "Cheers, darling."

I raise my glass to clink with the only other person in the world who believes in this product as much as I do. Partly because Nicola had participated heavily in the "research" portion of research and design, but mostly because we've been together since we decided we made better friends than lovers in college. Nic isn't afraid to tell me the truth, and I depend on her to do so. There is no better person to be my right-hand woman.

"In spite of all the misogyny, it was a good day. We talked to a lot of people, opened a lot of minds." *Maybe if I say it with enough conviction, I'll believe it too.*

"I don't know about minds, but their eyes sure opened wide," Nic teases.

I snicker, thinking of that cute reporter's face this morning when I explained what he was fondling.

"Next up, opening pockets! I hope this conference gives us the publicity I need to convince the venture capital folks MiO is a good bet. I need the next round of funding locked down before production runs start. I had some ideas about—"

Nicola covers her ears and groans. "Stop! Enough business! There's more to life than giving the world great orgasms."

"Bite your tongue! First of all, everyone deserves the kind of orgasms we can provide. And second, we are sitting in a bar in Las Vegas. Say that any louder and you're practically asking for some dude to prove you wrong."

"You're absolutely right. We are young, attractive women sitting in a bar in Las Vegas, talking shop instead of looking for new exes to O. Let's talk about that. When's the last time you were with a real live partner?" Nic sips her wine smugly as I contemplate an answer that doesn't make me sound pathetic. She knows as well as I do it's been quite a while.

"When's the last time a real partner could deliver half the pleasure the MiO does?" I match her sip for sip.

"Is a great orgasm really your only criteria for a relationship?"

I don't know what to say to that. It's been so long since I actually contemplated what I need in a partnership the answer feels foggy. Maybe it's time for me to take a clear look at my "needs" list. Make some new goals or, oooh a vision board… Maybe after Q2.

Shit. Maybe I should put it down on my work flow chart: Complete second phase launch. Find a life partner. Expand plan for global sexual domination.

This *is* pathetic, but I can't admit that to Nicola or I'll never hear the end of it. This is the downside to working with someone who has known you forever. Boundaries get fuzzy.

"Fine, don't answer, but I'm worried about you. Remember senior year?"

"You mean when I kicked ass on my senior thesis project and graduated with honors?"

"As I recall, you disappeared into the basement of the Engineering building for three months and emerged from your cave with a severe sleep deficit and carpal tunnel. You convinced the Chinese takeout guy to deliver to your lab."

"And I tipped him well. So what? All that proves is I know how to work hard toward a deadline." I raise my glass to take a sip, but Nic stops me with a hand on my wrist. She knows when I'm hiding behind a flippant response. Bringing her to Vegas was dangerous. She's not afraid to call my bluff.

"At what cost, babe? I also remember you turning to a string of one-night stands to get your rocks off so you didn't have to give anyone time or space in your brain or your heart."

"They're valuable real estate."

"They absolutely are, and they've been vacant for too long. I wish you'd consider a long-term tenant. Maybe a rent-to-own situation."

"After Q2. There is so much riding on this."

Nic shakes her head at me, and I know I've earned myself a follow-up lecture at the most embarrassing time. Nic loves an audience.

"Listen, I don't care what you do, but you've got to relax or you'll burn out."

"I'm fine. I promise."

She rolls her eyes, gathers her purse, and downs the last of her wine. "I'm not going to waste an evening in Las Vegas talking business with you. I'll see you in the morning. Put it on the company tab, would ya, boss?"

It grates on my nerves when she calls me boss, and that's exactly why she does it. I wonder what or who she's going to do, and remind myself it's none of my business if I want to keep her part of my business. Navigating work and friendship is a bitch.

"Sure, I'll claim this as an executive meeting for the taxes, shall I?"

Nicola snorts. "You're determined, I'll give you that. Promise me you'll do something a little fun and a little stupid tonight? Even if it's just ten minutes at a slot machine? Balance. Remember, what happens in Vegas, stays in Vegas."

"All right, fine. I'll add fun and stupid to my to-do list. Now, go. I'll see you in the morning."

I wave as my friend disappears into the crowd, and then turn back to my glass of Cabernet and contemplate her message. I've been nose to the grindstone lately, but I balance.

Budgets, P&L statements, the expectations of my employees against reality…

Getting this company off the ground has been more challenging than I anticipated, and really, who has time for meeting someone and dating anymore?

Luckily, I can get off efficiently and powerfully with MiO. Orgasms are fun and good for my health. I've worked damn hard to claim my sexual power, and now I'm going to share it with the world. Sure, my O's feel more like business than pleasure these days, but what is so wrong with being focused on my goals?

Still, Nicola might have a point about making time for fun tonight. I deserve a night to relax, and damn it, I'm going to take it. I'm too tired to navigate a one-night stand, but a one-night business break sounds like bliss.

Focus on the little things. Small drops of pleasure can add up to refill my well if I let them. I inhale slowly, controlling my breath, pushing deeper into a calm headspace. The clink of glass, the overloud laughter, and the chiming slot machines fade into white noise as I ruthlessly quiet my mind. One sound is more stubborn than the rest. There's no way his voice was that deep.

His voice. It's not in my mind. It's over my shoulder.

Any pretense of calm is gone as anticipation ricochets through my body. What are the odds in a conference of thousands of people spread out over two casinos, the only man I enjoyed talking to today would be at this bar right behind me? Not even Vegas bookies would take that bet.

I turn my head slightly and give him the once-over to confirm.

Yep. Same smooth olive skin. Same loose and rowdy curls. Same broad shoulders I'd imagined draping my knees over earlier. New are the glasses giving him a Clark Kent vibe.

A one-night stand might be in the cards after all.

When I first spotted him in my booth, I had braced myself for another techie dudebro, but he'd handled his confusion and consequent embarrassment with humor and humility, following up with intelligent questions. I'm a sucker for competence.

He is the first person I've felt even a flicker of attraction toward since my last breakup. And if I'm being honest with myself, it's way more than a flicker.

The deep rasp of his voice weaves through my brain, leaving a trail of flames along my nerve endings, and I decide. Fun and stupid. Check and check. I'm doing this.

As soon as he wraps up his conversation, I'll tap him on the shoulder and see where things go.

Another sip of wine mellows me. My ear is attuned to his voice now, and I can't help but overhear bits and pieces of his conversation.

"So the articles on the new video streaming app and the gaming console updates are done and in your inbox. The other three are in various stages of completion."

He must be talking to his editor. Another workaholic. I respect that. I can keep my thirsty ass on this barstool until he's free. My mind helpfully supplies images of all the things I'd like to do with his freedom. I squirm on my stool, trying to ease the sudden pressure.

Hopefully he won't be too long.

Although length should not be discounted, I'm more of a technique girl. *Gutter, meet brain. I'll be here a while.*

"Good. All you need is a few breakout articles, and I can pitch bringing you on full-time. We won't hit the benefits you had at RPGiga, but at least it's better than freelance."

"Sure, I'll keep that in mind."

"And how was your first interview?"

I glance at the mirror behind the glass bottles on the bar, trying to read the face that goes with the sarcastic voice. All I get is an impression of bloodshot eyes and a collection of shot glasses on the bar in front of him. Delightful. Thank God this guy didn't show up in my booth today.

Clark Kent takes a careful sip of his beer. I study his profile. His blank face gives nothing away.

"Oh, come on," his asshole boss teases. "That was funny, and you know it."

My con crush sets his beer down and gives his attention back to his editor while I hold my breath.

"Actually, it was a really fascinating story. Female entrepreneur nominated for a top award with a sex-positive toy in a traditionally male-dominated sphere? It'll make a great profile piece."

"Jesus, can't you take a joke, kid? I was just messing with you."

"Nah, it's a good story. Permission to run with it?"

"Sure, as long as you get the rest of them done. No guarantee I'll have room for it, but knock your socks off." He tosses back another shot.

I wish I could see Clark's face right now. I also wish I could give his asshole editor a piece of my mind for belittling my work and his focus. Clark must say something in reply, but I miss it under the noise of the bar. Unfortunately, I can hear his boss loud and clear.

"Okay. Workday officially done. This is your first big conference, right?"

He nods in the mirror.

"Time to pop that cherry. Let's go find a hot piece of ass for the night."

God, this guy is truly a gem. I deliberately shift my focus to the intricate wood grain pattern on the bar, hoping to escape his unsubtle scan of the room.

No such luck.

"Don't turn and look," the asshole drunk-whispers loud enough that I can hear him. "Great tits, right behind you. She's a little butch, but you never know."

Clark shifts uncomfortably on his barstool, suddenly very interested in the rim of his beer glass. He raises his pint for a sip, and glances at me from the corner of his eye. Those gorgeous brown eyes click with mine and hold before widening in recognition and then twinkling with humor.

I have to give him credit. He neither spits out nor chokes on his beer. And he doesn't give me away either. I raise my glass for a sip, and he mirrors me with a smile. The sexy dimple that caught my eye earlier makes a brief appearance before he carefully evens out his expression. I really like the vibe I'm catching from this guy. Now to get rid of his boss.

"Sssso, what'ssss a pretty girl like you doing alone?" The asshole slurs his words, leaning far around Clark to see me. I hope he falls off his stool.

I angle toward them, plumping my breasts up to the vee of my T-shirt with my forearm as I lean farther on the bar. The asshole's eyes track exactly where I intend. *Gotcha.*

"Honestly? I'm looking for someone who can give me exactly what I need." I finish on a breathy little pout that makes him grin like the idiot he is.

Mr. Kent leans back out of the line of fire. *Smart man.*

"Well, I'm your guy," T.A. leers. The smarm is thick with this one.

"I haven't even told you what I need yet." I giggle for effect, and Clark breaks and snorts a laugh into his beer. But his boss is too far gone to notice.

"Whatever you need, I've got you covered right here, babe."

T.A. grins and rubs his crotch suggestively. I fight back a gag, but I am committed to the bit now. I have to see it through.

"No, see? I knew you wouldn't understand." I pout and sip my wine.

"Told you she was butch," he whispers loudly to Clark. "What doan I unnerstand?" he asks me.

He is so far gone this isn't even a fair fight, but I'm not about to pull my punches. "I don't want *that.*" I wiggle my fingers in the general direction of his lap. "I'm into toys. And there's one here giving blended orgasms. It's like a whole out-of-body experience! Have you ever tried it?" I blink, doing my very best imitation of innocent.

T.A. shakes his head, entranced.

"I knew you couldn't help. I need someone who

knows what they're doing to come play with me." I turn to Clark who is pretending to be invisible. I shift closer to him, close enough to press my breast up against his arm and run a hand from his bicep to his wrist. "What about you? Do you know what a blended orgasm is?"

He clears his throat and suppresses a grin. "I, uh, do. That's when a woman comes from simultaneous stimulation of her G-spot and her clitoris."

"Oooooh, it sounds so good when you say it." I slide my fingers over his where they rest on the bar, caressing their dexterous length before interlocking our hands together. Satisfaction warms my ruthless soul as both men track the motion with dumbfounded expressions. "Simultaneous stimulation..." I linger over the S sound and turn up the Marilyn in my voice, my confidence growing as they shift their gaze in unison to my lips.

"It's...supposed to be quite the phenomenon." Clark's voice is low and serious, and a frisson of anticipation courses down my spine. I want to hear that voice growl.

"Have you ever given one to a woman before?" My breathy sigh is less acting and more instinct than I like, but fuck it. I'm getting the reaction I want. T.A. is about to trip over his own dropped jaw, and Mr. Kent licks his beautiful lips, as if already envisioning his strategy.

"No, I haven't."

Fun and stupid. I am all in on this bet. I bring my lips close enough to his ear to tickle, and whisper, "Wanna try?"

Clark quickly stands from his stool, moving right into my space. I lose my balance and brace myself. My hands land on his chest, and my fingers flex involuntarily into hard muscles. I stifle a groan, and pray. *Please God, don't let this be the only hard muscle he's got.*

He slaps some twenties on the bar, nods to his boss who still hasn't realized what is happening, and wraps a strong arm around my waist.

"Lead the way."

CHAPTER 3

DASH

On the walk to the elevator, I can't stop stealing glances at her. The red hair had made her stand out in a crowd, but the sweet and sexy blonde curls suit her better.

"It's so no one recognizes me off the floor," she says when she catches me staring.

My hand rises to tuck an errant curl behind her ear without conscious thought. *Silk and gold. Precious.* Impressions riot in my mind, but one thought makes it out of my mouth with pride.

"I recognized you."

"Yes, you did." She smiles at me and runs her hand over the curl I just touched, smoothing it down nervously. Where did the bold woman who talks about orgasms with strangers go? Maybe she's realizing she left a bar with one of those strangers.

I acted impulsively, no surprises there, unable to take another moment of public teasing from her or my editor.

She presented the opening and I took it. Hustling her away from my completely inappropriate boss seemed like the most expedient solution, but this situation is weird at best.

"Listen, I know we barely know each other, but I hope you don't hold my boss against me. He's a decent editor, but he can be a real jerk sometimes, especially when tequila's involved."

"Don't apologize for T.A."

"T.A.?"

"The Asshole. His actions aren't yours. Trust me. I heard you defend your article on my work."

I have a feeling I will forever think of Chad Brooks as T.A. now.

"You heard that, huh?"

"I did."

Another thought occurs to me, and my feet slow to a stop as she pushes the call button. Did I misread this situation? It wouldn't be the first time I've gotten social cues wrong. When Penny turns to look at me, I make the hardest offer of my life, pun fully intended.

"If you are using me as a safe exit from a difficult situation, I get it. We're out of sight now if, you know, you want to go. Or we could have dinner? Hit the casino? There are a million ways to chase dopamine in Las Vegas…" I trail off, waiting for her reply.

She still seems skittish, but she steps closer and takes my hand. "Or we could go up to my room and chase it privately?"

"Yeah, or that," I say, a little breathless.

The elevator doors open, and she hesitates. "I'm Penny Maxwell," she says, expectantly.

"Dash Hall." I squeeze the hand she's holding.

"Dash. Now I know exactly who I'm leaving with and why."

I follow her into the elevator. Is this really happening? I've wandered into a *Penthouse* story, and I don't think I want to find my way out.

Except this woman makes revolutionary sex toys. Would a man stand up to man-made? Or woman-made? And who the hell am I to put it to the test? I mean, I've had some experience, but not a ton, and if she thinks I'm going to be some incredible lover...

This doom spiral is threatening to make it no contest.

Going on impulse, I slide my hand along the small of her back, and she arches and turns toward me with her eyes closed. With slight pressure, I draw her flush against me and raise my other hand to cup her cheek and jaw. She shudders and I feel every tremble. I wait for her to open her eyes, and they glitter with want as I lean in close.

"Good," I whisper before I press my lips to hers.

As far as first kisses go, this one is pretty mild. Mouths closed, lips exploring lips, and yet it shakes me to my core. We briefly pull apart and stare at each other. She feels it too, that tremor of recognition, the same awareness from earlier when she'd touched my hands, magnified by a factor of ten. I'd bet money.

Certainty clicks into place inside me as she licks her tongue into the seam of my lips. Following her lead, I take the kiss deeper, opening my mouth against hers, letting my fingers flex into her hip. She opens for me just as the elevator doors do, and we almost miss her floor.

This is going to be fun.

Stumbling and laughing as the doors bump into my shoulder, I practically fall into the hallway behind her, and Penny fumbles for her key card. I deliberately slow my steps to enjoy the view, my eyes on her ass the whole way. The way her hips shift back and forth, lovingly cupped by faded denim, is fucking mesmerizing, and I feel drunker than the one beer I consumed should make me.

I want to know all the ways she moves her hips. Would happily spend a lifetime cataloging all the ways she can shake her ass. That flippant thought stutters my steps. It is too soon to be thinking in lifetimes. And yet the thought lingers.

When she stops in front of her door and tries to insert the key, I can't resist. I step up behind her and grip her hips, line myself up with the crack of her ass and press my already painfully hard cock against her tempting cheeks. She groans and presses back against me, encouraging my bad behavior.

"Keep it up and I'm not gonna make it inside." She moans and reaches back to grab me through my jeans.

"I'll keep it up as long as you need, but I'm not an exhibitionist. Open the damn door, Penny." I punctuate this command with a light tap against her ass which makes her jolt forward, luckily with the key card at just the right angle. The little light turns green, and I take it as a sign.

Go! Full speed ahead!

I reach around her, push the door handle down, and propel her into her room with my body. Before the door even shuts behind me, she whips off her T-shirt. Her breasts are lovingly cupped by a lacy contraption, and I am irrationally jealous that a scrap of fabric gets to hold her.

Caught up in the sight and my reactions to it, I miss her question. She snaps her fingers in front of my face to break my trance before reaching for the hem of her bra.

"Personal history time, Dash. Cards on the table before this comes off."

That gets my attention, and I rally my scattered thoughts. "No known diseases, last test was negative, no partners in…nearly a year. I'm good. You?"

"I got tested at my annual last month, and I'm good. I haven't had sex in six months, and I'm about to explode. Do you have a condom?" she asks.

"Fuck."

"No, not without one."

I pat my pockets frantically as if to will one into being, but I know damn well I don't have one. "All I've got are these handy packets of lube some amazingly prepared hot chick handed me. I wasn't planning on having sex at a conference."

"You clearly aren't going to the right conferences," she teases. She leaves her bra where it is, and I nearly whimper my disappointment.

Never again, I vow.

"We've got one last shot," she says as she crosses the room to a small table where a swag bag sits. Unceremoniously, she dumps the bag out on the table and begins rifling through the stress balls and branded keychains.

"Halle-fucking-lujah!" she crows, holding high a condom bearing the name of the VR porn booth.

Even as turned on as I am, I chuckle at the irony.

"I know, I know, a condom promoting virtual fucking. It's ridiculous, but beggars can't be choosers. And I'm gonna make you beg, Mr. Hall."

She pokes me in the chest to punctuate her intent, and the sharp little jolt makes my cock twitch. My knees are already made of jelly. Kneeling before her and begging is the next logical step. The image playing out in my head is fascinating, and I get caught up in the possibilities. Until she takes my chin in her hand and hauls me back to the present with a thumb pressing against my lower lip.

"Would you like that, Dash?"

"I think I would."

Her cheeky grin flips every last switch I have. I pull her back into my arms, needing to feel her pressed against me again. My glasses bump against her face and I wrench them off, tossing them on the table. Reaching behind her, I fumble for the clasp of her bra. She laughs and pulls out of my arms, and then whips the whole thing off over her head.

"No hooks," she says on a sharp inhale as I bend my head to pull her nipple into my mouth.

I lick and suck until her tits stand hot and hard against my tongue. I love the way she holds my head in place, wordlessly commanding me to give her the pleasure she craves, leaving no room for doubt.

My God, she is incredible. Smooth as silk, her skin flushes red where I squeeze and suck. I want to see her glowing by morning. Stepping her backward, I give her hips a gentle shove, bouncing her onto the bed so I can slide her jeans down her mile-long legs. She lies there, a feast of temptations spread out before me, covered only by a pair of lace boy shorts I imagine she picked out along with the bra. So, Penny is into matching. That knowledge will torture me if I ever see her again.

Will I see her again? Or will this be a classic one-night stand? Will we fuck our way through the conference and get this uncontrollable attraction out of our systems? Or maybe we can continue this once we get home? Where *is* home for her?

My mind spins with questions I can't answer, but I know one thing for certain: if this is my only shot with her, I want it to be memorable. I want to try a blended orgasm.

I pull back from kissing her chest, to catch my breath and ask as nonchalantly as a man with a raging hard-on can, "So, this blended orgasm…have you had one with a partner before?"

"Yes. An ex was good at giving them, and not much else. Once I figured out how to get them myself, I moved on to making them accessible to everyone."

She sounds nonchalant, but a shutter comes down

over her eyes, and I feel a distance even though we are skin to skin.

"Tell me about it again," I urge.

She pulls out of my arms and sits up, her arms crossed over her chest. "What is this, another interview? Did you miss the part where I said I made a machine for this?" she snaps.

"No, I just thought you'd enjoy it, and I'd like to learn how." I'm confused as to how this bright idea of mine cast the whole room in shadow so quickly. What did I do wrong?

"Listen, it's sweet of you to want to try, but I'm not a puzzle to solve. My machine isn't some challenge to your manhood. Plus I'm so fucking horny right now, I don't want to wait while you figure it out." She moves to roll away from me.

I wrap my arm around her waist and pull her back down to the bed beneath me, pressing my hot length against her leg to try and find some patience. "Now you listen. I'm not threatened. I'm intrigued. I like to learn." I punctuate each sentence with a biting kiss against her neck.

"Please," she whispers as she arches for me.

"I hear you on the impatience. Can you come more than once?"

She nods tentatively.

"Well then, first things first." I slide off the bed to my knees, recreating the scene I'd imagined moments ago. I settle one of her thighs on my shoulder and spread her other knee wide. I drag my index finger down over her wet pussy and in between her slick folds. *So pretty.* "Do you like this? My mouth here?" I ask. I want to know what she likes. How else can I make her crave more of me, so I stand a chance at a second date? My breath raises visible goose bumps on her inner thighs and I can't help but grin. She is so responsive, and just as turned on as I am. She nods frantically.

I drag my tongue slowly and firmly across her clit. Her hips arch off the bed, pushing her pussy harder against my mouth, and I groan. Her taste fills my head, sweet, salty, and clean. One hundred percent freshly showered horny woman. *Beautiful.*

I slide two fingers inside her warm channel and drive her passion higher as I explore what rhythms and textures she likes best with my tongue. Flat, pointed, slow, fast, short, long—I try everything, carefully cataloging what makes her pump her hips off the bed and reach for me.

"Oh God, yes, right there. Faster! Harder!"

Her wish is my command, and within minutes she has a vise grip on my hair and is riding my face to her climax. *Holy fuck that's hot.* She comes forcefully, locking her thighs around my head, inadvertently cutting off my air as she clenches me where she needs me. Her body continues to shake with the aftershocks of her enthusiastic orgasm, and my head begins to spin. It might be from denied pleasure or the lack of oxygen. Either way, I need a release. I tap her thigh, and she immediately eases back.

I haul a deep breath into my aching lungs, while she stammers an apology.

"Oh my God! I'm so sorry! I didn't mean to—"

I cup my wet hand over her pussy to stop her unnecessary words. "I liked it. If today is my day, that's a hell of a way to go," I tease and kiss her knee before joining her back on the bed. "So now we're warmed up, let's play."

She grins at me with an odd twist to her mouth, but rolls into my embrace when I join her on the bed. "And I can return the favor later?"

"Deal."

PENNY

Who the hell is this guy? A lover who listens to my needs, who is open about his curiosity, who gets off on me telling him exactly what I want? Is he a unicorn? Am I being pranked? Do I care? The man hasn't even reached for the condom yet, and I am way ahead in the pleasure polls.

"Okay, talk to me. Blended orgasms," he prompts, joining me in bed.

I feel exposed with him so close, so I sit up and prop my back against my padded headboard. He follows my lead.

"The blended orgasm occurs when the G-spot and clitoris are stimulated simultaneously to achieve a bigger and longer-lasting orgasm. Most people think the clit is just a small spot hidden by the vulva, but it actually extends up to five inches internally, and the G-spot is actually part of the clitoral gland." I try to think of a way to explain this he can relate to. "Think of it like a blow job where someone uses their hands to play with your balls and perineum at the same time."

"God, it's so sexy when you go into engineer mode. Do you have a pair of glasses? Maybe a pencil skirt?" He chuckles as he runs a finger down my arm.

There it is. The sarcasm. The subtle knock. I knew he was too good to be true. Yes, I reached for my rehearsed explanation. I'm still reeling from the orgasm he just gave me. But I don't deserve to be laughed at for it.

"Penny. Look at me."

My side-eye is less than welcoming.

"I mean it. Hearing you talk about how you like to come in that crisp voice of authority... It's like a level eight turn-on for me. The only thing better would be a demonstration paired with your sexy, scientific brain."

I hesitate, unsure if I should trust he's being honest. He has been so far, but I've known him less than twenty-four hours.

He doesn't give me time to spiral. Leaning over me, Dash grips my hips and tugs so I am flat on my back again. He leans on his elbow and brings his other hand up to stroke my breast. The low thrum of pleasure dampens my annoyance.

"So, Professor Maxwell, let me see if I have this right. If I stimulate your clitoris from the inside and outside at the same time, you go through the roof?"

At least he was listening. And he might have a teacher kink? I guess I can play along for a little while, but if it gets weird, I'm pulling the plug.

"Excellent summary, Mr. Hall. A+. As for method, there are many ways to achieve dual stimulation. Can you think of any?"

He exhales deeply.

"So many... Fingers and fingers, fingers and hand, cock and hand, fingers and tongue, fingers and toy, toy and tongue..." His eyes glaze over, and he swallows hard. "Fuck, Penny. I want to try them all. Do you have a favorite?"

"MiO is the best, hands down, so to speak, but I enjoy having my G-spot stroked while I get eaten out when I'm with a partner."

A pensive look replaces the lusty one he had on his face a moment ago. He slides his hand from my breast to my belly, following the path of his eyes with his hand. "I have a stupid question," he admits quietly.

"There are no stupid questions when it comes to sex. Ignorance is the enemy."

He nods, but doesn't look up. "So, that's different from what we just did because of your G-spot... How... Where... Do I...?" He stumbles over the question and I melt, my earlier suspicion gone. He's just so damn earnest and eager to please me.

I want that too, so I explain. "My G-spot is about two knuckles in on the front wall of my vagina. Go slow with these two fingers until you feel a spongy walnut. And then firm, consistent stroking feels good."

I expect another crack at that description, but he's looking at me so intently it's like he's memorizing everything I'm saying. I hold up my hand to demonstrate the position, and he mirrors me, and then looks at my belly like he has X-ray vision or something. Maybe he does now that those Clark Kent glasses are off. It's really fucking cute.

"One more thing."

His eyes flash back to mine. "Anything, Penny."

"If I say, 'Just like that,' you keep going. Just. Like. That." I punctuate my statement with pokes to his chest, and he laughs as he nods.

"Yes, ma'am."

With every intelligent question about speed and technique, asked with the banked heat in his eyes of an erection denied, I trust him a little more. All of those skills that make him a good reporter—a keen mind, a sharp sense of observation, and a facility with words—are being put to use for my delight. And I am here for it.

He slides back up until we are face-to-face, bits to bits.

"Thank you, Penny." I cannot deny the look on his face, and those words in his mouth give me a surge of feminine power.

"You're welcome," I reply, knowing that this is indeed a gift that will keep on giving for his future partners.

He kisses me then, obliterating any lingering thoughts with his skilled tongue. I can still taste hints of my last orgasm on his lips, and I want to skip to the good part, but he doesn't let me rush. I cede control, and he insists on building me back up slowly. This man can kiss. I can't remember the last time I've gotten so turned on from making out.

He keeps kissing me until I am lost and floating again, before tethering me back to my body with a sly finger gliding over my sensitive clit. I shudder and squeeze my legs tightly, his touch too light. I can feel him try to pull back, and I can't have that. I grip his wrist and pin him with my stare.

"Firmer is better right now. Not too light or it tickles."

Relief floods his face, sweet and satisfying. He immediately cups my pussy firmly and I relax, sliding back into pleasure.

It has been so long since my last hookup I'd almost forgotten how it feels to be the center of someone's attention. He doesn't need a single thing from me, except pleasure in this bed. And maybe again later in the shower. I can turn everything else off and just be me.

His beautiful fingers explore between my legs, and I spread my thighs wider. He does not take the invitation to come on in, and continues to tease. Two can play that game. I reach my free hand down to cup an impressive erection.

He groans and his hand stutters to a halt. "Fuck, Penny. Don't do that. Not yet. I'm trying to focus."

"You're thinking too much. I want you to lose control, get a little wild."

"All that and more in round three, I promise."

Oh, fuck me. Round three? I love a man with a plan.

Visions of what that might entail distract me, and he moves his hips out of reach. I pout at the loss, but he keeps sliding lower and lower, getting in position for our experiment, and I am instantly refocused on my plan, enjoying round two before we worry about three.

His focus is intense, like he's getting lost in his game plan. I want to tell him to relax and just have fun. I open my mouth, but he looks up and the emotion in his eyes dries up any flippant words I'd found.

"I'm going to make this good for you. I promise."

I can only nod. Without breaking eye contact he slides two fingers into my now desperate pussy, slowly, deliberately advancing and retreating. He crooks them just how I showed him and strokes along my inner wall. Engorged from my first orgasm, my G-spot is super sensitive, and I gasp and jerk when he brushes over it.

Dash freezes immediately. This man misses nothing. "You okay?" he asks, his voice rough with concern.

"Yep, ah, you found it."

His frown transforms to a toothy grin, as if I've given him a gold star. He is definitely an excellent student.

"Do you want to keep going? Or do we need to slow things down?" he asks.

"If we go any slower, I'm gonna scream."

"You'll tell me if you need something different."

It isn't a question, nor a command, but more a verbal confirmation we are in this together. "Absolutely. Carry on."

Still grinning, he puts his mouth to work, licking my

entire pussy, side to side, end to end, around his fingers relentlessly driving me higher.

I've known him for less than twelve hours, and he has already taken more care and time to figure out my needs than my last three partners combined. Maybe that says something about my choice of partners, but I'm pretty sure it says a hell of a lot more about him as a person. And I like what I'm hearing.

I want to keep puzzling him out, but his fingers moving inside me against the rhythm of his tongue when he settles on my clit shuts down my frontal cortex pretty quickly. I react with pure instinct, straight from my amygdala, and I love every second of it. He is driving me out of my mind, and I'm riding shotgun with the map.

"More. Up. There!" I barely manage to gasp single syllables, but he understands. He gets the rhythm just right, and words flow from my lips like water. "Yes, yes, just like that, yes, oh my God."

I am losing control, my body twitching against his, delirious for the epic release looming. I squeeze my breasts, needing the pressure, and he sucks my clit hard into his mouth. I shatter and scream, the tremors separating my mind from my body. It goes on and on as he holds on for dear life, keeping the rhythm as best he can.

This man is a fucking gem. I've never ridden a partnered orgasm for so long or so hard, and I am still shaking when he pulls his fingers gently from my sheath. He stretches his fingers wide, and it is every bit as sexy as when a certain Mr. Darcy did it. He licks his fingers clean as he watches me and I shudder, helpless to do anything but respond.

Mr. Macfadyen has nothing on Dash Hall.

I lift my limp arms, and blessedly he understands my request. He lies down next to me and pulls me flush against him. The heat radiating off his body warms me to my core, and I curl my head against his shoulder, luxuriating in the flood of sensations in my body right now.

"That good, huh?" he asks, a grin to rival the lights of the Strip gleaming on his face.

"Mmhmm," is the best I can manage as I lazily run my fingers through his mussed curls.

"Should I go and let you get some rest?" He trails a fingertip down my arm, and I shiver with delight.

"Stay." I anchor him on top of me with my legs around his hips. I'm not letting him go until I absolutely have to.

His eyes roll back in his head before fluttering closed. "Let go, babe."

"Uh-uh."

He groans and pushes himself back. "It's too good, Penny. You keep that up and I won't get a chance to use the condom."

"Go get it, then." I'm slurring my words, pleasure-drunk. My brain still feels scrambled with euphoria, but I know I need to give him some attention.

He fumbles the foil with shaking hands, and I love it. I wish I could take him in my mouth, my hands, my ass. Play with him in all the ways I know how. But he has reduced me to raw nerve endings, and I can only watch as he pumps his thick length in his hand before smoothing the layer of latex down. Even as blissed-out as I am, my pussy clenches at the sight. I want him inside me.

He rolls me to my side and curls up, big spoon, behind me. His arms hold me safe and secure, treasured as he positions himself, cock thick and heavy prodding my ass. I tilt my hips back in welcome. He slides his insistent length between my thighs, gliding over my sensitive folds, evidence of my pleasure easing his glide. With slow, short strokes he teases me, but I am beyond playing, operating on base need. I arch my back and the tip of his cock slips inside me. I grip his hip behind me and rock back until he fills me completely.

"Are you sure, Penny?"

"Yes, Dash. Please, fuck me hard."

Once again, this man does exactly as I ask. With my legs pressed together, it's tight, and yet he fits perfectly, in so many ways. I'm afraid to contemplate those ways too deeply, so I give myself over to the moment. This might be the stupid portion of the evening, but I'll take it. Full, even strokes, his balls slapping against me as he bottoms out, he takes me and erases any thought in my head beyond *more*.

Everything is so sensitive, it doesn't take many strokes before I'm reaching between my legs for one more release. He grips my knee and lifts it for me.

"That's it. Get there, Penny. I want you to come with me."

I frantically work my clit, desperate to give him what he wants.

"Good girl. That's right. Fuck me, Penny."

His words push me over the edge, and I give him everything. Every last ounce of energy, every breath, every pulse. This orgasm wrings me out. His grip around me tightens, and with a few furious pumps he comes with a shout and a laugh, before collapsing and holding me close.

He presses his lips to my neck and growls, and it's just as sexy as I imagined. "My God, you're incredible."

My heart is beating out of my chest. Tears well in my eyes and I blink furiously, overwhelmed. I can't let him see. I can't let him think he made me cry.

Fun. This was supposed to be fun.

This *was* fun. So why does his casual praise make me feel so intensely loved? Am I so out of practice a one-night stand breached my defenses? *Stupid.*

He slides his hand up the front of my body, startling me from my thoughts. I have no idea what he's after, but I'm game for anything at this point. When he takes my hand in his and holds it against my chest, hope flutters wildly beneath it along with my heart. He kisses the back of my neck and settles sleepily behind me.

Fun and stupid, Nicola had said. Between the three superior orgasms and me catching feels, I certainly managed both tonight.

CHAPTER 4

DASH

It is still dark outside when I wake. Well, as dark as Las Vegas gets at three a.m.

I slide out of the bed, careful not to wake Penny with my pre-dawn exodus, and begin gathering clothes. When I reach for my shirt draped across the foot of the bed, the spot on her neck that makes her shiver tempts me to kiss it and wake her for another round, but we both have busy days ahead. My brain is awake and flooded with dopamine, but that's no reason for her to lose sleep. She needs every minute of rest she can get after the night we shared. My helpful memory serves up the mental image of her falling apart spectacularly, and my impulse to make her do it again flares high and hot. I stub my toe on the shoe I couldn't find crossing back to her, and the pain is enough to shake me free of my fixation.

I grab my glasses from the table and refocus on reality.

I will see her later. Work now. Play later. Use my super-

powers for good. Ride the dopamine wave to productivity. All of my therapist's coaching is trying to speak loudly enough to be heard over Penny's soft snores. Her strategy catchphrases are shouting in my head, and I am dressed and on my way before my baser instincts can get a word in.

I tiptoe out the door and make my way back to my own hotel room, where a hot shower and shitty coffee make me feel nearly human on two hours of sleep.

Noise-canceling headphones on, 8D music on loop, phone set to DND, I put my head down and get to work. For three hours, I crank out drafts of my assigned articles, ideas flowing like wine. Deadlines and dopamine always help me click into hyperfocus.

Last night was the first time I've felt such intense focus with a partner. I can't wait to do it again. She was transcendent.

If I get ahead on some of these articles, I can afford to spend more time with Penny today. I shoot the other articles to Chad for preliminary approval. I work on her story last, barely fleshing out the details before saving it and closing my laptop. I can't write about her invention without thinking about her. And thinking about her makes it hard to keep my laptop on my lap. I need to see her again.

Then again, what better reason to go see her than needing more information for the piece?

I glance at my watch. I've been working for five straight hours. Time for a reward.

As I throw my laptop into my shoulder bag along

with the condom from my swag bag just in case I see her before I make it to the gift shop, I can't help grinning like an idiot. I head back down to the conference floor with a bounce in my step.

The number one tool I have as a reporter is asking questions. So my plan is to track Penny down and ask her a few of the thousands I've thought of since I left her bed. Starting with, "What's your phone number?" and "Do you want to have dinner with me?"

I weave through the packed conference floor, for once not distracted by the displays I pass. Nothing is tempting enough to divert me from my goal. But when I round the far corner, I realize the goal line has just moved. Instead of the sleek, polished display where I fondled her toy yesterday, there is only a partially disassembled rig and her colleague tossing literature into boxes.

"Hey, what's going on? Why are you packing up?"

The woman glares at me. "We won't stay where we're not wanted." She shoves more pamphlets into the packing box.

"What does that mean?"

"It means the judging panel is full of misogynist cowards with their heads so far up each other's puritanical asses they might never see daylight again."

What? I'm dumbfounded.

"Our application was cleared and submitted for the award by a preliminary committee. The full judging panel came by this morning and revoked their nomination and our permit to exhibit after they saw the product in action yesterday. Started spouting some nonsense about it not fitting into the health category. Called it immoral and profane."

"But they allow the VR porn guys to stay?"

"That's exactly what I said!" She slaps my shoulder. "Guys can get off in new and exciting ways, but heaven forbid a woman enjoy anything but dick."

"That's some bullshit. Where is Penny?" I ask. I definitely need to talk to her now, both to get a quote for the new article I need to write, but also to make sure she's okay.

"Last I heard, she'd given up arguing with them and went to arrange things with the union guys to move our stuff off the floor."

"Damn it." Despite my personal disappointment, my professional Spidey senses are tingling. I dig out a business card and hand it to the woman. "I'm Dash Hall. I spoke with her yesterday for an article. Can you tell her I came by to follow up?"

"Sure thing," she replies, already distracted by the mammoth task ahead of her.

Time to chase this story.

The VR guys are more than happy to spout off about their past win. I survey the other presenters in the personal health categories for the uses of their devices. I even track down the official rules for entry from the organization and email the address listed on the website for official comment. Which they promptly decline. Of course.

It doesn't matter. I have enough to start working.

The closest Starbucks closed at two p.m., but still has functioning Wi-Fi. I set up camp in the corridor to finish writing the piece. By four, it is emailed to my editor. This is the best thing I've written in a long time. I have a legitimate scoop. This is exactly what Chad said he wanted to see for a shot at a full-time spot. The idea I might actually meet a professional milestone has me riding high through cleaning up my notifications.

So when the email from Chad dings in my inbox, I open it immediately expecting a pat on the back, but it feels more like a slap in the face.

"Kill the story?" What the fuck does he mean *kill the story*? I read the email again, stunned at the perfunctory tone and brusque dismissal. Buried under a list of changes and approvals for the other articles is a one-line rejection of my most intriguing piece in years.

I need clarification. I pull out my phone and text him immediately.

Dash:
Why is it a no-go on the MiO story?

Chad:
It was a joke assignment.

But it's a real story. This is big.

It's too political and feminist.
Not our target demographic.

> Aren't we trying to change that?
> Expand our demographic?

It doesn't flow with the rest of your pieces.
I can't use it. Also don't want to piss off T-Con
and get uninvited next year.

> It's an important story.

You've got sex on the brain.
What ever happened with that girl last night?

> No comment.
> Permission to share
> the story elsewhere?

As long as it's anonymous
Knock your socks off.

It chafes that I can't take credit for this. But I'll be able to break Penny's story to the world, and that is vitally important. The requested edits to the other pieces fly, and I put them to bed. Then I do a quick edit of the MiO piece, and before I second-guess myself, I post it on several open-contributor news and opinion sites. God, I hope she sees it.

PENNY

I pace the airport, fuming. What a disaster! The T-Con organizers refunded my fee, but stood by the decision to revoke my status. I'll lose thousands of dollars on swag alone, not to mention the lost revenue in presales because I've just gotten kicked out of my biggest marketing opportunity. The loss is staggering.

Fuck them and their biased bullshit. They banned me because I made a brilliant robot to give women pleasure without a man. *Threatened much?*

I have to go. I have to get back to the office. I am spiraling out of control here. There is too much chaos I cannot wrangle into submission, and there's really no point in staying anyway, especially since Dash snuck out on me without a word.

I might have been persuaded to console my hurt feelings with a few more orgasms, but I woke up alone in a cold bed. Thinking of him spikes my anger even higher. He just left! Who the fuck does that? Dash Fucking Hall apparently. Name is destiny. I should have known.

It's truly a shame to have this red haze coloring what could have been a lovely memory. And I thought the stupid wouldn't come back to bite me... Needless to say, I wasn't in the best of moods this morning when the all-male panel of judges came by, which might have influenced their decision a bit too. Telling them where they could shove their archaic opinions was probably not the key to getting invited back.

This is why I don't do fun and stupid anymore. There's too much at stake. I can't afford the fallout. The patch job on my internal defenses is messy but it will hold until I get home. I need my familiar spaces. My office. My apartment. My couch with my cat Callie. Then I can figure out a new way forward.

I feel bad about leaving Nicola to finish packing up the booth, but she planned to stay a few extra days in Las Vegas anyway. If I'd waited one more minute, I'd have said something else I wouldn't regret but would probably pay for. So here I am at the airport, rage-buying an expensive plane ticket to LA.

These idiots didn't just pull a prize. They effectively pulled the plug on my three-year plan. All of my projections for the next six months are now bullshit. Projections I've been touting to secure my next round of venture capital funding.

My mind is already spinning with ideas for how to salvage this. This was the only major conference happening before our launch, but maybe there's something regional I missed. Direct advertising is out most places because sex is a restricted category. I need something big to get those preorders up and prove to investors this product is worth supporting. That I am worth supporting. I refuse to lose my momentum.

Fuck. All this because God forbid we celebrate the female orgasm without a man getting the credit.

I spend the hour before my flight crafting emails and finding enough caffeine to fuel my manic spin into damage control. By the time I board, I am wild and wired, and no closer to a solution. I have reached livid levels of outrage as I shuffle onto the plane for my hour flight home.

When the dude in the middle seat tries to manspread into my space, my rage finds an outlet. I twirl my pen in my hand and boldly eye him up and down.

"I bet you have nice balls. Do you like them?" The jerk nods with a smirk. I twist my grip on the pen to hold it like a dagger. "Then you'd better press your legs in real tight, and keep them safe."

It gives me small pleasure when he keeps his legs cinched together, and I have two armrests for the rest of the flight, but I hold tight to my rage. Anger is better than sadness. I just need to control my emotions for a little longer. If I lose it now, I'll be the single lady crying on an airplane leaving Las Vegas, and I refuse to be a cliché.

I just want to get home, curl up in bed with Callie, and cry over the stupidity of men and my bruised ego for a few hours.

I am thoroughly disgusted with men on all levels.

I make my way to baggage claim and grab my suitcase. Surely I deserve a rideshare after the day I've had instead of the shuttle. I turn my phone on to check the app for surge pricing, and it explodes in my hand as notifications flood through my restored cell service. Through the rapid-fire dinging and flashing text boxes, I try to make sense of it all.

Emails, texts, missed calls and voicemails, not to mention my social media apps all pinging like mad.

What the hell happened during the hour I was in the air? Scrolling back, the first missed message is from Nicola.

Nicola:
Hot Guy from yesterday came by.
Seemed sad you weren't here.
Left his card.

So he hadn't ghosted me completely. But no note? No text? No nudge on the shoulder, thanks for an amazing night, let's do this again, bye? An interesting development, but no way is this why my phone battery is ticking down percentages before my eyes.

The next five texts are from friends and employees asking if I'm all right. I may have a small community, but the grapevine is alive and thriving. I should have known better than to think I could keep this under wraps until I figure out plan B.

The next slew of texts stop me in my tracks, much to the chagrin of my fellow travelers who swerve around me and my bags. I open my email, ignoring their curses. That's flooded too.

Requests for statements from major news outlets. All wanting details about the MiO and my perspective on the gendered bias of T-Con.

How did this break so quickly?

I'm still trying to get my head around what I'm reading when my phone rings in my hand. "Hello?"

"Hello. I'm looking for Penny Maxwell."

"Speaking."

"I'm Irina Mendez's booking agent. We want you to come and do a live segment on her morning show to talk about your product and what happened."

Irina Mendez! *The* Irina Mendez? If I get on this show, the visibility would be huge. But...

"Isn't your show filmed in New York?"

"Yes, it is. We are happy to reimburse you for your travel expenses. Do you think you can get here?"

I pivot and make my way back into the airport to find out.

CHAPTER 5

PENNY

And that's how I end up back on an airplane, hustling through Kennedy Airport, and then girding myself for the battle to save my Phase One launch in a hotel room instead of scheming on my couch with my cat. Much better plan of action. Thank God I packed the extra prototype in my luggage!

My evening disappears in a flurry of replying to emails and phone calls telling my story to anyone who asks to hear it. Suitcase abandoned at the door, I set up camp on a hotel bed with my laptop, my phone, and my tablet, all plugged in and charging. News sites are already coming out with articles. I make sure our website is up and ready to handle traffic. I also check the XPTech website to see if Dash filed his story. There are four articles of his published today from T-Con, but not one featuring my product.

My rage from the plane rekindles. He'd been lying the

entire time. He never planned to write a serious article about a sex toy. He'd just been using the article as an excuse to flirt with me. Every lingering good thought I'd tried to resurrect about our time together burns to ash in the flame of my anger. I funnel my energy into a flurry of TikTok story time videos about my removal from the con.

My computer dings as another email hits my inbox. I automatically click over in spite of the fact it's nearly midnight, and I have to be up soon. *Just one more, and then I'll go to sleep.*

Subject: Dinner?
From: Dashhall@xptechmag.com

How are you holding up? Want to have dinner with me?
-Dash

The byline at the bottom includes his phone number, and I am tempted to call him and ream him out. Instead I center myself with a deep breath. I am an adult. I am in control of my emotions, not the other way around. I can use my words to express my feelings. Instead of ignoring it like I want to, I send a measured, thoughtful, carefully worded reply. I should get major adulting points with my therapist for this.

Subject: Fuck You
From: Penny@Mio.co

I'm fine. And no. I don't have dinner with liars and users.
-Penny

In less than a minute, he replies. I am really tempted to not read it, but curiosity gets the better of me.

Subject: Re: Fuck You
From: Dashhall@xptechmag.com

What are you talking about? Call me.
-Dash

I am just pissed off enough to call the number listed in his email signature. He answers on the first ring.

"Why do you think I'm a liar and a user?" he asks without preamble. His voice reverberates through my head and into my chest. My body has apparently imprinted on the sound, associating it with pleasure.

I can't help the shiver, but I can absolutely remind my lady bits we are angry. "Because you said you were going to write an article for your magazine, but that was clearly just bullshit. Everyone else under the sun wrote one today, but you? Crickets. Not to mention you bailed on me this morning without a word. I don't play with players."

"Are you done?"

I refuse to answer. I said what I said.

"Check your email."

I do, but only so I can sleep with a clear conscience

tonight. This time it's just a link. It takes me to an article written by Anonymous, describing the MiO and detailing the controversy. It catalogues everything that happened and offers historical background on past winners of the Innovator's Award. It is a really well-researched article. I can pick entire passages straight from my conversation with Dash.

My stomach sinks as the dots connect. "Did you write this?"

"I did."

"Then why is it anonymous and not in your magazine?" I ask, confused as hell and trying my best to make sense of it all through a fog of exhaustion and fading anger.

"My editor killed it. Said it was too political."

"Women's pleasure is always political."

"Which is why 'anonymous' took matters into his own hands."

I check the time stamp on the article. He had done this before I'd even gotten on the plane. He took my story and wrote about the unfair treatment I received in a clear, focused, yet sensitive article eviscerating T-Con for its hypocrisy. I'm floored. This is the article that sparked the media frenzy. God, I should be thanking him instead of cursing him out.

The words lodge in my throat. I hate being wrong. The silence stretches as I try to find the proper apology.

"You there?" he asks.

"I'm still here. Just trying to figure out how to get my

foot out of my mouth." I am already off-balance from this whirlwind of a day. This one-eighty on my opinion of him is making me dizzy. I lie back on the hotel bed and pray it passes.

"So is my editor. A modified version of the article will run tomorrow morning, but it won't be an exclusive scoop. He missed a huge opportunity. His loss…"

He sounds nonchalant, but I can hear the careful distance in his voice. I've hurt him. *Fuck.* I didn't think I could hurt him. It seems like I'm not the only one who caught some feels yesterday. You can't hurt someone who doesn't care.

"I'm sorry I jumped to conclusions." My voice softens as the last of the anger drains from my body, leaving me limp with exhaustion.

"It's okay. You can make it up to me over dinner."

"I wish I could." I am surprised by how much I mean it.

"Schedule suddenly booked up with interviews?" he teased.

"You could say that."

"Then why don't you let me buy you breakfast tomorrow morning?" A subtle change in his voice sets off another shiver. I know exactly what we'd be doing before breakfast if we were together. Now that I don't hate him, my mind is wide-open to a second-night stand.

"Unless you Venmo me, that's going to be a little difficult."

"Why?" His confusion is clear, and I am regretting my impulse to storm off to the airport.

I mean, I would still have ended up here for the shows tomorrow, but I could've ended things better between us. He had come by the booth, Nic said. What would have happened today if I'd been there instead of in the security line? Regardless, I can't let him linger in uncertainty. That would be cruel. I don't mind being mean when it is deserved, but cruelty is never appropriate. "I'm in New York."

It's his turn to go silent on the line. I feel his sigh as if we are in the same room, chest to chest again. After a long pause, he finds his voice. A true reporter, he leads with an open question. "How did you end up there?"

I recap the rest of my day, adding, "I have to be up to go live on a national morning show in a little over five hours. Thanks to your friend Anonymous I've gotten more exposure than I dreamed was possible. The article is amazing. I'm sorry I yelled at you." I curl the pillow under my head and wish it was his chest.

"If I'd known it would take you away from me, I wouldn't have sent it to so many colleagues," he grumbles. I hear a door slam and rustling on the other line.

"If you hadn't, I wouldn't be sitting here wishing I could kiss you again." I do wish I could see him again. I wouldn't normally share that information with a person I've just met. I shouldn't be giving him this ammunition. But the truth slips out.

"What's that supposed to mean?" he asks.

He lets out a huff, and I imagine him collapsing in the club chair in his hotel room at the end of an exhausting day on the conference floor. It's far too tempting a mental image, and I push it away with blunt words. I need to get myself back under control. I don't have the energy to wrangle chaotic emotions tonight. "As a rule, I don't pine for people who walk out on me."

"You're pining?" I can practically hear the smirk through the phone.

"That's the part you heard?" I shoot back.

"Last night was…" He pauses to search for words.

"Regrettable? A hit-and-run? A mistake?" I roll to my side, hugging the pillow to my chest as if it will ease the growing panic over my uncharacteristic behavior. So he wrote the article. So what? He still snuck out on me.

"What? Were we in the same bed? No! I was debating between amazing and unforgettable. Was it that bad?" His voice drops, crestfallen, and I feel a small, petty pleasure.

"What was I supposed to think when I woke up this morning alone?"

"You looked exhausted, and I had deadlines breathing down my neck. I couldn't wake you, or I'd never have left. I figured I'd go write and then see you down on the floor. Maybe convince you to have dinner with me. I never thought you'd leave."

Ooooh, you're good. The warmth of his response rolls through me, making it harder to shut the door between us.

Do I really need it shut? Maybe this one time I can make an exception and leave it open a crack. There's something about Dash Hall that's gotten under my skin. "Next time, wake me up. I can be quick," I say.

"So you're open to a next time?" he asks. The hopeful lilt in his voice makes me grin.

"Next time we're in the same place, we'll see."

"It's a date. Where do you live?"

"Los Angeles," I reply. How have we not talked about this yet? Oh, right. We skipped over the small-talk portion of the mating ritual yesterday.

"Damn it."

I do not like the sound of that. "You?"

"San Francisco," he groans.

"Same time zone at least." I try not to let the disappointment into my voice. I've already given him too much.

"Yeah." He sounds just as fake positive as I do. It strokes my wounded ego.

A yawn catches me off guard and I glance at the clock. "Right now it's tomorrow on the East Coast, and I've got to get up in a few hours to get ready, so I'm going to sleep. Give Anonymous a kiss for me?"

"I'll give him more than that... Sleep tight, angel."

The endearment throws me as I hang up. He's calling me angel and making future plans. My one-night stand is expanding rapidly, and on top of all the other complications of the day, my brain refuses to make it make sense. I lie back on the bed and contemplate my options. I can lie here and ruminate until I exhaust myself with anxiety, or I can bliss out my brain and body, burning off the questions, and get to sleep sooner. The tension our flirting aroused isn't going to go away on its own. His voice alone invoked all of the good memories from last night in a rush of heat. And I do need to sleep...

I get back out of bed and rummage through my bag until I find my personal MiO and lube. Closing my eyes, my imagination rebuilds the night before in my mind. I always visualize when I touch myself. Dash added plenty of content to my spank bank, and now that I'm not pissed at him anymore, I have no qualms about using our night together to turn the MiO into more than a silicone-covered machine.

The memory of Dash's tongue getting me wet is enough to do the same for me now. I warm the toy in my hands as I apply my favorite lube and get comfortable. I tease it into place, remembering his determination to please me. I close my eyes and let it work me inside and out. In my mind's eye, it's Dash's cock stretching me, teasing my G-spot, and his tongue on my clit instead of the machine I made. The most intense orgasm I've achieved with MiO to date shatters me, and I fall asleep with my toy in my bed and Dash in my head.

DASH

I set a ridiculously early alarm to catch Penny on the live show. She looks stunning, even sporting that red wig again. No one could tell by looking at her that she'd taken a major professional hit less than twenty-four hours before.

"Why don't you tell us a little bit about your company and your device?" Irina Mendez asks.

"Gladly. MiO's mission is twofold: educate people about their body's potential, and encourage better sexual health using that knowledge to design solutions. The more you know, the better you, well, you know. The exact numbers vary, but forty to sixty percent of women experience sexual dysfunction in their lifetime, with few easily accessible medical solutions."

Her engineer voice is turning me on again. Her intelligence and passion for her mission glow on her face. I can't wait to see her again. Maybe she'll talk dirty for me again about her sexual research. How much had they asked her to self-censor? The device isn't anywhere on set, likely a nod to the early morning time slot, and her words sound very rehearsed.

"And your invention helps with that?" Irina prompts.

"Yes, achieving regular orgasmic release has a variety of health benefits, from stress relief and hormonal regulation to improved circulation and cognition. The MiO is revolutionary in the way it uses biomimicry to create a completely customizable experience to fit everyone's unique anatomy and preferences. It's getting raves from our early beta testers. We even presented it at T-Con this year and were an early nominee for the Innovator's Award."

She is a master at weaving light innuendo through her words. Clever girl. I can't help the grin stretching my face. The powers that be at T-Con are going to hate this.

"How exciting!"

"It really was." Penny leans toward Irina like they are girlfriends chatting.

Damn, she's good at this. If I was on the show, I'd be stuttering and stumbling and probably saying something completely inappropriate like "When's the last time you had a screaming orgasm, Irina?"

But Penny has this interview in the bag. "The best part was getting to talk to so many people who'd never heard of a blended release before."

"And when can people get their hands on one?"

"We are taking preorders now and will begin direct shipping in time for Galentine's Day, with a full retail launch planned for the end of June."

"Congratulations. That all sounds wonderful. So what's all the controversy?"

"The day before the final awards ceremony, the judging panel disqualified us for being obscene and indecent and therefore not allowed in the robotics category, despite being qualified as a personal health device. I find it very interesting that a device for women's health engineered by women and produced by a female-led company is indecent, but other male-centered sexual health products were allowed to stay."

"It does make you wonder what their criteria is for drawing the line. What will you do? Are you considering litigation?"

"At this point, I'd love an apology and acknowledgment of the double standard so the next young girl who builds her dreams into reality will have a fair shot. Beyond that, I'm going to focus my energy into bringing this amazing device to as many people as possible."

"Thank you so much for coming this morning, Ms. Maxwell," Irina says with a light laugh, before speaking directly into the camera. "If you'd like more information about this miracle device, go to mio.co. I can tell you I've already got my preorder in! Up next, the perfect frittata."

I turn off my TV, and marvel for a moment at how well she did. So calm and collected. Gone was the disappointed woman I spoke to yesterday. How did she do that? She really has her shit together. What on earth would she want with a guy like me?

I'm not sure the bliss of a one-night stand is worth the mental gymnastics the morning after. I do know what I felt with Penny is worth a hell of a lot more than one night, but I am not at all confident she feels the same. I send her a quick text of congratulation anyway.

I do a horizontal surface sweep of my hotel room. I still have to cover the final awards this morning, but I've got a much better shot of making my plane if I'm packed before I leave. I toss cords and cables on top of the jumble of clothes in my carry-on before zipping it up. My flight home leaves this afternoon at two. Usually I love flying into SFO. Good wine, great food, and easy layout made it an excellent home hub. But today I wish I was headed for the chaos of LAX.

I leave my bag at the front desk and head to the main hall to get a good spot for the final awards and press conference.

The president of the board of directors for the

conference takes the stage, followed by the larger panel of judges who stand silent behind him, and begins presenting the various awards given for various categories every year. I dutifully note down the winners and their inventions for the list I will compile before I head to the airport. The award for robotics goes to a self-driving mop/vacuum combo unit.

I haven't even seen the MiO in action yet, but even I know it deserved an award on premise and design alone if this was the competition. An iteration of an existing household robot? Hardly groundbreaking or life-changing.

After the awards are all presented, the president congratulates everyone and thanks us for our attendance, and moves to leave the stage without addressing the hands flying in the air from the press box. I cannot let this opportunity pass.

"Why did the MiO get disqualified?" I cup my hands and yell at the top of my lungs.

People around me turn and quiet down, waiting for the same answer. I know he heard me, because he pauses in his exodus from the stage. I try again.

"Is T-Con a fundamentally sexist organization?" I yell.

He doesn't walk away but he doesn't answer either. The crowd is starting to murmur with interest. If they haven't already heard the story, they will by the time they get home tonight. I'm going to make damn sure of it.

"Will you be apologizing and reinstating the award?" I try one more time.

He turns back to the podium and scans the audience

as if to pinpoint the voice that is calling him out. "I cannot comment on that situation as it is ongoing. But I can assure you this organization is committed to equal representation for all sexes, races, orientations, and religions. I have no further statement at this time."

A quick scan of the stage reveals the lie inherent in that statement. Not a single woman stands on the panel of judges. I am not the only one who notices, and cameras begin flashing. I don't even think he realizes the optics have betrayed him.

But I have enough for a follow-up article, and I've sparked others to think about it as well. My work is done here.

Through some miracle, I manage to get through the Las Vegas airport with plenty of time. Security is practically empty, and my flight is only half full. Old reruns of *The Office* on my tablet entertain me for most of the flight, and I almost manage not to think of her constantly. Why did this amazing woman have to live four hundred miles away? I flip ahead through my scheduled events in my calendar, and nothing will bring me to LA in the next few months. San Francisco is home, because it's a tech hub and that's where the job action is. I don't generally travel a ton. Maybe she'll have events near me that I can pitch to cover.

I get off the plane with my carry-on, happy to bypass the rush to baggage claim and sit down to a meal before leaving. The seared salmon over greens and the white wine flight I pair with it hit the spot before I hop on the BART and head for home.

I drop my bag by the door of my room, too tired to unpack. I prep myself to converse with my roommates, and try not to wish too hard for things that cannot be.

CHAPTER 6

PENNY

I stay in New York for three more days, changing hotels based on who is comping my stay. I do talk shows, late-night Jimmy shows, and even a national news spot, not to mention countless phone and email interviews for print publications. I'm not sure what day it is, but I am sure that I owe Dash more than a kiss for breaking the story wide-open.

Preorders are through the roof. We broke one million in revenue within two hours of my spot with Irina Mendez airing. In between interviews, I've been on the phone with our manufacturer trying to ramp up supply, and formulating a cost-benefit analysis of shipping via boats versus planes. I haven't slept more than four hours a night. There is just too much to do. I have big problems, but they are the best ones to have.

Half dead with fatigue, I methodically pack my bags for what feels like the eighteenth time this week. Thank goodness for packing cubes! It isn't until I get to

LaGuardia and on a plane for LA that I let myself start to fall apart. I am so tired I can hardly keep my eyes open. Most of the flight passes in a blur. I don't even think they served me a drink. I probably slept through it. I am jostled from my travel fog when I am stopped exiting the terminal to have my temperature checked.

What the hell is going on?

True, I've been in my own little bubble for nearly a week, but what the hell did I miss?

On my way home from the airport on the oddly empty shuttle, I open my news app and read with a rock in my gut. All travelers are being advised to self-quarantine for fourteen days after contact with foreign passengers.

Between the conference and the airports, that's me.

Wash your hands. Don't touch your face. Don't leave your house. Don't get within six feet of others. Watch for fever and respiratory distress.

After this week on the professional roller coaster, I had been looking forward to things getting back to normal. I promised everyone we'd celebrate our nomination with a champagne happy hour at the office. Even if we got kicked out, this week has been a net win. I need to decompress from the conference at my desk, so I can log all of the contacts I made, and make notes before ruthlessly organizing the literature I brought home. All of the boxes from the trade show need to be inventoried and prepped for the next trip. I need to send thank-you notes to the people who hosted me this week. And I was really looking forward to a group hug with my team to celebrate our success before the work of actually managing the preorder begins. The next six months are going to be nonstop and I need to recover from this wild week so that I can handle it all.

Instead, I have to completely remove myself from the physical running of my company? Sure, I can call into meetings, but God, I want to be there. Instead I'm going to have to watch it all go down from my couch? I'm going to get people on the phone for every little update or answer I need? All of my work stuff will invade my home space? *Gah! Torture.*

Damn it. No. This can't be happening.

Eager to find any loopholes, I research every known detail on this virus that's sending people indoors. The few details we have are terrifying. No loopholes. No easy fixes. Just lots of people getting sick and trying not to die. And all signs point to the U.S. as the next hot spot.

This is happening.

I can't in good conscience ignore the order and risk getting everyone at my company sick. That would be an even worse disaster.

I'm screwed.

The shuttle drops me off at the front of my building and I duck into the grocery store on the corner, pushing a cart and pulling my suitcase behind me, to grab enough coffee and easy meals for the next fourteen days. On the bright side, at least I'll get to sleep in and rest after my insane week, right?

~

Wrong. I end up working even harder at home, trying to keep up with everything happening in real time at the office. Communication is ten times harder because I can't just walk over to a desk to ask. Scheduling a call for every question gets real old, real quick. And if I wanted to be my own IT department, I'd have gone to school for that. My engineering brain is working overtime to try and figure out the most elegant and efficient solutions for a situation that continues to spiral. I'm exhausted.

At least my cat sitter took pity on me and brought Callie home, since I couldn't go out to get her. So I'm not completely alone. I have my asshole feline roommate who howls her displeasure at being left for a week in between demands for food and tummy rubs. She has decided that her new favorite lounging spot is draped over my laptop keyboard.

Yeah, work-from-home is great…

One might think my massively busy days would help me sleep at night, but one would be wrong. Three days in and no such luck. My brain has designated the hours between one and four a.m. for general anxiety and panicked musings. So I do what any red-blooded American would do in that situation, surf the internet. XPTech ran two updates to the original article, fully credited to Dash Hall. Yes, okay, I googled him. I can't get him out of my head. My brain keeps asking questions that I cannot answer, and it is maddening.

Had he crowed when his editor changed his mind? I

wish I could ask him. Was he thinking of our night together when he was writing those follow-ups? Does he crave another night together like I do? I hope so. Is he home from Vegas yet? Is he awake? Surely not.

But the urge to text him in the middle of the night hits me hard and won't let go. A late text shouldn't disturb him if he is asleep, because his phone will be on do not disturb, right? What's the harm in reaching out? Am I really going to let texting etiquette keep me from finding the answers I need?

These are the thoughts that torture me as I toss and turn in my bed. Tonight, before I can chicken out, I tap his contact and send a text.

Penny:
You awake?

I wait, holding my breath, staring at my screen intently as three little dots pulse in the corner. Pulse and disappear. Pulse and disappear. The anticipation is killing me!

Dash:
Yeah. Are you home?

That's what he comes up with after two minutes and multiple attempts? What kind of writer are you, Dash Hall?

Penny:

Yes. On day three of fourteen in
self-quarantine because of the
flight to New York and the
conference.

Dash:
Same, but I'm three days ahead
of you. Working from home.
Getting caught up on game reviews.

Saw your article
finally got picked up.

Yeah, imagine that.
It hits national news and
suddenly it's not too political
to put their name on it.

I saw your interviews.

You watched those?

How else was I going
to get to see you?

You don't write, you don't call…

How are you holding up?
I know media days can

be intense.

> I was fine with the interviews
> and publicity. Honestly, it's been
> a godsend, so thank you for that.
> It's the being away from my team
> right now that sucks.

I don't mention the kiss I owe him, but I'm thinking about it. I don't want to go there. It opens a door to physical flirting through text that I'm not comfortable with yet, so I keep it casual. Friendly but professional. Totally normal tone to use with someone you nearly suffocated between your thighs… Ugh, why am I overthinking this?

Dash:
I'll bet.
Why are you awake?

> Penny:
> Can't sleep. Too many thoughts
> racing through my head. You?

New game release.
Got caught up.

More pulsing dots… I hold my breath.

Dash:
Do you want to talk?

Do I want to talk? It is one in the morning, and I won't be falling asleep anytime soon. Is this going to calm me down or keep me wired? Also, is this weird? I have never called a one-night stand for emotional support in the middle of the night. But I want to. What the hell?

He answers on the second ring.

"Didn't think you'd actually do it. I have you on my headphones, FYI." I can hear his smile through the phone.

"Why are you whispering?"

"Trying not to wake up my roommates."

"Oh, I didn't realize…"

"Everyone in San Francisco has a roommate," he teases.

"Should we go back to texting?"

"No! No, this is much better. I've been wanting to hear your voice again."

"Oh yeah? Then why didn't you call?"

"Thought you might still be slammed and wouldn't want to talk for one more minute." He pauses, and I wait, anxious to hear what he has to say. "If it makes you feel better, I was going to call you Friday. Figured I'd have a better chance at the end of the week."

"Better shot at what?"

"Getting some one-on-one time with the sexiest woman I've ever met."

"Good one." I'm glad he can't see me blush.

"It's not a line. The other night was fucking transcendent."

Okay. Maybe he's good with the words after all. "Mmm, agreed. It was amazing."

"Glad to hear you say that."

"Why's that?"

"Sleeping with the engineer of revolutionary sex toys is intimidating. I worried about how I measured up."

"Listen, a guy who takes direction is worth his weight in silicone. I had a great time."

"So did I. I wish you weren't so far away."

"You make it sound like you'd like to see more of me." I am probing shamelessly, but I don't care.

"I'd like to see all of you, anytime you want to show me." His voice projects his comical leering into my mind's eye, and we laugh at the same time and the tension eases. "Honestly, I don't meet many smart, sexy women in person, given how much time I spend behind a screen. So yeah, when I meet a gorgeous woman who'll fuck me senseless and is brilliant enough to design prototypes and run her own company, I'm bummed you live six hours away."

"Six? Lead foot. That drive takes seven, minimum."

"What is your pit stop?"

"Harris…"

"…Ranch." He finishes my sentence. "The brisket?"

"Of course! It's the only thing that makes that god-awful stretch of the I-5 worth it."

"I call ahead and grab it to go."

"That's how you hit six." I deliberately turn the

conversation to drive times, because I do not know how to respond to a man who finds my body and my brain equal turn-ons.

"Favorite meal in LA?" he asks, keeping the conversation rolling.

"The ramen place around the corner. This thing they do with deep-fried brussels sprouts is amazing. Yours?"

"In LA? Don't laugh. Shake Shack."

I settle farther into my pillow, and Callie yowls her displeasure at losing real estate.

"Was that a cat?"

"That or a demon spawn who has infiltrated my apartment and thinks the entire bed is hers to control."

"Didn't peg you as a cat person."

"Haven't pegged you yet at all." The sex joke slips out before I can catch it. He chuckles and I try to get us back to casual-friendly-professional-not-horny territory. We skipped all this small talk in Las Vegas. I'm not complaining, but I am enjoying this banter more than I thought I would. Maybe we just need to be in different cities to keep our hands to ourselves long enough to chat. Our chemistry has a way of derailing a conversation. "And in San Francisco? Favorite eats?"

"Broken Record. I can walk there, and everything on the menu is great."

"Maybe someday you can take me there. I'll show you mine if you show me yours."

"It's a date."

I grin at his choice of words even though he can't see

me. If we keep racking up these date plans, one of them has got to work. Hopefully I can make good on the promise in his voice. In the middle of the night, I can almost pretend we are chatting in bed in the dark. Together. The image snaps into place in my mind and refuses to budge. It's so normal and natural and…nice. If we were together, he could spend the night, and we might find new ways to enjoy the naughty and the nice. I yawn deeply, imagining the cozy scenario, unable to keep it silent.

"It's late," he says. "I should let you go."

"I wish you didn't have to, but I do have to be up early."

"Can I call you tomorrow?"

"I'd like that."

"Till tomorrow, then. Sleep well, Penny."

"I will now. Thank you, Dash."

"For what?"

"For being here when I needed you. Good night."

The next few days fly by. I am slammed at work for the best reasons. Preorders are through the roof. T-Con issues a formal apology and a reinstatement of my nomination even though the final awards have already been given out. Whatever. It prolongs the news cycle, and we will go back next year with our next toy and win it again.

My three-year plan has survived the pivot and is back

on track. And I spend the end of every day video chatting with a handsome, interesting man over dinner.

Life is wonderful, and I can't wait to head back into the office next week.

Until Monday, when the governor announces a shelter-in-place status for all nonessential businesses. We are sidelined for at least two weeks.

Turns out sex toys are nonessential pandemic items, though I seriously beg to differ. If people are stuck home alone, my product is very essential. I should know. I haven't left my apartment since I got back, and if I didn't have my MiO with me, I'd be going insane.

I pay my employees a two-week vacation and send them home, while I try to get any one of the venture capital funds to sign on the dotted line to extend their investment. But everyone has gone to ground to ride the virus out. How am I supposed to be a badass boss if I can't even keep the lights on? I have spent too much time on this project to let it falter now, but I cannot see a path out of these weeds. Every potential outcome feels shrouded in fog, and I'm just stumbling around in it, hoping I don't fall off a cliff before it clears.

The plus side of all this is I have more time to spend chatting about anything and everything with Dash. The last week and a half has felt like hyper-dating. Hours-long conversations cover everything from the fun to the fundamental, giving me the feeling I've known him much longer than I actually have.

It feels like literal years since I've been able to touch him, and with the added pressure of the stay-at-home order and the threat to my business, I really wish he was physically closer to help me relax. I am craving physical touch in a way I didn't know was possible.

"Why the frown?" Concern is the first thing out of his mouth when I answer his video call.

I lie down on my couch and set my laptop on the coffee table, so I can feel like I'm lying next to him. "Rough day."

"Me, too. You go first."

"Nope, I'm not going to let it spoil my evening. Why was your day tough?"

"I didn't sleep well and forgot to eat breakfast. And then I got distracted by a new game request and didn't get my article researched. So it's going to be a late night to catch up, which means I won't sleep well again."

"You forgot to eat? I wasn't aware that was something a person could do," I tease.

"Yeah, my ADHD fucks with me in a myriad of ways."

"You've got ADHD?" I ask, suddenly feeling shitty that I made it a joke.

"Yep, although my parents would tell you I just need to work harder and apply myself."

"Your parents would be wrong. Are you on any medication for it?"

"No, my parents wouldn't even let the school officially diagnose me, much less take me to a doctor for meds. By the time I tried the pills as an adult, I was used to how my brain works and they made me feel weird. So I use strategies and skills to manage. They work better when I sleep and eat regularly. But you don't want to hear about all of that."

I don't know what to say next. I feel like I have a million questions and no way to ask them that doesn't feel rude or intrusive.

"Thank you for sharing that with me. I do want to hear more about it, whenever you feel like telling me." I hope he can hear the honest truth in my voice.

"Okay, I will. I just don't want to dump it all in your lap tonight. You already said you had a bad day." His sincere words and quiet delivery soothe me. I'm already struggling to remember why I was upset. The peace he gives me with his voice alone... The only thing better would be if he was snuggled in next to me on the couch so I could feel his words rumble through my chest.

"I wish you were here," I say, my throat thick with emotions I'm not ready to claim.

"I wish I was too." He settles in on his bed with his laptop next to him, mirroring me, and removes his glasses, rubbing his tired eyes. "If I was there, what would you want me to do?" His voice goes low and gravelly, vibrating through my chest, leaving goose bumps in its wake.

I cannot help the violent blush my wild thoughts bring to my face, nor can I bring myself to answer truthfully. *I would strip you naked and ride you till morning* feels awfully forward, if one hundred percent accurate.

"Oh really?" He grins. "So naughty you turn beet red and can't speak? I think I like whatever just flashed through your mind... Want to know what I'd do?"

My eyes snap to the screen, and I draw in a deep breath. Am I ready for this? Once we open this door, there's no going back. I hate the idea of initiating sexy-times online. It feels so skeevy. But these are extraordinary times, and I am horny as fuck. And most importantly, I trust him more than any other man I've let into my life. I nod and my voice comes out breathy as I reply, "What would you do?"

I roll to my side so he can see me from the waist up. Crossing my arm across my chest, I deliberately plump my breasts higher. His gaze drops, and I grin at the look I see on his face. I believe the word is *smitten*.

"Before or after I get you completely naked?"

Maybe he really could see what flashed through my mind. Or maybe he's just as horny as I am. But he's still giving me the choice to lead us into temptation or not. I smile and arch my back, causing my nipples to rub delightfully against the inside of my shirt. One benefit to staying home is the ability to go braless. I am thankful for my freedom of movement right now.

"After," I whisper.

His gaze sharpens on mine, trying to read me. It's now or never. I want this too badly to pump the brakes. I squeeze my aching breast in my hand, deliberately pinching my pebbled nipple with a gasp, letting him see I am all in.

"Are your breasts all swollen and sensitive?" he asks.

I nod and squeeze the other one with a groan.

"I would take them in my hands and hold them to my mouth, so I could lick and suck on those pretty nipples of yours. They get so hard when I roll them with my tongue. I wish I could see them all red and rosy right now."

Wordlessly I pull my shirt up over my head, freeing my breasts and baring them to his gaze.

"Oh God, babe. Those tits…" He runs out of words as his eyes follow my fingers along the path of my exposed curves. I like rendering him speechless.

"What would you do next?" I prompt, wanting to know where he'll take this.

"I'd kiss you deep and long so you know just how fucking incredible you are and how much I've missed you." His hand dips off-screen as he adjusts himself and closes his eyes.

"Hey, no fair. I can't see you. Tit for tat and all that."

"You want to see my tat?"

"If your tat is on your cock, then yes. Yes, I do."

He growls and shifts his laptop so I can see more of him, and a groan escapes me as he palms himself through his jeans.

"Where would you kiss me?" I ask, my desire driving me to get to the good stuff.

"I'd start at your lips and move my way down your body. Your collarbone, those perfect breasts, your belly, until I get down to your hot pussy." I press my fingers to each spot he names, desperate to feel what he's imagining.

I run my hand along the seam of my yoga pants, teasing us both.

"Now who's not being fair?"

I shove my coffee table back with my foot, not caring about the papers that scatter on the floor. Now most of my body is in frame. "Better?"

"Much. Where was I?"

"You were kissing my pussy." I'm proud I manage to say it without stuttering.

"Ah, that's right. I'd give it a nice deep kiss and then…"

He unbuttons his jeans, and I can see his erection straining against the waistband of his briefs. One little tug and his thick, dark head would be free. I hadn't gotten to taste him during our one night together, and at the moment the lack of that detail in my memory bank feels tragic.

"And then?" I ask, shimmying my own pants off, my eyes fluttering shut as I cup my hand between my legs, trying to create and relieve pressure at the same time.

"…I'd ask you to get your MiO, and show me exactly how you like to come."

My eyes snap open, and I freeze. That is not what I expected to hear. Toy play has always been very private for me. This is…different.

"Penny, go get it."

"You want me to…"

"Yes, I want you to get your brilliant invention and show me how you like to use it. I want to see your favorite way to come apart."

Nerves pull me out of the moment. My MiO time is intensely personal. I've never pictured using it with a partner, although it's part of our marketing strategy. My brain wants to click over into business mode, but I know that's a cop-out. And I've already made the decision not to hide from this attraction. The longer he stares at me, the more I want to share this with him. My breathing quickens and nerves tighten my throat, making each gasp a wheeze.

Dash turns his computer and leans forward on his forearms so all I can see is a close-up of his face.

"You are a brilliant queen who knows exactly what you want and how to get it. Hell, you've made it an art and a science. That is so fucking sexy." He deliberately distracts me, and I appreciate his understanding. He gives me a breath to decide before continuing. "Show me, Penny. I want to know how you like it, so when I use it on you in person I can make it good for you. I want the image of you playing with yourself burned in my brain, so when I fist my cock alone at night, it's your face in the throes of an orgasm I see. Let me see."

Without a word, I rise from the couch, take my laptop to my bedroom, and pull my little yellow pouch from the bottom drawer along with a bottle of lube, although I am so wet already from his words I might not need it.

"This is MiO." I hold my personal device in my hands, warming it up. "I like to have a story going in my head before I start. Do you want to help me write it tonight?"

"Absolutely."

"So I'm picturing this guy I met in Vegas."

"I like where this is heading." He adjusts himself and settles in.

"He is so hot, and he's looking at me like he'd know exactly how to make me fall apart at the seams."

"Where are you?"

"On the floor of the conference, in my booth."

"Where is he?"

"Underneath the table at my feet."

"Oh fuck." Dash fists himself hard as he curses.

I run my fingers up my thighs as if I'm lifting a skirt for him. "No one can see him behind the stand, and I'm covered from the waist down, but I still have to try and talk to people while he's got his hands and mouth on me."

"That's right, Penny. Sell it. Use your sexy engineer voice. Don't let me distract you. You won't even know I'm here."

"Oh, I know right where you are. You're sliding your fingers into my pussy like you did that first night." I take the MiO and slowly tease the shaft into my vagina. "You know just where to please me." Once it's in, I start the fingering motion at the slow and steady speed I like. "You're fingering me so fucking slowly, driving me out of my mind. I want to grind against your face and come hard and fast, but you won't let me."

"I want to take my time with you, Penny. I want to make you feel good."

I tilt the external stimulator so it lines up perfectly over my clit, but I don't turn it on. Not yet. I'm so horny, it'll take me over too quickly.

"I want you to put your mouth on me, to lick and suck and tease me. A man comes up to ask about my product, and I can barely form words. You pick up speed between my legs, and I swear he's going to hear the wet slapping sounds your fingers make as they fuck me. You get me so wet." I turn up the speed on my G-spot.

"I love the way you taste, Penny. I love how wet you get for me. Let me lick your pussy, babe. Just a little. Just a taste."

I push the button to start the suction valve, and immediately flick it off. "I can't. It's too much."

"Good girl. Don't come yet. Let me just make you feel good while you tell that man how good your vibe is going to get his wife off."

I click the come-hither button again and hit my favorite speed. Usually I turn on the external bit at this point and come within a minute. My machine is nothing if not efficient. But tonight I find myself holding off, making it last. I linger on the edge longer than usual. I don't want this to end.

Everything in my belly tightens in anticipation. In my mind I can perfectly visualize him feasting on my pussy, fingers deep inside me, while I try and remain calm from the waist up.

"You look so good right now, Penny. If I was there with you, I'd take those pretty breasts of yours in my hands, in my mouth. Would you like that?"

I raise my hand to tweak an already hard nipple and sensations shoot directly to my clit, begging for me to turn the damn thing on already. I nod and do it again. "But then he'd see."

"Let him watch. I want to kiss that clit of yours too. Pull it tight between my lips. Flick it back and forth with my tongue. Lick you front to back and inside out until you're shaking in my hands. Until your knees buckle. Turn it on, Penny. Now."

I hit the button for suction twice, and the sensation combined with the mental image of Dash feasting on me immediately pushes me into an orgasm. My body jack-knifes in on itself, everything contracting and shaking. My legs clench around the MiO, holding it in place while it wrings every last ounce of pleasure from my body. With shaking hands, I manage to turn it off and collapse on my side.

"Penny…" Dash sounds as out of breath as I am. "Holy fuck! You're incredible."

I manage to make eye contact again, and I see him wiping thick ropey strands of come off his chest with his T-shirt. He came just watching me. And I missed it.

I'm currently too blissed out to care, but next time… Next time I'll talk him through his pleasure too. Next time…

I'm in so much trouble. Every last one of my barriers falls far too quickly around this man, and I don't know how to act without those careful walls in place. He makes me think dangerous thoughts, like *next time*, *again*, and *forever*. I look away and gingerly slide the device out of my body, needing a reprieve from the intensity.

"Penny." Dash says my name with such authority I have to meet his too-perceptive gaze. "I don't know what thoughts are causing that look on your face, but I need you to hear me. This is the sexiest thing I've ever experienced. I'm sorry I couldn't hold out, but watching you come like that…I lost it. I wish I could hold you."

"Me too," I say as I roll to the edge of the bed and my back hits the cold sheets. I need a little space, a little distance. "I'll be right back." I walk to the bathroom to clean up and collect myself.

How can this be moving so quickly and at the same time be torturously slow? He's got me all churned up, and he's four hundred miles away! But as I look at my glowing reflection in the mirror, I have an epiphany. We are living through a global pandemic. None of this is going to be normal. That has ceased to exist. I may feel like things are moving too fast, too wild. I may feel out of control and impulsive. I might also be a tiny bit afraid of how intense my attraction is. What I don't feel is regret.

CHAPTER 7

DASH

Lying in my bed, I try to focus on the game I'm supposed to be reviewing, but Penny keeps sneaking into my thoughts. I wish she was here. The exploration-based quest isn't holding my attention at all. My eyes keep darting to the clock.

My days in quarantine are running together. I barely see my roommates since I'm supposed to stay distanced. I can't remember the last time I showered, because who cares how I smell. I've taken to ordering all my meals through delivery services, and I've reviewed roughly a dozen video games, only half of which have made it into the magazine.

Chad tells me to slow down, but I can't. I'm so bored stuck in this little room. Gaming and Penny are the only things keeping me sane.

We have fallen into a routine of calling each other at six p.m. when she makes dinner. We eat in front of our screens and chat about our days. Some nights we talk for hours. Other times we have some mutual fun. It feels so…normal, and yet nothing about this situation is normal.

My real normal involves writing at a café, editing at a coworking spot, eating at a restaurant, or walking at the park, just to get out of our tiny apartment for a bit, before holing up in my room with the latest game. Variety and novelty are the antidote for the boredom that can sidetrack me hard. Living in San Francisco has given me the stimulation I need…until now.

I'm a little surprised I'm enjoying it so much, because maintaining focus, especially during long conversations, is usually a struggle. My mind likes to wander down rabbit holes without giving the other person a trail of breadcrumbs to follow. But with Penny it's different. Our conversations are new and exciting and the only goddamn thing I have to look forward to.

A knock on my door startles me from my musings.

"Your takeout is here," my roommate, Dan, says through my closed door.

"Thanks."

I put on a mask and open the door. Dan hands me my bag of pad thai from a distance. I don't know what I would have done without my roommates' help this week. They've been great about helping me stay cooped up, even though we are usually just ships passing. We are friendly but not friends, if you know what I mean. I turn to go back into my quarantine hidey-hole, but he clears his throat.

"Um, while you're out here, can we talk a minute?"

Shit. He never wants to talk. Now I'm going to be late for my date with Penny. Is this about the dishes in the sink? There shouldn't really be any of mine since I've been living out of plastic and styrofoam for two weeks. I'm not the cleanest roommate, but I try to keep my mess contained to my bedroom. "Sure, dude. What's up?"

"Listen, I don't want to put you in a tough spot, but I'm moving out. My job just announced we'll be work-from-home for at least two more months if not longer. If I move back home with my parents, I could save a shit ton of money."

"And get Mama Liu to cook for you," I tease as I process what this means.

"It's a factor." Dan smiles.

"Have you told Rishi yet?"

"This afternoon. He said he's been thinking of visiting his sister in LA. Same thing. Plus his nephews are home from school but his sister is still working in the ER at the hospital and sleeping in their guest room so no one gets sick. She needs all hands on deck."

What would it be like to have someone you'd move in a pandemic for?

As far as family goes, I only have my mother left and our relationship is…strained. Since Dad died last year, I'm no longer actively avoiding my childhood home, but I cannot move back home like Dan and Rishi can. Couch surfing with friends isn't realistically an option right now, but neither is holding my roommates to a lease they don't want. I'll have to figure out something quick.

"Man, I'm sorry to drop this on you while you're

quarantining, but I figured you could use the time to search. I'm giving the landlord notice tomorrow." Regret shines in Dan's eyes.

"Yeah, okay."

"It just doesn't make sense to pay this crazy rent if I don't have to be here for work."

"No, I get it. It's just a shitty time to try and find a new place."

"Do you have someone you could stay with?"

"I'll figure it out. Don't worry about me. You're right. It doesn't make sense. You'll send me your new address, right? Keep in touch?"

"Sure, man. Will do. Thanks for taking this so well."

I nod and bring my food into my room. I'm not actually taking it very well, but I've always been good at masking. My face is calm, but my mind is spinning in a thousand different directions, trying to process this information. I grab my controller to give my fingers a fidget, even though it's not turned on. Moving the buttons helps me sort through the tangle. Growing up, keeping any turmoil on the inside was the only way to survive. The skill continues to serve me well as an adult. Besides, it's not like I have any control in this situation. I can't make Dan and Rishi stay. We found each other through a Craigslist ad.

This apartment is just a place to lay my head. It has never been a home, just a room where I keep my stuff. Everything I own fits in two suitcases and ten boxes. I still have the boxes folded up in my closet. Getting this place was a compromise, so I could be in Silicon Valley chasing my dream. I'll just have to figure out the next compromise. Or maybe the next dream.

If I'm going to be spending the near future wading through housing sites, I need sustenance. Penny and dinner. If I talk to her first, maybe she'll help my brain calm down and find some solutions.

I slurp my noodles while I check for notifications from her.

Zero.

Odd. She usually calls by now.

I scroll my phone. Nope. No missed calls. No voice messages. No texts.

Well, I'm not some fuckboy who's going to get bent out of shape because she doesn't call. I'm a grown-ass man. I can text her just as easily as she can text me. I bolster myself with another loaded fork of spicy peanuty Thai goodness before I tap out a message.

Dash:
Hey, how was your day?

There. Not too needy, but polite and friendly. God, is this middle school? Why am I dissecting my tone and vocabulary choice? Three blinking dots save me from obsessing over modern textiquette.

Penny:
Ugh. Headache. Feel like shit

You got the 'Rona?

Not funny. 

> Sorry, bad joke.
> Do you need anything?

Just some sleep.

> Ok. Sleep tight

Talk tmrw

I set down my phone, unreasonably disappointed I won't get to talk to her after all. I am left alone with my spinning thoughts.

Did she have any water before she lay down? Take a Tylenol? Check for fever? All things I can't ask her now because she is sleeping, but not knowing the answers is only adding to my spiral.

If I lived closer, I could just pop over to check on her. If I lived closer, a lot of things about our relationship would be easier. Including sex. If I lived closer...

The idea percolates as I idly search rental websites. What if I move down to LA? I have to move anyway. What's keeping me in San Francisco? It certainly isn't the bustling nightlife with everything shut down.

If I'm being honest, the city lost its luster long ago. I've stopped trying new things for fun, but to try and outrun boredom. It isn't my job, which has gone fully remote for the foreseeable future. I don't even have lease loyalty holding me back now. I don't have a good answer. Maybe it's time for new questions…

PENNY

A piercing sound rips me from sleep and I blindly slap at my nightstand to shut my phone up. It isn't until it hits the floor in a blaze of light that I realize a) my phone was ringing with a call, not an alarm, and b) I'd slept in until eleven.

I never oversleep.

"Shit."

I half roll out of bed to get my phone and instantly regret the movement as my lungs protest the stretch with vigorous coughing.

I manage to get to the phone and answer it, but my coughing fit hasn't subsided enough for speech.

"Hello? Hello? Penny, are you there?" Dash's worried voice carries over the cacophony.

"Here," I croak.

"God, you sound terrible. Are you okay?"

"Hang on." I stumble to the sink in my bathroom and get a glass of water. It soothes my parched throat but the rest of me is burning up. I wet a washcloth for my forehead and head back to bed and my phone. At least I can speak now. "I'm here. I feel like shit. I just woke up."

I try to clear my mind and pull up my schedule for the day, but it's like trying to walk through quicksand. My fire swamp of a brain is pulling me back under the blanket of heat, and I don't have the energy to fight it. If any rodents of unusual size show up, I'm screwed.

"How can I help? Do you need anything?"

I am already climbing back under the covers. "No, I just need to go back to sleep…"

"Have you eaten anything today?"

I hear his question, but my eyes close before my mouth can open, and I give in to oblivion.

The next thing I know, it's nine p.m. and my head is throbbing. *Water.* It is the one thought I hold on to.

Crawling out of my bed, I make my way back to the sink in the bathroom and down an entire glass of water. I'm not convinced my legs will get me back to bed, so I sit on the floor to gather my strength. The icy tiles feel good against my overheated skin. Maybe I'll just take a nap here…

Pounding on the front door, coupled with my name being yelled at full volume, rouses me from my stupor. Who in the hell could that be? Is that what woke me up?

Still on my hands and knees, I crawl into my living room.

"I'm coming," I call out, sparking another round of coughing.

"Penny? It's Dash. Open the door."

Dash? Here in LA? I don't understand what's happening, but his voice radiates through the door, and I've never been so grateful to hear it. I reach up and undo the locks before slouching to the side against the wall so he can let himself in.

The door swings in and there he is, mask on and hands full of plastic bags he drops on the ground when he sees me.

"My God! Penny! Are you okay?"

I barely have the energy to shake my head, but it's enough.

He crouches next to me, sliding an arm beneath my legs and another behind my back, and lifts me effortlessly. I float back to my bed and I swear to God, the man tucks me in. As if I wasn't already struggling to keep my head around him…

"Have you eaten anything today?" he asks gently, with his hand on my forehead.

I shake my head again and wince as my brain rattles against my skull.

"Okay, try to stay awake until I get back. Give me five minutes."

He leaves and I really try to stay awake, but my eyelids are so damn heavy.

His cool hand on my shoulder wakes me with a start.

"I'm awake! I'm awake. Not sleepy at all," I say, and promptly prove myself a liar with a yawn.

"Here. Eat some of this and you can go back to sleep."

I look at the cutting board he's carried in as a makeshift tray. A small bowl of my favorite ramen, a mug of steaming tea, two Tylenol, and a large glass of water bring tears to my eyes. "You brought me ramen?"

"You said it was your favorite. I put the rest in the fridge so you can have some later if you wake up hungry. Take your medicine and try to eat," he urges.

I swallow the pills and manage to eat half a bowl, though I can't taste anything but salt, before I am nodding into my soup. He rescues the tray from my lap and heads for the kitchen. The last coherent thought I have is *don't leave me* before sleep drags me under again.

DASH

"Mrrrow!"

I open one eye a crack and find an orange tabby eyeing me suspiciously from the coffee table. What time is it? I turn my head to check my phone and wince. Sleeping on the couch, using the armrest for a pillow, was not my brightest idea, but nothing about the current situation is ideal. My stomach growls in angry agreement.

"Are you hungry too?" I squint my eyes to read the tag on her collar as I try and rub the kinks out of my neck. "Callie, huh? Let's see what we have for you."

Standing too quickly, my back protests and so does the cat, hissing and sprinting out of range. Great. Now I'm scaring cats. What's next, small children or the elderly? Hopefully not my sick patient in the other room. In hindsight, I can see how showing up on her doorstep unannounced could be a bit creepy, but I hope my actions will prove I am here with the best of intentions.

Callie peeks around the corner cabinet cautiously. Lesson learned: no sudden moves.

I shuffle into the kitchen wearing the same clothes I drove down in and pull a white takeout box from the fridge.

"Do you like brisket?" I pull off a piece of tender beef and hold it out for the cat, who allows my approach but has eyes on her escape route. She sniffs it and decides I'm not an intruder trying to kill her, before taking the meat from my finger. I offer another tidbit and she greedily licks my fingers this time.

Good. Her cat won't starve. I shred a bit more and put it in a bowl on the floor for Callie, who happily settles in to eat.

I pop a cold brisket chunk in my mouth and decide the cat has good taste. I rummage in the fridge for a piece of bread and some cold caffeine. *Jackpot!* There is a tortilla and a Diet Coke. Beggars can't be choosers.

I drink half the can of soda in one long swig to try and wake up more fully before fashioning a brisket burrito and eating it standing over the sink.

It's strange to be in her kitchen without her. Almost as bad as snooping through her medicine cabinet last night to find the pills for her fever. But if I'm going to take care of her for a bit, I need to know where things are. I pop the last bite into my mouth and begin my survey of her apartment.

The kitchen is immaculate and organized to the nth degree. All of her silverware is sorted by shape and size. She has not one but two wine openers in a clearly designated spot and actual chip clips for closing bags. Like, more than one! I open a cabinet and find juice cups and water glasses, stemless wine goblets and tulip pints for beer, all matching and lined up like little soldiers waiting for her next party.

My stomach drops.

Yeah, this kitchen isn't clean because she hasn't used it in a week. It's clean because this is how she keeps it.

Her pantry reveals neat rows of canned fruit and boxes of pasta and jars of sauce and jelly. No can of long-expired soup gathering dust or half-used bag of lentils spilled in a corner. No random niche ingredient bought on a whim and never used. She buys what she eats, and eats what she buys.

The feeling of dread deepens and I bring my soda into the living room. Sure enough, there is a coaster on the coffee table, ready and waiting for me when I set it down. No water rings allowed here. Her potted plants look a little peaked in the windowsill, and I am positive that is a result of being sick and not general neglect. I debate giving them the last of my soda, but even I know that's a terrible idea. Back to the kitchen for water in a glass. At least I know exactly where to find it.

I put some down for Callie too after I'm done with the houseplants.

It's barely nine, and I'm exhausted trying to process and maintain this apartment.

My hands shake with jittery energy. I do not belong here. I need to find my own apartment quick, before I scare Penny off with my messy habits and forgetfulness. I would go look today, but she needs me. I can't abandon her while she's ill. And I should probably quarantine as well, in case I've been exposed.

I'll just have to be on my best behavior while I'm crashing here. It'll be fine. I can fool her into thinking I can adult for at least another week.

But I can't leave my stuff in the car that long. In fact, I should have brought it up last night, but I got distracted doomscrolling the internet for any information on this new illness. I'll be lucky if it's still there.

It takes several trips up and down her elevator, but I manage to squeeze my ten boxes and two suitcases into the corner past the couch. I turn one suitcase into a makeshift dresser and actually attempt to fold my clothes so they at least look like a neater pile of laundry on the floor. I get my laptop out and charging, and open boxes until I find where I stuffed my pillow and a blanket. At least I can fix that part of the equation here.

With nothing left to do, I put my mask back on and peek in her bedroom door. She is still sleeping. I wonder if I should wake her or get her some water. I'm no nurse, but I try and remember what my mom used to do to make me feel better when I was a kid. I remember saltines and Sprite and kisses on the forehead. I don't think that will work here, but what do I know? I'm not a professional.

A professional. Rishi's sister! Without thinking about shifts or time of day, I pick up my cell phone and call.

"Hello?" He sounds groggy.

Fuck. I probably woke him up. "Rishi? Hi, it's Dash. I'm sorry if I woke you. I can call back."

"No, s'okay. I'm awake now. What's up?"

"I'm here, in LA."

"Cool, man. I hope you don't need a place to crash though. My sister is still quarantining after her shifts at the hospital."

"Actually, that's why I'm calling. I'm down here helping a friend. She's sick. Like really sick. And she was at T-Con and then on airplanes for days afterward. I'm worried she's got this new virus. I'm in her apartment, and I don't know what to do to make her feel better."

There is a heavy silence on the other end of the phone.

"Rishi? Still awake?"

"I'm here. Just processing. You, confirmed bachelor, gamer boy extraordinaire, drove to LA because this woman is sick?"

"Well, I had to move anyway so yes, I packed up and here I am." I pace the length of her kitchen and back, making myself dizzy with worry.

"Wait, you showed up on her doorstep with all of your shit?"

"Yes, and now I'm sleeping on her couch and hoping she doesn't die. Rishi, can you ask your sister? What do I do?"

There is another pause, and I know I'm probably never going to hear the end of this. But the next voice I hear is clear and professional. Doctor Amrita Singh has entered the chat.

"Do you have PPE?"

"What's that?"

"A mask, gloves, scrubs…"

"I have a mask, and I think I can find some gloves." I walk back to the yellow pair I saw hanging next to the sink. Those should work. I tug them on and immediately feel ridiculous.

"Good. Don't go near her without them. I need you to promise me that."

"I promise."

"Do you have a thermometer?"

I put my mask on and go into the bathroom through the hallway door. The one that leads to her bedroom is firmly shut, but this is going to be the area where we have to cross over. It's the only toilet in the apartment.

I put Rishi's sister on speaker as I open her medicine cabinet and drawers, determined not to feel like a lech as I search through Penny's personal bits and bobs for a thermometer. Her rigid organization pays off, and in the third drawer I find one that shoots a laser at the mirror when I push the trigger. Honestly, I wasn't sure if it was going to vibrate in my hand or not. Who knows what a sex toy designer keeps in her drawers? Well, I mean besides me who has been snooping all morning. "Bingo."

"Okay. Now, go take her temperature."

I open the bathroom door into her room a crack and peek in. She is still sleeping. I tiptoe to the bed and kneel down next to her.

"Amrita, she's so pale and her breath is rasping in her chest." I aim the laser pointer thermometer at her forehead and the display flashes red. "It says 103.2. Is that bad?"

"It's not good."

"Dash? Is that you?" Penny's voice creaks as she tries to speak.

"Yes, baby, I'm here. I'm just checking your temperature. It's high. Do you think you can swallow some pills again?"

"I'll try."

She pulls herself up to sitting, but immediately curls over in a coughing fit.

"Here, let me help." I put my hands under her arms to help lift her and her body is radiating heat. Like a lot. Like, warmer than I've ever felt a human be. She leans her head limply against her headboard as I run back into the bathroom for water and pills. Real terror that she might have the virus everyone is afraid of lodges in my chest. I hold her against my side while I help her take the medicine.

"Dash, everything hurts."

"I know, baby. Finish the water, please," I coax when I feel her flagging against me, and I curse this mask between us keeping me from kissing her forehead like I need to.

She is asleep before I close the door between us again.

"Dash?"

I realize Amrita is still on the phone, and I grip it like a lifeline. Horror stories I read online last night cycle through my head. People in the hospital. People dying. If this is Coronavirus, even I know enough to know this is bad.

I have never felt so helpless in my life. This amazing woman who was on top of the world a week ago is now teetering on the edge of leaving it, and that would be a tragedy. I can't let that happen. I don't realize there are tears on my cheeks until my voice cracks.

"Amrita, I'm so scared. She's really hot. Like scary hot under her arms. And she keeps coughing. She's barely eating or drinking at all, and everything hurts. I need to make it stop hurting. I need her to get well. What do I do? Tell me how to fix this. I just found her. I can't lose her. I won't."

PENNY

The next few days pass in a blur. I can't think straight. I keep coughing like crazy, and my chest is on fire. All I want to do is sleep. But every few hours Dash wakes me up to eat something or drink something. He even helps me into and out of the bathroom. It's annoying as fuck to feel this weak and dependent, but I'm glad he's still here. I don't know why he was at my door in the first place, but I figure that's a conversation for a day when I can actually string coherent thoughts together.

On the third day my fever spikes even higher. I'm on fire one minute and then shaking with cold the next. The hallucinations are really trippy. At one point I am convinced I'm being mummified and someone is trying to extract my brain through my nose. I'm so weak, I don't even fight it. Maybe it will relieve the throbbing in my skull.

On the seventh day, I open my eyes and the light doesn't burn. My stomach is empty but so is my head. The crushing pressure is gone, and I am lucid for the first time in a week. I scan the bed for Callie, and it appears she has abandoned ship. I groan and haul myself out of bed, wincing at the stiffness in my joints before making my way to the shower.

I glance in the mirror and the pale, gaunt face looking back at me is startling. I look over my shoulder to see who is in the room with me before I realize I am still alone. This flu has certainly knocked me on my ass.

Hopefully a shower will help wash away some of my sickbed pallor. The warm water flowing over my body feels heavenly, and I want to stay in this steamy cocoon forever. I feel almost human again. But I don't trust my legs to keep me vertical for much longer. Weakness hits as I try to climb over the side of the tub, and I stumble.

I hit my hip on the edge of the sink on my way down to the floor.

"Fuck! That hurt!"

The hallway door slams open, and there is Dash, seeing me in all my naked glory. His eyes fill with concern instead of lust, and it's lowering to realize what he's dealt with this week. Yes, he's seen me naked before, but this hits different. Sex is the bodily function I am *least* embarrassed about. Personal hygiene is a whole other level. I cover myself ineffectually with my arms, and he is quick to drop me a towel.

Bracing for a lecture, I sullenly wrap the terry cloth around my chest and try to stand up again. My lungs wheeze with the effort. How can I possibly be winded? I barely moved. When he tries to help, I know it's petulant but I jerk my elbow away.

"I didn't hear you get up. I was taking the garbage out. Can you walk back to your bed, or do you want me to carry you?" is all he says.

"I can walk," I snap, a complicated cocktail of shame and embarrassment and confusion turning my tone acidic.

"Okay." He follows half a step behind me, waiting to catch me if I fall again. "Do you want some clean clothes?"

I desperately want to get them myself, but the little energy I had is dissipating quickly. I nod and point to the dresser. "Underwear, top drawer, T-shirts just below."

He pulls out sensible undies, a pair of boxers, and a super soft T-shirt. He lays them on the bed and leaves. I wish I could see the expression on his face, but he is still masked.

By the time I struggle into my clean clothes, he is back with a mug of warm apple juice and some cinnamon toast cut into triangles, my traitorous cat weaving a figure eight around his ankles. Why is she being friendly with a stranger? And where the hell did he find apple juice in my apartment? More importantly, why the hell is he still in my apartment?

Thoughts become words that sail out of my mouth before I consider things like tone and timing, and he bristles.

"You…you asked. You said *don't leave me*. So I didn't."

At least now I can tell from his furrowed eyebrows he is annoyed right back at me. I didn't realize I'd voiced that fever wish aloud. And this man is probably the reason I am marginally alive this morning. I take a deep breath to reset my attitude and set off another round of coughing. *Fuck, this sucks.*

"I'm sorry. That was rude." I manage a few sips of warm cider between coughs. I can't taste it, which is weird, but it clears the tickle going down. "Thank you for taking care of me. I'm sorry I'm a grouchy patient this morning."

"Well, anyone battling Covid has a right to be grouchy," he replies.

"No, it's just a bad cold…the flu…" I protest.

"No, actually, you have Coronavirus."

"Okay, Dr. Smartypants, how do you know?"

"Because my friend's sister is an ER doctor, and she came to swab your nose."

He hands me a lab report that knocks me on my metaphorical ass. Covid. The thing everyone was worried about. The thing no one knows enough about. And I tested positive… A fever dream flutters from memory. "Ah, the ancient Egyptian burial rite…"

"What?"

"Never mind. So I tested positive?"

"Yes, you did. Amrita said to push fluids and watch your pulse-ox readings on your fruit watch, but so far you've stayed in the okay range. If it drops, we've got to get you to the hospital."

He keeps talking, and I try to piece together what I remember from the last week with what he must've done for me. He fed me and cleaned me and monitored my vitals and called in favors. This man kept me alive. This man I barely know dropped everything to come care for me.

The way he so casually tosses around "we" makes my chest feel warm from something other than a fever. Caused by the Coronavirus. That I currently have.

Appreciation tangles with fear of the unknown and makes my empty belly churn. My mind spins with unanswerable questions. Will I survive? And if I do, are there long-term effects? Will I fully recover or be a burden to whoever is in my life?

And, oh God, I exposed him! I don't even know if he still has a job or insurance or…

"Dash, I think you should leave."

"What? Why?"

"Because I don't want you to get sick too."

"Well, that's going to be difficult. Since I've already been exposed, I'm supposed to quarantine for at least another week without symptoms before leaving. Luckily, I've been wearing a mask this whole time and I feel fine, but better safe than sorry, right?"

"How is you staying here safe by any stretch of the imagination?"

"We've been in completely different rooms. And I sanitize every surface in that bathroom after you use it." His jazz hands in my yellow dishwashing gloves distract me. "It will be fine. Besides, I don't have anywhere else to go. I can't stay with Rishi because he's crashing with his sister. My plan was to get a hotel room and look for apartments once I got down here, but now I can't safely get a room..."

My eyes bulge at that information, and he trails off.

"You...you moved here? You didn't just come to visit me because I'm sick? You live in San Francisco..." None of this makes sense, and I don't know if it's brain fog or if the situation is just that bonkers.

"My roommates moved home to save money, so we let the lease go. I don't have to live in the Bay Area to do my job, so when I thought about where I'd like to live next, LA was looking real attractive."

The way he says that makes my cheeks burn. How can he still have the hots for me after this week of hell? I scared myself in the mirror on the way to the shower.

True, we've been internet dating for a while, and that one night had been...magical... But this feels very fast, and now he has all but moved in without me even knowing. He's literally been living in my space unattended for over a week! He's been through my drawers to dress me. Oh God! Did he find *that* drawer? I mean, the MiO is my current fave, but I did a lot of market research... What must he be thinking?

I try to rally my filters so I don't say something rude again, but I am struggling to keep it all straight. My utter exhaustion is not helping. "I'm glad you came when you did. I clearly needed the help, but this is all moving so fast. I don't—"

He holds up a hand, and I stop.

"I'll be honest. I did not expect to move in with you, but this virus put a spike in my plans. I'm not trying to push anything on you, and I will get my own place as soon as possible. But you clearly needed help, and I am not the kind of person to turn their back on a friend. Whatever else we may become, you're my friend, Penny. Let me stay on your couch and help you until it's safe for me to leave."

Well, when he put it like that... "I'm not the kind of person to kick a friend out into the cold."

"It's LA. It's never cold."

"Smartass. But while you're here we are just friends. No benefits, no pressure, none of that."

"Deal. No offense, but I'm planning to drop your meals at your door since you're conscious again."

"How did you even get food? My fridge was practically empty."

"I found an app that delivers. I've got enough to see us through the next week or so. I'm not a gourmet chef or anything, but you won't starve."

"I can't taste anything anyway, so not starving is literally the bar."

He chuckles and heads for my bedroom door. He turns back at the threshold. "Thanks, Penny, for letting me stay. I know it's awkward as hell, and we didn't plan on any of this, but I'm glad I was able to be here for you."

I want to put my hand on his forearm, or even lean in for a hug, but I stay where I am on the bed and he lingers safely six feet away in my doorway. While my independent streak is pitching a fit, my logical problem-solving brain concedes I'd have been in real trouble if he hadn't come when he did. Yes, it's awkward, but I'm grateful under my grouchiness.

"I'm glad you came."

CHAPTER 9

PENNY

I close my laptop and toss it to the end of the bed, frustrated and tired. My team is trying really hard but there are no easy answers. Or any answers at all, really. They are all stuck at home too and I'm trying to run meetings from my sickbed. All of the unknowns weigh heavy on my shoulders along with a head that feels like it's full of lead.

On the one hand, it's great so many people want to preorder our product now that they're stuck at home. On the other, it's super stressful that I don't have firm time-lines for when we'll be getting those units in or when we'll be able to ship them out again.

I keep teetering between hope and despair.

Add to it the exhaustion and brain fog and… What was I doing? It doesn't matter.

I flop back on my pillow, not caring if my silk blouse wrinkles. It only had to look good for that meeting, and I'm too sore to take it off. My flannel sleep pants complete the outfit as I slide farther under the covers. Even just sitting up and talking, trying to make sense of my employees' reports, has made me sleepy again. My eyelids weigh five pounds each.

I think the worst part is that I can't turn to any of my usual stress relief activities, so it's just building up to critical mass inside me. I can't clean or organize. I can't plan. I can't fuck. I'm so exhausted, the MiO is too much right now. I can barely breathe let alone run. I'd walk if I was allowed to go outside.

Even the puzzle I started is too much. Instead of calming me down, it's stressing me out. I started crying while finding the edge pieces. All I can do is sleep and worry, and it's making me cranky.

My phone rings in my hand. I forgot I was still holding it, my lifeline to the outside world. It's Dash, calling me from the living room.

In some ways, going back to video calls with him has been great. I feel like we're back in our separate apartments, chatting our evenings away. It's blessedly normal, until he shifts the camera and I remember he's not at home. He's on my couch, and my apartment is a mess.

"Hello, beautiful. What do you want for dinner tonight? I can make pasta or heat up a can of soup."

"It doesn't matter."

I can't even muster the energy to care. All of my hard work, my hustle for funding, my triumph in the media over T-Con, all of that momentum is slipping away into this sea of uncertainty, and I don't know how to make it stop.

"We offer only the very finest in cuisine here at Chez Maxwell. Every shelf-stable staple is here for your convenience. Simply say the word."

I know he's just trying to help, but I'm fighting back tears and I really don't care. If I open my mouth I'm going to cry.

"We're going to get you back on your feet, but you need to eat."

I know he wants me to laugh at his terrible rhymes, but I'm not in the mood to be cajoled. I want to wallow. "Make what you want. I can't taste it anyhow."

His shoulders fall, and I feel like a bitch for being so cranky with him. I'm just so over all of this bullshit, and my filters burned up with my fever.

"Ok, pasta it is," he says.

Damn it, I hurt his feelings. Why is he still here, putting up with my shit? The tears I was fighting win the battle and slide down my cheeks.

"Hey, or soup. I can make the soup. Or I can put the pasta in the soup?"

"Why are you being so kind to me?"

"Because you're sick and need help with dinner?"

His genuine confusion sets me off. "What is the point? I can't do anything! I can't eat. I can't exercise. Christ, walking to the bathroom gets me winded. I can't be with you. I can't be alone. I can't work, but I can't stop thinking about everything I should be doing either! This just sucks!" Once my frustration overflows its banks, it floods my brain and exits in an angry stream from my mouth.

"It does. It completely and utterly sucks."

His ready agreement acts as a temporary dam, halting my rant. "What? No cheerful advice about keeping my head up?"

"No. This whole situation is completely fucked up, and I wish I could wave a magic wand and fix it but I can't. It absolutely sucks. I think admitting that is just as important as continuing to try anyway."

Somehow the acknowledgement that the situation is genuinely shitty—and not just my fever brain coloring the way I see the world right now—makes me feel the tiniest bit better. Enough to dry my cheeks and attempt a smile. "When did you get so smart?"

"Can I get that in writing for my mom?" he jokes. "So, pasta?"

"Sure. Pasta."

*D*ASH

Three weeks into isolation, I am damn lucky I can effectively do my job from quarantine. This lockdown has thrown everything into chaos, and people are leaning more and more on technology to make life function from the boundaries of their homes. My articles are in high demand. I know there are so many struggling to work from home, but for me it's working.

Although this isn't exactly home. My meager possessions sit in boxes shoved up against the wall. I've only unpacked what I absolutely need. Even that has managed to explode all over the couch and the floor.

It might be better if I had a dresser or a closet or a bed that wasn't also the couch, but I don't because I don't live here. Right now Penny is stuck in her bedroom so it doesn't matter, and once she's back on her feet I'll be finding my own place. Also, to be honest, even with my own space it would probably still look like a tornado hit.

Why doesn't organizing give me the same dopamine hit as video games? My life would be a whole lot easier if it did. Unfortunately, if I can't see things, I lose track of them completely. So I tend to leave everything out, all the time.

My watch beeps, and I realize the morning has flown by. Time to make some lunch for us. I'm falling back on classics I remember from my childhood sick days. We've gone through cinnamon toast, canned chicken soup, saltines, jello. Today, tomato soup and grilled cheese. It's a classic for a reason. I even manage not to burn the bread this time.

I fix a little tray, don my mask, and knock on her door.

"Come in!"

I balance the tray on one yellow-gloved hand, turn the knob with the other, and nudge the door open with my foot. I've gotten good at this balancing act over the last few weeks. When I see Penny, she is sitting up in bed and grinning like she's won the lotto. I'm so surprised, I bobble the tray and spill a little soup. After weeks of despondent at best, downright angry and sad at worst, a smile is a welcome change.

"You all right there?" she asks.

"You're smiling," I say, still stalled in the doorway.

"I don't have a fever!" She grins wider and aims the laser thermometer at her forehead for confirmation. "98.8!" she crows.

"That's great!" I grin back behind my mask. This is absolutely worth celebrating. "Do you feel up to eating lunch?"

"I probably won't taste it, but yes I am hungry for the first time in weeks." She claps her hands like a toddler at McDonalds and reaches for the tray. I set the tray on her lap and retreat from the room. I connect to the video call on my computer in my lap, and she answers immediately. This has become our routine. I watch her take a hopeful bite of the sandwich.

"Anything?" I ask.

"Nope, just warm salt, but I'm not going to let that bring me down."

"You are certainly in a good mood."

"I feel like I've turned a corner. I can't wait until I can get back to work. Panicking about my business between involuntary naps and useless meetings has been driving me nuts. I need my brain back!" She dips the sandwich in the soup and takes another bite. This is the most she's eaten all week. I can't help but hope she has truly turned the corner on this virus.

"Don't worry about work. Just focus on getting better."

She takes another bite. "I really wish I could taste this. My mom used to make this for me all the time when I was a kid."

"Really? Mine too. What else did she make? I'm running out of ideas."

"Campbell's chicken noodle, oatmeal, and chicken nuggets. I didn't ever get to have chicken nuggets unless I was sick. Such a weird thing to remember."

"My mom always babied me when I was sick. The rest of the time I ate what my father wanted for dinner, and I'd like it, damn it. But when I was sick, Mom would make all my favorites. Grilled cheese and tomato soup, homemade chicken soup with those little oyster crackers, jello with marshmallows on top…"

She grins. "I wondered where you got the idea. Your mom sounds great."

I go quiet. Was she? The woman who raised me had largely been a bystander to my father's anger. Sure, when I was home sick and he was at work she had cared for me. But what about all the other times she stood by while he badgered me about my grades or my focus, refusing to even hear the letters ADHD from my teachers?

But that's too heavy to lay into this conversation, so I shrug and divert. "What about your mom? Tell me about her."

Penny stirs her soup and answers without looking at me. "Yeah, not winning any mother of the year awards there. My dad decided pretty early on he wasn't cut out for family life. He provided for us, but he worked late a lot. And I'm not so sure he was working alone, if you know what I mean. Mom coped by drinking. And doing whatever recreational drugs she could get her hands on. So she was there, but not really there, most of the time. Notice my sick foods were just 'add hot water' or fast-food takeout? I learned how to take care of myself early on."

"Well…" I trail off. I don't know what to say. I didn't mean to bring up bad memories while she already feels like shit. "Where does ice cream fall on your list of sickbed foods?"

"Ice cream is always at the top of every list."

"Ah, but what flavor?"

"The one with the most chocolate. You?"

"Plain vanilla."

"Vanilla? With all of the options, you pick vanilla?"

"I don't like being surprised by things in my ice cream. I like to add my favorites and make it just how I want. Don't judge me!"

"Oh, I am judging hard." She might be judging, but she's also laughing again.

"Okay, Judgy McJudgerton, you can just finish your lunch by yourself."

"Noooo! Don't go!" She laughs as I slowly lower my laptop screen and cut her off.

I'm relieved she's feeling better. I hadn't realized how heavy the worry had been until just now when I set it down.

I know I should get some more work done or start tidying because she'll likely be up and about soon, but just seeing her all curled up in bed and happy has gotten me too excited for any of that. I've kept to her request of just being her friend while I'm stuck here. She's been too sick to even think about anything else. But now that she's on the mend, I can't help but wonder what comes next.

My brain fast-forwards to all the things I'd like to do with her if we were not-just-friends, and soon I am hard as a rock. That smile on her face, her silk blouse hanging low and loose, her hair tousled from the pillow, looking all satisfied and sleepy... I imagine all the things I could do to make her look like that again.

I should pull up my apartment searches to see if anything has shifted, but sitting in these jeans right now is going to be uncomfortable. Maybe a hot shower. Clear my mind. Maybe clear my pipes too.

The hot water flowing over me does little to calm things down, and after weeks of abstinence I need to handle this. My mind starts to spin a fantasy. I am back in that hotel room with Penny, and in my alternate reality I don't have any deadlines so we have time to wake up leisurely together. I imagine she joins me in the shower and runs her hands all over me as I soap up.

My own hands don't even come close to hers. Too big, too rough, but for now they'll have to do. I grip my shaft gently, the way she would, and give myself a long tug. I pretend she's on her knees in front of me, eyeing me greedily as she pumps her hands up and down my cock. I want this woman so badly, I have no restraint. In an embarrassingly short amount of time, I've forgotten to be gentle and slow. I'm jacking myself hard under the hot water spray, grunting and panting, ready to blow.

The image of her cupping her gorgeous tits for me to come on sends me shuddering over the edge. Relieved, I rinse the soap and everything else down the drain, dry myself roughly, and wrap the towel around my waist to go get dressed in the living room.

PENNY

Feeling halfway human, I put on a mask and carry the tray into the kitchen myself, anxious to see the world outside my bedroom. The shower running tells me I'll have the space to myself. The main room of my one-bedroom apartment has an open concept kitchen and living space, so limiting contact is hard. But I really need to get out of my bedroom now that I'm physically able.

Dash has been so good to me while I've been sick. I want to start pulling my weight again. My legs feel fine and sturdy beneath me as I leave my confinement, but the level of chaos in my normally well-organized and spotless space threatens my newfound balance.

Plates and coffee mugs sit stacked up in the sink, food caked on the porcelain. The stovetop is covered with seemingly every pan I own, all used and stacked with abandon. I look for a place to set down the tray and settle on the floor, since it's the only clear space I can find. The counter holds a loaf of bread, a bag of apples, and jars of peanut butter and jelly.

I survey the living room in a daze, taking in the

details and piecing together the story. This poor man! He's been waiting on me hand and foot, living on my couch, and trying to hold down a job remotely. He literally packed up his life for me and parked it on my couch when I needed him. This level of chaos would normally drive me insane, but all I can see is the evidence of a life upended on my behalf.

Luckily, this is all just temporary. Dash has done so much for me. The least I can do is not harp on his housekeeping skills. The only roommate I've ever been able to tolerate was Nicola in college, who is just as neat and driven as I am. Even that had only lasted as long as our ill-fated relationship.

But Dash isn't my roommate or my lover at this point. Just a friend who cared enough to help. Soon, I'll be back to full strength, and he can find his own place down here in LA. We'll get back to normal, and then we'll see where things go.

Before I've roused from my shock, the bathroom door opens and he comes out, wearing only a towel, his chest still wet from his dripping hair. All worries about the state of my apartment disappear as I remember the glory of his chest under my hands.

For the first time in weeks a hint of lust percolates and all I can think is *thank God*. If Covid had taken this too, I'd have been pissed. As it is, I'm frustrated I can't touch him until I'm completely sure I'm not contagious. His hand flexes and tendons dance as he grips his towel more firmly, and I wonder if he feels the same. I know we agreed to take things slow, but this feeling in my gut (and lower) just confirms I'd definitely like to take things somewhere.

"Penny! What are you doing up?" he asks.

My eyes jerk from his abs to his face. "You were in the shower, and I just wanted to bring my dishes to the sink."

"Here, let me take those." Still gripping the towel, he bends to pick up the tray and I hold my breath as the towel stretches, molding to his thighs. "I was going to clean up a bit before you came out. Thought I had another day or two." He starts collecting coffee mugs and plates one-handed and piling them in the sink. All I can think of is how strong and nimble that hand can be.

"Dash, stop. It's okay. You've been taking care of me and working full-time during a freaking pandemic. Go get dressed. Please."

He glances down as if just realizing he's still half naked. "Oh, right. Um." He picks up a T-shirt and clutches it in front of him, looking at me expectantly.

Because I am standing in his bedroom.

"Right. Okay, I'm going to go lie back down."

As much as I hate it, I hustle back into my bedroom so he can have some privacy. His strong hand follows me, tucked securely in my horny memory. So what if I imagine it when I touch myself under the covers? It takes my mind off the mess in my apartment, and gives me a shot at keeping my hands to myself long enough for him to find a place and for us to see if this has a shot at being a real relationship.

CHAPTER 10

PENNY

I drop my head on the kitchen table that is serving as the de facto command center for my startup. This is too hard. The office is still closed; my shipments have been dropped off at the warehouse but there is no one there to unpack them or ship them out to customers. Investors are spooked, and I'm trying to solve problem after problem with a Covid-fogged brain and video calls from my kitchen. I've cleared the Covid infection. So why don't I feel better? Why can't I fix this?

The guttural yell of frustration explodes from my throat, and it feels great to scream into the void. When Dash's hands land on my shoulders, I sit up and yelp. I forgot for a moment that there is another human in my space.

Dash is so quiet when he writes, curled up on the couch with his laptop, that it's easy to forget he's here. Still here. His apartment hunt has stalled, and I haven't pushed. There is really nowhere for him to go, and to be honest, I don't want to be alone right now. But we aren't really together either…

Everything is stuck, and it's breaking my will to keep hustling.

"What's wrong?" he asks, puttering at the counter behind me.

"Everything."

"Want to talk through the specific everything that made you scream bloody murder?"

"No, I want my brain back! I want to be able to fix things like I usually do. I need to talk it out with my teams and find the creative, flexible solutions I know are hiding out there. I want things to go back to normal."

"Normal is my nemesis. It's completely overrated. Come talk to the chaos junkie in your life, and we'll see what we can come up with. What is your biggest worry right now?" Dash slips into the kitchen chair next to mine and hands me a fresh coffee with cream and two sugars, just how I like it. I can feel the lovely heat and support he radiates like a sunbeam.

I lean my head on his shoulder and let my stress spew. "I can't get these preorder units shipped out. We had all that fantastic buzz which turned into sales, but if I can't deliver them, I'll lose all that momentum. I promised my customers that they would have their toys on time, and nothing is functioning at full speed, least of all my brain. I am failing, and I hate it."

"And how many preorders are there?"

"Thousands." I sip the coffee and hope it jolts something loose.

"I see. So you can't deliver everything, but what if you could deliver some of the things?"

"What good would that do? People will get pissed off if they see other people getting goodies and they aren't."

"Not if you focus on sending out the ones to the big influencers, celebrities, and media folks you met who happen to be on the list. People always think those folks get stuff earlier. And if they're already on your preorder list, you aren't sacrificing stock."

Puzzle pieces shift and move in my head as I struggle to wrap my mind around the proposed plan. It's completely different than what I had planned, and I don't have the brainpower to think through it clearly right now. Dash keeps talking, but I only catch bits and pieces.

"...keep the buzz going, and if you keep it exclusive, it should be small enough that we could handle the shipping from here."

I've had my eye on the goal of shipping out one hundred percent of preorders on time for so long, this shift is disorienting. Could it work? Is it feasible? This is just the kind of solution that I was looking for though. A sidestep that is manageable but doesn't pull us too far off course.

I hadn't expected him to have a viable solution, and here he is stepping up with a possible winner. I need to vet it with Nic and the team. Just figuring out if this is a possibility is making my head hurt. The logistical questions and current Covid restrictions swirl in my mind, and I want to cry. Dash's warm hand rubs my back, and the comfort helps calm the hive of angry wasps swarming in my skull long enough that I can stop the spiral.

I have the units in LA. Can we liberate a crate or two? I can't ship out thousands by myself, but if I could ship out, say, twenty to targeted users, maybe even some of the connections I made through my interviews...it just might work.

"You're a genius."

"Nah, just thinking it through from another angle." Dash sits back in his chair and takes his hand with him. I instantly miss the connection.

"I'm usually excellent at pivots, but my brain still isn't a hundred percent. And I've been staring at the forest for so long, I've forgotten there are trees I can climb. Thank you."

"My pleasure." He smiles and retreats to the couch.

I think about all of the pleasure he's forgone over the last month, both while taking care of me and by agreeing to keep anything more than friendship in cold storage while we are living together. That's a lot of pleasure we've missed out on.

That part of my brain perks up with a vengeance. There is something intensely sexy about a man who put his entire life on hold because I needed him. He has taken such good care of me, and as I side-eye him sprawled on my couch, I really want to *take care* of him too.

I'm not sure I'm ready to start a real relationship with him staying here in my space. But I am also still ridiculously turned on by him, and he's been such a sweetheart taking care of me.

Like the thousand-piece puzzle I started and had to set aside, this feels like another problem with a lot of moving pieces that I can't quite sort through right now. But also like the puzzle, I'm hopeful we'll find solutions together.

DASH

I settle back on the couch, ridiculously pleased that one of my ideas might be helpful. I've largely kept my nose out of her business. After all, what do I know about the sex toy market? But she'd looked so beaten down I had to try.

One thing my brain is never short on is ideas. Execution is another matter entirely, but I am a great brainstormer. Hell, some days my head feels like my own personal hurricane. The fact that my suggestion might actually help makes me feel ten feet tall.

Taking care of Penny while she was sick but being unable to make her feel better was humbling. I've never worked harder and felt more helpless in my life. This is a nice change of pace.

The pesky voice inside my head keeps piping up. The one that tells me there's nothing she could possibly see in me, and I should cut and run before I get in too deep. I refuse to listen. This...thing...still has potential. I have never been this attracted to someone before. I just need to give her enough time and reasons to feel the same.

I watch from the couch as she takes my idea and runs with it. She gets Nicola on the phone, sends an email to the warehouse, and starts making a list of influencers and press who should get one, muttering under her breath all the while. She is incredible. What's it like to have an idea, make a plan of action, and then see it through to completion in one sitting?

That ability eludes me, despite years of searching, but I could watch her do it for hours.

"Are you hungry?" she asks, pulling me from my musings.

I realize I've been watching her for nearly half an hour, absorbing every detail. "Sure, I could eat."

"Want to order Thai?"

"On it." I open the delivery app on my phone. "Spicy pad thai with shrimp and tom yam soup?"

"That's right. You remembered." She smiles and turns back to her laptop.

My chest warms at her praise. I add my order and send it off. This is what I can do for her. I can take care of her needs and support her path to success. Speaking of success, I forcibly turn my attention back to the article I need to finish on the ten best streaming services. Fixating on how amazing she is will have to wait.

PENNY

I don't know what I'd have done without Dash. Thanks to his idea, we get thirty units out the door and into the hands of excited influencers. It is small progress, but progress nonetheless.

Even that small effort wiped me out though. He carried up the boxes, unpacked everything, built and filled the shipping boxes, and carried them back down to the car to drop off at the post office. All I did was the digital legwork, and I am exhausted. Messaging people, printing labels, and writing a quick note to everyone shouldn't have drained me this badly, but I am falling asleep at my computer by three in the afternoon.

Dash rises from the couch and stacks his stuff haphazardly on the floor. "Okay, I'm calling it. Break time," he says.

"But there's still so much to do," I protest. I'm too far behind to stop.

"And none of it that can't wait a few hours while you take a brain break."

I cross my arms and refuse to stand. "Calling a nap a brain break doesn't make it sound better."

He looms over me, crossing his arms in a stubborn imitation of me. I am not amused. "Regardless of what you call it, it's what you need right now."

"I'm not two."

"I'm aware."

Not even the deep timbre of his voice as sexual tension sneaks into the innocent statement distracts me from my funk. "I don't need a nap," I insist, immediately hearing how petulant I sound.

Dash takes my hand and tugs me toward the couch. "Okay, how about a movie break?" he suggests.

"I can't watch a movie in the middle of the workday!"

"Why not?"

The honest confusion in his tone sets me back. "Because it's the middle of the workday." Shouldn't this be self-evident? Work. Day. If it's day, I should be working.

"Let me ask you something. Stay with me for a second." Dash frowns and looks at his hands. "What do you consider 'the workday'? Nine to five?"

"Sure, close enough."

"Okay. Do you work late into the evenings?" He holds up a finger.

"Sometimes."

"And through lunches?" He raises another finger.

"On occasion."

"How about weekends?" A third finger rises, and I'm starting to get annoyed.

"What's your point?"

"My point is that if you can choose to work during nonwork hours because it is more efficient, the converse should hold true as well."

I let that sink into my tired brain, still struggling to let go of my high expectations for myself.

"Listen," Dash tries again, "your brain and body are still recovering. We are in the middle of a pandemic that has turned the world on its head, and we still managed to get good work done today. You are allowed to rest."

Why does that last statement have tears welling in my eyes? His argument is compelling, and I am tired. I blink rapidly, barely resisting.

"I'll even throw in a foot rub…" Dash wiggles his eyebrows over that enticement.

Fine. He wins. I'll rest, but I'll do it on my own terms. "How can I resist? But I get to pick the movie."

"Deal."

He pulls my grandmother's afghan up on the couch and props up a pillow, while I get comfy. The six-hour BBC version of *Pride and Prejudice* is the perfect comfort watch in my opinion. But to my chagrin it isn't streaming anywhere, so the two-hour 2005 version will have to suffice. Thinking of Darcy now makes me remember Dash stretching his hand after making me come so hard I forgot my own name. I hadn't anticipated getting this turned on before he's even touched me, but here we are.

I start the movie and lay my head on the arm of the couch, stretching my legs toward the other end where Dash sits with an adorable frown on his face.

"Problem?" I ask innocently.

"No, not at all."

He tucks the blanket he's been sleeping with around my shoulders and I am surrounded by his scent: citrus and sunshine, with an undertone of ocean. It's not as powerful as when he gets out of the shower, but still intense enough to fill my head with decadent dreams. I try to pick up the threads of the Regency conversation on the screen, but it's difficult when all I want to do is snuggle in and be his little spoon again.

"That wasn't convincing," I tease.

"Shut up and give me your foot," Dash retorts.

With a laugh, I poke one foot out of my cocoon. He grasps my ankle and pulls my heel firmly into his lap.

"I've wanted to get my hand on this ankle since T-Con. So pretty."

I try to focus on the screen, but Dash pushes the pads of his thumbs into the arch of my foot and my eyes flutter closed on an involuntary and indecent moan. The sounds he's pulling from my throat would make me blush if I wasn't already feeling so relaxed and aroused. He works his knuckles into tired muscles and tight tendons. He pulls each toe, squeezing along the length. He doesn't miss a single trick. My body is molten with pleasure, and my pulse thuds beneath my skin, thick and slow.

About the time Mr. Collins compliments the potatoes, Dash switches feet. As Mr. Darcy proposes the first time, I nod off, exhausted and blissed-out.

Maybe I did need a nap.

I wake with a start to find the end credits rolling, my feet still resting in Dash's magical hands. Head tipped back, mouth soft, lashes long against his cheek, he looks so peaceful sleeping sitting up. Careful not to dislodge my feet and wake him, I shift so I can better admire him.

Physically, he is a beautiful man. I clocked that the minute I saw him in Vegas. And after all the time we've spent together, his personality has only made him more attractive.

The way he leapt into action to care for me while I was sick, and the way he continues to care about my well-being now that I am struggling with work and recovery... He is a good man on top of being a great lover. He's been such a good friend, but I don't want that. I mean, I don't want just that. I want the friend and the lover. Can't I have both?

My recently awakened libido perks up at the memory of just how great he was in Las Vegas. Grateful, I send up a silent *thank you* to whichever sexy gods hadn't abandoned me for its slow but steady return. For a long time, I'd worried Covid had taken it from me.

But the familiar tension low in my belly and the gathering heat between my legs let me know systems are back online. Lusting after him while he sleeps feels a little creepy though, so I roll back to my side, my feet accidentally brushing the very hard evidence of his own arousal.

Good lord, how can he sleep like that?

I glance back up at his face and realize he is no longer sleeping.

His hands begin caressing my feet again, and he smiles sleepily. "Do I lose points for falling asleep during your movie?"

"No."

"Good. Your nap—sorry, brain break—was catching, apparently. Feel better?" he asks, petting my calf.

NO! I want to shout. *No, I am all mixed up and turned on now and I asked you for distance and you gave it to me and now I don't want it but I'm afraid to let go of it and I don't know what to do because I can't think past you putting your mouth on me again!*

After what feels like an interminable pause for such an innocuous question, I gather my courage and honesty and shake my head no. This does not feel better at all.

"No? Does your head hurt?"

I shake my head again. "Lower."

"Your feet? I can keep rubbing them." Dash does just that, and I close my eyes and groan at how good it feels, but I've made my decision and I'm committed to my mission.

With regret, I pull my feet away from his gorgeously talented hands, sliding them past his cock deliberately before tucking them beneath me on the couch and rising to my knees. "No. I need you to rub me a little higher."

Dash closes his eyes on a gasp and clenches his now empty hands as if he's holding on to a very thin thread of control. "I need you to be very clear, Penny. Where do you want me to touch you?"

"It's easier if I show you." I scoot closer on the couch and hold out my hand. He places his in mine, eyes wide and fine tremors shaking his fingers with the effort to stay still. I turn his hand and lay it against my cheek. "Here. I miss your hand here."

He relaxes a fraction and smiles. *Good.* I guide his

hand down my neck, tease his fingers over my collarbone, and clasp it firmly over my breast. His eyes track every move, hungry.

"And here. I really like it when you touch me here."

"Penny," Dash growls in warning. A warning I welcome but choose not to heed.

"And here, Dash. I need you here." I tug his hand down past my navel, pressing it between my legs, rocking my hips forward to grind against his strong fingers.

Dash coughs and tries to speak. "Are you… Are we…what?"

I take inordinate pride in the fact that I've rendered him speechless. "Remember when I asked you to keep your hands to yourself?"

He nods.

"I've changed my mind."

His fingers flex against me, gripping my hip and my clit. I gasp and instinctually lean into the pressure. That seems to be all the confirmation he needs to bring his other hand to the party. Sliding it around the side of my neck, holding my face steady before his intense gaze, Dash pins me with a basilisk stare. "That's my hand, Penny. How do you feel about my mouth?"

He is so close his words tickle against my lips, and I lick them in anticipation.

"Kiss me, Dash."

CHAPTER 11

DASH

This is happening. This is really happening.

I fell asleep holding the ankle I've been admiring since T-Con. I woke from a delicious dream replaying my one night in the flesh with Penny to find her rubbing her feet against my erection.

After weeks of keeping my desire on lockdown, it breaks free now with a vengeance. When she tells me to kiss her, I take her mouth like a man in a desert takes his first sip of water.

It was easier when we'd both been wearing masks and I couldn't see her lips at all. Since she's recovered and we've stopped masking at home, everything is harder. And I do mean everything. Constantly. Being able to see her mouth but not touch it had felt like a reward and a punishment in one.

She returns the kiss with equal passion, tangling her tongue with mine as we reacquaint ourselves with each other's taste.

The heat radiating from her pussy warms my fingers, and I am torn. I don't want to move and bring her to her senses. I want to go slow, so that this lasts forever. I want to charge full speed ahead and give us both the pleasure we've been avoiding, damn the consequences. Her stretchy yoga pants are doing nothing to contain her scent or warmth, and they tempt me to madness.

I push her shoulder until she lies supine on the couch. Her baggy T-shirt comes off easily, exposing her beautiful breasts to the sunlight. If I'd realized it was a no-bra day, I'd have been too distracted to fall asleep during the movie. But now I can only be grateful because it gave her time to decide and me easy access. I growl my gratitude, because words are beyond me.

I'm not sure if it's the growl or the tossed T-shirt, but Callie abandons her catwalk along the couch cushions for the safety of the bathroom with a disgruntled yowl. Penny laughs, but I am not letting the cat distract us.

Squeezing and plucking until her nipples pebble against the sensation, I pull her back into the moment and into my mouth, soothing the sting and absorbing every taste and texture I'd missed.

She has never tasted sweeter.

My hands meet in the middle, one tracing down her curves from shoulder to hip, the other reluctantly rising from between her legs. Hooking my fingers into the waistband of her pants, I drag them down her legs and toss them aside. I slide down to kneel next to the couch and splay her legs wide.

Her whispered, "Oh yes!" and gasped, "Please!" are all

the encouragement I need. I reacquaint myself with all of her beautiful secrets, already slick with desire. Sliding one, then two eager fingers into her tight sheath, I hook them gently, searching for the spot that makes her twitch.

Ah, there it is.

Slowly, deliberately keeping her off-balance, I alternate strokes of my fingers with flicks of my tongue until she growls and grips my hair in her fist.

"Quit fucking around, and find out already."

"Make me."

She grips my hair hard and holds me right where she wants me. "Fuck, that's so good, Dash."

With a grin and a firm tongue, I diligently work her clit, pushing her hard for her first orgasm until her pussy contracts with pleasure and her thighs clench around my head. Light-headed euphoria streams through me as she comes back down.

She's completely limp, panting, her chest heaving with the exertion of pulling oxygen into her lungs. *Fuck! Was that too much?*

She's only just recovered from Covid. I shouldn't have made her come so hard. Why didn't I ask Amrita about protocols for sex post-Covid? I'm an idiot.

"Whatever...put that...look on...your face...stop." Penny smiles up at me and rests her hand on her chest while she catches her breath. "Go...get a condom."

"No, I'm good," I demur. It's hard, but also the easiest no. Reality hits me like a bucket of cold water. I will not forget again that she is still on the mend.

"Bullshit." Her sharp tone pulls me from my spiraling thoughts. "You touched me. I want to touch you too."

She reaches for the button on my jeans and I bat her hands away. "You're still recovering. You are literally gasping for air."

"That's right, because you just delivered an orgasm that took my breath away. I would like to return the favor." She grips me through the thick denim and tugs, and I deliver the gasp she wants.

"But…"

She tucks a finger into my waistband and pulls me back on top of her. "Did you think you were the only one who missed this? I need to touch you. I want to feel again. I wish I could taste you. I need you, Dash."

I turn my head to the side to absorb the truth in those words. She needs me. That's a novel experience. Far be it from me to deny her what she wants. When I look back, she is waiting patiently.

"Do you trust me?" she asks.

"Yes." That answer rolls off my tongue without a second thought.

"Then trust me to know my own mind and my body."

I nod.

"Good, now go get that condom. I want you inside me for my next orgasm."

I reach over the edge of the couch to rummage in my backpack for the foil packets I optimistically packed over a month ago. Penny keeps busy undoing my zipper and freeing my cock, so it takes longer than I want to find them. Finally, condom in hand, I straighten to find Penny on her knees. She pushes me back on the couch and takes me in her mouth.

The sudden shock of heat and pressure threaten to pull my orgasm immediately. *Must. Not. Come.* I gasp and clench my jaw as she pops her lips off me like a lollipop.

"Gasping already?" Penny teases. "We can't have that."

She wraps her fingers around the base of my cock and squeezes until they meet, trapping the blood inside my already swollen member. It throbs uncomfortably, but it does help beat back the urge. I force a few deep breaths, desperate to hold on until I get inside her, but it's difficult when she is eyeing my cock like it's candy on Halloween.

"You know, prolonging this stage of arousal is excellent for your health. All kinds of hormonal and circulatory benefits." She says all of this while still eyeing my twitching cock.

"Are you telling me that edging is good for my heart?" I ask.

"Studies show—"

I cut her off with a kiss. Her voice in that tone, the brilliant engineer saying filthy things with authority, threatens to send me over. Another night I'll take my time and let her play, but tonight I need her too much. "We'll have to explore those health benefits another time."

Scooting back, I quickly roll on the condom and surge forward, reversing our positions and pushing her back on the couch. The head of my cock unerringly finds her, wet and waiting, and she rocks her hips greedily, encouraging me. I am helpless to deny her anything. With slow, even pressure, I push inside her tight pussy and watch her eyes flutter closed.

"God, I missed this," she moans. "You feel so good."

"Worth the wait," I murmur against her neck as I kiss and lick along the sensitive line to her shoulder that I remember makes her shiver, while I pump thickly inside her. Already primed, her second orgasm is not long in coming once I move my thumb to her clit, circling firmly. I chase her over the edge, my hips pistoning hard to keep pace. My release racks my body with wave after wave of pleasure as I try to give her everything. Anything to prove my worth. Hopefully enough that she'll let me stay.

As we both come back down, Penny wraps her arms around my back and her legs around my waist, holding me in a full-body embrace.

And for the first time since I moved in, I feel at home on this couch.

Riding high on our renewed relationship, I get inspired to impress her. My editor has yet to pull me back onto gaming reviews, reasoning that pandemic tech content is more marketable right now. So I'm reviewing a new cooking app for an article, and treating Penny to a fancy meal at the same time.

The concept is great: they ship fresh food to the door, provide app-based cooking instructions and tutorials to guide any chef through the cooking process, and there's a social component where users can share plate snaps, feedback, and substitutions.

As a very basic home cook, I am the perfect demographic to try it out. I picked a stir-fry because it feels both healthy and easy to assemble. I hope Penny likes it. After last night's shift in our dynamic, I replayed the high points in our time together, and I realized we've never actually gone on a date. Tonight I'm going to fix that.

Opening the box, I lay the chicken, veggies, and rice on the counter along with the little packets of spices, seasonings, and sauces. The app on my phone recommends doing a *mise en place* whatever the hell that means. From the picture it looks like putting chopped thingies in a lot of little bowls. I rummage through Penny's kitchen until I unearth relative approximations for the cutting board, knife, pot, and frying pan they show, plus a few cereal bowls because those tiny glass bowls do not exist in any of her cupboards.

I press play on the next video and chop up the veggies like they showed me. The way they disassemble the bell pepper blows my mind. I would have never thought to unroll it with my knife.

Feeling confident, I chop the other veggies and the garlic before side-eyeing the chicken. *Ugh. Raw chicken.* I hate the texture. It is soft and slimy and gross. Just thinking about it makes me gag. This is a big part of why I rarely cook from scratch. The things I love to eat often squick me out in their raw form. But I am determined. I can do this.

I haul in a deep breath and click the chicken tutorial

video. The tip offered is to cut the chicken while it's still partially frozen to make smaller slices easier to manage. I open the bag and pour the chicken out onto the cutting board. It lands with a clunk. Willing to give it a go, I take the knife I found and aim for thin, even slices. Apparently the chicken is too frozen because my knife is barely making a dent in the hard surface, chipping off tiny shards of crystalized meat. It looks nothing like the video.

Going off script, I grab one of the cereal bowls, dump the garlic on the counter and throw in the chicken. A quick defrost cycle in the microwave should help. Unfortunately, this idea leaves the edges rubbery and over-cooked while the center of the chicken is still solid. The idea of eating this turns my stomach, but it is indeed easier to cut, and oddly, the different texture makes my aversion easier to handle.

Finally the damn meat is sliced into thin strips for the stir-fry, but my hands are covered in chicken goo. How the hell am I supposed to touch my phone to watch the next video? I scrub up with hot water and soap twice before tapping the autoplay feature in the app. There. Now I won't have to keep touching it.

Rice rinsed and into the pot, oil in the pan followed by the chicken. Keep it moving, Hall. *Check. Check. Check.*

When the video tells me to take the chicken out and put the veggies in, I can see that the chicken is still pink, so I get out another bigger pan and start heating oil in that one for the veggies. By the time that is hot, the video is showing all the veggies being tossed around.

Crap! Is there an order? Does it matter? I can feel the recipe getting away from me. Did they add the seasonings yet? Trying to catch up, I dump all the veggies in at once along with the garlic, ginger paste, chili flakes, soy sauce, and sesame oil packets.

On the back burner, my rice begins to boil over. I snap off the heat as rice starch oozes over the side of the pan and onto the cooktop. An acrid smell singes my nose and catches my attention. *Is something burning?*

I check the chicken which has turned orange on the side facing the pan. *Damn it.* At least it's cooked through. I scrape it into the veggie pan, and give it a toss. My eyes widen as I realize the acrid smell is coming from the veggies. Just then the video chimes in with, "Now for a finishing touch, add the sesame oil off the heat so it doesn't burn."

Crap. Too late for that now.

Hustling to salvage the meal, I put the stir-fry into a big bowl, spilling some on the counter as the pan is difficult to lift one-handed, and the bowl is smaller than the rim. Gluey rice plops into another bowl, and I slap off all the burners. I am done. Spent. Finished. How do people do this every day? Multiple times?

The chaos I've created on the counter is overwhelming. I need sustenance before I tackle cleanup. And maybe booze.

I knock on the bedroom door where Penny retreated for a video call. No response.

Quietly opening the door a crack, I spot her, fast asleep on the bed, laptop closed and clutched like a pillow. I go closer and smooth her blonde curls back from her face.

"Hey sleepyhead. It's time for our date."

"Uh-uh," she murmurs and rolls over. "Don't wanna eat. Can't taste it anyway."

"Penny, come eat. And then I promise you can go right back to sleep."

She stirs and rolls toward me, adorably rumpled. Sitting up slowly, she holds a hand to her head. "What time is it?"

"Six-thirty. How was your meeting?"

I hold out my hands and help pull her to standing. She keeps going right into my chest, snuggling in for a sleepy hug. I wrap my arms around her and my heart beats thickly in my chest. Screw dinner. I'm just going to exist on hugs for the foreseeable future.

"I think it went okay. We're trying to figure out damage control."

It takes real effort but I turn our hug toward the door. Taking her right back to bed is super tempting, but I don't want the food to get cold. "Tell me all about it on our date."

"You keep saying that," she grumbles as she follows me into the living room. "Did I miss something?"

"You and I both missed a first date, so I'm fixing that. I cooked."

She pulls back from my arms with a smirk on her face. "You cooked. No shade, but does that mean we're having grilled cheese again?"

"Why do people say 'no shade' right before they start throwing it? No, smartass, chicken stir-fry."

"Wow! Look at you, getting all fancy."

"Right this way, madam." I guide her to the couch and the coffee table I cleared and set. I even found an emergency candle in her drawer while I'd been hunting for spatulas. I'm quite proud of my attempt at ambience, and the candlelight makes her skin glow like the goddess she is.

I seat her on the couch before ducking back into the kitchen to bring out the food.

"Here we have a chicken, broccoli, and red pepper stir-fry over jasmine rice," I say in my best snooty accent, earning a chuckle.

"I'm sure it'll be delicious."

"Honestly, I'm kind of banking on the fact that you still can't taste anything."

CHAPTER 12

PENNY

I am charmed. I didn't expect to wake up from my nap to a date night, but this is a delightful surprise. He's clearly gone to some trouble to make a nice meal for us both. What a sweet man! I do wish he'd given me a heads-up so I could have primped a little bit, but then again what difference would lipstick make when he's already seen me at my worst? I love the fact that he's thinking about us and wants to surprise me.

So what if the rice is a little wet? I scoop some onto my plate and cover it with the tasty-looking chicken and veggies. I'm sad that I won't be able to smell or taste much of the meal, but I've learned that recovering from Covid is a long path lined with disappointments. At least I am healing and no longer contagious. And maybe he'll add this recipe to his repertoire, and I'll get to taste it again soon. There's the silver lining.

"So tell me more about your triage plans," Dash

prompts as he wrestles with a bottle of wine and trips over a pile of laundry he's shoved behind the armchair.

"Well, we've got the website updated to reflect the challenges. We also sent out the review form to the people who got early units. We are hoping to get some good buzz from that. Still no word on when we'll be able to get back into the office, but everyone is working out the kinks of these remote meetings. Poor Emmie has her kid home from school right now while she's trying to keep designing. She's considering moving home to Palm Brook to stay with her parents for some help. Nightmare. And Zarah might need to move out of her apartment, because with everyone working from home, the internet keeps crashing. Thank you."

I take the small glass of wine he offers, ignoring the tiny bobbing flecks of cork. My first sip leaves a glimmer of sourness tingling on my tongue, but mostly I just register sensations of cold and wet. At least it will help me get back to sleep.

Dash finally sits down and raises his own glass. "To our official first date. May it be the first of many."

I grin at that, warmth spreading through my body that has nothing to do with a fever or the wine, and everything to do with this sweet man. We skipped a lot of the courtship stages and jumped right into "in sickness and in health." I love that he wants to slow down and savor what we missed. Once I get back to full energy, I'll have to make sure I plan some nights like this too. He deserves to be spoiled a little after all he's done for me.

We might've gone about this relationship ass-backward, but it's working for us so far.

"To our one-night-stand, long may it last." I clink my glass to his and smile. "How was your day?" I ask.

I take my first bite of the stir-fry while he contemplates an answer, and my eyes begin to water. With a small cough, I reach for my wine and down what's left.

"You good?" Dash asked.

I nod, not trusting my voice to not give away the lie. Holy hell, that's spicy. My mouth is burning. My taste buds picked a hell of a time to wake up.

Dash raises his fork to his mouth, and I am caught between warning him and hurting his feelings. Before I figure out where to land, it's too late. The food is in his mouth. And then the tears are in his eyes, and the water is at his lips.

"So where did you get the recipe for this?" I ask politely while subtly scraping the seasoning off a piece of chicken.

Dash coughs and clears his throat before answering. "It was one of those all-in-one meal boxes." He stares at his plate, and I am stunned to see him scoop up another bite and force it down.

"Mmmhmm, and you followed all the directions?"

"As best I could," he confirms before a coughing fit sends him to the fridge for a glass of milk.

"Can I see the recipe card?"

"Liked it that much?" He grins and swallows hard, and my phone chimes. "I sent you the link. It's all on an app." He drinks down half the glass on his way back to the table and sits heavily in his chair. When he reaches for his fork again, his face stoic, I have to end the madness.

"Stop! I can't watch this!" I cover his hand with mine. "My mouth is on fire, and I can only taste the barest hint of it. How can you eat that?"

Dash lets the fork fall out of his hand and he chugs the rest of the milk. Tears stream down his face, and his shoulders shake. "Oh, thank God. It's terrible!"

His laughter is contagious. I try to speak through a bad case of the giggles. "How much chili flake did you put in?"

"I just used what they sent!"

"You poured in the whole bag?"

"I guess I should have paid more attention to the measurements." He chuckles at his mistake. "I think I burned off my taste buds."

"Nope. If you had, it wouldn't hurt so bad. Why did you keep eating it?" I wipe my eyes on a clean napkin, careful to avoid getting any chilies on my face. I don't want to be crying for the rest of the night.

"I thought you couldn't taste it. You haven't been eating much lately, and I didn't want to put you off it. Plus I didn't want to ruin our date if it wasn't bothering you."

"Dash, that's sweet, but for the love of all that's holy, don't take another bite."

I get up to grab bread, peanut butter, and jelly. My steps stutter to a halt as I take in the state of my kitchen. Apparently a war occurred during the preparation of this meal, and casualties were left where they fell. It certainly explains the nuclear heat levels. I find a clean butter knife and back out slowly, steeling myself not to say anything. He isn't the only one who doesn't want to spoil our first date.

Back at the table, I assemble two sandwiches and hand him one.

"Cheers!" I grin and raise my sammy in salute.

He taps his to mine and takes a resigned bite. "Some first date this turned out to be." He hasn't looked at me since I came back with the PB&J.

I lean my head on his shoulder and kiss his neck. "At the very least it's memorable. I know I'll never forget it. Someday we'll—" I almost say "tell our kids about it" but I catch that rogue thought before it can escape my lips. "—laugh about it over dinner with friends, and I'll tell them we stick to eating me out and takeout, thank you very much."

Dash finally smiles down at me, and I know this is a memory I will treasure.

"I'll take that." He kisses me, his tongue brushing against mine before he jerks his head back. "Damn, you're spicy."

"So I've been told." I wink and begin to clear the table.

"Leave the dishes. I'll take care of that later. I want to write up this article real quick before I forget how terrible it was."

I know how he gets lost in his work, and his nightly nine o'clock deadline is fast approaching. "Go ahead. You cooked. I'll clean."

"You sure?" he asks.

"Yeah. It'll feel good to get back in the groove."

"You're the best."

Damn straight I am. I find a certain zen peace in the monotony of washing dishes. It's a meditation on cleanliness. At least that's what I tell myself as I clean every pan, bowl, and utensil I own.

DASH

It is three p.m. on a Tuesday. I am cocooned on the couch, noise-canceling headphones on, completely immersed in the world on my screen. *Call of Anarchy* is my happy place when I'm not reviewing new games for the magazine, even if it's now bittersweet. I've had the same account since college when it first came out, and a group of old friends meet up online to play at least once a month. This is the game that convinced me I wanted to be a game designer.

My fingers fly over the buttons and levers on my controller without conscious thought. It's an extension of my hand, responding directly to impulses from my brain. I nimbly dodge and duck, before firing again and taking out my opponent.

I win the level and the cut scene of my player talking to the Boss takes me straight to my memory bank. I helped design this. This bastardization of my dream. Glimpses of *Astraia* are still visible if you know where to look. I was such a fool, but I can't stop coming back to my creation.

Astraia. Just thinking that name fills me with shame. For my senior thesis in undergrad, I designed the framework for a game. Going above and beyond as I do on projects I love, I poured my heart and soul into its creation for months.

I fully fleshed out the storyline for a space odyssey based on the ancient Greek goddess of justice who fled to the heavens to escape how terrible humanity had become. In my game the descendants of those horrible humans who had completely destroyed Earth looked to the skies for escape, bringing them once again into her sphere of justice. Post-apocalyptic earthlings venturing into space had to adapt and make good choices in the face of unimaginable odds to earn her favor and blessings which helped them survive and thrive in their harsh new environment.

If I couldn't have justice in real life, I could at least earn it in my pretend world.

In terms of my thesis, I wanted to prove that a game based around positive play and rewarding engagement could be just as compelling as single-shooter games that relied on violence and the thrill of vicarious lawlessness.

And I succeeded. Everyone who played it became obsessed, striving for an ounce of approval from the fickle goddess.

My little game about putting thoughts into action to please the goddess of justice in space blew away my advisors. The graphics had been basic but clear. The decision trees? Complex and flawless. The gamer feedback? Ninety-five percent positive. I not only graduated with honors—no small feat for a video game junkie who struggled all the way through middle and high school—but I came away with a coveted job offer from RPGiga. Powerhouse firm and legend in the industry, it's the very firm that designed the game I'm playing right now.

When I took the job, I naively brought my project with me in hopes of finishing it and producing it through RPGiga's impressive pipeline.

Instead, my IP got chopped up and integrated into a *Call of Anarchy* update, taking my dreams along with it.

Memories of that conversation with my idol telling me my project was dead still haunt me.

The next level starts and I blink from my daze just in time to take a grenade to the gut. I rub my chest, trying to ease the impact of both the virtual and mental attack. It doesn't work.

I emerge from my nest and creep carefully past where Penny is set up at the table on a video call, to get another cup of coffee. She smiles at me and turns her attention back to her screen where she has her camera off and mic muted. So far we are managing this shared workspace situation great. Noise-canceling headphones have been a godsend. I make a note in my phone to pitch a top ten tech list for headphones to my editor. Maybe I could ask different companies to send samples.

Hot coffee in hand, I go to the bedroom for some privacy on my call, and immediately lose my train of thought. Sitting on the edge of her bed, surrounded by her scents and textures, does little for my concentration and everything for my fixation. I can't wait until the work for the day is done so I can show her just how much I've restrained myself.

My cell phone ringing in my hand successfully pulls my head out of my pants and back into the present.

"Hi, Chad. How's it going?"

"Good, good. That last article you wrote was hilarious. Who knew that a recipe could be screwed up that badly?"

I hope the meal service isn't too disappointed. I tried to use my foibles as a cautionary tale for anyone attempting the service, while still outlining the positives. With a few user tweaks, I'm still convinced it would have worked out fine.

But I laugh at my own expense because it seemed like the response Chad Brooks expects. He likes to be laughed with and never at.

"I'll never take a stir-fry for granted again."

"I'm seeing a potential new series for you. Like a pandemic-centric, tech-based Try Guys. I'm making a list of products to pitch."

"Hey, put noise-canceling headphones on that list. Just a thought."

"Hmm, good call. I'm always down for an article that comes with free product."

"Just a heads-up, the *Fall of Pharaohs* launch is coming up next week. Did we get a review copy yet?"

"I gave it to the new intern, Lyam-with-a-Y. I don't want you distracted. We need to ride this wave of popularity. If you keep bringing in these numbers, there's a possibility that I can bring you on as a full-time staff writer."

In what department? I keep my eyeroll internal and play the game. After all, isn't full-time employment with benefits the endgame goal?

"That would be amazing. I've got a few other ideas for product reviews that might work. I'll send you an email."

"Sounds great. Keep up the good work, kid. I'll need at least two of them written up by next week. The funnier the better."

"You bet."

I hang up the phone and sigh. I should be happy. Hell, I should be elated that someone wants to offer me an actual job for my writing. Healthcare! Salary! Retirement plans! My father would be over the moon at this glimpse of stability for me.

But when have my emotions ever done what's expected of them?

CHAPTER 13

PENNY

I glance up from my staff meeting in full swing as Dash comes back in. He walks behind me to put his coffee cup in the sink. Didn't he just fill that? Something definitely happened on the call with his boss. He looks spooked, but I can't ask him about it right now.

I deliberately turn my attention back to the screen where everyone is staring at me. We've only gotten halfway through my agenda, and my team is squirrelly today.

"Nicola, how are we looking on shipping timelines?

"Um, sorry, I'm too busy shipping you and your conference booty call who just walked past. Are we just going to ignore the fact that he's in your apartment?" Nic asks.

"Hold up," Emmie chimes in. "Who did what when and how? I need details!" As a single mom currently parenting through a pandemic, she is always hungry for stories from the dating world.

"Conference booty call? That sounds like a story," Zarah teases as she twirls a curl around her finger.

"Oh my God, did he give you Covid?" Jen, always jumping to the worst-case scenario, asks.

Mike, my warehouse manager, is the only one on the call who holds his tongue, but he might also have us muted while he watches *Star Trek* reruns. It's a fifty-fifty shot. He usually doesn't tune in until he needs to.

And just like that, my carefully crafted agenda for this meeting flies out the window. No one tells you this is a hazard of working with friends.

"What happened to 'stays in Vegas'?" I glare at Nicola.

"I don't know. You tell me why he didn't stay in Vegas? How long is he staying? How long has he been there? More importantly, why are we only finding out about this now?"

It's a fair question. This group of people are more than my colleagues. They are my people, my inner circle, the friends who are family. They took a leap of faith with their finances and careers to come open this business with me. Why hadn't I been more open about Dash?

I peek over my shoulder to confirm that he has his fancy headphones on again before I reply.

"At first, we hooked up in Vegas, and I thought it might turn from a one- into a two-night stand. And then everything went sideways and we scrapped that plan."

"He's Anonymous," Nicola blurts.

"He didn't tell you his name? Hot!" Emmie leans closer to her screen as if we're sitting across from each other at a bar and the story is about to get good. I smile and long for the day G&T nights are a thing we can do again. Girl talk and gin and tonics are now forever linked in my mind. I do owe them the story, even if I don't have a bubbly beverage to ease its flow.

"No. He's the Anonymous who broke the story." Nicola corrects her.

"Oooooooh, that's even hotter. Hold on." She grabs a lime seltzer water and pours it into a fancy glass and takes a sip. "What? I'm on the clock. It's the best I can do."

"G&T call!" Zarah chimes in and disappears from the screen.

"Keep it sober! We are not done with this meeting!" I plead. Everyone except Mike ducks off-screen to grab their bubbly water of choice. It gives me a chance to compose my thoughts. This was not how I anticipated this meeting going. Jen sits down last. She cut an actual lime and is squeezing it over her beverage.

"Okay. Keep talking," Jen says, taking a bracing sip.

I really love my friends.

"That's exactly what we did. At first I thought he was just following up and keeping track of the story. But we kept talking and texting, and it turned into more."

"I still don't understand how he ended up on your couch," Zarah prodded.

"We were on the phone every night, since he was in San Francisco and I was between New York and here. So when I missed a call because I was sick, he drove down here to check on me."

"Swoon!" Emmie squeals.

"Yeah, his roommates bailed and he was headed down here to find a place, but he stayed to take care of me. And with everything else going on, it's been hard for him to leave."

"Which is why you didn't tap any of us for help?" Jen asks. She's not judging, but I can tell she's hurt.

"In the beginning I couldn't even keep my eyes open, let alone think to call anyone. By the time I was aware, I didn't want to risk any of you catching this, and he was already here and exposed."

"Do we need to come roust him out of there? He's been there almost two months at this point," Jen points out.

Two months. That reality hits me in the chest. Has it really been that long? What is time anymore? It feels like he moved in a week ago. *Two months...* It's probably time for us to have a conversation about his sleeping arrangements. "Not yet."

"Hmm, he must be taking *excellent* care if you're okay with him disrupting your space," Zarah observes.

"Two words." I lean closer to the screen and my friends mirror me. "Foot. Rubs," I whisper.

My friends do not disappoint. Falling off chairs, fanning themselves, chugging bubbly drinks, they cut up and make me laugh in the best way. All except Mike, who is still staring slightly off-screen, confirming that whatever is happening to Spock and Kirk is far more interesting than the rest of us. It feels so...normal. Lately, every bit of normalcy feels like a gift.

"His, ahem, foot rubs are excellent at shutting my brain off. I think I'll keep him around."

"If you decide against keeping him around, you can send him my way," Emmie teases. "What I wouldn't give for some quiet brain nights."

Touch is one of her love languages, which, along with her engineering degree, makes her an excellent fit to run research and design.

"I'll let you know." I hold up my agenda on my phone and try again. "Now, if we're all done picking apart my personal life, can someone update me on the preorder numbers?"

That night, halfway through a shared frozen pizza and bottle of red wine at my kitchen table, I broach the subject that has preoccupied me since the meeting. I don't know why I'm so nervous, but I can't seem to find the right words. I know I do better with speeches when I can practice them and prepare. But when I tried to plan this conversation there were so many unknowns that everything I said sounds wrong. I can't keep going over and over it, so I'm just going to wing it. We talk about everything else. Surely we can talk about this too.

"Dash, can we talk about something?" Nerves shake my voice and I draw in a deep breath to steady myself.

Mid-sip of wine, he lowers his glass cautiously. "Of course. What's up?"

"You are still sleeping on my couch."

He runs his hand over the back of his neck and winces. "Yeah, I know. I keep checking the listings but nobody is moving right now, and people are real skittish about new roommates…"

I stretch my hand across the table and wait for him to take it before I speak again. "I think we need to figure out a new arrangement."

"Okay." His face tightens, and he pulls out his phone.

No, this is not going well. Panic shortens my sentences. "You shouldn't have to sleep on the couch. I want you to move."

"I know. I'll look again in the morning. Maybe I can just head back north."

I swear to God I can word better than this. "No. Into my room. With me. Fuck, I'm not saying this well." I grip his hand harder as I take another sip of wine and try again. "Look, I just think it's ridiculous for you to keep contorting yourself to fit on my crappy couch when there is a perfectly good bed ten feet away that we have established I enjoy having you in, so…"

Dash blessedly cuts off my ramblings with a kiss. My shoulders relax and the tension in my neck melts away along with my knees as he does that thing with his tongue that I love.

He moves to my neck and kisses his way up to my ear, his whisper sending a shiver down my spine. "Are you sure?"

"It…it makes sense, doesn't it?" I stutter on an exhale.

Dash pulls back and leans in his chair, his face blank. I miss his touch immediately. What did I say?

"Not what I asked. I can make do on the couch until I find a place, if this is a logic thing. I don't want to be a logical conclusion."

I can practically see him drawing the shutters down. I hurt him with my fear, and I can't stand that. Words explode from my mouth, no filter, no preparation, pure emotion.

"Good. Because nothing about the way I feel makes sense to me right now. I shouldn't be tied up in knots over a man I've known barely two months. I shouldn't be asking him to move in during a global pandemic. This feels impulsive and out of control and…right." I take a steadying breath and try again. "All I know is when you talk about leaving, it gets hard to swallow. And when you tell me about roommate listings, the butterflies in my stomach turn to hornets. I want you to stay. I want you in my bed and in my life. I want to take another step toward logic with you in this world gone mad."

Dash smiles wide enough that his dimples come out to play. I'm toast.

"Okay."

"Okay?" I smile back, relieved we're on the same page. Why can't all relationships be this easy? What was I so worried about?

"I'll stay as long as you want me here. In your apartment. In your bed. In your life."

"About that bed part…" I tease, eager to work out some of these nerves that have had me tied up in knots.

And so a planned evening of binge-watching Netflix fast-forwards to "chill."

DASH

I wake in the middle of the night to soft hair tickling my nose. This is new. My spot on the couch never tickled me awake, but the tradeoff of waking with Penny in my arms is worth it.

The bare shoulder a hair's breadth from my mouth belongs to the naked woman I'm spooning, and this pleasure outweighs any irritation I might feel over being woken up in the wee hours of the morning.

If making love until we're exhausted and falling asleep in each other's arms is logical, I am here for it. With distance, I can see how her mind took apart the problem of how to get me in her bed and laid out a solution. Her approach nearly broke me, but the reward is worth it.

Kissing her shoulder, I notice that she doesn't shiver the way she does when I kiss her neck. I add the observation to my mental list of Penny's Pleasures. I am quickly becoming obsessed with learning all the ways to make her feel good.

I'm not going to mess this up. I slide my arm around her waist, bringing her snug against my chest. When she arches to move her ass closer to my hips, grinding sleepily against me, I kiss her curls and grin. "Good morning, sunshine."

"Mmm, what time is it?" she asks.

"Early. Time enough to play before the day." I tilt my hips to slide my now-hard length between the welcoming cheeks of her ass and try to hold back a moan. *Be cool, man. Be cool.*

"After last night, I'm so sleepy." Her words say *I'm tired*, but her rolling hips say *Wake me up!*

"Leave-me-alone-I'm-going-back-to-sleep so sleepy? Or I'm-just-going-to-lie-here-and-let-you-wake-me-up-right so sleepy?"

"Oooh, I like options." Her sleep-tinged voice is deep and sexy. "How 'bout number two with a possibility of number one if it's not happening?

"As you wish."

"All right, Wesley."

I turn her laughter into a gasp with a gentle bite at the nape of her neck. "How do you know I'm not the Dread Pirate Roberts?"

My hands trace over her shoulders and down her back, and she practically purrs. Her eyes close with plea-sure when I comb my fingers through her hair, scratching her scalp gently. There are so many ways I want to make her feel good. It'll take years to discover them all, and I'm going to love every second of it.

I hook my thumbs at the base of her skull and massage away the tension she stored there this week. Continuing down her spine, I turn her into a soft marshmallow of joy next to me on the bed. Moving to her lower back and hips, I wring moan after moan from her beautiful lips.

She is every bit a goddess, wrapped in white sheets, glowing in the faint light of her charging phone, and I am the mortal content to worship her any way she'll let me.

"Roll over, Penny."

Eyes still closed, she rolls toward me, clearly still lost in sensation. The sheet catches and wraps around her waist, exposing her breasts to my greedy gaze. I cannot resist, increasing my pressure with each pass as I run my hands over her curves, noting what makes her gasp and what makes her twitch away. A squeeze that goes too far flattens her back against the bed as she pulls back from my touch and I immediately make amends, licking and kissing her pretty red nipple until she is writhing toward me again.

Switching to the other side, I resume my experiments, testing, teasing, learning what she likes until she weaves her fingers through my hair and grips it tightly, pulling my head back far enough to meet my eyes.

"Dash! Enough! I need more."

"Which is it? Enough or more?"

"Enough of that." She grabs my hand and lowers it to her clit. "More of this." She turns her own hand over to cup me through the sheet. "And definitely a lot more of this."

I circle my fingers over her clit, and she is wet and ready. A more detailed and leisurely exploration of her lower topography and its features will have to wait for another day. I've gained as much knowledge today as she has patience for. It's time to sprint for the summit. She knows what she wants, and I am eager to please.

Grabbing a condom from the pile I left sprawled the night before, I am sheathed and poised above her in seconds.

"Is this what you need more of?" I run the head of my cock between her slick folds, and she nods frantically, hips jerking to rock against me.

"Yes. I need you, Dash. Please!"

Green light given, I slide home in one slow, deep thrust, and she screams into her hand. I freeze. Did I do something wrong? Did I misread the signals? "Too much? Should I stop?"

"If you stop right now, I swear to God, Dash—"

"Not stopping, not stopping!" I withdraw and thrust again, and this time the sound she makes is pure pleasure.

I turn my words into action, finding the right rhythm to match her jerking hips.

"Fuck, you feel so good." She drops her hand to her clit, and I try to watch without losing my focus. It's difficult as her movements grow more frantic. She is getting close.

"Give it to me, Penny. You feel so good. Come on my cock. Now."

I grab her breast again possessively, squeezing her nipple, and she erupts. Hips bucking, hand clutched firmly over her clit, her entire body shakes and she locks her legs around my hips, holding me buried deep inside her.

I try to keep my pace steady as she winds down, but the contractions of her sheath around my cock feel too good and I lose control. I sprint toward my own finish line, my hips moving of their own accord, until I come with a shout. Sated, I collapse on top of her, not ready to lose this connection yet.

"Good morning?" I say, more question than statement.

"Very," she murmurs as she snuggles into me and promptly falls back asleep.

But rest eludes me, my brain spinning at three thousand RPMs. *Was that good? Did she like it? Is she ignoring me by rolling over? Physically, she enjoyed that, but what about emotionally?*

I'm sure there are things I could have done better, things I missed, things I should have known about. It's only a matter of time before she realizes she could do so much better than me. I will enjoy it while it lasts. Which I would be able to do a lot better with a full night sleep.

I wish my brain would just shut the hell up sometimes.

I could ignore it, except no, I can't. I could give it free rein, but then I'd never sleep again. Which leaves me with option three. Write down the spinning thoughts, and hope that funnels enough out of my head that I can get some rest.

I carefully roll out of bed, propping a pillow behind Penny to support her back, and grab my laptop. It's charging so I sit against the wall next to the outlet and open the lid. The spreadsheet I've made about Penny is already open on the screen. Rows of her physical reactions, columns detailing time, date, situation, context, and perceived enjoyment.

Callie emerges from beneath the bed and leans her warm body against mine. I scratch her behind her favorite ear, and she settles down next to me. Like cat, like owner. I just have to find the right places to scratch.

I add the things that made Penny gasp and squirm this morning, as well as the too-hard nipple pinch that went awry. Her physical reactions are the easy part—cause and effect. She is so responsive, I can tell right away if something feels good or not. But her emotions are beyond me. I'm out of my depth. I think she's into me, and not just letting me stay out of pity, but the voice that lives in the back of my head keeps trying to convince me otherwise. It's really hard to ignore him.

But writing all of this out, codifying and organizing it, helps. Slowly, my brain begins to quiet. Callie brings me from my trance with a gentle tap of her paw on my hand, pulling it from the keyboard. I look up from my laptop and realize Penny's watching me with a quiet frown. How long has she been staring?

"Can't sleep?"

"No. Had a bit of inspiration I needed to get out. I'm sorry I woke you."

She shakes her head softly and pats the bed next to her. Was that a flicker of sadness I saw? *Damn it! What did I do now?*

"Clearly I didn't wear you out enough. Come back to bed and we'll see if I can fix that."

I may be an idiot when it comes to love, but I'm no fool. I close my computer, give Callie a final scratch, and slide in next to Penny's warm, sleepy body for round two.

PENNY

I awake with a start and glance at the clock. Ten a.m.! I can't remember the last time I slept so long when I wasn't ill. True, I'm still recovering, but today's exhaustion I can lay firmly at Dash's door.

He is a force of nature. The way he touches me, keeping me guessing, always wanting more, is addictive. And when he tells me how good I am, how much I've pleased him, it pushes some button installed deep inside and I lose it. I become pure euphoric sensation, existing only to earn that praise. I could get used to this, but I shouldn't.

Dash Hall sets a very high bar.

Nic would tell me to "grab his pole and vault that sucker," but I'm already moving way faster than my usual pace. I prefer a reasoned approach, involving logical steps toward intimacy and maybe a timeline. For goodness' sake, Dash has already moved in! This is way out of my comfort zone, and I haven't had the brainpower or strength to give this relationship my usual vetting. But if he keeps wearing me out like this, I might never have the energy. I'm not so sure that would be a bad thing. Isn't Nic always saying—

Oh God! Nic! I promised to call at nine!

Flinging back the sheets, I sprint into the living room in a panic. Dash is sitting with his back to me, legs extended on the couch, cell phone in front of his face. He turns at the sound of the door slamming against the wall and his eyes goggle wide.

He immediately lowers his phone to his chest and coughs. "Good morning," he says.

"I missed a call with Nicola."

"I know. I think you also missed something else." I follow his gaze down and yelp.

I'm standing in the middle of my living room completely naked while he is fully clothed and on a video call. *Fuck!*

I turn on my heel and duck back into my bedroom, hastily throw on a cotton sundress and underwear, and rush back out. "Sorry!"

"It's okay. It's nothing I haven't seen before." Nicola's muffled voice chuckles from Dash's chest.

Dash looks back and forth between me and his screen, trying to make sense of that comment and the tone with which it had been delivered.

"We make better friends than lovers." I brush past the curious questions lurking in his fine brown eyes, and narrow in on the one that is bothering me. "Why are you on the phone with my business partner?"

Dash holds up a hand to protest his innocence, and I realize my words came out harsher than I'd intended.

"She called me when she couldn't get ahold of you." Dash leans back against the cushions, wary.

"Why does she have your number?"

"Because I put it in my phone after I sent it to you at the conference. I figured a good press number was worth keeping," Nicola chided. "And now that I know he's living with you, I tried him when you didn't answer."

Mollified, I move closer to Dash on the couch and run my hand down the back of his neck in apology. "Sorry. My system jumped to eleven when I woke up late, and I overreacted."

"Understood. I was just chatting with Nicola about the supply chain issues you've got going."

"Mmhmm. Do I smell…pancakes?"

"You do indeed. Here, sit and have your meeting while I reheat your breakfast. Bye, Nic. It was nice chatting with you again."

Dash hands me his phone and heads for the kitchen. I sit down, blushing, and Nicola smirks.

"So morning sex *and* breakfast? You bitch! If you tell me his cock is better than MiO, I'm going to have to hate him on principle," Nicola teases.

My cheeks flame even hotter. "No comment."

"Holy hell! No wonder you were knocked out."

"Can we have the conversation we were supposed to be having? Please?"

"Sure. New product development idea. Do you think he'd let us cast a mold of it?"

"Nicola!" I hiss, glancing at the kitchen to see if Dash heard that, but his back is to me.

"Oh come on. You can't just say he's amazing and expect me to drop it."

"I didn't say anything, and I absolutely can expect you to drop it."

"Nope, this is way more fun than supply chain hiccups. Does he have any annoying habits?"

I shake my head at her persistence. "I'm not answering that."

"Not even in the name of science?" Nic pleads.

"How could that possibly be in the name of science?"

"Okay, fine, then in the name of marketing. 'MiO: all the pleasure, none of the socks on the floor.'"

"Oh my God." I cover my face with my hand and groan. *Work with your friends, they said. It'll be fun, they said.*

Nic pauses for a sip of coffee. "Seriously though, you good?"

"Yeah, I'm good."

I think about just how good he made me feel last night... *What does his schedule look like today?* Nic slaps down her coffee mug, and I jump.

"Ugh! Enough with the moony grins from both of you!"

"He had a moony grin?" I ask.

"I did indeed." Dash appears at my shoulder, a plate of warm pancakes with syrup and strawberries in his hand. He leans down to set it on the table in front of me and presses a kiss to my bedhead hair.

I didn't think it was possible to blush harder than I already am, but my circulatory system is determined to prove me wrong. I can feel my pulse from my temples to my collarbone. Is that from embarrassment or attraction? Or some weird blend of both? "You heard that, huh?"

"Uh-huh. Most of it. Better than the MiO, huh? Don't worry, I won't tell," Dash teases.

"Go enjoy your, uh, breakfast," Nic says from the screen I had momentarily forgotten about. "Call me when you're awake and ready to talk."

"I will. I'm sorry."

"Quit apologizing. You were late. The company did not crumble to pieces in your absence. The sky has not fallen. The world continues to turn. Now that I know you're okay, I can wait. Eat. Have some coffee. Fuck the poor boy senseless again. I need more data."

Before I can formulate a retort, Nic disconnects the call. I fall silent, well aware that Dash heard all of that last bit. I dig into my pancakes to buy time to figure out what exactly to say. I'm used to Nicola's lack of filter, but her teasing could be seen from the outside as inappropriate at best.

"So, she's an ex?" Dash breaks the silence, sitting down with a fresh cup of coffee.

I chew my pancakes carefully before answering. "A long time ago. Sophomore year of college."

"So you are…bi?" he asks cautiously.

When I get this question, I try to get a read on the person asking. Are they titillated by the idea? Grossed out? Turned on? Curious? It helps me determine how to answer. I can't read Dash at all right now, but I trust him so I share as openly as I can. "Pan. I fall for people, not parts. As we've seen, I can make any parts that I want to play with. It's the person that attracts me, their personality that makes me stay."

"Got it."

"Got it? That's all you have to say?"

Dash nods calmly, his face still so blank that I don't know what he's thinking. "That covers it pretty well. Neither of us came into this with a blank slate. I'm just glad my personality hasn't driven you away."

I sit back against the couch, stunned. No one has ever accepted me that easily. Now I'm the one with nothing to say.

"Do you want to talk about what Nic said?" He takes another sip of his coffee.

"About us being better friends than lovers or how you compare to the MiO?" I tease, trying to get a rise out of him. Anything to break this awful controlled blankness.

He doesn't even look up from his coffee when he speaks. "No, I want to know if I have any annoying habits. You didn't answer her. I'm not always the most aware of how my actions or lack thereof bug people. If I am really staying, we should probably talk about stuff."

"Wait, what do you mean *if?*" I ask, panic rising unbidden in the back of my throat. "I thought we covered this last night."

"I'm not holding you to a statement made while under the influence of my dick. It's been known to provoke unreliable outbursts." He finally looks at me, his awful mask breaking a little at the seam of his mouth with the beginnings of a smile.

"Oh really?" I chuckle. "Like what?"

"'Anything you say' or 'Don't ever stop' are pretty common, but it's the 'I'll love you forever' that really hurts when the power of the D fades."

Suddenly this conversation isn't funny anymore. I set my plate on the coffee table and crawl over to his end of the couch to straddle his lap. I need to hug him right now. He holds me close with one arm, his cheek nestled against my chest.

Who hurt you? I want to ask, but I don't want that awful mask to come back.

"I just…I want to have a clearheaded conversation so no one gets hurt or disappointed." He sounds like he's been down that road before, and frankly so have I.

I kiss his head and climb off. "If you want clear-headed, I need more coffee, a bra, and at least ten feet of distance from your dick."

Dash

I can't help but smile as she disappears back into the bedroom where she'd blown me away. But in the resulting quiet of the living room, doubts assail me. *Why am I rocking the boat? Is she already retreating? Is she really pissed I chatted with Nicola? Was I too nosy with that question about her sexuality? Is it too early in the relationship to be opening up sensitive topics?*

Then again, we're practically living together. Is it too late for these conversations?

I go into the kitchen to make her coffee—cream and two sugars—but I get stalled again at the fridge door, looking for the half-and-half.

What if she has a real hard line that I can't toe? It would break my heart to lose her now. And oh God, when did my heart enter the fray?

My brain continues its panic spiral until Penny shakes my shoulder and gets in my face.

"Hey, I said your name three times and you didn't blink. Where'd you go?"

"Got stuck in mental *Mario Kart*. It's like getting on the highway in a bumper car. Each new ricochet sends me further off track, and I end up spinning against the guardrails going sixty miles an hour. It can be hard to pull out of it."

I scrub my hands over my face and really look at her. Bright as sunshine and warm as summer, in her sundress with her short blonde curls teasing her face, I am struck again by the unanswerable question: What the hell could she want with me?

"I was asking if that coffee was for me," she says.

My panic flares for a moment, thinking I've said that last bit out loud. "You…you said you needed caffeine." I try to calm my racing thoughts, but my mind is stuck in overdrive.

"I did. Thank you." She reaches past me for the cream.

"The sugar is already in there."

"So thoughtful." She sits down at the kitchen table and fiddles with her steaming mug before drinking.

I mirror her sip without tasting my coffee at all. Is this Covid or has this conversation simply subsumed my other senses? It would not be the first time.

"So…let's talk. I agree that last night was amazing, if kind of a fast one-eighty. But in my mind we've been building toward that for weeks." She pauses and sips her coffee again, while I try to analyze the spaces between her words and fail miserably.

But I have to say something… "I was completely caught off guard, but that doesn't mean I didn't want it to happen," I clarify, staring at my coffee because looking her in the eye right now feels too exposed. "I just… You have to know… I will believe what you explicitly say over your actions every time. I can't read between the lines at all."

"Got it. I will try and be as clear as possible."

I haul in a breath and gather my courage to ask the question that will allow me to hush the others. "Do you really want me to move in with you? Like officially?"

"I do. You've been so wonderful, helping me recover."

God, more of this gratitude! I don't want her to let me stay out of obligation. I want her to want me in her life. Period. I cut her off, before she can go any farther down the path that will crush my soul. I slump in my chair, all of my strength draining with disappointment. "I don't need to move in because you're grateful."

"You said you need my words. Let me get them out." She waits until I nod before continuing. "I've gotten to see a lot of you the last few weeks. The way you think, the way you love, the way you care. And I like what I see. I'd like to see if this relationship can keep growing, and the only way I can guarantee that I'll get to see you during this lockdown is if we are living together. Do you…want to be in a relationship with me?" This time she's the one who can't meet my eye when I snap to attention at her question.

I reach across the table and put my hand over hers where she picks at her watchband. "Absolutely, I do. And I want to give it the best chance possible. Can we talk chores and responsibilities?"

I offer, but let's be real—now that she's said she wants me to stay, I will agree to anything she wants to keep that true. Besides, this is her place. I don't want to throw off her groove while I'm here. She's clearly got things running smoothly, or she did before she got sick and had some dude crash uninvited on her couch.

I don't want to disillusion her, but my ADHD and tidiness don't really go together well. If I put something away, I tend to forget it exists. So when I'm working on a project or a game, things stay spread out so I can find what I need. And given how many projects go unfinished, it leads to a lot of project piles around my space. One way I combat this is by keeping my life and possessions fairly minimal and by restricting projects to my own space. I don't have that option here. But if Penny needs me to be neater, I'll do my best to give her that. I'll just have to hustle to stay on top of things. I lean back in my chair to better focus.

"As for chores, I say we both just pitch in and do what needs doing. If you see it needs doing, do it."

"That sounds fair." I like that she's willing to keep things open and flexible. I rummage for my notebook and a pen and begin to take notes. If I don't write the details down, I'll never remember. "So what is your list of chores that you normally do to take care of your apartment?"

Penny begins rattling off tasks and I dutifully write them down as best I can, but at the end of two full hand-written pages, I hold up my hand to stop her, my brain stumbling over the rapid-fire panic this list is generating.

"You do *all* of those things? Every week?"

"Yes. It soothes me to have a neat and tidy space."

I drop my head into my hands, elbows propped on my knees and groan. "We're doomed!"

She laughs. We'll see how long she thinks it's funny.

"Switch off cooking?" she asks.

I chuckle at that one. "Mine might be takeout more often than not. You've pretty much experienced the breadth of my cooking knowledge."

"Maybe we could pick some new recipes to learn together?"

"I'd like that." I smile at the image of us in the kitchen together. "Rent, fifty-fifty?"

"Deal."

I hold out my hand and she shakes on it, but I don't

let go of her hand. I lean closer and, desire making my voice deepen, I ask, "Last but not least, orgasms?"

"Fifty-fifty?" she suggests.

"I was leaning more eighty-twenty in your favor. When you factor in recovery time and your natural abilities, it's only fair. I mean, it's science. If Nic wants data, I can give her data."

I press a kiss against her collarbone, and Penny's entire body responds with a shiver, just like yesterday. I am trying to keep this conversation light and playful, but I need her. Now.

I grip her ass and stand up, and she clings to my neck with a gasp. Her ass in my hands feels so damn good, but if I put her down, I can make her feel even better. I set her on the edge of the table and lean until she's flat on her back and I've got her penned in with my arms extended. She tries to pull me down to her, but I resist. There's one last thing I need to have clear between us.

"Dash, please. I need you."

I move my palm to her chest, her heart racing beneath my fingers, urging mine to catch the fuck up. "I need you too. If anything ever changes on that front, tell me."

Penny reaches up and cups my face with her hands. "Same goes for you. If this stops working for whatever reason, please talk to me."

I nod and lean into her caress, closing my eyes as she runs her fingers through my hair. "I really want this to work, Penny. I've never felt this way before, and I'm going to do my best to keep you happy."

"Should we seal the deal with a few orgasms now that

we've got a ratio to aim for?" Penny teases, running her hand over the seam of my jeans.

Two can play at that game. I stand up straight and flip her skirt up to her waist. Sitting back down in my chair, I yank her panties down and spread her knees wide, propping her heels on the table. "Abso-fucking-lutely."

PENNY

I open my email for the eighty-third time and want to cry. There are five more emails waiting for me. I glance at the clock in the corner of my screen. Six thirty p.m. I haven't eaten since eleven. Haven't had coffee since two. Can't remember the last time I peed. I have got to get better about setting boundaries for myself.

Just as soon as I answer these emails, I'll—

Dash pushes a finger into the back of my screen, lowering it just enough to break my gaze. He's leaning across the kitchen table with that grin on his face, the one that melts my heart and my panties simultaneously.

"Come play with me," he says.

I cannot resist that dimple. "Okay, just let me…"

"Is something on fire?" he asks, his voice urgent with concern.

"What? No."

"Is someone injured?" His *concern* escalates into parody.

"No."

"Is the company going to implode if you ignore that last email for a few hours?" Sarcasm drips from his words, and I cross my arms and glare. He is unfazed. "It's six thirty on Friday night. You've given the company enough. You deserve to rest and play too, just like your customers. Come on."

I reluctantly slip my hand in his and let him lead me from the kitchen. Not having to "leave the office" to get home has led to very blurred lines between work time and downtime. And he's right, even if I don't want to admit it. It's time to rest and have a little fun. Halfway to the bedroom, Dash takes a hard left and pulls me down on the couch with him.

I don't understand. There is a perfectly good bed literally fifteen feet away, but if he wants to make out on the couch, I'm game. When he hands me a controller, I realize I have misunderstood.

"A video game." I state the obvious, as if he might refute it. I wouldn't have left my emails for this. I have never been a gamer girl. I don't get it.

"I got a new game, and I'd love your opinion on it."

"Who's working on a Friday night now?"

"I'm not getting paid to review it so technically it's not work, but I can see how you'd come to that conclusion since my job is often fun and entertaining." He grins at me and gestures to the TV.

I roll my eyes hard at that, but it doesn't deter him at all. All excitement, he rolls right into an explanation.

"So, it's a quest-based reboot of a classic game, but the princess who always needed rescuing in the original is now a playable character and has to rescue the various other players who fell into traps trying to get to her in the first place."

"Sounds fun." I'm not sure my voice is convincing, because he arches a brow.

"It is fun. More fun than answering emails. Play with me and give me your honest opinion. Please?"

It's the please that kills me.

"Okay, okay, fine. How does this work?"

He puts the controller in my hands and reaches around me to carefully place my fingers, explaining what the different buttons are called and what they control. I flash back to our first meeting, when our roles were reversed, and giggle. I struggle to focus because he is so close and he smells so good. If I turn my head just a little I could lick his neck. He leans back and takes his hands from mine. The loss is profound. I don't know what gave me away, but he's definitely on to me.

"Behave. If you play your game like a good girl, I'll reward you. Later."

I press my lips together and try to follow along. The game starts off pretty quickly with some easy challenges to learn the ropes. Before long I am running and jumping and sword slashing with the best of them. Then I hit a wall. A literal wall that I cannot get past.

"Try AABB on quick repeat while flicking up."

"I don't know what that means. Here, you do it."

I hand him the controller and snuggle in next to him to watch. I try to pay attention to the game, I swear, but his hands are right there. I'm sure Princess What's-her-name kicked some ass and took some names, but all I can see are the tendons in his forearms rising and falling and the veins on the back of his hands twitching with excitement.

He demonstrates the AABB/UP combo, his eyes focused on the screen, and I am shook.

That. Thumb.

The way he flicks it back and forth over the control stick is seriously hot. No wonder he can stay consistent when I say, "Right there, just like that."

Do other women know about this? I feel like someone should have told me. Here I am, ready to boil over at the discovery, and if someone knew about this and didn't tell me, I'm going to be pissed at the years of missed opportunities. Holy fuck, he can maintain his rhythm without even looking at it.

Something is happening on the screen. Beeps and clashes and trumpets are coming from the speakers, but I am transfixed. My pulse picks up and my blood thickens in my veins until I can feel it, throbbing, everywhere. Suddenly the clothes which seemed perfectly appropriate for work this morning feel super tight. I unbutton the top two buttons on my collared shirt, needing fresh air and easier access to the girls. I slide closer to him so I can brush up against his arm while it's all tense and hard. Fuck me, I want this intensity on me. Now.

He gets to the end of a level and fireworks go off. That's it. It's a fucking sign.

"Can I have a turn?" I ask.

"Of course," Dash says and hands me the controller,

which I promptly toss on the ground behind me. I straddle his lap while he's lost and confused and take his hands in mine.

"What? I—"

"What's that combo again?" I ask. "AA." I move his hand to my left breast and flick his fingers over my already hard nipple. "BB," I hiss as I raise his other hand to repeat the motion on my right. "And then a whole lot of ups and downs?" I grin and grind my hips against the rapidly hardening cock between my legs. I knew he'd catch on quick.

I let go of his hands, and pull my shirt wide-open. He takes care of tugging down the lacy cups of my bra so he can better push my buttons. With those skilled fingers, thumbs, and occasionally his lips and tongue, he proceeds to drive me out of my mind by paying attention just to my breasts and nowhere else. I'm not going to lie—it's hot as fuck, and I'm sure I've drenched his jeans where we are still pressed against one another. But I'm greedy. I need more.

"Your thumb," I gasp.

"This one?" he asks, holding up his right thumb in the universal sign of approval.

"Yes, that one." I hike my skirt up to my waist and tug my lacy undies to the side. "I need you and your gamer's thumb to come work some up up down down magic."

He groans at the sight I've presented him, before looking me straight in the eyes.

"Don't worry, princess. I've got this."

He takes his other hand back to teasing my tits, which

I love, and puts his thumb directly where I need him. He circles and flicks and makes me come fast and furious in his lap. I cry out and clutch his head to my chest. *How? How can it feel so good every time?*

When I return to my body, he is looking at me with that naughty gleam in his eyes.

"How about a challenge round?" He hands me the controller. "Restart the game. If you finish out the level, I'll let you come. If you don't, you'll have to wait."

"Challenge accepted."

"Game on." He chuckles before lying down flat on the couch. "You agreed to that too quickly."

"What are you doing?" I ask, but he's already got his hands on the hem of my skirt, lifting it high.

He turns me so he can palm my ass before pulling me back. "Come sit down so you can play."

"I can sit fine where I was."

"Penny. Come sit down." He tucks a pillow under his head and holds out his hands.

"Do you have a death wish?"

"I'm going to count to three."

Before he gets to two, I am scooting back, my thighs on either side of his chest. "Are you sure?"

He answers without words, gripping my hips and pulling me back where he wants me. I brace my forearms on his thighs, clutching the controller and trying to hover. I can't put my full weight down on his face, but I am too greedy to turn down a chance at his mouth on my clit.

"Eyes on the screen, or you forfeit," he says before licking straight down my center.

I blink twice, trying to remember what it is I'm supposed to be doing.

"Start the game," he reminds me.

I push the buttons on the controller, and he rewards me with another gentle lick. I try to remember what he taught me, but my mind is completely blank with pleasure. His hard cock is outlined by his plaid pajama pants directly beneath me and I am so tempted, but my hands are already full.

These tender kisses are driving me mad. I need more, faster, harder. I'm about to say something to that effect when he slaps my ass and pulls his head back as I jerk forward.

"Are you as frustrated as I am?" he asks.

Verbal communication is beyond me so I moan and nod, hoping he understands.

"Then when I tell you to sit, you better fucking sit. I can't give you what you need if you don't do what I ask."

With another moan, I shift farther back and he hauls me fully onto his face. He licks and sucks at my labia, his tongue strong and firm, and my thighs start to tremble from a different pressure.

I try to keep the game going, but before I know it the sad music is playing. I've lost the level. He stops.

I am not a whiner. I take what life throws at me and make the best of it. But when he shifts my hips from his face and stops his rhythm, a sound so pitiful wells up in my throat that I close my eyes so I don't have to witness my own pathetic weakness.

"Penny."

I turn and look over my shoulder. He staring at my ass and counting to twenty under his breath.

"It's later."

He grips my hips and pulls me back down on his mouth, tonguing my clit with strong, sure strokes until I quake so hard I'm positive my soul has left my body. The orgasm races through me, shaking my foundations, and I collapse. I fall forward, my head landing on his thighs, controller bouncing on the ground as it falls from my nerveless fingers. The video game song plays on loop, waiting for someone to start another round. His hard cock is right there. I grin and pull him through the gap in his pajama pants while I have him pinned with my pussy.

Time for a new game.

When he grunts at my teasing licks, I move to take him deep. I take him as far back as my throat will allow, and then push a little farther. I set a steady pace, covering what I can't take in my mouth with my hand. He's not the only one who can keep a rhythm going. I slide my other hand beneath his balls and give a gentle tug. His hips jump beneath me, and I hear him press a curse against my inner thigh. I am so sensitive that I jerk and pull off him with a pop of suction.

"You had your fun. Now it's my turn," I tease.

He might have said something, but I'm already bobbing my mouth over his cock, faster this time. I'm done with the teasing. I want him to come hard and fast.

I want to be the one who makes him lose control. I revel in every filthy word that leaves his mouth, until with a shout, he comes and coats the inside of my mouth.

I lick his twitching cock clean and rise, leaving him spent and disheveled on the couch. He looks so cute and my heart does a weird little leap in my chest. I'm not ready for that. Not at all.

Despite my knees still feeling a little weak, I stand and wobble to the kitchen. I need some distance to put myself back together.

"I'm hungry. Are you hungry?" I ask.

I open the fridge to hunt for leftovers and peace of mind, but I get distracted by a funky smell and a large bowl of something that looks alive.

"What the hell is this thing in the fridge?" I call over my shoulder. "Should I call the CDC or the FBI?"

Dash strolls up behind me and grips my hips where I'm bent over to inspect the vegetable graveyard.

"It's sourdough starter. It's for an article."

"It's trying to escape. Uh-huuuuuh!" My sarcasm ends in a shriek as I am lifted over his shoulder, the fridge door swinging shut with a gust of cold air against my hypersensitive and now partially exposed bits. He carries me into our bedroom and drops me bouncing on our bed.

"You know what? I am still a little hungry," he teases, prowling across the bed toward me.

Game. On.

CHAPTER 15

When I finally I get the okay to go back into our office space with strict Covid protocols in place, I am militant about six feet between employees at all times, masks, handwashing, temperature checks, the whole nine yards. I will jump through a flaming hoop spraying hand sanitizer from a hose if it means I can salvage my business plan.

I can't hug my friends, but I can see them. We can't really work in the same room, because of the layout of the office space, but just knowing they are right next door is a gift. Every laugh or conversation feels precious, even if they're a little muffled by the masks. Even that small glimpse of normal feels amazing after months of being cooped up.

I can't afford to hire the launch staff I'd anticipated because we've had so many delays and setbacks. So Emmie, Zarah, Nic, Jen, Mike and I all pitch in and pack the remaining preorders ourselves. We print shipping labels and build an entire wall of empty boxes around the conference room. We even figure out how to arrange for contactless shipping pickup. Even Dash drops by to help fetch and carry.

At last, my dream is getting off the ground. Soon word of mouth will spread, and more and more women will be empowered to take control of their orgasms. Vibe la revolution!

A sharp buzzing interrupts my daydream of world clitoral domination, and I realize I've been sitting at my desk with a dopey smile on my face for at least twenty minutes. I answer my phone and try to get my head back in the game.

"Hey Nic, what's up?"

"Don't panic."

I lean back in my chair with a heavy sigh, instantly deflated. How can two little words pop my happy bubble so effectively? "Oh God, what now?"

"I told you not to panic."

"Has that line ever worked in the history of bad news? The fact you said it at all implies there is something I might panic about." I can feel it licking at the back of my throat. Nic wouldn't warn me if there was nothing to worry about.

"Well…" Nicola prevaricates.

"Spit it out," I snap.

"So we've been following the MiO hashtag and mentions hoping for some reviews from the early influencers we managed to ship out a few weeks ago."

Yes, I know that. This was the plan.

"And?"

"We've had a few great ones, really gushing about the product."

"Oh my God, did they really say 'gushing' in the review?" I can't hold back the chuckle. If this is the bad news, we're fine. I can spin that in one TikTok video.

"Only one, with a wink and a nod. It was funny. But… we also got a few bad reviews."

Nope, there's the bad news. Still, we knew we weren't going to please everyone. We just wanted to come close.

"Oh no! From who?" I ask.

"Hayley Prescott."

The other shoe drops like a ton of bricks. Hayley Prescott. The famously sex-positive singer. The person we hoped to approach at a later date for a celebrity endorsement.

"What did she say?" I scramble to pull up her Insta-Snap account. This is bad. This is so bad!

Like she can read my mind, Nicola replies. "It's not all bad. She talks about how great the orgasm was but that it was hard to use and had a steep learning curve. She criticized the appearance too, saying it looked a little too industrial."

"Oh for fuck's sake. It's a machine." I'm still reeling from losing Hayley's potential support, and hearing that my design isn't visually pleasing pours salt in the wound.

"Yeah, but we're not marketing to Comic Con. According to her and the comments section, a lot of women don't want to have sex with a machine. They want a toy that more closely simulates the real thing without reminding them it's not the real thing."

"Well, the real thing can't suck your clit and hit your G-spot with a dick at the same time, so..." I snap.

"I know. Just the messenger here."

I shouldn't bark at Nic. She's right. This isn't her fault. It's my responsibility to fix. I have to find a bright side. Something we can rally around. "Okay, this is just one bad review..."

Nicola coughs.

"Actually, a full twenty-five percent of the reviews we've been tagged in have mentioned the user experience being tricky. We just ran the analysis today."

I cover my eyes with my hand and through sheer dint of will manage not to cry. Big girl CEOs don't cry over bad reviews. I need to keep it together right now.

"Can you or Emmie reach out to those folks specifically with a detailed survey? Thank them for their time and feedback, but dig into what was so hard to figure out? We've got to get ahead of this before we ship these new units out."

"You got it, boss. It's going to be okay." Nic knows I hate when my friends call me boss, so of course she does it at every opportunity to rib me.

I hang up and drop my head to my desk, barely resisting banging it hard against the glass surface. Nicola's last word echoes in my corner office. Boss. I am the boss. The success and failure of this dream rests squarely on my shoulders, and I feel every pound of it. Not to mention the fact that I've linked my best friends' careers to this crapshoot.

My phone rings again, and I answer without opening my eyes or lifting my head. "What now?"

"Penny? Are you okay?" Not Emmie or Nic following up. Dash's deep voice tickles my ear and makes me actively wish I was back home, curled up in bed, little spoon to his big spoon.

"I'm fine. Just got some bad reviews. We'll get through it."

"I was calling to see if I could order you anything for dinner."

"What, you're not cooking?" I tease.

"Ha ha. No brain-melting stir-fry tonight. Sorry to disappoint. I was thinking pizza?"

"Mmm, with cheesy garlic bread and a Caesar salad?"

"You got it. Hang in there, babe. I'll see you soon."

I square my shoulders and draw in a deep breath. So we had a few bad reviews. Fine. It happens. What doesn't happen every day is stumbling across a guy who will order me dinner because I'm having a crappy day. Or who wakes me up with kisses along my neck because he knows it drives me wild. Or who can right my day with a thirty-second phone call.

With my mental train wreck sidetracked, I regain a little perspective. A little positive momentum.

I email Nic for the report she put together, but get impatient waiting and dive right into the raw data. I read the negative reviews in question and start a spreadsheet to track the common complaints. I read the positive ones to remind myself that it is working for a majority of users. I go through the packaging and onboarding materials we shipped out with the preorders and look for improvements. I white-board some ideas for changes to present to the team tomorrow. I look at our competitors' packaging and user manuals, and judge ours far superior. Where is the disconnect?

If anyone is going to find it, it's going to be me.

After all, I designed the thing, and I'm the one who convinced everybody to follow me out here on this ledge to launch it. When things go wrong, I should be the one to fix it.

It works wonderfully for me, but if there's one thing I've learned in this industry, it's that I always have more to learn about people's sexual experiences and their relationships with their bodies. I've done my best to make the MiO accessible for everyone, but clearly something is off.

If I could fly to everyone's house individually and show them how to use it… No, I still wouldn't do that. But everything up to that line is fair game. How can I take this feedback and adjust my plan so that I can still succeed?

When my stomach growls its displeasure, I look up to see if it's time to go. *Shit.* It's almost nine! Where did those hours go? I hope Dash isn't too upset that I missed dinner. I fire off a text to Nic requesting to be added to the calls tomorrow before shoving the contents of my desk back into the tote bag I'm using to cart everything back and forth.

Time to go eat my boyfriend for dinner, or eat with him. Either way, win-win.

~

DASH

I get off the phone with Penny and order the pizza quickly so I can feed her immediately, and then get on to the funsies, as she calls them. I've got something to celebrate, and I don't want to waste a minute.

Today I got another article approved, and the check hit my bank account. This article outlines the back-to-work protocols. Penny was incredibly helpful as I peppered her with questions. She deserves to share in the reward for a job well done.

I look around the apartment, pondering where to set up the food, and grimace. The kitchen table is small and currently covered with my laptop, papers, and the sour-dough starter that's ready to escape its bowl again. I swear I used half of it today in my breadmaking fiasco, but it's already filled the bowl again. It's worse than a goldfish.

The end table is hosting the small collection of house-plants I bought for a different article. I think the snake plant has the greatest likelihood of survival. It's definitely the Katniss of the crew. The rest are already wilting from neglect, but the snake plant is reaching for the sun. I take a glass of stale water from the collection on the coffee table and reward its persistence.

The array of other dishes still there attest to the fact that my work has made the table unusable for days. And the kitchen counters are a disaster from my earlier attempts at sourdough art. Pizza wasn't the first option, but it is the only option. On the plus side, with all the windows open I aired out the apartment. I don't think it smells like smoke anymore.

Time to dig in. I dash around the house, picking up my hoodie from the couch before setting it down in the chair to free my hands for the coffee mugs and dishes. Taking them into the kitchen and setting them in the sink to soak, I brush an armful of flour and dough scraps into the garbage can. Half of it hits the floor, so I go broom hunting. When I see the notebook Penny's left on the counter, I decide to put it on the bed on my way to the hall closet for the broom.

Once I hit the bedroom, my plan unravels. Callie objects to my tossing the notebook on her perch, even though it lands feet from her, and I must appease her pique with pets and reassurances. I sit down next to her on the bed and she claims my lap as hers. My game controller is right there, plugged in on my side of the bed and now fully charged. The idea strikes to celebrate with a quick round of a new game. We relocate to the couch and settle in.

The company reached out directly to me for this review, so my editor hadn't been able to hand it off to someone else. It's been weeks since I've gotten my hands on a fresh game. *Just a few minutes to get a taste for it... I'll be done with level one before Penny even gets home.*

I load the game and begin exploring the fictional world. Rich graphics pull me in deep, and the clever quest keeps me there. Whoever designed this really put in the work to make the game beautiful and engaging. I am delighted.

Until Penny steps into my field of vision, blocking the screen. Then I am panicked.

"Hey," she says.

"Hi! Oh my God, hi! I didn't hear you come in." Callie leaps from my lap with a yowl of protest and I follow to my feet and look around, chagrined at the mess I still see everywhere. A glance at my watch says it's been over three hours since I called her. How did I lose so much time? *Fuck!* I start running around snatching things from surfaces and putting them down on other surfaces, making absolutely zero net change in the messiness balance sheet. The apartment is still a disaster, and Penny is holding a pizza box with a bag balanced on top and looking at me like I've lost my marbles.

"Oh, you picked up takeout? I ordered in."

"Yeah, this was sitting on the mat out front. I guess you didn't hear the delivery guy."

I take the food from her, palming the bottom of the box, now ice-cold. I really played through a doorbell? It wouldn't be the first time, but it's been years. She deserves better than this.

"Crap, it's gone cold." I head for the microwave, setting the cardboard on top of the floury stove.

"It's okay. We can just reheat it after," Penny says, grinning and prowling toward me.

"After what?" I'm still so worried about the pizza and feeding her and losing the thread on the cleaning I was planning to do that I'm still spinning when she corrals me against the stove with her arms.

"After dessert."

"What's for dessert?"

~

PENNY

Dash looks so cute when he's confused. I step into his personal space. My breasts press against his chest, and I skate my hands back over his hips to grip his ass.

"You are."

His answering grin melts me. The raw panic recedes from his eyes and he wraps his arms around me. He catches on quick, I'll give him that. I love that he did the same thing for me with a phone call. We get each other. I want to thank him for calming me down earlier, and I don't want to wait any longer.

"Oh really? What if I want you for dessert?" he asks.

"I'd say you'll have to wait. I called dibs." I drop to my knees on the kitchen floor and go to work on his jeans, unbuttoning and tugging them down to his knees. "Do you know how horny I got just thinking about coming home to you? And then you have the audacity to look all sexy and intense, wearing *glasses*, when I walk through the door?"

I palm him through the thin cotton of his underwear and he groans, his hips rocking forward. The way he is game for anything is such a turn-on. I can feel him growing as he catches up with my plan. How long has it been since I had a partner who liked to play?

Too long. I smile, but I am impatient now. I pull down the remaining barrier in one swift motion. His thick, hard cock bounces right in front of my face. Taunting me. Daring me to take him all at once.

I've never backed down from a dare.

I lick his swollen head with the flat of my tongue before running my mouth down the length of his shaft, getting him nice and slick on each side. His hands reflexively tighten in my hair, and I gasp before taking him inside my mouth, pushing forward until he hits the back of my throat. I fight my gag reflex and bounce my head until he is making the most deliciously filthy noises come out of my mouth. It pairs nicely with the stream of expletives he is chanting above me.

"Fuck, Penny. I love it when you take all of me. Swallow that cock like a good girl. That's it."

He holds my skull steady as he picks up his pace, and I let him fuck my mouth. I love every thrust, every tear that leaks from my eyes, every thread of saliva that drips down my chin. I love that I can be filthy with him.

This giving is something I can't replicate with my toys, and I am enjoying having a partner to please again. I didn't realize how much I missed that aspect of sex until I got it back. But judging by how quickly this blow job turned me on, I'd do well to think more on how to achieve it when between partners.

Dash grunts and thrusts deep, pulling me back into the moment. His movements become jerky, and he coats my throat. He twitches and curses above me, vulnerable in my mouth, and I lick him clean, wiping all thoughts of work and future droughts from my brain. Worries for another day.

He slumps back against the counter, and I rise shakily on knees gone numb.

"So what did you order?" I tease.

"You, on a fucking platter," he growls, pulling me close. "If you think we're done with dessert just because you've gotten your craving satisfied, think again." He slaps my ass through my work pants, making me jump and teeter in my heels. "I want this ass bare and up on the edge of the bed, now."

I drop my slacks to the floor and step out of my heels to free my feet.

"Put the heels back on," he calls over his shoulder as he disappears into the bedroom ahead of me. I step back into my heels over the protest of my toes and follow him, unbuttoning my blouse as I go. He turns with one hand behind his back, and gestures toward the bed with the other.

"Face down, ass up. I'll be right back."

I shed my bra and panties and climb onto the bed on all fours, careful to leave my heels hanging over the edge. Water runs in the bathroom, but before I can figure out what he's up to, he's back and running warm hands over my ass and thighs.

"You look so pretty like this, Penny. Ass in the air, bare and waiting for me."

I shudder as he runs his hand from my tailbone up my spine, pausing at the top to squeeze my neck lightly and turn my face against the bed. My body is so sensitive to his touch, I can feel him before he makes contact.

"Now," Dash says, moving the fingers of his other hand over my clit. I'm ridiculously wet from going down on him, and he is quick to take advantage. "I know what you like here." He circles my clit, impressively hitting my self-pleasure rhythm and rotation perfectly. My nerves instantly jump to eleven.

And then he stops. Before I can protest, he slides those same fingers into my pussy, stretching me wide before curling downward against the front wall of my vagina to stroke gentle pressure across my G-spot.

"And I know you love this."

I gasp and nod, the spike of pleasure stealing my wits and words. My hips jerk backward of their own accord, chasing his fingers on the withdraw. My thighs were already shaking with anticipation. I've never gotten this close this quick. If he paired this petting with his mouth on my clit, I'd hurtle right over that edge embarrassingly fast. And I get the feeling he knows it too.

"You've been taking notes."

But he's not done showing me what he's learned. He holds his fingers stiff and still, withholding the glide I crave. I rock my hips, trying to find it, and turn to meet his eyes when an amused chuckle escapes him.

"Nice try, darling. But I've got other plans. I can't help but wonder what you like…here." Dash withdraws his fingers, and I cry out at the loss before immediately catching my breath on a gasp as he moves them higher to tease the rim of my ass. "Do you mind if I learn what you like here?"

The temperature in my bedroom has just gone up a hundred degrees. "Mmm, I love helping you with your research," I say.

Dash's grin lights up the room. "Good. Step back and put your feet on the floor."

With my heels on I am practically bent in half, resting my elbows on the bed. Dash grabs the towel he'd dropped on the bed and unfolds it to reveal a bottle of lube, a wand vibe, and my favorite anal plug. It's a silver bulb that I can take pretty easily and the flared end is capped with an amethyst crystal cabochon. It's almost more art than toy.

"I picked this one because it's pretty, but if you have one you like better, tell me now."

I shake my head over his thoughtfulness. "I love that one. Which lube did you grab?"

"The water-based one from the drawer next to your bed."

I nod and grab a pillow for between my elbows. "Next time we'll try the CBD lube. I got some samples from a new supplier."

"Mmm, I like the sound of that."

"Of a new supplier?" I ask.

"Of a next time." Dash holds the plug in one hand, warming the metal, while he drizzles the lube on my exposed ass. I bite back the urge to tell him what to do, and then realize this is exactly what I coach my customers against. What's the use in gaining knowledge of my body through experimentation with toys if I'm not going to share that information with my partner?

"You know what I like the sound of?" I say.

"Tell me." The sincerity twined with command in his deep voice has me baring my soul and my ass.

"Going slow, teasing as you stretch me, and then, your hand lightly spanking me once the plug is in, while your cock stretches my pussy."

His growl and tightened grip on my ass cheeks, holding me open, send a bolt of pure lust through me. With a firm, slick finger, he explores, dipping inside to tease me before circling the sensitive rim.

The metal plug is delightfully warm from his hands, and he teases me as requested, before sliding it in easily, thanks to the lube and foreplay. The fullness in my ass only highlights how empty my pussy is, and I am increasingly more frantic for him to fill me there too. I push back against him, delighted to find that he is hard again, his cock bouncing against my thighs as I sway. Recovery time, my ass.

Dash tugs the amethyst head of the plug just enough to increase the pressure and make everything clench against the fear of him pulling it out, before smoothing his hands over my lower back, my round cheeks, and my trembling thighs. I want to purr and arch into his touch. When the stroke turns into a firm swat, I jerk forward and tense, clenching around the plug.

I love that he listens and genuinely wants me to feel good. I love that he approaches life as an adventure. If I'm not careful, I could end up loving everything about him.

Would that be so bad?

That dangerous voice in my head needs to shut up and let me enjoy this. Falling in love is not in the plan. We've barely gotten to know each other. We're still in the honeymoon phase. I don't want to think about this yet. It's pulling me out of the moment.

Dash to the rescue with a well-timed spank followed by a soothing squeeze pulls me right back in.

By the time he reaches for a condom and slides his cock inside my pussy, my limbic system is on fire. I've gone beyond rational thought. I'm a roiling ball of sensation and need. His steady strokes push against the plug from the inside, driving me wild. I'm so full.

"You feel incredible, Penny. I need you to come for me, baby."

When he kicks my feet closer together everything tightens, each stroke pushing me closer to my limit. Barely breaking rhythm, he grabs the vibrator and flicks it on before tucking it between my legs, directly against my clit. Like he's figured out some fucking cheat code, I erupt.

I collapse on the bed, a shaking, gasping mess as my

orgasm rips through me. My voice goes hoarse as I scream into the mattress.

Dash yells and whips off the condom, furiously pumping himself to completion and shooting a warm stream across my ass and lower back. The vibrator is still buzzing beneath me too much against my hypersensitized skin, but I am too boneless to find it in the tangled sheets. All I can do is twitch away from it instinctively.

Once again, Dash comes to my rescue, carefully lifting my hip to remove the wand before flipping me back on my belly and easing out the plug. Tucking both in the towel, he carries them into the bathroom before returning with a warm washcloth to clean me up. With gentle, thorough strokes, he wipes off every trace of lube and come from my cooling skin. The tender emotions in my heart combine with the delicious friction from the nubby fabric to leave me shaking by the time he's done.

My bones are still liquid, but Dash seems content to remove my shoes and tuck me into bed before heading back into the bathroom. My eyes drift shut, and I vaguely register running water, before Dash is back, curling up behind me and turning off the lights. It's not even late, but I could sleep for days. Longer if he stays right where he is.

CHAPTER 16

My growling stomach wakes me long before morning. I'd been so intent on making up for spacing out on dinner and tidying that I'd gone too far in the opposite direction and skipped eating entirely. Sliding as silently as I can from our bed, I tiptoe back into the kitchen to reheat the pizza we'd happily ignored. I inhale one piece cold while a full plate of slices reheats in the microwave. The piquant tomato sauce, cold cheese, and assertive basil and oregano combine with the orgasmic afterglow to create a wild alchemy. This is the absolute best pizza I've ever eaten, and I need to share this revelation with Penny.

Carrying the warm pizza into the bedroom, I pause in the doorway, struck again by how beautiful she looks sprawled out in our bed, face relaxed and sleepy. Too often tension holds her face tight and her body rigid. *I did this.* Pride flares in my chest. Taking care of her needs is quickly becoming an obsession. I want to be the person this woman turns to for comfort and peace and pleasure, with an intensity that scares me. A thought to dissect another time.

I wake her with a kiss and offer her pizza on a platter instead of my heart. We've been moving on warp speed since the beginning. I know I can be too much. I don't want to push her away. This is enough for now.

"Pizza? Naked? In bed?"

"Pizza, anywhere, anytime. Your slice, milady." I bow before climbing back in next to her.

She offers me a piece, but I decline. All of the warm feelings bouncing around in my chest need an outlet. "You eat. I'm good." I scoot behind her, with my back against the headboard, and pull her into the vee of my legs. She is my queen, and I'll be her throne. As she eats her pizza with gusto, I rub her shoulders, gratified by the way she melts against my chest.

"Mmm, my God! You've got magic hands, Dash. A girl could get used to this."

I wish you would.

"I like learning you and your body, what makes you tick, tick, boom. I love exploring and playing with you. I've never had a partner I connected with like this." I am shaken to realize it's true. I am twenty-seven years old, and I've never felt anything close.

"Me too. You see everything, every reaction, every need. It's a little intense, but I like it." She leans her head back on my shoulder, and I slide my arms around her torso.

"I'm taking notes so I don't forget." I kiss her neck and she shivers. "Like that right there."

"I love a man who is studious." She grins and squeezes my thigh. "You're still wearing your glasses."

"You said they were sexy."

A soft quiet settles between us as she finishes eating, but my brain will not let it last long.

"You seemed upset when I called and then you came home late. Want to talk about it?" I ask. Penny sighs and puts the crust back on the plate. I take it and set it on the floor.

"Some of the early reviews came back and mentioned that the MiO was difficult to get the hang of. Obviously not the first impression we want gearing up for the third-party resellers launch."

"Is it hard to use?" I dig my fingers into the space between her shoulder blades and she slouches forward to give me access.

"It does take some experimenting. Because everyone's anatomy is different, finding the G-spot can be tricky, and then figuring out what makes yours feel good is another layer. But that experimenting is part of the process."

"That makes sense. Do people know that going in?" I ask.

She sits up straight and flails her arms as she turns to explain. "We included it in the user directions. With diagrams! And suggestions!"

I chuckle at her vehemence. "Well, no wonder they

had trouble. Horny, excited people reading directions before playing with a new toy? I can see it now. 'Honey, get your face out of my pussy and come up here. We have to read first.'" I protect my face as she swings a pillow playfully at my head.

"What else can I do? I've gone through so many edits of those damn directions trying to make them as easy to follow as possible…"

I hug the pillow to my chest so she can't bop me again. "Yeah, but once they have the toy out, it's too late. I know I wouldn't have the self-control."

"I need to reach them before they get the toy… Oh my God! That's it! Onboarding before the toy even gets there! We could send out a video demo with the order confirmations so they hear the information when they are excited about the toy but haven't gotten it yet. Dash, you're brilliant!"

"No, baby, you're brilliant. That was all you." I slide my hand up to cup her still-bare breast, and she leans back into my chest, trusting me to support her. "I like these naked business meetings. Have I mentioned how much that fucking sexy brain of yours turns me on?"

"Not today."

"My bad." I tweak her nipple lightly, earning a gasp and a moan. "You know what, I think I am a little hungry. You keep plotting your global sexual revolution, and I'm gonna have a little snack."

Turning her in my arms, I lower my head and show her exactly how hungry she makes me.

~

The next morning dawns well before I am ready to rise, and I roll, hoping to convince Penny to play hooky, but the spot next to me is already empty and cold. With a groan, I pull on fresh boxer briefs and search for her.

I find her hunched over her computer at the table with a phone to her ear.

"No, we didn't talk about that. My mouth was a little busy. It seemed like a better use of my time… Stop it. But yes. It's just so much easier to fuck it out…"

I cough softly to alert her to my presence.

"Nicola, quit laughing. We found the problem. We need to get the customers learning before the device arrives. I was talking with Dash last night… Ha ha very funny. Behave yourself. I'm putting you on speaker because he just walked in." She mutes the phone and holds it to her chest. "Good morning! I hope I didn't wake you. I was too jazzed to sleep, so I came out here to work. Nic and I were just getting into it. Want to help?"

I grin and nod, pleased to be included. She sets the phone between us on the table and hits the speaker button.

"Okay, Nic, so I was thinking that we send out an email with a training video to everyone with their confirmation email so that we can explain the setup before the device arrives. Dash made the point that people are too excited for close reading when the toy actually gets there."

"It's a good idea, but we don't have that produced. And where are we going to host the video so that only folks who've ordered can see it?"

Problems and solutions chase each other through my head. I snag the most likely and easiest pair and jump into the fray. "I assume you have a website constructed?"

"Of course, but it's mostly a sales site," Nic explains.

"What if you make a members-only page, where you compile demo and instructional videos?"

"That's great, Dash, but that's two years down our timeline. I don't have anyone to do that right now or make the content."

"I can." I make the offer impulsively, but it's not an empty promise. I have a computer science degree, for God's sake. I can program a website to have a password-protected page.

"You're going to make videos on how to use a sex toy for people with vaginas?"

I can practically hear Nicola rolling her eyes through the speaker phone.

"No, I can design and code the website. I'll make their customer number their login and have a generic password sent out with the shipping confirmation. And I'll build the page for the videos to live. Maybe Penny could make the videos here or at the office?"

The more I talk it through, the better it sounds. We can totally make this work.

Penny picks up where I've left off. "It doesn't have to be perfect, Nic. It just has to work for now, and we can polish the process later. Are you on board?"

"I'll help however I can. What do you need from me, Dash?"

I think through what I'll need access to. "Do you have editing privileges with the web host?"

"I do," Nicola answers.

"Are you comfortable sending me your login, or adding an admin login for me to use?" I look at Penny for approval on this and she nods.

"Of course. I can send our current customer list too." Nicola's fingers are already clacking against keys on the other end of the line.

"Great! Send those over and I'll get started."

"No problem."

Nic hangs up on us, presumably to get busy knocking out tasks, and Penny grasps my hand across the table.

"Are you sure you have time for this? I know you've got articles to write and—"

"Penny." I cut her off. "I wouldn't have offered if I couldn't do it. I know how important this is for you. Trust me to know what I can handle."

Penny nods, eyes glassy. "It's just… It was just me in the beginning, and then I slowly brought on my friends to help me run the business. No partner has ever really taken an interest beyond how many hours I was working and how that impacted my availability for them."

"Then they were shortsighted idiots. I'll do anything I can to make you glow like this."

"Anything?" Penny purrs.

My exhausted cock pulses inside my boxer briefs, helpless to resist her flirting.

"Anything." I link my fingers with hers and raise our joined hands to my lips.

"Like washing the dishes in the sink and emptying the dishwasher, since it was your turn yesterday but we got distracted?"

"Ooof. Walked right into that one. But yes, I'll take care of the dishes today. The distraction was worth it. But you need to go put on more than my oversized T-shirt if you want to keep me from getting distracted again."

I wiggle my eyebrows like any good horndog, and laughter crackles from her lips, a little rusty but full of energy and life. A morning where I can make her life easier and make her laugh? That's worth a few hours of soapy torture.

~

PENNY

I retreat to the bedroom to put on actual clothes and get ready for my day. I am loath to give up Dash's T-shirt, and I tuck it under my pillow before hopping into the shower. His soap is in my shower, and I can't resist opening it and taking a deep sniff. That scent is hard-wired in my brain with intense pleasure, and I touch myself under the hot spray just to take the edge off and clear my mind.

I've never had a lover like him. Hell, I've never had a *partner* like him. Sure the mind-blowing O's are great, but the way he genuinely cares for my mental and physical well-being too blows the rest of me away. And stepping up to help my company this morning? Icing on the cake! I try to remember the last time I felt this seen by a lover and come up blank.

Dash is dangerous for my equilibrium. It would be very easy to start depending on him. I don't know if I'm ready for that. But oh how my heart wants to trust him with everything.

Shaking the deep thoughts along with my wet curls, I push aside my fears and walk naked back into the bedroom.

"Penny, I wanted to—" Dash stops mid-sentence, both in words and motion, frozen halfway through the bedroom door, his laptop balanced on his forearm.

I toss the towel I'm using to scrunch my curls on the bed and stand there naked and amused. I wait for him to finish his sentence. It's supremely gratifying when he can't.

"You wanted to…?" I prompt, barely holding back my chuckle when he looks at me like an owl through his glasses, all wide-eyed and stunned.

"I…I can't remember. Jesus, Penny. How can you expect a man to think when you're there, all naked and warm and wet?" Tossing his computer on the bed, he wraps his arms around me and kisses me like he means it.

I could really get used to him meaning it. Scary thought indeed. His lips obliterate any remaining scrap of humor and shoot me straight into the fire that sparks at a moment's notice between us. I kiss him back, happy to let my conflicted thoughts burn.

The rest of the day passes in a blur of spot fires to be put out and anxious emails from my team as I change gears on them yet again. I can't expect them to keep their balance on shifting sand, so I try and do as much of the legwork as I can before I hand the tasks off. Exhausted, I flop on the couch at the end of another long day and drop my head into Dash's lap. He sets aside his laptop to pet my hair, and I very nearly purr.

"Tough day?"

"Lots of chasing my tail. I feel like it was an all-out hustle just to hold our ground. It's frustrating not making progress."

"Wo—" Dash cuts himself off with a shake of his head.

I study his face from below and watch the muscle in his jaw clench and release as if he's literally biting his tongue. "What were you going to say?"

Dash shakes his head again. "Nothing. I'm sorry you had a tough day."

"That's not what you were going to say." I sit up and turn to face him. "Spit it out."

"I was going to ask if it would make sense to delegate some of the decision-making responsibilities so that you have more time to do the actual growing of the company? You keep having late nights, and I wonder why you are the one handling it. But then I thought, 'You idiot! She's the CEO and founder and knows what she's doing. I'm sure she's already thought of that.' So I didn't say anything."

I grin at both his cuteness and his thoughtfulness. "I think I followed that. And yeah the ultimate goal is delegation, but we are too new and still unsteady so my people aren't comfortable making big decisions on their own. And at the end of the day, it's my company, my call. Today just happened to have a lot of big decisions coming to a head." I kiss him on the lips. "That's for trusting me to know my business. But I don't want you to feel like you can't ask questions."

"Okay. Just know that when I ask a question it's because I don't understand, not because I'm questioning your decisions."

His soothing hand down my back makes me want to curl up like Callie. No wonder she's traded her allegiance to him. Well, that and the table scraps he thinks I don't know he's giving her. "Deal. Want to watch a show?"

"Sorry, I have to finish this article before I can relax."

Speaking of Callie, she comes and settles on the back of the couch against his neck. I swear she would read over his shoulder if she could read.

"Yeah, I can see your editor is really breathing down your neck," I tease as I lift her from her perch to cuddle on my belly. "What's the game?"

"Ha ha, I wish. I'm not back on the game beat yet. My editor still has me 'temporarily' assigned to pandemic tech and funny reviews. This one happens to be about the challenges of sharing space, and how to ensure that your Zoom background doesn't accidentally catch your partner in the nude."

"You are not!" I sit up quickly, much to the chagrin of the cat I'd just placed in my lap. Callie leaps from the couch, but not without voicing her displeasure and leaving me with a few claw marks on my thighs as souvenirs of her love.

"I am too!" Dash turns his screen so I can see. "Look at all the cool green screen choices there are."

"Oh my God! I'm mortified." I cover my face with my hands.

"I'm not using your name, or any personal references, but curating your background and being thoughtful about privacy is a big deal. You're simply my muse."

"You're sure no one will know it was me?" I ask between my fingers. I know he wouldn't deliberately embarrass me in an article, but I need confirmation.

"Positive. Zero personal references."

"Okay." I'm not totally convinced, but I don't know what more to say.

"I tell you what. You give me two hours to knock this out, and I will get you naked again and keep you well off camera this time. I'll be yours to command."

"Deal."

I snuggle into my couch with a throw blanket and my phone, using Dash's thigh as a pillow. Opening up my social media apps, I scroll the feeds, deliberately sticking to my personal accounts. News of pregnancies and pandemic pups gives me the smiles I need. I just want to turn off the business brain for a while. Unfortunately, news stories creep in around the edges, and after reading about spiraling Covid shutdowns and cruise ships being kept at sea, I tap out and close my eyes. Maybe sleep will help me shed some stress. At least until Dash is free.

CHAPTER 17

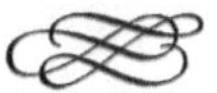

DASH

I wrap up my article and glance at the clock. Shit. I got lost in an image search for green screen background replacements, and now I'll barely make my deadline. Callie has returned from her pout and is conked out, draped over my shoulder, and Penny is fast asleep on my thigh.

Given the hour, I let them both sleep and keep working so I won't disturb them. Penny looks so peaceful curled up next to me. I'm tempted to brush a curl away from her cheek, but I know I will not stop touching her if I start. I keep my hands to myself.

Besides, my mind is finally in a work groove. Might as well ride it out until it fizzles. The chores I still need to do today and my plans for Penny fade from my mind as I shift into excitement over a fresh challenge that will actually help people, as opposed to the fluff articles I've been turning in lately.

I log into her website host and begin structuring the

platform to contain the preorder videos she wants. I set up the password page with an age verification to keep out minors and begin designing the actual pages of what I hope will become a community forum.

Wouldn't it be great if there was a place where people could talk to each other about their experiences and connect through shared pleasure? And an FAQ section for sure. A video library. Links to the customer service department. A tagging system to make searching easier. A connection to their point-of-sale email so that every order confirmation email will go out with a link to set up their login and a discount code on their next purchase for doing so.

My list of things to build and design is growing, but I want this portal to be robust and flexible for her to use long into the future. I won't always be able to help with coding, so I need to give her a solid start to grow into.

Where did that thought come from?

Why am I already thinking about a time when I won't be here?

This is the happiest I've ever been in a relationship. And in the middle of a global pandemic, that's really saying something. But that old doubt creeps up the back of my throat, burning a path of bile. No other relationship has ever lasted. I've always been too much to handle for the long haul. Penny will come to her senses and realize she deserves better, because she absolutely does. She deserves the world, and I'd give it to her if I could. But I can't. I'm not built for forever.

But as long as she is happy, I am happy. I won't borrow trouble tonight.

My eyes droop and I blink hard to wake myself back up. How long have I been drifting? A glance at the clock shows it is now nearly two, and my brain has finally run dry. Carefully setting my laptop to the side, I hold Penny's head steady as I slip my thigh from beneath her and stand. I stretch to make sure my legs are awake, scoop her up off the couch, and carry her to the bedroom.

The way she snuggles into my chest makes me feel like a hero. Yeah, I'm going to hold on to this feeling for as long as I can.

"Hmmm, wha' time zit?" Penny asks on a yawn.

"It's late. Go back to sleep."

"What about the movie?"

"You need sleep more. We'll watch it tomorrow."

"M'kay." Her sleepy disappointment tugs at my heart.

I lay her down and carefully tuck her in, this time not repressing the desire to brush her hair back. She smiles and rolls over, already asleep. Shucking my clothes, I climb in on my side, smug that I have a side, and close my eyes.

PENNY

I groan as I wake and reach for my phone, which isn't on its charger. Right, because I fell asleep on the couch. Dash probably hadn't noticed it. I have no idea what time it is, but the sun peeking through my curtains tells me I'm late. Again.

What is it about Dash that makes me sleep so much better than usual? Careful not to wake him, I sneak into the living room and gasp at the clock. I slept for over ten hours! That has to be some kind of record since becoming an entrepreneur. I go cushion diving and find my phone. Completely dead. *Great.*

I set it on the charger while I make coffee. Before I even add my cream and sugar, my phone is buzzing to life with notifications. I scroll through them as I mainline my hot caffeine.

This is why I don't sleep.

Fuck.

A message from Zarah about the price of gasoline and silicone fluctuating and eating into profit margins.

An email from Jennifer about a shipment we are expecting from the manufacturer, stuck on a boat that isn't being allowed to dock because of active COVID onboard.

A voicemail from Nicola following up on damage control for the reviews.

All needing my opinion before they can act.

I leap from well-rested to stressed in a heartbeat. Any one of these events could put us under if I can't fix it. Together? I'm screwed. Every day more problems chip away at my belief that I can do this. My resolve is crumbling under the impact of these setbacks. My plan is in shambles.

I have always been the person with the answers. The one who figures things out and saves the day. It's been a point of pride that I can take care of myself and my responsibilities. Maybe my childhood was rockier than I'd like, but it did give me a killer work ethic and a desire to be in charge. Now that I am, running my own company, employing my friends, making million dollar mistakes, that desire is flagging and I don't know if I have the energy to keep going. But I have to. Failure is not an option.

A kiss on my shoulder from Dash startles me. Had there been any coffee left in my cup, I would have scalded us both.

"Good morning. Do you have a minute before your day gets hectic?" he asks, taking my hand in his.

Too late for that, but I nod and let him lead me to the couch where I'd fallen asleep waiting for him to finish last night. I don't want to be salty about it, but I had a free evening and he'd chosen to work through it. I had hoped to unwind with him, and I'm a little miffed that an article about Zoom backgrounds took nearly seven hours to write.

He opens his laptop and sets it on my lap before reaching across me to pull up my website.

"You fell asleep yesterday and looked so peaceful that I couldn't wake you. So when I finished my article, I got to work on the client portal."

He clicks through a few of the pages while I try to catch up. It's hard to pull out of a pity spiral on a moment's notice. He's saying words, but I'm not taking any of them in.

"You can see the basic functions here, but I didn't want to do the full design until I knew I was on the right track. What do you think? Is there anything I'm missing? Anything you'd like to change?"

I sit back against the sofa cushions and feel my soul shrivel a little. I am a horrible person. Here I am, pissy that he hadn't set aside his work for me, and he'd been letting me rest and doing work for my company instead. That sticks like a fish bone in my throat, and I cough to clear the sudden tightness.

"Dash, I don't know what to say. You outlined so much so quickly. This looks amazing."

With his jazz hands flared to the side, he grins and croons in his best sea witch voice, "This is what I do…it's what I live for!"

I can't help but laugh. "And what will I have to give you in return for this…favor?"

Dash laughs with me but quickly sobers. "I know you want me to play along and demand your voice so you'll have to use body language, but I can't. You don't owe me anything for this. I'm happy to help and shake the rust off my skills."

"You never told me why you stopped coding." I don't want to pry, but I really fucking want to pry.

"That is a long and sad story, and now is not the time. The pages are all saved in draft form so you can look them over in detail today and tell me anything you want to add or change. Be as specific as you can, and I'll keep working on it this evening. Have a great day, babe." He kisses me on the lips and beats a hasty retreat toward the bedroom. "I'm gonna hop in the shower."

Message received. Touchy subject. And he's right. First thing in the morning, as I'm triaging my company's failures, isn't the best time to tackle an emotional memory. I'm distracted and not likely to be able to give him the attention he deserves. But I'm not going to forget. I owe him some slack after the way I misjudged him, so I will save my questions for later.

As I sit there, trying to get my analytical brain to function, a message pops up on the screen from his former roommate, Rishi. Dash's reply from his phone flashes almost immediately.

Rishi:
How goes things with sex toy babe?

Dash:
Things are going great.

I hope he doesn't ask about my giddy grin when he comes out of the bathroom. If he does, I can truthfully say I'm ecstatic about his design work, because I am. I sit for another few minutes, scrolling through the page mockups, making notes and brainstorming functionality. This is going to be amazing when it's finished, and I can see how he's setting up places for community to grow once I have customers in the pipeline.

I can't believe how well he's solved this problem for me after one conversation and a coding binge. With this solid win under my belt, I switch his computer with mine and join the Zoom call to save my company with a lighter heart.

CHAPTER 18

DASH

I drop my phone down on the couch, my hand gone boneless, my jaw slack. Adrenaline and dopamine fight for supremacy in my bloodstream as excitement and fear fire simultaneously. I can't believe it. In the middle of the uncertainty of a global shutdown, I've been promoted.

The lowest man on the ladder, the last one hired, the gamer boy.

Now XPTech's newest staff writer, assigned to cover breaking pandemic news and relevant tech developments.

This buzzing in my brain and tingles down my spine must be excitement. It's certainly not panic, right? A full-time job with benefits and stability? A regular salary? No more cobbling together freelance work and side hustles to pay the bills? All the things a functional adult should want.

The American Dream.

At least, I'm sure my mom will think so. My father definitely would have. He might even rise from the grave to say, "I always said you could do better." I wouldn't put it past him.

But I stopped seeking their approval a long time ago. I tried very hard for a very long time and it never came. I was never good enough. To save myself, I had to stop caring. But the ingrained desire for my parents to be proud of me has apparently been lying dormant, waiting for a professional win to jump out and sabotage me. I shake my head to clear some of the static and clap my hands.

It is really time to celebrate. This is a big step in my career, and I couldn't have gotten here without Penny! She's going to flip!

I rouse myself from the couch, and cross to the kitchen table where she sits with her head propped on her hand, noise-canceling earbuds in.

I touch her on the shoulder, and she jolts and slaps her laptop closed. Her eyes look tired, but the light in them gradually sparkles back as I watch her mentally pull herself out of her work and into my giddy joy.

"You look like you got some good news. What's up?" she asks.

"I got it." I bound around the kitchen like Tigger on speed.

"Got what?"

"The job."

"What job? I feel like we're in an Abbott and Costello bit."

"Who?"

"—is on first." She waves her hands at my confusion. "Ignore me. I thought you had a job."

"I did. I do. And I'm doing well enough with all the pandemic articles that they hired me on full-time! You're looking at the newest XPTech staff writer." I puff up my chest holding my fake suspenders and win the laugh that turns my insides all sparkly and golden.

"I didn't know you had applied."

"I didn't. But Chad has been teasing the possibility for a while, and I didn't say I didn't want it, so he must've taken that as affirmation."

"Good old T.A. I'm so happy for you, Dash," Penny says.

"You know what this means? A salary! Benefits! Retirement accounts!"

"Woohoo!" She pumps her fists in the air in a victory dance, laughing.

"I know it's ridiculous to get excited over entry-level, and my articles are just fluff, but—"

"Don't knock your work! The world needs fluff and joy now more than ever. Your work has just as much value as mine."

That sets me back a moment. I'd never considered my work on par with hers, and hearing her say that feels damn good.

"I've paid my own way freelancing and hustling for so long, it feels good to have some guarantees."

"Well then, I'm glad you've got them. I'm so happy for you. We should celebrate! Don't worry. I'll plan everything! Why don't you go shower while I get things set up?"

I plant a kiss on her forehead, because if I kiss her anywhere else in this state, we will be celebrating in a very different fashion. Not that I'd mind, but I am trying to be better about remembering to eat.

I lean back before her nearness can distract me from my goal. Shower. Dress for dinner. I smile, soaking in her joy and praise.

"Don't mind if I do." I strut into the bedroom, closing the door behind me, flush with pride in this win. The pandemic has changed so much for the worse. It's nice to have something change for the better.

PENNY

When the door closes behind him, I let out a heavy sigh. That was a close one. I didn't hear him come up, and could barely summon my poker face in time.

I am happy for him, truly. He's been working so hard on these articles, and he is a really talented writer. It's wonderful to see his hard work recognized.

I hate the tickle of resentment that itches in my throat.

Days like this make me miss working for someone else. Having a boss tell me I did a good job wasn't something I thought I'd miss when I struck out on my own.

There are just times when I wish I had someone pointing me in the right direction. Well, the way things are going, I might be going back to that soon.

I'll tell him everything later. I don't want to bring down the vibe, and I certainly can't afford to lose my composure now. I refuse to let my fear or sadness show. I am the face of the company, and my friends are counting on me.

Resignation thickening my throat, I join the four o'clock call with bad news on the tip of my tongue but a calm smile on my face.

"Hello, everyone. Thank you for being prompt. I've done an analysis of our numbers and accounted for all of the current shipping costs and delays, and it's not looking good. There is no way we can keep to our targets now, so we're going to have to cut some costs."

Everyone starts talking at once. Their fear and panic wash over my open wounds like salt water. This is exactly what I didn't want to happen.

I raise my voice. "Don't panic!"

"When in the history of bad news has that line ever worked?" Nic asks, tossing my words back at me. *Smartass.*

"Let me explain. I have a plan to keep us going until I can secure another round of capital, but it's going to mean big changes."

"How big are we talking?" Emmie asks with a smirk, and I appreciate the attempt at levity, but I can see her nerves simmering just below the surface. I know just how much this job means to her, professionally and personally. I took a chance on this engineer fresh out of college, eager to get some work experience while tackling her master's, who also happens to be a single mother. Our partnership has been great for both of us, except it really needs to pay her bills.

Every one of my employees has a similar story. I hired these people because they are exceptional and needed to catch a break. They have devoted themselves to the success of this company. Now I need to hold to my end of the bargain, namely keeping them employed.

"Let me start by saying no one is losing their job."

"Shit, that big?" Nic winces.

I repeat myself, steel in my voice. "No one is losing their job, but we are all losing our office space. I'm breaking the lease on the building. What we save in rent will keep us afloat until I can get more investment money in, and with Covid and new variants it's probably safer to work from home for now anyhow. It's more important that we keep the warehouse paid up, so we can keep shipping orders."

"So no change for me?" Mike asks.

"No, you'll still be managing the same space and skids." He nods, relieved. Change is hard for Mike. I'm glad I don't have to disrupt him...yet.

"I am also reducing my salary until we get through this."

"Wait, how is that fair?" Zarah asks.

"It's my company. Logically, I have the most to gain from its success, so I should also have the most to lose."

"This isn't making sense." Jen holds her head in her hands. "Shouldn't we all take a pay cut?"

I push onward.

"That's not on the table. You were hired under certain expectations, and I'm going to hold to that. We'll take the money we save from these cuts and put it into advertising, both for the product and for the web portal Dash is building, to try and boost direct internet sales while everyone is home. For a lot of folks it's been months since they've been able to casually date. I want an angle on that."

"You got it, boss." Nicola scribbles a note.

"And Zarah, I want you to prep pitches for bigger third-party vendors. Once we get these reviews up and more product in stock, we need to be ready to move."

"Absolutely."

"I want to be very clear. This is a rough patch, but we are going to get through this, and we'll do it together."

Nods on the screen confirm their agreement, and I inwardly let go of one small thread of worry, while keeping the rest tightly clenched in my fist lest they unravel. Even with everyone on board, I'm still pulling the strings. By the end of this, I'll be a master puppeteer. Let's hope that end is far in the future.

"You'll have time this week to go in and clear out your space. I've made a digital sign-up so we can be isolated while we're there. Take anything you'll need to be comfortable at home. Chairs, monitors, plants, and send me a list. If you take it with you, I don't have to store it. I don't know how long we'll be without an office. Take everything personal. I'm not even sure we'll be able to rent back the same space, but it will save us a substantial amount of money each month. And keep pushing on all fronts. We've got this!"

"We've got this!" Voices clamor out of my screen as everyone chimes in. I'm the luckiest CEO in the world.

I drop off the call and begin drafting the notice to the leasing agent. *Two steps forward, one step back. This is just a step back.* So why does it feel like I stepped back to the edge of a cliff?

Luckily, Dash is there to break my free fall into disillusionment.

"You finish your work?" he asks, his hands kneading my shoulders.

"Just. Give me ten minutes to get ready, and we'll celebrate."

CHAPTER 19

DASH

She comes out wearing a pretty, flowing wrap dress that clings to her frame in all the right places, makeup done and hair styled…and wearing shoes. I thought we might order in for a nice meal, but Penny has other plans.

"Follow me, good sir. Adventure awaits!" She tucks her hand in my elbow and leads me to the door, so I can add shoes to my outfit of slacks and a button-down. "Tell me more about this new job!" she prompts as we climb into her car.

"It's a great opportunity. More stability, benefits, a chance to move up in the company. And all I have to do is keep writing articles about how the pandemic is affecting tech usage and making a fool of myself. Easy-peasy." I lean back in the seat, trying to project a nonchalant joy I do not feel.

"Do I detect a hint of resignation in there?"

I can't hide my grimace. My earlier euphoria evaporated with the steam in the shower, leaving behind some serious reservations.

"It's great. Really. I just…" I run my hand over my head and grip the back of my neck tightly, as if that might ease the strain from the boulder balanced between my shoulder blades. "All my life I've disappointed people. My parents, teachers, employers, lovers… My ADHD is great sometimes, but other times it makes me look lazy or late or not reaching my potential. I had a great gig reviewing video games. It played to all my strengths and paid my bills. The deadlines were motivating, and concentrating on a game was super easy. Games are literally built to deliver dopamine and keep you engaged. Now? Writing all this stuff about the pandemic? It's depressing. I'm having to bribe myself to get the articles in on time. And now it's going to be a full-time gig? I just…yeah. I'm worried."

As my rant winds down and my words slow, I realize that I just spewed words for an entire mile without a filter. God, she must be bored to tears. I brace myself for disdain or chiding about being grateful.

"It can be hard to embrace risk when you don't want to let people down. It's a lot of pressure," she says, eyes on the road. Every vulnerability is sitting just under my skin, waiting for a punch. "This is a big shift, and change can be scary."

Now I feel ridiculous for having worried and for spilling out my trivial anxieties. I know this is nothing compared to the pressure she faces every day as CEO.

Why am I bringing us down when we should be celebrating?

"I'm sure the pressure you're under is a hundred times worse, starting your own company from scratch," I say.

"It's not a competition, and me being stressed doesn't mean that you can't also be feeling pressed."

Her soft words hit me in the solar plexus, stealing my breath. I have no idea what to say to that. I've gotten so used to minimizing my reactions so they don't become problems for everyone else that I'd forgotten what it's like to feel entitled to my feelings too.

"Can I ask you a question?" she asks as she flicks on her blinker to turn left.

"We're on a date. I believe conversation is customary. Ask away," I tease.

"You said that your degree program was in computer science. How did you end up in journalism?"

I take a deep breath and settle lower in the passenger seat. "That's a long story."

"You said that before. I've got time."

I take one look at the honest interest in her face and decide to trust her with my deepest failure. I want to trust her, and be worthy of her trust in return. I want to open up my entire life for her to browse. I just pray she likes what she finds.

My mind is spinning, unraveling the threads of the tale, trying to decide where to start. If she wants this story, I will find the courage to tell it. And somehow it's easier with her focus on the road and not my face.

"Just remember when I'm still rambling in an hour that you asked for it."

She chuckles, as I hoped, breaking the tension.

"When I was a kid I always had trouble at school. My behavior was all over the place. Impulsive, couldn't sit still, disrupting other students...but my grades were solid, so they never had me tested for anything. Just the class clown. The screw-up. When middle school knocked me on my ass, my counselor had his suspicions and asked my parents to do the assessment. ADHD. Four big letters that broke my parents. I wasn't put in special ed. They wouldn't even consider it. See, when they thought I was just goofing around, they could punish me and think they were fixing it. When I had those letters attached to me, I was confirmed broken. They couldn't have that, so they ignored it and kept punishing me, because that's what they knew."

"Dash, you aren't broken."

"I know."

"No, Dash." She turns to look at me, tears in her eyes. "You're not broken. They were wrong."

Hearing her defend me shakes loose a bit of the anxiety I've been holding close to my chest. "Middle school added hormones to the mix. I was still getting in trouble, and also distracted by girls. So I spent a lot of extra time in detention with the computer teacher who set me up with game-based tutoring. I really liked the games and started showing up, even when I didn't have to. Thus began my love affair with video games, yet another thing my father never understood. It became one more thing he could hold over my head to punish me with. Didn't get good grades? No Xbox. Phone call from the teacher? No TV."

"You know that was absolute crap, right?"

"I know it now, but back then? When your mother looks at you in the principal's office and just shakes her head and walks out? I was a Problem with a capital P. Thankfully high school was somewhat better. I got paired with a guidance counselor who actually had some chops, who connected me with the special ed teachers to learn specific strategies. Through all of it, playing video games was my escape. I'd sit in my room, hyperfocused for hours, just swimming in the dopamine. I joined a coding club that claimed to be a place to build your own video games, and I was hooked. They met every Tuesday at lunch, and I found my people."

"I can just picture you in a room full of teenagers geeking out over some new game."

Happy memories with my friends flood my brain, and I smile. "The faculty advisor for the club was Mr. Anderson, and before you ask, yes, we teased him mercilessly about *The Matrix*. He really saw something in me and encouraged me to apply to his college, and lo and behold I got in. My parents were so excited. They thought they were getting a computer engineer."

I turn to look out the window, remembering how proud my dad had been when I got that acceptance letter from my first-choice school. The pride hadn't lasted long, but it was sweet while it did.

"I worked so damn hard to make it through college,

and I did it. When I was eighteen I saw a doctor through the university and pursued medication as an option. I gained a little traction. I worked with tutors for the classes I hated, and did extra credit for the ones I loved."

"I see." She glances at me, waiting for me to keep talking as she scans the highway.

Now I'm getting to the hard part, and I brace myself for her disdain, gripping the car door handle.

"To graduate with honors, I built this amazing game, *Astraia*, as my final project. My goal was to prove that a game seeking positive approval and justice could be just as entertaining as a single-shooter, 'break all the rules'-type game. Everyone thought it was great, and it got me a job offer with RPGiga right after graduation. My parents encouraged me to take it, and I listened, wanting to make them happy. And for a hot second they were proud of me."

I hesitate. God I was so young and such an idiot. I still can't believe that I just walked in there completely blind. It's been years, but these memories still have the power to shred me from the inside out. I stare out the window at the slow-moving traffic.

Penny reaches over and takes my hand in hers, squeezing her support. How do people know how to do that? Did I miss that day at school? Or is it just another innate understanding I lack? I take the comfort offered and rally my words to share just how stupid I was.

"When I started at RPGiga, I signed a bunch of intake paperwork that I didn't really read closely. I thought it was just standard, *you're working here, we need your tax forms* kind of stuff. But mixed in with the forms was a contract that claimed anything I worked on while I was an employee was technically included under their intellectual property rights."

"Oh no!" Horror dawns on Penny's face and I know she's put together the pieces. Her beautiful brain works just that fast.

Where was she when I was signing away my rights to my own brain at twenty-two?

"Yep, I kept working on *Astraia*, making the decision chains more and more complex, and then I got assigned to work on a project update. *Call of Anarchy*. Maybe you've heard of it?"

"Uh, yeah. Even I've heard of *Call of Anarchy*."

"I was instructed to integrate my beautiful scaffold into the latest and greatest shoot-'em-up clusterfuck. I balked. I said no. They showed me the contract I had signed without reading, and said I could do it or I could walk away. Either way they owned *Astraia*. I tried to toe the line, tried to do a good job, but it broke me. So I walked. And they broke my baby into bits and pieces, and I haven't been able to design anything since. Mr. Anderson was shocked. My parents were appalled. 'Unprofessional and a disappointment' were the words they used."

"Oh Dash! I'm so sorry! That's horrible. How could they not understand?"

I shrug. I have asked myself the same question a thousand times over, and still have no answers.

"Where does journalism fit in?"

"Video games are the one thing I'm good at. For years I had been running a blog reviewing games, and I needed to pay the bills and get off friends' couches. So I pitched freelance articles and got picked up by XPTech and here we are. My dad wasn't thrilled when I told him I was playing video games for my job, but this… This full-time job might have made him happy, but I don't think it will make me happy. And how twisted is that? Did we just drive around the block?"

"We did. I wanted to give you time to finish your story." She parks the car in a garage, turns it off, and shifts to face me. "I have things to say. Brace yourself. First of all, you are only responsible for your own happiness. You do not have to do anything in your life to make your parents happy anymore. In case you needed to hear that. Second, you're incredible, you know that?"

I don't know how to take that, so I default to defense. "What do you mean? What did I say?"

"No! No sarcasm! You legitimately amaze me. You chased one dream job and had your work stolen from you, so you found another job that let you pursue your passion, and got promoted out of that one. I have no doubt you'll figure out your next step to getting back on a path you love."

Her faith in me is humbling. The way her brain so succinctly finds the through line makes me feel seen. Maybe I need to let her see my fears. Maybe she'll help me understand those too. I let my worry escape its cage and fly out of my mouth, even though it sounds ridiculous to my ears.

"Then why am I balking at this opportunity? Shouldn't this be a good step? I mean, it's a lot more money, more security, more benefits…"

"More joy?" she asks pointedly.

I have to be honest with myself. I shake my head no.

"Exactly. So say you keep this job for a while, enjoy the stability if that's what you're craving. You can always keep your eyes and ears open for the next opportunity. Be ready to ride the next wave when it comes, because it will come if you keep paddling your board out."

"I thought I was the writer. Look at you, Ms. Metaphor." I tease to break the moment, overwhelmed by her confidence in me. She floors me with her generosity and faith. I climb out of the car and don my mask, eager to leave conversation in the car. "So, where are you taking me for our date?"

"Well, restaurants just reopened, and you once told me that your favorite restaurant in LA is…"

"Shake Shack?" I blurt out, bouncing on my toes. Penny laughs at my enthusiasm.

"Yes, Shake Shack. It's right across the street."

"What are we waiting for?" I take her hand in mine and squeeze it before tucking it back into the crook of my elbow where it belongs, and we hustle across the street to join the line that stretches down the block, everyone spaced six feet apart.

CHAPTER 20

PENNY

My phone keeps vibrating in my purse as I shift from side to side trying to ease the aching in my arches.

"Go ahead and check it." Dash gestures toward my bag.

"I don't want to." That is a lie. My fingers are itching to dog through my purse and see what the notifications are about.

"You'll feel better once you check."

I sigh, knowing he's right, and give in to temptation. Email updates from the team needing clarification or decisions made on every single item I gave them before we left. I'm so tired of this back-and-forth on everything. I switch my phone to silent and tuck it in my purse. There is nothing I can't deal with after we've eaten. In fact, I'll just handle things directly in the morning. I don't have the patience left tonight to be polite.

"Everything okay?" Dash asks.

"It's fine. It can wait until morning. What can't wait is my stomach! I'm starving. Why is this line so long?" I shift feet again, trying to see and give my toes a break at the same time.

Dash rises to his toes and looks over the heads in front of us. "Someone from the restaurant is walking up the line. Maybe they are taking orders?"

I cross my fingers. I need to eat or my hanger is going to ruin the evening.

When the employee gets close, the expression on his face fills my empty stomach with dread. His words confirm the worst.

"There is no food left. Thank you for coming. There is no food left."

He comes even with us as he's repeating his message and I step in his path. I need answers. "What do you mean there's no food left?"

Waiting in line for forty-five minutes just to be told to go home empty-handed pushes me past my breaking point.

"I'm sorry, ma'am. We've been keeping stock low because no one has been coming in. We weren't prepared for the reopening because the governor didn't give us any warning. We've got a delivery coming in Thursday. You can try back then." The beleaguered employee continues shouting down the line, explaining that the Shake Shack is indeed out of shakes, and burgers, and fries.

Dash runs his hand down my arm and I jerk away, beyond pissed and not wanting to be placated. All the frustration I've been tamping down for weeks explodes. All I wanted to do was treat him to his favorite meal. All I needed was one night of normal. One night for things to go right.

But of course that's too much to ask for.

The noise I make frightens the dog in line behind us into hiding behind his person. *Great, now I'm scaring small animals.* I cover my face with my hands as if I can hold back the sweep of emotions rioting through me. The heels of my palms pressed against my eyelids fail utterly to stop the ridiculous tears forming.

"Babe, come on. It's okay."

"No, it's not okay! None of this is okay! I'm tired of being held hostage by this virus. I'm tired of my plans being caught in the crossfire. I cannot keep pivoting and rebounding every time some new complication pops up. I needed a win here." My voice rises in speed and pitch as I rant, letting my accumulated frustrations fly.

I totally understand all of the safety measures in place, and of course I don't want people to get sick. But operating in a constant state of flux is exhausting, and I simply don't have the energy left to pretend everything is fine while the world around me burns. I'm not against change as a concept. Hell, I'm CEO of a startup. I thrive in chaos. But regular chaos ebbs and flows. This is too much, too constant. And suddenly I've hit my limit. I drop my hands, and a few tears escape into the seam of my mask.

Dash is right there to take my hands in his.

"You're right. It sucks that we can't eat here tonight. But we can eat. And that's something. Here, I have an idea. Give me your keys."

I let Dash lead me back to the car. He opens the passenger door, and I drop heavily in the seat, hunting in my center console for takeout napkins to dry my face and coming up empty. Right. I haven't stopped for fast food in months.

What a disaster! Nothing is going right. It's my job to make good decisions, and every call I make these days seems to be the wrong one. My plan is in pieces on the floor and I don't even know if it's worth figuring out a new one. Hell, I can't even pick a good place for dinner!

As I sit alone in the car waiting for Dash to get in, the weight of the world presses me into the seat. Tears fall with abandon. I whip off my mask so that I don't accidentally waterboard myself. *Pity party for one.* This doesn't just feel like another mistake. It feels like I am a failure. Like I can't even feed the person I care for. Like I've lost every gain I've made since moving out on my own. Who am I if I'm not the girl who made it?

It takes me an embarrassingly long time to realize Dash hasn't just not gotten in the car yet. He left.

Where the hell did he go? Is he just letting me cry it out in the car by myself? Is that a kindness or have I scared him?

I scan the parking garage for any sign of my lover but he's vanished. More negative thoughts swarm my overwrought brain and each prick from the sharp edge of failure sends another tear down my cheek. I have a deep affection for this man, and it scares me. I want to celebrate him and keep him around, but I am terrified that if he sees the mess of a woman behind the curtain, he'll run just like everyone else. Every disappointment, every mistake, every loss looms large in my mind's eye. And I break.

The dam holding back my emotions lies in rubble. Tears run unchecked down my cheeks. Sobs rack my chest. Anger forces its way out of my throat in raw screams of frustration. A full-on nuclear meltdown.

I hate this feeling, which was why I do my very best to avoid it. Failure.

Growing up, trying to please my parents into paying attention to me, I pushed myself hoping they'd notice or care. Grades, science club, looks, student council—I always reached for excellence and often found it, even if I never did quite find that love and acceptance I craved.

My father worked all the time to avoid my mother, and my mother drank to avoid reality. Neither had time or attention for the little girl they'd created between them.

But my teachers and coaches did. Little Penny soaked up their approval and praise like a dry sponge. I learned that if I succeeded I would be praised. It was well-reinforced that people would only like me if I didn't push them away with mistakes. Soon I had a reputation to uphold. And my drive to achieve took me to the places I wanted to go. Valedictorian. Summa cum laude. CEO of my own company before thirty.

But I still don't know how to exist in an imperfect world. How to be human and fallible and not beat myself up for it. Every imperfection is like a grain of sand under my skin that I work away at under the surface, trying to turn it into a pearl. I have no idea how to relax and just be the clam.

Lack of parental support? I turned it into a stunning work ethic and a praise kink.

Have a partner give an amazing orgasm and then ghost? I built a revolutionary toy to recreate it for everyone.

Get laughed out of the room by the bank manager when I asked for a loan to start a company and share that toy? I start the company on a shoestring and aim higher to venture capital funding based on a proven sales record.

I am well versed in taking shit and making it shine, but I cannot keep it up forever. The overload of a pandemic on top of my regular shitty stressors is just too much to bear. I'm so tired and afraid all the time. And I can't risk Dash seeing it and deciding I'm too much. That would break me. With focused effort, I wrangle my emotions back under tight control.

By the time Dash returns and sets a bag in the back seat, the choking has ceased and my nose has quit running, but evidence of an ugly cry is still all over my face, from the puffy eyes to the red splotchy cheeks.

"Sorry, that took longer than— Oh my God! Are you okay?" Dash asks, climbing into the driver's seat. "Penny, talk to me."

"I'm fine. Just overwhelmed, and not being able to treat you to your favorite meal on your special day pushed me over the edge."

"Then you're in luck."

"What?"

"Nope, you just have to wait and see. It's my turn to surprise you."

Dash pulls out of the parking garage and onto the road. Without much interest in the lighter than usual LA traffic, I gaze vacantly out the window, letting my mind drift.

"Do you want to talk about it?" he asks.

I shake my head. I really don't want to lance the wound again with an audience. This sweet man has already witnessed more than I'm comfortable with.

"Penny, look at me."

I do, and he is looking me straight in the eye, serious and sincere. "It's okay to fall apart. It's okay to cry. It's okay to get messy and make mistakes. I'm here."

How do I tell him that's what I'm afraid of? He's here watching me fall apart. No one wants to see this side of me. At least, no one ever has before. My parents' reaction to my big emotions was disdain and distance. Lovers never stayed lovers long enough to let them in.

Even Nicola figured out that I could use a friend more than a girlfriend after I fell apart over stress in college. Don't get me wrong, I'm grateful she's in my life in any capacity. But the sum total of my experience tells me love doesn't stay when things get messy. People don't love me when I'm out of control.

And yet Dash has only ever seen me out of control. This man has only known the spiral. T-Con, then Covid, then business stress…he's seen it all at quarantine range. And he's still here.

Maybe, just maybe, this time will be different.

I haul in a deep breath and let it go.

"I feel like the weight of everything is on my shoulders. I'm stretched thin because my routines have been obliterated and every plan I make falls apart before I can execute. I'm pivoting so fast I'm running in circles. Today I made a lot of decisions at work and at home and all of them were disappointing. My pivot is exhausted and I got stuck. I'm sorry I lost it."

Dash lays his hand on my thigh, gentle and comforting, and I turn to watch him drive.

"I'm still here," he says quietly.

"What?"

"I'm still here. All of those decisions that went wrong, they're in the past. I'm still here, and you're still here. I still think you're an amazing, kick-ass, smart, and sexy woman. You still have the opportunity to try again tomorrow. Failure doesn't mean it's the end. If you need to fall apart again, go ahead. I'll be here to hold you while you pick up the pieces."

This kind man… I cover his hand with mine and nod before falling into sleepy silence for the rest of the drive, exhausted by my tornado of emotions and contemplating the novelty of having a partner who stayed through the storm.

~

*D*ASH

I park the car behind Griffith Observatory and walk around to open Penny's door. I offer my hand, channeling that Prince Charming shit, and help her out of the car and into my arms. The long, quiet hug isn't just for her, although I am gratified to feel her melt into my embrace. The tension drops from her shoulders and she lets me tuck her close. I hold her firmly against my body, being the physical support she needs. I press a kiss to the top of her head and inhale her scent.

"It's okay. I've got you."

She wraps her arms around my waist and nods. I don't know how long we stand entwined. It could be minutes, hours, days. All I know is that I'd gladly stay there, holding the woman I love in my arms, for as long as she'll let me.

Eventually though, Penny pulls back, much sturdier on her pins, and looks around.

"Griffith Park?"

"My favorite view of the city." I jog to the other side of the car and retrieve the bag of food I picked up.

"What's that?"

"Walk with me."

She follows me around the observatory to the deck where LA at night spreads below us. Setting the bag down, I pull out one bowl of ramen for her and one for me.

"I know it's not from your place, but I could only run so far. So we get to have my second favorite meal for dinner."

Penny smiles and tears well up in her eyes again, and my panic switch flips my brain into no-filter mode.

"Oh no! No! This is a good thing! A favorite spot, a favorite meal with you, my favorite girl."

"It is a good thing," she says on a hiccup. "A very good thing. Thanks for salvaging the evening I wrecked."

"Oh so you're taking the blame for the pandemic and supply chain issues now? Good to know. I'll be sure to work that into an article. Thanks a lot, Penny." When she doesn't chuckle as I hoped, I realize I need to be more direct with her right now. "Penny. I appreciate the effort you went to. I'm sorry the plan didn't work out, but it's okay. There will be other trips to Shake Shack. It's not your fault. You cannot control everything."

"Then why does it feel like I have to do exactly that or fail?" she mutters, not meeting my eye.

"Let's talk about that."

"No, I'd rather eat this ramen with the handsome man who bought it for me and enjoy the view."

"Penny…"

"Later. I can't handle another crying jag tonight."

I let it drop, and noisily slurp my noodles. That earns me the laugh I wanted. As we eat, we talk about friends, trips to LA and other places, funny childhood memories, recent reads, and a whole host of other little things that make a person unique and interesting.

Being in the same space together all the time gives us

a familiarity and banality that often keeps our conversations perfunctory and mundane. We discuss the Zoom schedules and meal planning instead of philosophical positions on dessert as a meal or favorite Tom Hanks movies.

This step out of time into the outside world opens up familiar patterns of date-night conversations that feel really good. Normal. Real.

I am so gone for this woman. The more we talk and share thoughts and memories, the closer we knit our shared experience. I want this woman's future history to be inseparable from mine.

Notably, we don't talk about work, neither my insecurities nor her struggles. An unspoken truce is called. No more pushing the hard buttons tonight. And it is lovely to spend a fun evening with a beautiful woman I care for. The Hollywood sign towers on the hillside above the glowing Los Angeles sprawl, weaving its magic, and for a few minutes I forget that we are living in a world I no longer recognize.

Penny is quiet on the way back to the car, and I resign myself to a somber drive home. But when we get back on the freeway, she breaks the silence.

"Thank you for tonight, Dash."

"No problem."

"No, don't dismiss what you did. When things fell apart, you stepped in and fixed it. That's special. You're special."

It wasn't that special. "I did what anyone would do."

"No, Dash. Not everyone would. My parents never did. I was on my own to figure things out a lot."

I can't help but compare her parents' neglect to my parents' constant disappointment. Which is worse? Does it matter, if we both still bear the scars? Gratitude for the adults in my life who did support me blooms as I realize just how lonely the alternative could have been. "I'm so sorry."

"Don't be. I've put it behind me. After years of trying to earn the love and care that should have been free, I gave up and walked out."

"Yeah, but you shouldn't have had to reach that point, and I'm sorry you did."

"Well, it sucked when I was eight and broke my wrist biking. I didn't get it set for a week because no one believed me when I said how bad it hurt. But learning to take care of things by myself from an early age has made me the CEO I am today."

"Just because you learned to be good at something through trauma doesn't mean you should have to keep doing it once the trauma is removed."

"Really, it's fine. This way the things I want to do get done. In my friend group in college, we never hung out until I made plans. I've never had a partner who would plan something like this without asking me to handle part or all of it. Even my friends and coworkers now text me constantly for guidance on what to do. But the flip of that is I often get what I want. Which is why it's doubly frustrating when I don't through no fault of my own."

Something has been off since this afternoon. *Let me in, Penny.* "Did something happen at work today?"

"Oh, you know, just had to tell my entire staff that we'd be working from home indefinitely, so that I can break the lease on our office building and save the rent to pay for our warehouse and shipping woes. And I'm just praying our direct shipping targets can weather the bad reviews."

Yep, that's a shitty afternoon all right. Maybe I can help her find some bright sides. It worked before.

"Is everyone still gainfully employed?" I ask.

"Yes." She picks at her cuticle and doesn't look at me.

"Are you still sending out product and taking direct orders?"

"As best I can." She shrugs as if this isn't a major win.

"Then you have failed no one, certainly not yourself."

"I just hate looking at what I've built and seeing only mistakes and disappointments. Honestly, at the end of every day, I feel like I'm failing." She watches the lights of LA flash past and I give her the same courtesy she gave me earlier of keeping my eyes on the road while I deliver some tough love.

"Well, quit looking at it through the expectations you had a year ago and look at the reality of what you managed during a global health crisis. You built an amazing prototype that will bring joy to thousands, and built a company around that mission that is flexible and fierce. So what if you don't look like the vision you had in your head yet? Don't you dare call my girlfriend a failure."

"So I'm your girlfriend now?" She finally looks at me, a teary-eyed smile on her face.

"When you say it all singsong like that it sounds ridiculous, but yeah. Girlfriend, lover, partner, friend, all that and more. But most importantly, you're mine."

"I like the sound of that."

CHAPTER 21

DASH

Buzz! *Buzz! Buzz!*

I reach for my phone and tap the screen blindly until it shuts up. It's been taking me longer and longer to write my articles, and I've been hiding from my failures in video games. After another late-night gaming marathon, I'm exhausted.

This is my third slap of the snooze button, and I am still unable to even contemplate the thought of rising from bed yet. With a sleepy yawn, I roll over and Callie is staring at me with unblinking green eyes from her perch on Penny's pillow. Penny must already be up, unless Callie is smothering her so she can claim Penny's side of the bed for herself. I wouldn't put it past her.

With that avenue of fun procrastination out of reach, I try to close my eyes again, but the clatter of pans in the sink keeps me from falling back asleep.

Pans. In the sink.

That sound rattles through my brain, trying to

dislodge some half-buried memory. I let it roll around, a bit like a pinball wizard trying to hit the bonus.

Crap! The pans are still in the sink. I told Penny I would clean them yesterday, and then I'd gotten distracted by work and the game and I forgot. Maybe if I stay in bed long enough she'll move past anger before I have to face her.

My phone beeps again, calling me on my bullshit. Before I can silence it and my guilt, Penny slaps open the bedroom door, and I sit bolt upright. Callie hisses and hits the ceiling before disappearing under the bed.

"For God's sake, just turn it off!" Penny barks, before loosing a frustrated growl and stalking back out.

Shit. So much for waiting her out.

I yank on a T-shirt and some sweatpants and make my way to the kitchen.

I look at the clock and realize what time it is. Nine forty-five a.m. On a Thursday.

"Aren't you supposed to be on a call right now?"

"I canceled the meeting. I can't lie and tell everyone the world isn't ending with a straight face today."

"Here, let me do the dishes. I should have done them yesterday. I'm sorry."

"No, it's fine."

It is clearly not fine. I can feel the waves of anger radiating from her. "Penny, stop. I'll do them."

Penny steps aside and gestures to the sudsy sink. "Fine. They're all yours."

Half of the dishes are already in the dishwasher. I wince. I blew it again. Why don't chores work like video games? Why can't I just remember to do what I said I would? Maybe I could design…

Penny clears her throat and snaps a towel against my butt. I yelp and put my hands into the hot water for a dish. "Yes, ma'am."

With a quiet snort, Penny wipes down the counters. Then she sprays down the handles on her cabinet doors and wipes those clean. When I lean over to rearrange the load pattern, she is scrubbing out the microwave. I step out of the way as she sweeps around me, and yelp when the wet mop hits my bare feet moments later. I let the water out of the sink and retreat, careful to stay on the dry path she left me.

"Do I want to know what caused this cleaning spree?"

"A messy roommate? Maybe I should make a chore chart with stickers."

My shoulders drop and I grab my hoodie from the table along with the hint and quietly leave the kitchen. Anger tries to make an appearance over being spoken to like I'm five, but sadness and resignation keep a firm hold on my emotional reins.

It's happening. Penny is realizing she deserves more than I can give her. The fact that she's talking to me like I'm a child who can't remember to flush the toilet grates on my nerves, but I can't deny I'm not pulling my weight.

Back in the bedroom, I pick up my phone and open the real estate app, hoping to find new rentals on the market. The governor said real estate is being moved to the essential services list soon. Maybe I'll get lucky. I can feel my time with Penny coming to an end.

She deserves a real partner. Sure, I can salvage a date night with my imagination and impulsivity. But I lack the executive function to carry out tasks from start to finish on a regular basis. I don't think those balance out on the relationship scale.

Everyone has their limit of how much Dash they can take.

Unfortunately, my name seems to fit. *A dash will do.*

I scroll through studio and one-bedroom apartments, since I can maybe afford my own space now with this salaried gig. Of course that means I'll have to keep said salaried gig, which whittles away more of my soul every day. My fingers begin to pick twitch against her bedspread, picking and pulling, as my anxiety spikes.

I find a few listings decent enough to save. I'll have to ask Rishi about neighborhoods I can afford, because I'm still clueless about large swaths of LA. I really don't want to try and acclimate to yet another round of roommates. If I can find my own space, I can keep it however I like.

Penny comes in and plops on the bed beside me, and I flip my phone facedown on the bed.

"I'm sorry. I shouldn't have said that. It was mean, and you didn't deserve it. I'm in a shit mood, and when I'm pissed, I rage clean. It's not your fault."

"The dishes in the sink were my fault. And the laundry I forgot in the washer, again."

"Again? It's gonna stink!" Penny stops herself and waves her hands in front of her face. "That's not the point. You didn't deserve to have me snap at you over some stupid dishes. You're not why I'm pissed."

"But I'm part of it."

"No, that's not—"

"Penny," I say quietly, cutting off her protest before I continue. "You don't have to lie. I'm messy and complicated and not worth the trouble. I forget to do things all the time. I'm a shit roommate. Don't sugarcoat it."

"Don't put words into my mouth, Dash."

"I don't have to. You said as much in the kitchen."

Penny sighs and grips her knees with her hands until her knuckles whiten. "I think I'm going to have to close the company."

My head snaps up, self-pity party shelved for now. "What do you mean?"

"I think we've reached the final straw. Our factory had to shut down because of Covid outbreaks. They are going to be several weeks behind on production at least."

"That sucks."

"After all of the earlier delays, I don't have any buffer. I have orders coming in I cannot fill and have to refund. Without those orders, I can't pay the bills or cover payroll beyond the end of the month. I have tried every venture capital firm I can think of to get bridge funding. Several have notices of suspension of applications due to Covid. Even more have posted waitlists of up to six months. Half of them don't even have anyone answering the phones. I know because I've called them all over the last week, trying to sweet talk my way into a deal to float us until the enforced quarantine in our factory ends, but who even knows when that will be... I've cut every corner I can cut. I can make it through the end of the month on duct tape and a G-string."

I can hear how every hit she's taken this morning has dented her confidence a little more as her voice gives away her anxiety. She must be reeling. Not only is her professional life spinning out of control, I'm throwing a wrench in her orderly home life as well.

She runs out of steam and collapses back on the bed. I can't think of anything to say. There is no bright side here. I don't even know how I can help her.

"I'm so sorry." The words feel empty, useless, like me, but they're all I can find.

"So am I. I've been crabby about it all morning, since your first alarm woke me up early and I read my overnight emails. I couldn't fall back asleep for worrying."

God, I'm an asshole. I hadn't even thought about my snooze alarm bugging Penny. Maybe I'm truly not cut out for cohabitation.

"So you see? It's not your fault."

I don't see anything of the sort. I see a woman I care about at her wits end, and I am not helping the situation at all.

"What were you doing when I came in? It looked serious," she asks as she sits up next to me and smoothes the covers between us flat again.

"Just paying some bills." The lie trips off my tongue and shames me, but I cannot add one more worry to her life right now. I can only do my best to remove a few.

~

By lunch, tensions have cooled to a simmer. I put together fancy grilled cheese sandwiches for us, so I can wrap up the pandemic paninis and wine pairings that will come out tonight. But when I sit down to write a new required article for the week, I've got nothing. Nada. Every idea is stupid or trite.

Who the hell wants another article about the pandemic? I sure as hell don't. I've run out of ways to make isolation funny. And now that there is all this pressure attached, my brain has noped itself out of the situation. This is exactly what I was afraid of when I took the promotion. Why can't I just write about the farm game that everyone and their brother is playing right now? The daily price of turnips sounds a lot more interesting than whether or not I put avocado on my toast.

When I'm excited about a project, deadlines are fantastic motivators. When I'm not, they are the ultimate energy suck.

Scrolling through TikTok for a while, searching for inspiration, I find dance challenges I will never learn and sourdough art which reminds me to feed the mutant growing in the back of the fridge, but nothing screams "technological advances." I switch to doomscrolling other platforms and come up empty-handed several hours later, having been distracted by the cat and cucumber videos.

Now all I want is fancy toast and a Callie snuggle. But Callie is eyeing me disdainfully from the top of the fridge, as if she knows the thoughts in my head are worthless. I have no toast and no idea what to write about.

My recent articles have all had a funny bent to them, but I want to write something more substantial, like my breakout article for Penny. Even when I was doing game reviews, I always took it seriously, digging into the structure and authorial choices in the games. I desperately want to write something that engages my brain at that level. And the world feels too fraught right now to do another "best houseplant for quarantine" update. Besides, the snake plant is the only one still thriving.

I want to write something important. Something interesting and real. Something that will make a difference in someone's life.

The only interesting thing that has happened today is Penny's revelation that she is on the brink of losing her company because of raw material and capital shortages.

The lightbulb in my head that's been flickering annoyingly for hours glows dimly as an idea starts to form. Maybe I can kill two birds with one stone. Opening a new search bar, I pull up contact information for several venture capital firms that have a track record of supporting tech innovation. Maybe I can get my article done and find data to help Penny out. It's enough inspiration to break the scroll.

The deeper I get, the more frustrating the results. Everyone is afraid of what might happen to the stock market, the job market, the global market, insert-other-economic-indicator-here, because of the pandemic. The wallets have all closed until they can sort out the new landscape of funding in a post-Covid world.

On the one hand, I can understand their hesitation, but on the other, my frustration for Penny keeps growing. How many other entrepreneurs are being affected by this? I open a survey thread on LinkedUp, and the responses come pouring in. I aggregate the data into a spreadsheet and look for patterns.

The results are stark. Established or late-stage firms looking for funding to bring information technology or healthcare concerns to market are getting money just fine. Smaller first-time applicants, especially women and people of color, are getting shut out of the market. I wish I could say it surprises me, but it doesn't. I'm not too jaded to feel dismay at the injustice.

"Hey! Earth to Dash!" Penny waves her hand in front of my face.

I look up from my computer, surprised to find that it's gone dark outside the windows. "Sorry! I got caught up in work."

"I can see that. I asked what do you want for dinner."

"Whatever is fine."

CHAPTER 22

PENNY

I suppress a growl. I wish he would just answer the fucking question! If I have to make one more goddamn decision today, I'm going to snap. Every time I turn around, someone else needs an answer and none of mine have been good ones.

If I can't get an influx of funding from someone soon, I'm going to close my doors within six months of my initial launch. I don't have time or energy to be dealing with dinner on top of it all.

"Leftovers it is. You can forage for yourself."

"Mmhmm. Sounds great."

Dash has already turned back to his laptop perched on his thighs, engrossed in whatever he's doing. That's fine. I can make food for myself, and he can eat when he feels like it. I'm not his mother. Or his wife. Or keeper. He is a grown-ass man who can take care of himself.

Heating up a bowl of leftover green curry, I sit on the

opposite end of the couch and click on the TV, desperate to zone out for a little while.

"Do you want to talk about it?" he asks.

"About the show?"

"No, about your funding."

"What about it?" God, can I please just shut down? I am so over today, and now he wants to chat? Where was supportive Dash when I was spiraling? I could've used some funsies to quiet my thoughts. But he was clearly busy with work, so I chose the next best thing, reality TV. I don't know why watching other people's lives run off the rails makes me feel better about my own struggles, but it does. The last thing I want to do is replay my failure right now.

"Why do you think it's been so hard to get investors to sign on?"

Okay, so we're doing this. I click mute on the mother/daughter modeling duo currently screaming at each other on-screen.

"It just seems like everything has dried up because of the pandemic. I can't even get people to respond to an email." I swirl my spoon in the rich sauce as if some sort of pattern will emerge and clear everything up. Unfortunately, my prospects are about as thick and murky as this green curry.

"Well, I did a little digging, and it doesn't look like it's dried up for everyone."

My phone dings in my pocket. Dash sent me a note from LinkedUp. "What's this?"

"Just a little informal survey I put up, but look at

who's getting funding and who's not."

The data in his poll is crystal clear, if anecdotal. "But how many of these were in the pipeline before the pandemic hit?"

"I don't know. That's a good question. A lot of these companies getting funding seem to have high pandemic product demand and are well-established firms."

"Not a single small entrepreneur on the list," I murmur, scanning for other names that I know are in the same boat.

"Why do you think that is?"

"I think VC firms are covering their asses in case the market tanks. I think they are fucking cowards if they can't see that products from small companies, women-owned companies, POC companies are just as valuable to a stable market."

"Have you been pitching your product as a quarantine-specific health device?"

"Health aides for stress relief of all kinds deserve funding right now. If people can't connect the dots between being stuck at home, afraid to breathe around other humans, and needing a device to help fill the gap, so to speak, they are idiots."

"Can I quote you on that?" Dash asks with a laugh.

"I don't even care anymore. This has been such an uphill battle from the start." I futilely press my palms against my eyes to stem the burning before it can summon tears. I've cried enough today. "Why would I expect it to get easier the farther in I wade?"

"Because you've made so many gains! Don't lose sight

of the goal line just because the hits keep coming. The product you are making is so important, not just for women, but for everyone who wants to have better sex! We just need the right pitch to get people to take notice."

Dash rubs a hand on my back, and I cannot deny how good it feels to have someone on my side. But I'm exhausted. I don't know how many different ways I can pivot and not lose sight of my plans. I'm dizzy just thinking about it.

"I'm just so tired." I drop my head onto his shoulder, too exhausted to even engage with his pep talk.

"Why don't you go to bed early? You've been up late all week. Maybe it'll feel more manageable after a good night's sleep."

"Are you going to join me?" I ask hopefully. There is nothing better at shutting down my brain and relaxing my body than an orgasm from Dash. I think my MiO might be too triggering tonight.

"I need to finish this article, ride the wave of inspiration. But I can certainly wake you up when I come to bed." Dash wiggles his eyebrows.

Honestly, I probably need the uninterrupted sleep more, but I give him a knowing smile anyway as I head for bed.

When I wake the next morning, the first thing I register is that I did indeed sleep through the entire night. No lingering O buzz, no tiredness from being woken up, no stubble rash on my neck or chest. Just a brain tired from chasing itself all night and a body that miraculously doesn't want to immediately sink back into the mattress. My happiness over decent sleep is tempered slightly by the knowledge that Dash hadn't woken me.

I roll and discover his side of the bed undisturbed.

Had he even come to bed at all?

I wander into the living room, still rubbing sleep from my eyes, to find him on the couch, headphones on, engrossed in a video game. He doesn't look away from the TV, doesn't even register my presence in the room. *At least he didn't leave.*

Even as I think it, the irrationality of that fear hits me. Where is he going to go?

Just because other partners had retreated in the face of my need for control and order doesn't mean he will.

This is his job. He reviews video games so it stands to reason he needs to play them to give adequate feedback. He is just being as focused on his career as I am. *Except he isn't reviewing games right now, is he?*

He is not required to come at my beck and call. His time is his own. *But it would have been nice if he showed up when he said he would.*

I told him I was going to bed. He knew I was tired. He was respecting my space! *Which would have been fine if I hadn't been counting on him pounding the stressful thoughts right out of my head.*

I continue arguing with my inner bitch as I retreat to the shower. The warm water sluices down my skin, and I let my worries wash right down the drain with the soapsuds.

Enough.

Today is a fresh start, a new opportunity to thrive, another day with Dash. I dry and dress, donning full makeup and professional attire for another day hunting for funding. I may have been beaten yesterday, but I'm not giving up on my dream that easily.

Primed and ready for caffeine, I go back to the kitchen in search of coffee. I stutter a step at the plate in the sink and the bags of snacks left out on the counter. There is even a stale beer on the table. I deliberately set aside that conversation for later and make my first cup of coffee for the day. I drop the beer in the sink and get my workspace at the table organized, making sure my background is nicely arranged. I don't like using the green screen ones, for all that Dash might tout them. I might have to work from home, but I am determined to present as professional an image as possible.

As a female CEO at the helm of my first company, I already have enough strikes against me. Looking sloppy or unprofessional is not allowed.

With my coffee in hand, I walk into the living room to see if Dash has come up for air yet. He startles and yelps when he sees me, which in turn startles me, shaking my still full coffee mug and spilling piping hot brown liquid down the front of my blouse and onto the floor. *Fuck!* Another mess to clean up before I can even start my day.

"I didn't see you come in!"

"So I gathered," I say as I turn to grab paper towels in the kitchen. I blot the stain ineffectually before stripping to the waist so I can pre-treat the stain and get it right into a delicate cycle. It soaked through to my bra, so I take that off too.

"Are you okay? Did it burn?" Dash tries to stop me as I stalk into the bedroom to grab a new shirt and a different bra, so he can inspect my bared skin.

But I'm so frustrated, I'm not having it. I don't need another obstacle this morning. I need support. I need something, anything to go right.

The fact that my bra won't match my underwear is irrationally irritating.

Everything is irritating this morning. It's going to be one of those days. I can feel it. I just have to start it so I can get through it. "I'm fine," I mutter tightly, not wanting to unleash the temper simmering just below the surface.

I rush past him again so I can finish getting the laundry in before my call. When I open the washer to find a funky-smelling load of towels still sitting inside, my last thread of patience snaps. The walls start closing in on me, and rage and panic form a toxic sludge in my throat, ready to flow when I open my mouth. Every failure, every set-back, every loss presses against my brain, telling me I'm not good enough to succeed, and I refuse to hear it. I can't hear it or I'll lose myself. And when caught between losing myself or someone else, my self-preservation instinct kicks in hard. Pushing Dash away is the only logical conclusion. My heart tries to step in and protest, but I can't afford to listen to that bitch right now. She's the one who got me in this mess. And the bees in my head are buzzing so loudly I can't hear her anyway.

"How am I supposed to do this?"

"Do what?" Dash asks warily.

"Function in a space that is falling apart at the seams? I can't be a badass boss bitch if I'm constantly distracted and having to clean up after you!"

"You don't have to clean up after me," he says quietly, not meeting my eyes.

"Apparently I do," I say, swinging my arms wildly. All of my frustrated rage comes flooding out. "Food on the counters, dishes in the sink, stinky laundry in the wash. If the kitchen is going to be my office, I need it to be tidy. I can't work with your stale beer and bags of chips all over my desk. And yet this is what I walked into this morning!"

I shove the bag of chips into his hands forcefully, spilling some on the ground. *Great. Fucking perfect. Something else to take care of.* I let loose a growl from the back of my throat and my temper revels in the loss of control. I've kept it on such a tight leash for so long, refusing to lose control. Now that leash has snapped, and my anger is running free and wild, trampling everything in its path.

"You're sure you're not burned?" he asks quietly.

"No, I'm fine."

"Go get ready. I'll take care of this." He takes the damp clothes from my death grip, and turns away, eyes on the ground.

Damn it.

I'd kept my frustrations over work and the pandemic and our relationship bottled up inside me, like a can of soda left in the trunk, shaking and bouncing against every turn and bump. Now, even letting a little pressure out triggered an explosion.

I'll fix it later, but I'm due on camera in five minutes, I'm pissed off, and I haven't managed more than a sip of coffee. How can I be living with someone twenty-four hours a day and never have a good time for a conversation?

Back in my bedroom, I take a moment to center myself in front of my mirror. Deep breath in, deep breath out. "I can do this. Today is not the day I fail. I can overcome any obstacle in my path." I look into my reflected eyes and nod. *I can do this.*

Slicking on fresh lipstick, I whirl back into the kitchen, ready to work. The washer and dryer are running and the dishes are rinsed and stacked in the dishwasher. Counters have been wiped down and food put away. A fresh, hot mug of coffee sits next to my laptop.

I breathe a sigh of relief. My entire body feels calmer in this clean and functioning space.

Five minutes. It had taken him less than five minutes to get things tidy. Why can't he do that without me having to blow up at him?

"I didn't want to start the dishwasher too. Figured it would be too noisy. And I will rewash the towels when they come out of the dryer." His voice is still low and devoid of emotion. Maybe he needs some time before we broach this conversation as well.

"Were you up all night?" I ask.

"Yeah, I powered through my deadline and was still wide-awake at two a.m. I peeked in, and you were sound asleep and Callie had claimed my pillow. So I came out and started a new game that I got pitched for a freelance review. It's really good, and I got caught up." He fiddles with the pen is his hand, rolling it back and forth across his knuckles.

"You should go take a nap this morning. You look exhausted."

"That's not a bad idea."

He leaves the kitchen without another word. No "have a great day," or "you've got this." No kiss on my head or cheek or lips. No acknowledgment of the blowup we just had.

It bothers me, but I don't have time to hash it out right now.

These quarantimes are messing with my head. It's a strange dichotomy of being together literally all the time and yet having no time to talk. Bottling everything up clearly hasn't been working. But I don't know that airing our grievances with nowhere to go will work any better.

Normally, I'd suggest we take some space, but there is no space to be had. He's as stuck as I am. My routine is shot to hell. My company is falling apart. My stress is at an all time high on all fronts, and there is no end in sight.

I can't keep going like this, but I also have no idea how to fix it. Because fucking Covid.

I settle in for my day of video calls and emails, trying to bridge the funding gap so everyone can get the orgasms they deserve and I don't lose my shirt. Once in a day is quite enough. I paste a happy smile on my face and imbue my voice with an energy I don't feel as I start the first meeting with my team.

"Good morning! Let's jump right in. I've drafted some questions to use when we interview the preorder reviewers. They are in your inbox—"

"But I thought Emmie and I were handling that," Nicola protests.

"I had thoughts last night so I just figured I'd get started on it. I'm going to spend the rest of today reaching out to VC firms again. Maybe something will have shaken loose. Any change on the factory front?"

My team goes suspiciously quiet. No one is looking at their screen. The hair on the back of my neck stands up and bile rises in my throat. Stress is a vise tightening around my temples. How much more of this can I take? The hits just keep coming.

"Oh God, don't tell me there's a bigger problem with the raw materials!" I brace for the worst.

"No, no change there, but you might not want to call the VC folks today," Jen says cautiously.

"What? Why? I'm sure if I just keep calling, someone is going to give." My team never pushes back against my ideas, and I don't like that it's happening now.

"Ask Dash," she urges.

"What does Dash have to do with it?"

"Have you read his most recent article?" Nicola asks.

"The one about pairing your paninis and wine to match your pandemic anxiety? Yeah, it was pretty funny."

Nic isn't laughing. A link to an article appears in the chat. "No, this one."

It is dated this morning. The conversation we had last night plays out on the page. He shares his informal research and the deeper dive into funding disclosures. He makes the case that venture capital firms are playing it safe, funding companies with proven track records over smaller, untried firms. Then he quotes me. Calling venture capital firms cowards. At least he's left out the "fucking." *Dear God.*

Words escape me as I stare at my name in print, condemning the very people I need to woo. How could he? What in the hell was he thinking? Why would he just throw me under the bus like that? And for what? A click-bait article that isn't even front page? I can see… No. No, I can't see how he could think this is okay at all. Not ever.

I keep scrolling to the comments section, and it's worse. The bees return, an entire hive of angry static filling my head.

NotUrFeminist24: No wonder she can't get funding. No one wants to put men out of business, not in the market or the bedroom.

MamaJoLo_TN: Those devices are immoral and profane. They ruin marriages and break down good Christian families. No one should give her a dime.

NotABot_8675309: I'd give her some funding to come over here and suck my d—

I push away from the table without reading the rest of

the comments. I don't need to. I know what they'll say. Half will call me a whore with disdain and judgment, the other half misogynistic interest. None will take my business seriously. Everyone will say I deserved it when my business crumbles because I didn't kiss the right asses. With my back to the camera, I brace my hands against the sink and try to regain my composure. I'm suddenly frustrated that Dash got everything put away. Smashing a glass right now would be very satisfying, if counterproductive. As it is, I can only try—and fail—to get my anger under control.

"Are you okay?" Emmie asks softly.

"I...I need to go. Can you...?"

Nic fills in the blanks without me. This is why it's great to work with friends.

"I'll finish running the meeting and send you an update."

"Yeah."

I slap my laptop shut, rage flowing like lava through my veins, burning up any sense of caution or restraint. I stalk into the bedroom where Dash is coming out of the bathroom in a towel, still wet from the shower. I notice and dismiss that fact in the same breath. I have to let these words out of my head or they will burn me alive.

"What the actual fuck, Dash?"

He stops drying himself and drops heavily onto the edge of the bed, shoulders hunched. "What did I do or not do now?"

"Don't play all wounded puppy with me. You know what you did."

"I'm gonna need a hint. I have no idea why you're yelling at me. Did I miss something in the kitchen?"

"The article?" I prop my hands on my hips and wait for him to catch up.

"About paninis?"

"No, you asshole. The one about venture capital where you quote me *by name* calling them all cowards."

"It was an excellent point."

"It was also meant to be a private conversation."

"I asked if I could quote you."

"I THOUGHT YOU WERE KIDDING!"

I back up a step and haul in a deep breath, working hard to make my next words calm and logical. I never yell in an argument. That isn't the way to win. My voice comes out loud and strained anyway.

"Why would I be okay with you alienating me from the very people I need to sway? Who do you think is going to give money to the woman making sex toys who called them out publicly? I told you that getting funding to tide us over was our only shot at survival. I didn't think you'd shoot me in the foot. I'm done, Dash. An entire year of my life, all my savings, my professional reputation, my plan, my creation… All of it, gone."

The reality of that statement hits me in the gut. The weight of that failure sits heavy in my heart. My pulse throbs in my head, and my fingers begin to tingle and go numb. I can barely think over the angry static. I failed. I gambled and lost. I have nothing left. I can't even begin to process the loss, but I do know that I am moments from complete meltdown.

I absolutely don't want to break down and cry in front of him. After this betrayal, he hasn't earned the right to my tears. A week ago, I'd have bawled my eyes out in his arms. The loss of that comfort, that unflagging support, slashes at my battered heart. It hurts just as much as the loss of my dream.

I'm done on so many levels right now, running on fumes, but I have just enough left to find the words I need to throw walls up behind me as I retreat.

"And for what? So you could make your deadline? Get a juicy headline? Clickbait fodder?"

"No! Penny, I—"

"No, Dash. There's nothing you can say that fixes this. I can't…"

Admitting failure ties my tongue for a moment, but I push through.

"I can't keep doing this. I tried. I let you into my life, but you keep using me. I can't trust that my private thoughts and my feelings won't end up in a headline. We gave it a shot, but I'm done."

I haul in another deep breath and try to look him in the eyes, but he's staring fixedly at the floor. I say what I need to say anyway.

"I'm going to go for a long walk. You need to leave before I come back." I snatch up a mask and leave before I can change my mind.

DASH

I've been floating outside my body since she told me to leave. I watch her grab a mask and her purse before storming out but it feels like I'm watching a movie, not my life. The door slams shut behind her, but I don't even flinch. The distance protects my heart from the imminent implosion. It's like this is happening to someone else, and that is sad but not soul-crushing.

But eventually I come back to myself and reality resumes at full pain. I have no idea how long I sat there, staring at the fringed edge of the carpet by her bed.

Dissociation is a scary strategy for me, but sometimes it's the only one that works to stop the pain. I got too good at it as a kid. It was an efficient escape from my dad's lectures. But I can't always pull myself back out of it, and I lose hours this way. Paralyzed. Removed. Safe but stuck.

I've been expecting this. I knew she'd eventually come

to her senses and call it quits. I always manage to fuck things up.

The stuff about her space and me being a mess, totally valid. I get tired of cleaning up after me too. It's not fair for her to have to cover the executive function I lack.

The part where she can't trust me with her thoughts and feelings cuts deep. That was the one thing I thought I could bring to the table. I could care deeply and be there for her to vent. And I fucked that up too.

And for what? An article? She's right. I wrote the story as it came to me, pressed against a deadline. I never even second-guessed if it was a good idea to quote her. Quotes give articles more gravitas, more authority. They also put a public name on unpopular ideas.

I'm clearly not cut out to be a feature writer any more than I am to be a boyfriend. I don't come with the right filters installed. I just wanted to get her story out and shed light on a troubling topic. I thought it would help. I also rushed to finish the damn article so I could spend time with her, and didn't manage that either.

When I write reviews about video games, it's expected that a few feelings might get hurt in the name of an honest review. I've certainly never single-handedly tanked anyone's company that I know of. Taking this new job was a horrible decision.

Add another career failure to my list of sins. Make it two this time.

Is she really going to lose her business over one article? I know she's struggling, but surely she can't be that close to the edge. Her launch numbers were so strong…

But the guilt sits heavy on my heart, because I know all of my protestations are simply my id trying to soothe my ego. In reality, I know exactly how close to the margins some companies run, especially while getting off the ground. The pandemic has done a real number on everyone. She likely isn't exaggerating how dire the situation is, which makes me a proper asshole.

Part of me wants to wait for her, argue, fight for us, beg her for another chance. But there's another, stronger part of me that says that's selfish and I should give her what she needs.

She deserves better than a thoughtless, messy, distracted boyfriend who can't get out of his own way.

How long have I been spacing out here on her bed? I have lost all track of time. If me gone is what she needs, me gone is what she'll get. It's the literal least I can do.

I stand to leave and realize not only I am still dressed in a towel and have left a wet spot that she'll probably be upset about, I've also frayed the edge of her towel with my nervous picking. Damn it. I put on actual clothes in a daze. I open my suitcases and put them on the bed so I can fill them.

Callie claims half of one and voices her concern over my actions. I pet her behind the ear the way she likes, but I can't let her distract me from my mission. She runs off disgruntled when I begin tossing clothes from the drawers and hangers that Penny had cleared for me into the cases willy-nilly. My books, comic book collection, linens and gaming gear all go into the cardboard boxes I'd folded up in the back of her closet, anticipating this day. Three of my boxes never even got unpacked.

Ten boxes stacked by the front door. Two suitcases bulge at my feet. The sum total of my life still fits in the back of my car.

Why do they feel heavier going down than carrying them up?

I fill the trunk and back seat of my car, and make one last pass through Penny's apartment. Callie circles my ankles, tripping me up until I pick her up for a cuddle. She butts her head against my chin and my throat clinches tight.

"Goodbye, sweetheart. You need to stay here with your mama. She'll remember to feed you."

Setting the cat on her favorite perch on the top of the couch, I finish the rounds. I will give Penny this one last gift, the gift of a clean parting.

I pull the laundry out of the dryer and put it back in the wash, and cycle the other load in to dry. I start the dishwasher and wipe down the table. A pass of the living room reveals stray papers, pens, wrappers, and cords, all of which I shove into my backpack, before I fix the throw pillows how I've seen her do it.

In the bedroom, my efficiency falters. I can smell her. That scent that's uniquely her fills my head and triggers every sensory memory I've been hoarding all at once, overwhelming me with joy and passion and a warmth I dare not name. And hot licks of shame over fucking up yet again. I'm a selfish bastard, because even knowing I will continue to disappoint her, I still want to stay.

I make the bed, smoothing the covers, remembering how she looked naked draped on top of it. I fluff the pillows and think of how her hair tickled my nose when she curled into my chest in the night. I think about stripping the sheets, but that would mean waiting for another laundry cycle, and I am determined to at least give her this one thing she's asked for.

I will be gone before she returns.

I can't be the man she needs in her life, but I can be the one who gets out of it when asked. I can listen to her boundaries and respect them.

In the bathroom, my gaze snags on my toothbrush still in the cup next to hers and tears well in my eyes. Hers, so neat and tidy, barely bent as she replaces it every three months. Mine, mangled and missing bristles, chewed and ready for the trash. If that isn't an accurate metaphor…

I snatch up the offending toothbrush and drop it in the garbage bin, tears spilling over. I have to go. I don't want her to see me like this. I refuse to add one more emotional burden to her load. The negative talk in my head is spiraling, and I need to get gone before it paralyzes me again.

I lock the door and slide the key under the mat, shouldering my backpack and running down the stairs, too impatient to wait for the elevator.

I don't glance around as I climb into my car. If she's lingering nearby, I don't want to see it. She is absolutely going to be better off without me. I just need to get somewhere I can fall apart.

But my problem remains. I don't have anywhere safe to go. I toss my backpack on the passenger seat and start to sweat as I pull into traffic. I really only have one option, and it's the last one I would have chosen. I am dreading the next five minutes of my life. Gathering myself and wiping my cheeks, I dial.

The phone connection in my car surrounds me with a voice that lives rent-free inside my head, but that I haven't actually heard in over a year.

"Hello?"

"Hi, Mom."

PENNY

Two hours walking the scorching summer pavement in LA does little to calm me down. I circle my building in wide loops until I see that his car is gone.

When I get back inside, I funnel my anger into more rage cleaning. My kitchen counters are spotless, even under the toaster. The grout in my bathroom gleams thanks to his old toothbrush I found in the trash. Using it to bleach away every stain in my shower feels cathartic. I sweep *and* mop the floors for good measure. My couch blankets are carefully draped, and my throw pillows are floofed and chopped to within an inch of their lives. By the time I've ruthlessly restored order and erased any trace of his presence, my blood has cooled somewhat and there are no longer flames burning from the sides of my face.

With a calmer mind, I replay the morning. I can understand that he didn't mean to harm me with the article. But he still did. I can understand that he didn't mean to ignore the state of the apartment, but he did. I know I wasn't in the best frame of mind to open the conversation, but I cannot regret what I said.

He might not have meant any of it, but it still happened, and it still sucked.

This is why I don't leap before I look. This is why I approach life with a carefully constructed plan. When I don't, utter chaos reigns.

Six months of my life, gone absolutely ass-backward. How many signs did I ignore because I was swept up? How could I let him into my life, into my company, just so he could use me for inspiration and hang me out to dry?

I keep going over the litany of his faults and reminding myself that I deserve better as I pace my apartment with a dust rag. Because there is part of me that wants to call him right now and apologize. Part of me that is afraid I just fucked up, big-time. The part of me that can't believe he actually left so quietly.

Well, that part of me can just shut up. I am a ruthless, badass, driven lady boss. I will get my approval on my own terms. The traits that make me a great CEO are the same ones I'll use to protect my heart. I will turn that energy back toward my work where it belongs.

As I look around my clean and tidy apartment with

satisfaction, a calmness settles in my chest. I hadn't realized how much anxiety I was carrying about the disorder in my space for weeks until it was gone.

Riding the wave, I sit down and make a list of all the things I need to do that I've been slacking on. I could be sending more emails, making more calls, researching STEM grants for women. I really need to do a walk-through of the warehouse to see just how dire things are, and then maybe I can send Emmie my ideas for the MiO version two and some other things I've been noodling. I wonder if an analysis of department duties could turn up new areas for efficiency that I might've missed. I've got users to interview... Ooh, interviews! Maybe I could reach out to the people who had me on their shows to do a follow-up piece and turn the tide.

Feeling more steady, I pick up my phone and dial. Nicola answers on the first ring.

"You okay?" she asks.

"I'm fine. It's over. I kicked him out. Things can get back to normal now," I say, proud that my voice doesn't even waver.

"Wait, what?" Nicola's incredulity surprises me.

"I told him to pack his bags. We're through." Why is she so surprised? She's usually the first to agree with me when I break things off with a partner. I lean back in my chair and contemplate getting a cup of coffee for this conversation. But that would require me to make coffee and that just feels like too much in this moment.

"Penny, don't you think that's a little rash? I mean, rip him a new one, but I thought you really liked him..."

"I did. I do. But I can't live like this. Little things have been piling up for weeks, and I've either been picking up the slack or letting him distract me with sex. It wasn't working, and now he torpedoes my company and says, 'Oops. Sorry. I didn't think about that.' No matter how good he is at melting my bones, I don't have room for his kind of chaos in my life right now."

Nicola mutters something.

"What was that?"

"Nothing."

"Good. Bring me up to speed on the meeting. I have a whole list of things I want to address now that I have my head on straight." I pull my list in front of me, ready to get lost in work.

"Penny. Stop. You are spinning in circles and the rest of us are getting dizzy!"

"What's that supposed to mean?"

"It means you need to let us do our jobs. You are so panicked about the company that you're doing that thing you do where you try to control everything by doing it all yourself."

"I am not."

"Bullshit. Do you remember when we broke up?"

"Yes, you said you needed space and that you thought we'd be better as friends since you were going to study abroad in Spain the next semester."

"I remember you researching my program, building sightseeing maps for efficiency and daily schedules for my free time. I remember you wanting to color-code my packing list. You were spiraling because I was leaving, and I couldn't watch you do that. And I couldn't let you control my big adventure. I would have resented the hell out of it. I loved you, so I let you go."

"You…what? Wait a minute…"

"We are definitely better as friends and colleagues, but you are doing it again. You're trying to control what you can't because you're scared. Do you trust us to do our jobs?"

I'm still reeling from the new perspective on our breakup. I can hardly keep up with the gear shift to the present.

"Of course I do," I protest.

"How many emails a day do you get, asking for clarification or a decision on something?"

I hate it when she gets that know-it-all tone in her voice. I also hate that it prods me to answer in kind. "A lot. I'm the CEO. It's my job to make decisions for the company."

"No. It's your job to set the course and trust your people to carry out your plan. Everyone is so afraid of setting you off by making the wrong call and bringing your attention to their office that they won't work on their own. You keep reinforcing that with your insistence on doing the legwork on these new projects yourself."

"I'm trying to save my company!"

How can she of all people not see this?

"You won't have a company to save if you keep it up. You are so panicked about losing it that you are micromanaging it to death. You're sending the message that they can't do their jobs, so you have to. Morale is at an all-time low."

"I just… I feel so fucking helpless to fix any of this. I have to do something."

"That something might be to trust your team to do what they were hired to and let things calm down a bit before making any rash decisions."

I slouch back in my chair, defeated. I wish I'd taken the time to make that coffee. "Is this what you talked about in the meeting?"

"Partly."

"What was the other part?"

"I'm not going to tell you. Send me the list of things you wanted to work on, and I'll distribute the tasks if I think it will help. I will table the ones that are just creating busywork for you to hide in."

This is why it's terrible to work with friends. They think they know what's best for you and boss you around.

"Do I need to remind you that I am your boss, not the other way around?"

"I only call you boss to piss you off. It used to piss you off because you insisted you were part of the team, remember," Nicola reminds me firmly. "Besides, everyone knows I actually run the company. You're just a pretty figurehead."

I scoff as intended, and I can hear her smile.

"Do you still trust me?"

"What does that have to do with anything?" We are

wading into muddy waters, and I hate not being able to see what's ahead.

"Do you trust me?" she repeats.

"With my life." I do. I trust that she absolutely has my best interests at heart, even if she's annoying me right now.

"Then let me do this for you. You've had a really rough day on top of a really rough few months. Take the weekend. Take care of you, okay?"

I want to argue with her. I want to take the control my subconscious is demanding to make the bad feelings go away. But I don't, because deep down I know what I really need to do is fall apart. "Okay."

"One more thing."

"Don't push it." I stand and begin making the coffee I need, because I'm going to need it in earnest if this conversation goes on much longer.

"Don't lose the life you started to enjoy just because Dash is gone. If I see you start to pick up your workaholic ways again, I'm calling bullshit and ordering in a puzzle and some tequila."

I have to chuckle at that. It's just so...Nicola. "That does not seem like a good combination."

"I know you. You'll start the puzzle thinking, 'oh how fun,' and then you'll get super focused and competitive about it and not be able to let it go until it's done. That's where the tequila comes in, to get you dancing on the table because you no longer care about losing a puzzle piece or two, and finally relax enough to fall asleep."

"That scenario is scary specific." I can actually see the

entire thing playing out, down to Callie deciding that the last corner piece is hers to chew on and me not caring after margarita number two. I pour the coffee in my mug and add my own cream and sugar.

"I know, but it comes from a place of love. I'm sorry things didn't work out with Dash." Nicola's voice finally softens and I'm talking to my best friend again, not my chief marketing officer.

"Me too."

CHAPTER 24

Alone in my apartment, I twiddle my thumbs. I said I would give Nic and the team the time and trust to handle today, but what does that leave me with? An empty apartment that feels too quiet? A brain that can't stop spinning? This grief beneath my sternum that I've been steadfastly ignoring?

If Dash were here, we'd play a video game together, or maybe cook a delivery box meal together. Or maybe we would try Shake Shack again, or head back to Griffith Park once the heat of the day has passed. Or maybe we'd go into the bedroom and play until everything in my head goes quiet.

I poke each memory now to test how painful it is before putting it back away. Nicola was right. I need today to wallow, so I can move on tomorrow.

I don't know how long I sit, lost in thought, but when I pick up my coffee again it's gone cold. I give Callie a scratch while I wait for the coffee to reheat in the microwave. She yowls her displeasure and stalks off.

Fine. Be that way.

I open the fridge to scavenge for dinner. A few leftovers from our last takeout nights and my stash of emergency protein drinks that I haven't touched since Dash began feeding me. Reaching for one now, I drink it like the fuel it is, with alacrity and a grimace. I wish I had ramen waiting for me but didn't think to order it ahead. I don't need someone else to get the takeout I want. I am perfectly capable. I stare down the protein drink that calls me a liar.

As I sit back down at my table-turned-office, my laptop calls to me. I could just do a little work to craft another proposal. That way I can hit the ground running on Monday. Nicola's words ring in my head but I push them aside. I have been guilty of overworking myself in the past, but I haven't done a thing all day. Just this one letter of interest, I promise myself, and then I'll go sit on the couch and binge-watch something entertaining like that tiger show or a fresh season with the Fab Five.

That is a promise broken. My coffee goes cold a second time, and the clock ticks past midnight before I look up again. *Damn it.* I got caught up. Too late for a marathon now. I shut down my laptop and head for bed.

Maybe Nicola has a point. I do find comfort in control. And maybe that's not the healthiest habit. I'm already falling back into old patterns and coping strategies. But when that pattern is the only thing that feels familiar, it's hard not to clutch it close.

I thought it would feel better to get back to normal. If I could just get back to the place where my plans were things I could make reality, maybe I could catch my breath.

My bedroom feels different without his presence. Emotions press against my closed eyelids. Why am I missing a dirty clothes pile on the floor? If I'm being honest, it's the man who's slept in my bed that I miss, but I cannot admit that right now or I will crumble.

Determined not to let the emptiness of my room mess with my head, I change into my comfiest pajamas, brush my teeth, and wash off my makeup. I climb into bed and starfish right in the middle of the mattress. I can sleep as spread out as I like. Callie leaps off Dash's pillow and stalks into the dark living room, annoyed I've woken her.

Time to recharge before another wild day. My dream is in a death spiral, so trivial things like repairing my heart will have to wait. Tomorrow. Tomorrow, I'll attempt adulting again. Today, I'm just scraping by, and that's okay. See? I can give myself grace…

I pull my pillow into a hug, and my fingers snag on soft cotton. His shirt is still here. My fingers stroke the fabric of their own accord, and before I can think better of it, I inhale deeply. His scent fills my head, triggering all sorts of erotic neurons. I am flooded with desire and memories of all the ways he made me feel good. *Fuck.*

I shove the T-shirt under what used to be his pillow and roll back to my side, turned on and exhausted at the same time. I need to work this out of my system so I can sleep. Escaping difficult feelings with the endorphin rush of an orgasm has been a solid coping mechanism of mine for years.

Good thing I have the perfect toy for just this situation. I pull my poor, neglected MiO from my drawer, and the orgasm fairies are smiling on me because it is still charged. I lie back, clear my mind, and let my wonderful machine take me away. In under three minutes, I build and clench and release. The easy climax wrings the tension out of my body.

But my chest tightens when I realize that though my body is taken care of, my toy hasn't touched the parts of my soul that are aching. The control I've been clinging to gives way, and my chaotic feelings break through. Sobs rack my chest, and memories and regrets chase me into the wee hours of the morning. Once again, there is no one here to help me put myself back together. I'll have to do it myself.

DASH

I lie on a twin bed and stare at the ceiling.

I am a grown-ass man sleeping in my childhood bedroom because I have nowhere else to go.

The reality of my situation sits like a brick on my chest and I struggle to calm my breathing. Everything about this situation sucks the air out of my lungs. The last thing I need right now is the panic attack waiting to pounce. I've held it off since yesterday with a combination of dissociation and denial. But Penny's angry words combined with the childhood memories of disappointment are almost too much to bear. Add in having to tell my mother that I'm a failure again, and my heart begins to race in time with my worst fears.

Hi, Mom. I have nowhere to live, my job sucks, my relationship just imploded, and I think I'm having a heart attack.

I'm sure that's exactly what my mother wants to hear. She was very kind when I showed up at her door last night after an eight-hour drive north, and had let me climb into bed without questions. But I have no illusions that the inquisition won't begin as soon as I head into the kitchen, followed closely by the accusations and recriminations. If I had anywhere else to go, I would have. The memories made in this house pile on top of my anxieties, and oxygen becomes even harder to find.

I can still hear my father's voice in my head.

"Video games? How in the hell are you going to make a living making video games? Why don't you put your brains to good use?"

That was the litany after college. When I washed out of game design in under two years, he hadn't gloated per se, but the criticisms had become more pointed. Contrary to the old nursery rhyme, sharp words do leave scars.

"Now you're just playing video games? How are you going to support yourself? A family? Why don't you grow up and get a real job?"

I was a disappointment and a failure in his eyes, and there's no changing that now.

Dad has been gone for over a year now, but I can still hear him in my head.

"My roof, my rules."

While Mom hadn't joined in the ranting, she hadn't disagreed with him either. Her silence was damning. Condemned for following my passions in my way, I left rather than stay and keep defending what my family found indefensible. I deserved to succeed on my own merit, and I couldn't do that with the constant negative feedback. It's bad enough it still pops into my head uninvited.

I wasn't there when my father passed, though I knew he was sick. I couldn't risk having his last words of disappointment branded on my brain. I came home for a day to pay my respects before leaving again. The memories and the painful emotions had been too difficult to reconcile with the persistent tug of love I felt for them both.

I let my mother handle everything on her own. I'm ashamed of that, but if I'd stayed then, I would have suffocated.

And yet here I am. Suffocating. Nothing has changed.

I have been lying here for two hours already, unable to move through the hurricane of thoughts and memories swirling through my head, until my stomach violently protests its empty state with a wave of nausea.

I still can't quite face the kitchen, so I haul myself out of bed and into the shower. The hot water eases my sore muscles and the tension in my shoulders loosens. Visions of Penny and that time in the shower flash in my mind, before I remember that I won't have the pleasure again. I ignore the morning wood that's grown insistent and flash the shower to cold before rinsing quickly and throwing on a T-shirt and well-worn comfy jeans.

No more avoiding. It's time to face the music.

Mom is sitting at the table, halfway through a cup of coffee when I walk into the kitchen. I open the cabinet where the coffee mugs have always lived and find the plates.

"They're above the coffeemaker now," she says. "I rearranged the kitchen after your father died."

I shift to the other cabinet, grab a mug, and fill it with liquid life. Other subtle changes catch my eye now that I'm looking. There is a pile of bills and letters on the end of the counter, and dishes from last night's dinner in the sink. And my mother is wearing a housedress. I've never seen her in her pajamas outside of her bedroom.

I sit in the chair I occupied for my entire childhood, staring into the dark abyss of caffeine, waiting for her to start in where Dad left off. I am bracing so hard that I startle when her hand comes to rest on my arm.

"Are you okay?"

The quiet concern in her eyes is unexpected. Thrown off guard, the question sneaks past my shields. I don't have the strength to dissemble, so I tell the truth. I shake my head and close my eyes against the welling tears.

"No, Mom. I'm not."

"Come here, baby."

My mother stands and opens her arms, and despite

being a solid eight inches taller than her, I step into the hug that healed boo-boos and dried tears until I'd gotten too old for that sort of thing. Little did I know, there's no expiration date on a mom hug. As she wraps me up in strong arms, soothing a hand up and down my back, I thank God that they still hold that magic.

CHAPTER 25

DASH

"I'm sorry, Mom."

I barely get the words out through the tears as I lean into her hug, but they feel right.

"Why are you apologizing?"

I pull back to look her in the eye, and find genuine confusion there. No judgment. No disappointment. *Huh.*

"Because here I am, a grown-ass man, turning up on your doorstep because I have nowhere to stay?"

"Anytime I get to see my son is a gift. You've been away too long."

"I didn't think I'd be welcome."

She has the grace to look down at that. "I can see how you would have gotten that impression, but your father missed you too."

"More like he missed having something to complain about…" I grumble.

"No, he found plenty to criticize in your absence."

"How could he criticize you? You did everything for him."

"And if it wasn't done the way he wanted, or exactly when he thought it should be done, you can bet I heard about it. It was easier to put on my mask and do as he asked than argue. I figured I had earned it for all those years of not putting myself between the two of you."

Though she smiles as she says it, I suddenly feel like an asshole for leaving my mom alone to bear the brunt of Dad's verbal abuse. Of course, I'd only seen my parents' marriage through the eyes of a child. What else had I missed?

I pull her back into a hard hug. "No. Never. Neither of us deserved the things he said."

"No, we didn't. But I should have protected you better. Thankfully, we won't ever have to put up with that again."

"Do you miss him?"

"Not as much as I thought I would." She looks over my shoulder, as if the air behind me holds the answer. "I don't have to keep the house immaculate and the meals hot and the clothes pressed anymore. No one complains about how I organize the kitchen or what I put on the TV." She looks me right in the eyes, and doesn't shy away from the truth. "I've got my life back. So no, I don't miss him as much as I should."

Me either sits on the tip of my tongue but that feels too hard to say.

"Quit should-ing all over yourself, Mom," I tease, trying to lighten the mood, but Mom's not having it.

"I *should* have protected you. I will carry that regret for the rest of my life. And I am learning. I'm learning a lot of things... But I will not let that man cast his shadow over this visit." Mom lets go of the hug and bustles around her kitchen, pulling out a plate and a loaf of bread.

I run my hand over the back of my neck. "It might be a long-ish visit."

"Good." She puts two pieces of bread in the toaster. "Now start at the beginning. Why are you here? What happened? How is everything at work?"

"I was writing game reviews for XPTech, and they sent me to T-Con to help cover the conference. I ended up breaking a major story, and they were impressed. Once the pandemic started, they asked me to write more quarantine-tech related pieces, and I got promoted to staff writer. Health insurance and a 401k."

"And?"

Here it is. Here come the questions and judgment I'd been expecting. For all she seems different, she's still my mom. My walls come snapping back up and so does my tone. "And what? Isn't that enough? I thought you'd be happy about a full-time gig."

"You wouldn't be here if you were excited about it. And how I feel about it doesn't matter. Are you happy at this full-time gig?"

I lean against the counter next to where Mom is puttering. She takes the toast from the machine, butters it, sprinkles it with cinnamon sugar and cuts it into triangles, no crusts. My sick-day breakfast. The exact right food for this kind of morning.

"I should be, right? Like this is a big step forward for me."

She hands me the plate and shoos me back to the table. "Who's should-ing themselves now?"

I chuckle. "It's harder than I thought. I'm not interested in the topics I'm supposed to be."

"Ah, no dopamine," she interjects, so casually that it throws me for a second.

"So I was looking around for inspiration since they won't give me games to review, and I ended up writing things I shouldn't have about the woman I was involved with. I put her business at risk to write an article to keep a job I don't want." I take a bite of the cinnamon toast and I feel five again. "I really messed up."

"Did you apologize?"

"She didn't give me the chance and I didn't stay long enough to try. Besides, what is there to say? She's right. I'm a mess, and she deserves to live her private life the way she wants."

My mom is persistent and doesn't let me hide behind the easy answer. "Are you going to apologize?"

"I don't know how." I want to say I'm sorry I hurt her, sorry I put her work in jeopardy, but I also know there's no changing who I am. So is an apology disingenuous? Also I have no idea if she'll ever speak to me again, so it's a moot point. "It's not like I can fix the root cause. My ADHD isn't going anywhere."

"No, it isn't. But you deserve love just as you are. Just

be honest with her. It may not fix anything, but she deserves the closure."

I don't know what therapist my mom has started seeing, but she is clearly earning every penny.

"I keep hearing Dad in my head telling me to quit being lazy and fix it."

"He hated to see you struggle. His way of helping was to tell you how he would have done it. I know that wasn't the most supportive, but he loved you." My mother wrings a napkin between her fingers as she speaks.

I take a sip of coffee before I reply. "I hope you're not going to tell me that his verbal slaps were just him showing that he cared."

Her eyes flash to mine, glassy but wide-open. "No. I'm not. He had a temper and a loud mouth and could often only focus on the faults of a situation. He wasn't perfect and made many mistakes that he never apologized for. But I do believe that he loved you. I love you too, Dash, just as you are. In fact, I've been reading some books..."

She rises from the table to duck into the family room and comes back, arms laden. She drops the pile of books on the table between us. They have a rainbow of sticky note tabs and notebook paper hanging out the edges and the spines are cracked and bent.

ADHD and You. ADHD: Unlocking Your Superpower. ADHD For Adults.

"Mom, what's all this?"

"I needed to understand you. And myself. These books weren't around twenty years ago, and your father sure as hell wasn't open to learning he was wrong."

"What do you mean, yourself?"

"Oh, honey. I started reading them to learn about your challenges and how to better communicate with you. I didn't expect to see so many parts of me reflected on the pages. I've never been diagnosed, but I connect with so many of these traits as they present in older women. A lot of things make sense now. Anyway, the books have been very helpful, and maybe we could talk about them later?"

"Sure, Mom. I'll go through them."

She smiles, and the five-year-old in me is stupidly happy about earning that smile. I crunch my last piece of cinnamon toast and grin as she continues talking.

"This one in particular talks about supercharging your powers. You're attracted to things that give you a dopamine boost. I think that's why you took so well to video games. And when your job gave you that hit, you did great because your brain was in a happy place. But it doesn't seem like this current job is giving you that."

"No, it's really not."

"And that's why it's harder. Is there a way to get dopamine from somewhere or someone else before you start working?"

It's an interesting question, one I don't know if I've considered in that light before. Can I hack my brain to make it do what I want? What *do* I want?

Possibilities are swirling, because my brain always works best in a storm, but one realization pushes its way to the fore.

I have never truly understood my mother.

~

After that emotional coffee break, I retreat to my old hangout, the garage, one of mom's books in tow. I thought for sure my dad would have reclaimed the space when I left for college, but shockingly, not much has changed. The weight system Dad bought me that I used for two months in high school, convinced I could bulk up and impress the girls, sits dusty in the corner.

The ratty old sectional couch is still crammed against the wall. The scuffed coffee table, that I jumped on frequently for victory dances, is still standing. My old gaming system is gone, but the stand is still there. The only thing that has been upgraded is the TV. A large flatscreen hangs on the wall. Dad must've bought it for fight nights.

I flop on the couch and flip through one of Mom's books on ADHD. The things she's highlighted are fascinating. It seems like we have a lot in common. The periods of distraction followed by the hyperfocus. The trouble finishing projects without external motivation or deadlines. The spacing out during conversations. But the parts that have red tabs stop me. They are on every page of the ADHD and relationships section. I know she probably marked them to process her relationship with Dad, but I read them now through the lens of my failure with Penny.

Too little communication on both sides, too much resentment and misunderstanding as a result. I had no idea there were ADHD relationship strategies. I'd only ever learned what I needed to survive school. Clearly, I have a lot to learn. It's too much too soon, but I'm going to come back to this when I'm not so raw from losing Penny. Maybe if I can learn from this, I won't mess up my next relationship too badly.

I toss the book on the floor and curl up into a ball on the couch.

Just being in the garage is comforting. This space was my cocoon, my incubator. This is where I nurtured my love of video games. Away from my parents' arguments, in my little cave, I escaped into races and quests and alien worlds. Every click of the button fed my obsession, and when I discovered that I could learn how to make my favorite games, I knew I wanted a career in game design. I loved my computer science classes, because they taught me how to codify and build sense into my world.

This room more than any other feels like home. All of those early dreams and primal memories flood my brain. Where did that kid go? I kinda missed the scrawny little guy.

Running out to my car, I grab the box that has my gaming gear in it and hook everything up through the screen to my laptop. When I lift my laptop, my Penny's Pleasures spreadsheet is still open. My eyes scan the columns and rows, remembering every minute of our time together, and I am hit with an intense longing.

Damn it. I can't have her. It's too soon, and I am too brittle to handle the emotions this spreadsheet unlocks. Tears well and fall, and I close the sheet quickly. All I want to do right now is hide away with a new game and get out of my head for a while.

I had a review request from an indie game designer at my alma mater, looking for eyes on her final project, come through my neglected blog space. Even though the rest of my world is falling apart, this is something I can do. I'll help this young woman out with some feedback, and I can shut down my own worries for a few hours. I load the game, settle back into my familiar butt divot on the couch, and let the story take me away.

It's a good game. I hope she gets some funding to spend on cleaning up the graphics a bit, but the premise is interesting. It's a game for teen girls to explore inter-personal relationships within a friend group on an adventure. Largely geared toward the middle school market, it's a clever way to build relationship awareness and communication practice into a fun quest.

Someone should make something like this for teen boys trying to figure out teen girls. God, I'd have been so much cooler in high school if I'd been able to figure out girls in a game before actually asking one out on a date and having to *talk* to her. Hell, I would still benefit from that kind of game, if my recent interactions with Penny are anything to go by.

As I play, I search for the inherent structure behind the game. The decision-making trees are nuanced and intricate. I'm even more impressed. What would Penny think, playing this in two-player mode? I'd love to have her input as a former teenage girl. I wish I could ask her to play with me. I wish a lot of things.

By the end, I figure out how to keep the friends together and achieve the goal. My review practically flows from my fingers. I can't wait for this game to find its target audience.

This is what I love. Being inspired by a new game and sharing that with the world. I don't want a fancy title or retirement plan… Well, the retirement plan maybe and a decent salary, definitely, but the rest of the bells and whistles can fuck right off. I just want to make a living doing the work that brings me joy.

What would Penny say to that? She'd probably encourage me to chase my dreams. But would she mean it? In five years if I'm still freelancing, would she resent the instability?

Why am I even still wondering what Penny would say?

For fuck's sake, I'm a mess. My entire life fits into ten boxes and two suitcases. And I still manage to leave my shit all over. She deserves a guy who can follow through, no matter what. A guy who sees her ambition and pushes her forward instead of pulling her off course. A guy who can bring more to the table than college debt, a stack of video games, and a comprehensive knowledge of local takeout spots. She deserves someone she doesn't simply tolerate because they deliver good soup and excellent orgasms.

But I deserve to be more than tolerated too.

No. It is well and truly over. I drove away the best person that had ever walked into my life. I can't fix it, because I can't *fix* who I am. I don't want to. And she'd rather have sex than discuss our problems, and that's not going to solve anything.

With my mother's words echoing in my head, and a new understanding of our dynamic, I realize something for the first time in my adult life. I am worthy of love, just as I am. I deserve to be loved and supported by my person. My ADHD isn't an illness or a burden. It's simply how my brain functions in the world. It's my superpower and my kryptonite.

I am worthy of love just as I am.

That truth blows the doors off my heart, leaving the tender bits exposed. But with my hard shell cracked, my belief in my own worth has room to grow. I believe, and for today that's enough.

CHAPTER 26

PENNY

I pull myself out of bed and sigh. How is it seven a.m. already? Every morning this week has been a struggle. Where has my energy gone? Callie jumps from her gargoyle perch on my bed frame onto my chest, the better to wake me with boops on the nose and disgruntled yowls. Why did I ever think that was cute?

I thought it was cute that she claimed Dash's pillow as her throne too, until I realized it doesn't smell like him anymore.

Shuffling to the kitchen, wearing only underwear and Dash's T-shirt, I drop cereal in Callie's bowl and cat food in mine. It's not until I pour cold coffee into the water bowl that I catch my mistakes. Callie on caffeine? That would be a disaster!

Brewing a fresh pot of coffee is first thing on my list. Dash made excellent coffee. I push away the thought. I've been an independent woman for many years, perfectly capable of making my own coffee and feeding my own cat, although there's an apparent order of operations there that I've neglected.

While Callie enjoys her blend of Cheery-O's and Kitty Kibble, I sip my first cup of coffee, black because I've run out of half-and-half, and try to wake up. Dash's never-ending alarms drove me nuts, but I was wide-awake by the time my day started. I pass the snake plant he left in my living room, but I don't attempt to water it because God knows what I'd pour into it. I should probably research how to keep it alive though.

Good thing it seems to thrive on neglect.

God, that's a depressing metaphor for the way I care for things…all or nothing…

Plodding back into my bathroom, I strip and step under the shower spray, desperate to wash away the fog of lethargy that has settled over me during the last week. I am happy to be able to focus solely on work, but my brain is not functioning at peak power. Also, happy is an exaggeration.

I'm not an idiot. I know exactly what's wrong with me. I screwed up with Dash, and I can't see the path to fixing it. Normally I would just push through, put it behind me, date someone else, replace the memories.

But I don't want to. I don't want anyone but him. I revisit our memories so often for comfort that I would cry if I lost them. But I also don't know how to fix what I broke. I really laid into him and he just left. He didn't even argue. He gave me exactly what I asked for, space and time by myself.

How was I supposed to know I would hate it? That it wouldn't fix anything?

I dry my hair and apply my makeup, determined to cover the bags under my eyes, but my head is still underwater. Every thought is harder to form, every action more difficult to complete. I struggle to make it through my normal workday, and my company needs me now more than ever. Everything is resting on my shoulders, and I can't seem to straighten my back under the pressure.

I thought that sending Dash away would make things go back to normal, but it hasn't. I'm not the same person I was before I met him. I've changed, and stepping back into my old patterns feels like putting on a wet swimsuit —cold and uncomfortable. Much like my bed, now that he's gone.

Dammit! Enough! I can't go through my day mooning over a man I shoved away with my shitty temper. I've well and truly lost him. The best I can do now is pull up my big girl panties and keep trying to save my business.

I grab a random bra and underwear, not caring that they don't match. They are both clean, and I haven't done laundry in a week. I pick a red silk blouse because it is dry-clean only and therefore still hanging clean in my closet. The blue plaid flannel pants I pair it with cannot claim the same, but no one will see them beneath the table. I pad back to the table barefoot, ready for work. If six-months-ago me were here, she'd slap me upside the head, but I can't find the energy to care.

I'm here on time, and that's a win.

I check my phone for my video conference call schedule. My first meeting is with the group of beta screeners using the community platform Dash designed. Nicola and Emmy are going to sit in too and take notes, but I am going to lead the feedback session. I love talking to my customer base. I thrive on their input for coming up with new ideas.

I survey the space that will show on camera, and it is clean and organized. My entire apartment is clean and organized again, but instead of bringing me the calm I needed, it just feels cold and sterile. Lonely.

I pour a second cup of black coffee and sit down at the table. Two cups on a stomach as empty as my apartment makes me a little jittery, but it's fine. Everything's fine. I'm going to be high energy Penny today, exactly what I need. Maybe I should buy an espresso machine…

I log into the call and find Nic and Emmie already waiting.

"You ready, boss?" I narrow my eyes at Nic, but she just grins.

"Absolutely. I've got my questions and notes. You both good?"

"Yep. Ready to take notes, although we are also recording the session," Emmie replies.

"Are you sure you're ready?" Nicola prods.

"Don't I look ready?" I shoot back. I really do not need her prodding me about how shitty I look right before we open the panel. I know I'm not sleeping well, but—

"You're not wearing your wig."

Fuck. She's right. I haven't had to be Public Penny for so long, I completely forgot about her. And I can't just plop it on my head. It requires a cap and makeup and blending. And, goddammit, a wardrobe change because I'm wearing a red shirt. *Fuck!*

"I'm going without it today. It itches. Besides, isn't everyone doing drastic changes with their hair these days? It's fine. I'm fine."

I am far from fine and can't believe I forgot, but it's too late to fix it now. The virtual waiting room is filling with people.

"Sure. Whatever you say, boss," Nicola says as she taps something into her phone.

"Good. Let's go."

Marshaling every last ion of positive energy, I nod at Nic, who opens the floodgates.

"Good morning! And welcome to the MiO community! I'm Penny Maxwell, CEO and Founder, and this is Nicola Stern and Emmie Rich, my marketing and design mavens. I want to thank you so much for taking the time to talk to us today. We believe that everyone deserves to find pleasure and joy in the way that works best for them. Your feedback today will directly impact our plans, both for devices and the community platform you were asked to test. We truly couldn't do this without you. So let's get started. First, I'd like to do a quick visual survey. Thumbs up, thumbs middle, thumbs down, how did you like the product you received?"

All of the twenty-five participants hold out their hands, in a nearly equal split of ups and downs. It seems like those who liked it really liked it, and those who didn't really didn't. I grab a quick screenshot to capture it.

"Same question for the community section."

This time the reactions are more generally positive to middling. Only a few thumbs down. That's encouraging! This community engagement platform just might work. Thank goodness Dash got the web design done so quickly.

A pinch of guilt squeezes my heart at the way I lashed out at him, when he'd done so much to help me. But I hit my limit. Aren't I allowed to have limits? Everyone keeps talking about boundaries. Surely I'm allowed to call it quits when he tramples through mine. But if I was right, why does everything feel wrong?

"Penny?"

"Hmm? Oh yes." I shake my head. *Get back in the game!* "I'd love to hear more specifics about what you liked or wanted more of in the community section. Does anyone have thoughts to share?"

A woman in her forties raises her digital hand, and I unmute her. "Yes, Jessica?"

"I like the articles and the user guides. It made getting the toy adjusted a whole lot easier. That was a bit of a steep learning curve. But once I figured out my specific configuration, whew! It was incredible! My question is about video content or maybe intimacy coaching. I bought this toy because I was intrigued by the concept of a blended orgasm. Now that I've had one, I want to experience it with my husband. We've had...less than stellar results. He feels like I'm bossing him and criticizing his technique, and I don't have the words to explain what I'm trying to do. Will there be videos demonstrating the technique or perhaps even showing a couple enjoying this that I could watch with him?"

Jessica mutes herself again, and I stare, struck quiet by pride. When I started this journey, I thought single people with vaginas would be our main target audience. I am continually surprised at how well MiO is being received by different demographics. The fact that our device is being used to make married sex better is next-level goals. It gives me hope that it is truly a universal pleasure tool. I am so happy that it takes me a beat to respond.

"We hadn't considered offering video content beyond the product demonstration videos. But that is a great idea. Maybe something we could expand into in the future. I want to reiterate, though, that clear and open communication is the bedrock of a relationship."

Nicola coughs violently, and I swear I hear the word *bullshit* beneath the bark. I ignore it and carry on.

"It sounds like you and your husband are aligned in your goals, so to speak, but that receiving feedback in the heat of the moment is breaking the mood. I'm not a therapist or sex educator, but I might suggest having the conversation about what, where, and how you want to try something before clothes come off to make it less intimidating? I'm so happy that you are exploring together."

I make it through the rest of the focus group asking

good questions, taking notes, and getting inspired for new ways this platform could help my end users. It's the best hour of work I've managed in ages. As I say goodbye to my early adopters, I am more determined than ever to make this company a success.

Once the room clears, I turn to Emmie and Nicola for a debrief. "That went well! I'm so excited. Let's go through the feedback."

"You're not even going to talk about it?" Emmie asks, incredulous.

"I just said I wanted to talk about it." I'm truly confused.

"I told you she was clueless." Nicola leans back in her chair, her lips pursed as if around something sour. Emmie is just staring at me, waiting for me to catch up.

"Well, by all means clue me in. What do we need to talk about? And when did you two decide to gang up on me?" I cross my arms and lean back in my own chair.

"Don't worry," Nic reassures me. "It's not just us. Jen and Zarah are on their way."

"We've been texting during the panel," Emmie says. "We didn't want to distract you, but I can't believe you're truly that oblivious."

"What did we miss?" Zarah asks as she appears in a new window, sitting side by side with Jen at her kitchen table.

"That's what I'm wondering," I mutter, my happy high quickly evaporating. I want to cling to it, the first fleeting bright spot in a shitty week, but my team has other plans.

Nicola leans forward, sarcasm dripping from her

words as she asks, "Remember Jessica? The woman you counseled to try open and honest communication with her partner *before* things got heated?"

"Yes… What's wrong with that advice?"

"Nothing, except that is one hundred percent not what you did with Dash."

Ambush! I didn't expect my recent breakup to be a topic of discussion today.

"What the hell does that have to do with anything?"

"I just find it hypocritical for you to tell this woman how to fix her marriage with a strategy you yourself refused to use."

"What happened between me and Dash isn't at issue here."

"I disagree." Emmie cuts in. "It is an issue. It's impacting you and your ability to lead. It's a pattern. A boundary only works if it's communicated in advance. When he ran up against one of yours, did you talk about it?"

"Kind of."

"Body language does not count."

"We used our mouths…"

"Doesn't. Count. How about afterward, when things were calm? Did you circle back and clarify what you needed? With clothes on?" Emmie adds with a smirk.

I sit back in my chair and refuse to answer that. We had talked about chores before. Did I say it was a hard line for me? No, but it was pretty clear that I was frustrated.

Except Dash told me from the beginning that he

needed words over actions. And what did I do? I avoided words and opted to mask my frustrations with positive actions like sex. These realizations hit hard. I fucked up, but I still don't see what it has to do with work.

Luckily, Zarah doesn't require a response from me to jump in, trying a different tack.

"Ever since he left, you've been on a tear, running yourself in circles, trying to be everything for everybody. Nobody can get anything done, because you keep changing course midstream and we're afraid to get in your way."

"What the hell does me trying to save my company have to do with Dash?" I have no idea where she's going with this.

"When you were together, you were calmer. Happier," Jen says gently.

"Distracted," I retort. "And where did that get us? Almost out of funding and thrown under the bus."

"Was that really his fault? True, the article was damning, but we've been struggling to cope with challenges created by the pandemic for months now. One person writes one article and the whole company is in jeopardy?" Zarah points out.

"It was just the final straw." I feel like I'm crawling out of my skin, being called to account like this by my team. I hate feeling defensive. My patience for this intervention is growing thin.

"My point precisely."

"What?"

Nicola jumps back into the conversation. "How did it

get to be the final straw? Why was there a pile of straw in the first place?"

"Because he's a messy slob who was pumping me for article fodder while keeping me sidetracked with his video games and stupid quarantine hobbies?" I snark.

"Or is it because you still bottle your frustration up inside, determined to stay in control, so you can pretend everything is fine and not get hurt? Instead of having clear and open conversations with clothes on to address things that annoy you and setting respectful boundaries?" Nic tosses back. "No, surely that couldn't be it."

Working with your ex-lover and best friend of ten years is a real bitch sometimes. Because, dammit, she is right.

"Fine. Yes, I let things build up, and no, I probably wasn't in the best frame of mind when I confronted him. With everything going on right now, maybe I just don't have it in me for that kind of commitment."

"You didn't have it in you seven years ago either," Nicola mutters. "What did he want you to do that was so frustrating?"

"Ooooh, I hope it's juicy. Was he into bondage? Did he tie you up for hours?" Emmie, always quick to take it somewhere dirty, butts in.

"No. He…wanted me to play games with him." I try to find examples that won't make me sound like a fool but pickings are slim.

"OoOoOoh, sexy games?" Emmie asks again, wiggling her eyebrows. "Should I go get a bubbly lime water for this?"

"No, like video games. If he was reviewing one or just playing, he'd offer to set up a second player for me. And then I'd lose an hour or two to a video game." I try to explain, but hearing it out loud, it does sound ridiculous.

"He wanted to spend time with you, enjoying a leisure activity. How very DARE he!" Jen teases.

"Shut up." They want details? I'll give them details. "The real problem was the mess! He's like a toddler dropping his shit everywhere in my apartment. His hoodie on the couch, dirty dishes in the sink, food on the table. He was just...everywhere! I mean he couldn't even remember to take the laundry out of the washer! I felt like I was having to clean up after him the entire time just to keep my apartment functional."

"Yeah, doing all of the work for him and then kicking him out instead of discussing your concerns really made the situation easier on you. Remind me, who is doing all the housework now that you're alone?"

I'm about done with Nicola's tone of voice. "Whatever I say right now, you are going to tell me I'm wrong, aren't you?"

"You've always been a smart one," she tosses back.

"Except when she's being an idiot," Emmie chimes in cheerfully.

It is really tempting to slap my computer shut and walk away, but I cannot indulge in any more bridge burning. The first one is still too hot to touch.

"So I should have just added 'personal maid' to my already exhausting list of duties and kept cleaning up after him?" I ask.

"No. You should have told him you hate cleaning up after him when it first became an issue, and brainstormed ways to handle it."

"But it was still so early in the relationship. I didn't want to push him away by asking him to help me more." I'll be honest with myself even if I can't say it out loud to my friends. I was afraid to ask him for more, because every time I have asked a friend, a partner, a parent for more support, it has ended badly.

"Play that one back in your head." Nic pauses. "Do you hear it now?"

Dammit. I do. I pushed him away because I didn't want to push him away. It makes zero sense, but emotions don't always make sense, and I am drowning in them.

"Why are you so adamant that I acknowledge that I screwed this up? I did. There. I clearly don't have the time or emotional bandwidth to successfully handle a relationship. I would have screwed it all up sooner or later." Dash's impression of the sea witch leaps into my head, and I don't know if I want to laugh or cry. "This is what I do. He's better off without me."

"Did you ask him if he wanted that? He seemed happy," Nic points out.

"Was he though? Was he happy that I was harping on him all the time?"

Zarah shrugs. "I don't know how he was feeling, but you seemed so much happier with him than with any of your past partners. We would hate to see you lose this because of stress over the company," she adds, concern clear on her face. Jen nods next to her.

"Screw the company. They're just some sex toys." Nic's temper is getting shorter the longer this conversation goes on.

"No, they are not!" I explode with frustration. "It's the company I built that employs all of my best friends. If it folds, everyone I love will be out of a job! I will be a failure."

"No, the company will fail, and you will learn from it. There's a difference. Can we just acknowledge what you've achieved to get us here, Ms. Forbes-Thirty-Under-Thirty, and that no one could have predicted a global pandemic messing everything up? Stop beating yourself up, and own your wins. As for putting your friends out on the street, don't hide behind us. We are all resilient, well-educated women who will land on our feet, just like a certain brilliant CEO I know. What is behind this really?"

Nic and the peanut gallery give me silence as I work around to it.

"I...I was trying so hard to get it right. I had this plan. The business, the launch, the relationship, the quarantine...and it all failed miserably. And the more stressed I got, the more I tried to keep things under control. Including him. And I didn't talk to him about it. I just did it all and resented him for it because I'm a terrible human being. He deserves better." The tears I'd managed to hold back begin to fall.

"I think he's the only one who can make that call. And Penny, you don't have to be perfect to be loved. We know you, and we still love you. And that won't go away even if this company fails."

I cover my face with my hands as if I can hide. I hate when my friends go all therapist on me. I really hate crying at work. But they know exactly where my buttons are installed and don't hesitate to push them for my own good. And, admittedly, they have a point. I didn't give Dash a chance to be part of the conversation I constructed in my head. That wasn't fair to either of us.

I miss him. My space feels cold and empty without him. I'm cold and empty without him. I miss the fun and the laughter, the care he showed, the supportive faith he gave. Why was I so afraid to talk to him about the things that weren't working? Did I think he'd leave me if I was too difficult? Too emotional? Too messy?

I don't know how he would have reacted because I didn't let him in to see any of that.

That was my mistake. I have to fix it. Will he even give me a chance? Only one way to find out.

Maybe we will still be over, or maybe we'll find a path to another chance. Maybe I will find the words I need to discuss clear boundaries or maybe I'll bungle it all again. Either way, I have to try. I'm not happy without him.

I blot my face and rally, decision made.

"Next time can we do this after work? I'm going to look like hell on the rest of my calls."

"As soon as the bars reopen, we promise to move this G&T to a more public venue," Nic teases.

"In the meantime, call the man and fix it," Zarah says.

CHAPTER 27

DASH

I sit in my darkened garage, the space barely illumined by the blue glow of my laptop screen. I haven't showered in three days. Food is a distant memory. Empty energy drink cans litter the floor at my feet.

But I am in the zone, and damn, it feels good.

After I sent off the game review, I couldn't shake the idea of a relationship game. Going back to basics, I built out the structure for a role-playing game with a focus on rewards for learned behavior. I created a female avatar first, since that felt more complex for me to write.

As I sit in the dark, lines of code flow like water from my fingertips. It isn't until she's nearly complete that I realize I've created a digital Penny. All her likes and dislikes, her wants and desires as far as I know them, even her annoying habits and quicksilver temper. My Penny's Pleasures spreadsheet is being put to good use. The same fixation that felt painful a few days ago is now fueling the most detailed character development I've ever done. And yet there's still so much I don't know. Might never know.

That thought makes me irrationally sad, but I have to be realistic. We are over. She said so. I told her from the beginning to tell me when her feelings changed, and she did. I have to respect that.

And yet I can't stop thinking about her. Instead of moving on to the male character, I play with graphics, just for the chance to think about her skin. Every curve I committed to memory appears on my screen, and I torture myself with the memories of all the ways I brought her pleasure, adding every detail to the character.

Then I torture myself more with everything I did wrong.

Setting up a slate of events to challenge each couple in the game is easy. Chores. Date night. Hygiene. Conversations. Problem-solving. Ethics. All things I failed at with Penny. All things I wish I had a second chance to figure out.

My childhood didn't prepare me for any of this. My dad just kept telling me to work harder, do better, quit being so…Dash. None of that gave me the functional skills I need, and unfortunately I am still Dash. It's no wonder I had no trouble believing Penny when she said she was done with me. Haven't I wished the same thing at times? That I could be done with me? Done with ADHD? That if I just tried a little harder, I could be normal.

Talking with Mom this week has helped a lot.

Without Dad talking over her, she has been able to open up about the therapy she got after he died and her journey to understanding ADHD. Knowing that my mother shares my struggles has shifted something. I'm no longer alone. And she loves me. She is still trying to mother me, sharing strategies and skills she wishes she'd had thirty years ago, but knowing it comes from a place of love and a desire to support me changes everything.

Fuck normal. I don't need to try harder. I might need to try different. It's been eye-opening.

Eventually I build myself into a shell of a male character that can learn from the interactions with the female player. I am just getting ready to start playing when my laptop lid slaps down.

"Hello! Earth to Dash!"

I blink twice, trying to make my eyes adjust in the dim room. Mom flips the light switch, and I cringe like a vampire at dawn.

"Jeez, Mom! It burns. It burns!" I joke, but I also cover my eyes from the intense fluorescence trying to bleach my brain. *Come on, pupils. Don't fail me now.*

"Maybe if you didn't sit in a dark room for three days straight, ruining your eyesight trying to type in the dark, you wouldn't be hurting right now."

I honestly hadn't noticed time passing, because I'm so amped about the game. Her lecture feels familiar and completely different at the same time. "Did you need something, Mom?"

"Proof of life?" She picks the cans up off the floor and I feel like shit.

"Leave those, Mom. I'll get them."

"No, it's okay. Your high school computer teacher, Mr. Anderson, is here, and you can't see him with the room a mess."

"Yes, Mom. I can." I take the cans from her. "But I will tidy the space."

"Thank you. Put those in the recycling, and then you can have a nice visit."

Will I ever not feel like a child in this house?

I make a quick sweep of the garage and put on a mask before my mentor comes in.

"Mr. Anderson." I hold my elbow out for a bump, which my teacher returns, eyes crinkled in what I hope is a smile beneath his mask. If my father's voice holds the negative real estate in my head, it's Mr. A I hear encouraging me.

"Dash! How are you? Your mother let me know you were back in town, so I figured I'd come over, since no one is really out 'running into' one another right now." Mr. Anderson sits at one end of the couch, and I reclaim the other.

"I'm glad you did. Still running the computer club after school?"

"Virtually, at the moment, but yeah, you bet. The group has never been bigger. You inspired a lot of kids around here when you got that job at RPGiga."

"And washed out in under two years. Big deal," I scoff.

"It is a big deal, Dash." Mr. Anderson holds my gaze. "Your game was brilliant."

"*My* game never got made."

"I beg to differ. Remember, you sent me the beta version to look over in college. I can see the bones of *Astraia* in *Call of Anarchy*. It is elegant and nuanced and completely wasted on a first-person shooter game, but it's there."

"I wish I'd never given up the rights to it. It's the best thing I've ever made, and now I can't touch it." Well, maybe second-best thing, if the game I'm working on now continues to flow.

"Why did you walk away?"

"They were never going to let me make the game I wanted. And the day-to-day coding, on a game I resented... I couldn't do it. I couldn't focus, distracted by literally everything else, and I was failing."

"You were learning. 'I never lose. I either win or learn.' Nelson Mandela."

"You had that on a poster."

"Every year I pray my students actually read it. My computer club loves your game reviews in XPTech."

"I haven't written one in ages. I got hired on as a staff writer and got assigned to pandemic coverage. I'm hanging on to that job by a thread."

"Why?"

"I'm not getting to write what I like, so my brain is in full revolt. I'm blowing deadlines and pissing off my editor."

"No, why are you hanging on?"

"Because I thought I needed some stability and a regular paycheck, but it turns out I can't even hack it. So yeah, I'm fucking up on all cylinders. I'm no role model for your students."

"That's utter shit."

My jaw drops, and I'm pretty sure my eyes widen. In all the years I've known Mr. Anderson, I have never heard him utter a curse word. "Are teachers allowed to swear?"

He ignores my attempt at humor. "You are absolutely a role model. You chased a highly competitive job you wanted and got it. When it turned toxic, you had the strength to leave. You've spun into various other gigs, always playing to your strengths and never lingering in bad situations. In today's workplace, that is a much more positive role model than seeing someone get into one career and stay there for forty years. It just doesn't happen that way for a lot of my students. I'd rather have them look up to someone who hustles."

"But I've failed at every job I've ever had."

"Have you? Or has the job failed you?"

That one sinks into my brain like a jackhammer, breaking up the old toxic concrete. I have beaten myself up over my shortcomings for so many years that looking at the situation from the flip side now throws me for a loop.

"You know what I remember about you from high school?"

"No, what?" I ask, still trying to process the seismic shift in perspective happening in my head.

"When you were excited about a project, nothing could stop you. You would work on it day and night until it was finished, and they turned out fantastic. But when you were bored? God help us, nothing was getting done."

"I know! I'm still like that. If I could just work harder—"

"No, Dash. Stop. The world needs the kind of creativity your brain is capable of. You have to access that in a very specific way. Keep chasing the projects that allow for that, and you'll be fine."

Is that really something I can do? I sit silent on the couch, letting it all sink in. A question tickles my curiosity. "How did you say you ran into my mom?"

"She tracked me down through the school's website and emailed me, asking if I would come talk with you. She's worried."

"Worried I'll end up living on her couch forever."

"Worried that her son is struggling, and she couldn't find the right words to help. Direct quote from her email."

"Thanks, Mr. Anderson."

"You can call me Scott."

I try it in my head, but the name feels too strange. "Nope. For better or worse you will always be Mr. Anderson in my head. At best, Mr. A. You know, I made you an NPC in *Call of Anarchy*."

"I loved that. Everyone thinks that character is a nod to *The Matrix*, but you made him a helper instead of an antagonist."

I nod, proud that he'd caught it. "Thanks for everything, Mr. A. I wouldn't have gotten this far without your support in high school. I think you're the first person who really saw what I was capable of, not just what I couldn't do."

"Maybe the first, but certainly not the last. Hang in there, kid. Don't give up. Just find the next passion project to chase."

"I might have something there."

"Can I see it?"

I open my laptop and walk my mentor through the idea. We brainstorm ideas, play a little *what if?*, and Mr. A leaves as excited about the idea as I am. It's solid and could potentially help a lot of people.

With my teacher gone, I glance back at my laptop, thinking about the game waiting for me inside, and that old familiar excitement sparks in my chest. I am absolutely going to chase the dopamine.

Mr. A is right. I'm not a failure. I just need to play to my strengths. And now, for the first time in months, I'm excited about a project. I'm going to dive in and refill my well.

And maybe I can figure out which of my strengths can win Penny back. Deep down, a little voice insists that programming her into my game won't fix the empty space in my heart, but I can't afford to go back to that bleak place of despair. I want to level up and win her heart. But to do that I need to improve my knowledge and skill stats. Good thing I can build a game to help me with that.

One thing has become crystal clear: my happiness is worth the effort it takes to keep chasing my dreams.

I reach to pick up my computer again, and catch a whiff of myself. *Gag.*

I will absolutely keep chasing my dreams. But first, a shower.

I pace my apartment trying to gather my courage. Callie thinks this is a great game and proceeds to see how many times she can dart between my moving legs without getting stepped on. The answer is not many.

YEEEEOOOOOWWWWLLL!

My cat's annoyed cry breaks my train of thought and I pick her up for a comforting hug, only to have the ungrateful demon spawn scratch me and leap from my arms onto the couch. She curls up in Dash's spot and glares. I can feel her judging my life choices from across the room.

I wash the scratches in the sink, but I don't scold her. If I was her, I'd be mad at me too.

Dammit. I miss him. Everything feels gray without him. And it's all my fault.

It's been over a week, and he's disappeared completely. No phone calls, no texts, no "hey can I come by and pick up the charging cord I forgot" voicemails. I don't even know where he went. I was so angry, I didn't ask.

I need a plan to fix this, but I also recently got my ass

handed to me for overplanning things, so I'm stuck. But I've never been one to let challenges slow me down.

I've done all I can for my company. We worked hard this week, and I stayed out of their way. Well, I tried. Baby steps.

My team is working the plan. We can carry on through the end of the month, and if we survive, we survive. If we don't, we don't. My friends were right. I have to let them do what I hired them to do. After all, I will have done what I set out to do. I'll have gotten my product into the hands of people who deserve excellent orgasms. And I can take the lessons I've learned into my next venture.

Now it's the weekend again. Since I'm no longer hiding in busyness, Dash's absence is intolerable.

I cannot accept this empty apartment and broken heart. I have to try. I pick up the phone and call him, no plan, no practiced lines. I'm just going to pour my heart out and hope he forgives me.

I get sent straight to voicemail.

"Hi, Dash. It's me. Penny. Um, I was hoping we could talk. Call me back."

That night I try again, worried I haven't heard from him. Straight to voicemail once again. Still unwilling to bare my soul to a machine, I stumble through another message.

"Dash, it's Penny. I'm really sorry. I...can you please call me back? I need to talk to you."

By noon the next day, I am frantic. I've lost track of how many messages I've left on his phone. He's never not responded before. And this doesn't feel like something I can do over email. He has disappeared and my brain fills in the blanks with worst-case scenarios.

Where did he go? What if he's sick? What if he caught Covid because I kicked him out of our safe apartment? What if he's so sick he can't answer the phone?

I remember how sick I was, and how no one would have known if he hadn't been there. I would have starved, unable to care for myself. What if he's in a hotel somewhere so sick he can't move? I have to find him. I have to.

Losing Dash is not a failure I'll learn from. It's a failure that will break me if anything has happened to him.

My heart flutters in my chest, matching my energy as I fly around my apartment, trying to think through my fear.

In my panic, I call XPTech and asked to be transferred to his line. They inform me he no longer works there. The pit in my stomach widens to a chasm, and I wish I could fall through it and disappear. Did I cost him his job too? *Fuck!*

I log in to my LinkedUp account and catch my first break. He hasn't blocked me yet, but he's also listed himself as a freelancer again. *Damn.*

I feel lower than low now. He's not going to want to talk to me.

But my concern for his safety pushes me on. He can accept my apology or not, but I need to know he's okay. I cannot even think of a world that doesn't have Dash.

Each minute that passes, my terror grows. I click through his links looking for the friend in LA he mentioned and luckily there's only one Rishi.

Pushing aside that little voice that is insisting this isn't an ethical use of the site, I send Rishi a message asking for any information on where to find Dash.

When his response comes back, I'm not surprised at the undertones of animosity couched in professional language.

Subject: Re: Do you know where Dash is?
From: Rishi_R89@gmail.com

May I ask the nature of this inquiry? Why do you need to know his physical location?
-Rishi Ravinder
he/him

Subject: Re: Re: Do you know where Dash is?
From: Penny@MiO.co

Look, Rishi. I know this is highly suspect, but I need to find him and apologize. I screwed up, and he's not answering his phone, and I'm worried that he's sick or worse. If he's not with you, could you call him and see if he answers? If he's just blocking me, I'll let it go. But I'm truly worried. What if he's sick somewhere by himself?
-Penny

I stare at the screen with its blinking cursor for fifteen minutes with no response. Just as I resign myself to another dead end, a message flashes into my inbox.

Subject: Re: Re: Re: Do you know where Dash is?
From: Rishi_R89@gmail.com

He's not answering for me either which is odd. I talked to him right after you kicked him out, and he mentioned going home. I know his mom has a place in Roseville, but I don't have an address.
-Rishi

My guilt is eating me alive. For a second I consider dropping it and letting Rishi follow up to make sure Dash is okay. It's the longest second of my life. But I quickly discard the idea. It seems work isn't the only place I struggle to delegate.

But waiting for others to do what I need done has never served me well. It certainly isn't how I became CEO of my own company before thirty, and it isn't how I'm going to fix things with Dash. There is a time to take control, and a time for compromise and taking a back seat. I've got to work on those last two, but I sure as hell recognize the first.

Pulling up my search engine, I begin to dig. High school yearbooks, birth announcements, obituaries, newspaper articles… I pull up every piece of information about him I can find. A picture from a high school coding event shows a young and gangly Dash next to a beaming teacher. The caption identifies him as one Mr. Anderson, who, according to the current school website, still runs the computer lab and IT for the building. The mentor he mentioned from high school…

With one impulsive click I send him an email, asking if he remembers Dash and might have any information on his family's current whereabouts.

His response is not at all what I expected.

Subject: Re: Dash Hall Info Request
From: Anderson_S@rosevillesd.org

Is this the same woman who kicked him out and broke his heart? I'm not sure I should share that information with you.
-Scott Anderson

The fact that this man has seen him recently enough to know about the breakup gives me hope. And I am glad Dash has such loyal friends watching his back.

Subject: Re: Re: Dash Hall Info Request
From: Penny@Mio.co

This is the woman who screwed up big-time, needs to know he's okay, and would like to apologize and fix things, if I can. Even if his answer is no, I think he still deserves the apology.

-Penny Maxwell

As I wait for a reply, I begin to pace again, this time keeping an eye on Callie. I am so close to finding him. Every second feels like minutes until a ding pulls me back to my laptop.

The reply has only one line. An address.

I don't plan what to do next, or strategize until I've found the best route or the perfect thing to say. I have to go. Now. On impulse, I grab my purse and Callie and head for my car.

CHAPTER 28

DASH

I am still sitting on the couch in my mother's garage. I managed another shower this morning, and Mom insisted on breakfast, but the game has me by the throat. I'm pretty sure the couch cushion beneath me is permanently flattened.

I am deep in code when the door to the house opens.

"Not now, Mom. I'm not hungry. I'll grab a sandwich in a little bit."

"Not even for Harris Ranch brisket?"

I snap my head around to see if the voice I hear is actually coming from a real person, or if I've somehow manifested her from my game since I've been thinking about her nonstop. I mean, AI is amazing, but spontaneous creation would be wild.

But no, there she is, beautiful and bold as ever, holding a white plastic bag of takeout containers.

"Penny?" I ask, afraid to believe what my eyes are telling me.

"Hi, Dash. Can I…come in?"

"Of course." I stand stiffly and set down my computer. I step toward her and stop, unsure if a hug would be welcome or wise. She keeps her distance and I gesture to the other end of the couch, waiting until she's past me before I drop back into my custom-grooved seat. She sets the food on the coffee table and grips her hands together in her lap, focusing on them instead of me.

"Are you okay?" Penny asks quietly.

"Don't I look okay?" I reply, still not quite able to believe that she is here.

"You look thin and a little tired." She reaches across to put her hand on my forehead, and seems relieved. "When you wouldn't answer your phone, I panicked. I was worried you might be sick." She snatches her hand back and clutches the bag in her lap. "I needed to make sure you were okay. And also I wanted to apologize, but I wanted to do it right. In person. Face-to-face. With our clothes on because I'm done hiding my feelings behind sex. And I brought you brisket because you said it was your favorite road food, and I thought you might be hungry."

God, she's cute when she rambles. My eyes dart over her, hungry for details. She looks tired too and a little disheveled, but still just as beautiful.

It's so unusual to see her nervous like this. In the months we lived together, this woman handled meetings with her teams, the press, and investors with grace and poise, all while adapting to the ever-changing restrictions of the pandemic. She's confidence personified. The fact that she is this unsettled to talk to me bizarrely gives me hope.

Surely she wouldn't have driven seven hours just to apologize and leave.

The scent of brisket tempts me to open it immediately, but we should probably get through whatever this conversation is going to be first.

Something else she said taps my brain for attention. "You called me?"

She looks up at me like I'm speaking in tongues. "I've called you at least fifteen times in the last three days."

"Fifteen times?" I'm shocked both by the number and the fact that I hadn't heard a single one.

"Panic may have gotten the better of me," she demurs.

I search through the couch cushions, feeling between them and down the back crease of the couch, until my fingers brush up against aluminum and glass. I emerge triumphant with my phone. My completely dead phone. "Huh. I wonder where my charging cord is?"

"You left it at my place. I have it in the car in case this doesn't go well. Callie is also waiting in the car. She's been inconsolable since you left."

She drove seven hours with brisket and her cat? It's impressive there is any brisket left and she arrived in one piece. Someone who is still angry wouldn't go to the trouble.

"And you?" I ask, needing confirmation I'm reading this correctly.

"Me?"

"How have you been feeling since I left?"

"I've been scrambling to keep the company afloat, but I was recently reminded I don't need to do everyone's job for them. I only need to do mine."

"That's not what I asked."

"No, it isn't." She hauls in a deep breath. "Don't be a coward, Penny. This is why you came," she whispers under her breath. When she looks back at me, I'm surprised to see her eyes glassy with unshed tears. "I've been…miserable. Dash, I owe you an apology. I am so sorry I lashed out at you like that. You didn't deserve it."

"I did though. My article hurt you in ways I didn't foresee. And I didn't keep up with my part of the chores. I'm impulsive and messy and forgetful. I'm a terrible roommate and you deserve better."

"Quit bad-mouthing the man I love. I'm bossy and controlling and have a terrible temper. I hide my insecurities with sex and have trouble communicating boundaries. You deserved better too."

"I don't see what's changed. Nothing you've said about me is untrue."

"But I didn't say everything that is true. When I look at you, I see a man who cares so much he would drop everything and drive the length of a state because I didn't answer the phone. I could do no less."

I am stunned and can't find words. Penny keeps talking, as if she's afraid to give me space to argue.

"I see a man who livens my days with spontaneous adventure and fun, things I forget to make time for. I see a man who unlocked my heart *and* my body, learning all of my secrets. A man who knows how I take my coffee and brings me some because he was thinking of me." She rests her hand in the crook of her neck. "And who knows I like to be surprised with kisses right here." She drops her hands back into her lap. "And who I cannot replace with my own creation, no matter how hard I try, because silicone cannot replace your affection and your laughter and the connection we have. I'm the one who fucked up here, Dash, and lost the best person in my life."

I lean back into the couch, trying to understand. Is it possible Mom and Mr. A were right? I mean, I understood them theoretically, but I've never felt recognized and loved just as I am, so I assumed it wasn't for me. But hearing Penny value the things I bring to our relationship, I'm struck. Maybe I am worthy of love just as I am. The thought is too tender to hold too tightly, so instead I let it float between us, like a kite hoping for a gust of warm air to lift it toward the sun.

"Please, say something." The tears she'd held back before slide down her cheeks.

"I...I don't know what to say."

"How about, I forgive you for being a trash human who didn't know a good thing till it was gone, and I'll come back home with you and we will figure out how to make this work because you're the love of my life?" Penny suggests. "Or something along those lines...not that I've visualized it on the drive up here or anything."

"Are you done?" I ask.

When she nods, I open my arms, and Penny shifts across the couch into my embrace.

I kiss the top of her head and my world shifts back

onto its proper axis. "Quit bad-mouthing the love of my life."

Her wet chuckle vibrates against my chest as I pull her more fully onto my lap.

"I missed you," she whispers.

"I missed you too," I whisper back, afraid to break the moment.

The weight of her in my arms, the scent of her hair in my nose, the way my hair rises in goose bumps beneath her soft exhale—I am vitally aware of all of it in this moment. I don't think I'll ever know everything that makes Penny special, but I'll gladly spend a lifetime learning them. The second chance I was afraid to ask for has fallen in my lap and I'm going to grab it with both hands and never let go. I hug her tightly, fighting my own grateful tears.

She climbs out of my lap and puts a careful distance between us again, and I hate it.

"Can we…talk about what happened? Without touching?" she asks softly. "I can't think clearly when you're touching me."

I want to rejoice at that revelation, but I hold back because she's right. Instead of avoiding our problems with sex, we need to face them head on if we're going to make this work. I tear off the bandage and go first.

"Sure. Like I said before, you were right to be upset about the mess. I tried to warn you at the beginning. I have ADHD. There will always be messes, and I may not always see them. At least, not with the same urgency you do. I just get distracted by other things, and can't follow through if there are multiple steps with time in between for me to get distracted."

"Okay. I do see the messes. And you're right, they do bother me. But what I should have done—instead of trying to ignore it with orgasms and bottling up my frustrations until I exploded—is ask, 'What can we do about that?'"

I shrug. I hate disappointing her, but I know this is beyond me to manage consistently on my own.

"Don't shrug. Let's dig into it and find solutions. You brainstormed for me. Now it's my turn to brainstorm for you. What are the parameters? Challenges? Past strategies that work or don't?"

This is new—a discussion of my challenges that doesn't sugarcoat them, doesn't dismiss them, and doesn't vilify me for them. She wants to address them head on with me and look for shared solutions. It is hard to follow her request because my mind wants to explore the novelty of the sensation of being seen, accepted, and valued, but I haul in another deep breath of her scent and let it wipe my mind and fill it with her. *Focus. Strategies. Right.*

I pick up Mom's book from the floor and flip through to the relationship section before handing it to her. "This might help us find suggestions. Um, challenges. Okay. If I can't see it, it doesn't exist. I lose things constantly because I don't remember where I put them down, like my dead phone. And if I see something else along the way that's more interesting, I will forget what I was looking for and not finish the task. My brain chases dopamine. If something feels good, I want more, and will forget there are other things I needed to do like eat and sleep. I am great at ideas, but follow-through is a struggle."

She takes out her phone and her thumbs start flying. "Okay. Visuals, need to see things to remember, distraction is high, pleasure improves attention, and starts strong but hard to finish," she mumbles as she types. "It helps me to see things in a list. What about strategies that work for you?"

"Strategies... I like lists too, because they give a thought object permanence. So a to-do list is great, until I lose it or forget to check it. Also, the switching back and forth between chores makes it harder because I will never remember which one I am supposed to do on which day. Half of the time I'm not aware of what day it is. I'm good at starting things, but I'm a terrible closer."

She looks up from the flow chart she's sketching. "Why didn't you tell me any of this when we were setting up chores?"

"I didn't want to rock the boat. I was in your space, so I went along with what you wanted done."

"So going forward, can we talk about *our* space? And figure out how *we* need it to work?" she asks.

I let out a sigh and bury my face against her neck. I am so thankful we are finally having this conversation and she's not bolting for the door. "I would really like that," I say into her skin before she leans back.

"No touching until we figure this out." She holds her hands out between us jokingly. "Six inches, sir."

"It is decidedly longer than that, as you well know."

She grins at that, but maintains her focus. How? I'd love to know. Maybe sparring with me gives her dopamine too.

"So tell me if any of this is wrong, but it sounds like a consistent expectation would be better, rather than trading off?"

I nod.

"And you do better with regular reminders to get it done. Writing is good but it has to stay visible."

I nod again.

"I…I don't want to feel like I'm nagging," she admits softly.

"I don't want you to feel that way either. I know it's a lot of emotional energy to keep reminding me. But if we have the conversations regularly, maybe it won't feel that way. Honestly, your executive function blows mine out of the water, so a lot of this is going to fall on your shoulders because I just won't see it. But if we plan together and check in on expectations, I will have a better grip on what you need done when, and I can pull my weight."

"So maybe we chat once a week and make a list. What about calendar reminders or alarms on your phone?" I hear the excitement building in her voice around a new plan of action. Before we get too far ahead of ourselves, I need to address the elephant in the room.

"I know my alarms drove you nuts before, but we can try that. I mean, if you want me to come back after… Are we going to talk about the article?" We were making such good progress, I hate to bring up my thoughtless actions, but she came all this way to apologize. I need to do the same.

"Yeah, that was not a good feeling."

"Tell me about it."

She fidgets with her fingernails, picking at her cuticles repeatedly. I cover her hands with one of mine until she looks at me.

"No, really. Tell me about it. I need to hear how it made you feel."

"I felt…betrayed. Like I had shared my frustration, venting to my partner, in what I thought was a safe space, and you printed it for the world to see. The article hurt my business, sure, but it broke my heart."

My hand spasms around hers, taking her pain as my own, as guilt squeezes my heart. "I am so sorry. I never should have written the quote down. It won't happen again." Her hand squeezes mine back, giving me the courage to go on. "What I'm about to say isn't an excuse, but it's the reason I've come to understand as I've gone over and over this since I left. When I got promoted to staff writer, I panicked. I thought it was the job I should have. A logical promotion. Another step toward stability. For fuck's sake, here you are, running your own corporation. I should at least be able to contribute a regular salary instead of gig work."

"It's not a competition. If we were both CEOs, we'd be miserable. And there are many ways to bring joy and add value to the world."

"I know, but…I've always felt like my career choices were mistakes, irresponsible choices, things I've fallen into. There are a lot of voices that live rent-free in my head, reminding me every day that I'm a failure."

"Those voices need to hush."

Her vehemence makes me smile. "I'll be sure to tell them that, but at the time I was really trying to make this stable job work. The only problem was it was boring as hell. When I write my game reviews, good or bad, at least it's something I'm passionate and educated about. I've never had a problem meeting my deadlines because the articles are so interesting to write. Pandemic panini trends? Houseplants and the best way to grow your own sourdough starter? Not so much. I was grasping at straws to try and find interesting things to write about so I didn't lose my job. And you..." I trail off, searching for the words to explain my obsession without scaring her off.

"Me?"

"You fascinate me. I could listen to you talk for hours. That night I had a deadline looming and nothing in the hopper. So when the conversation about funding came up and sparked an article idea, I jumped at it desperately. I researched, thinking it might help you too, and included your quote because it was succinct and logical. I was in such a rush, my filters never caught up to me, and I sent it off to publish right before the deadline without even reading it through a second time. It was a huge mistake, and I shouldn't have quoted you. But I did, and the damage is done. I am so sorry, Pen. The last thing I wanted to do was hurt you."

"I want to say it's okay, that I understand. But how

can I be sure it won't happen again? In hindsight, I realize I don't want my struggles to be your inspiration."

"Well, for starters I quit my job."

"Dash! No! Why? I saw the job change online, but I assumed… You worked so hard for that promotion."

"You assumed they fired me?"

She nods sheepishly.

"They nearly did after I left and missed deadlines for a week straight. But I made the decision to quit, because it turns out I didn't like the job I thought I should want." *That was confusing as fuck. Try again, Dash.* "I was reminded by an old friend that it's okay to walk away from something you thought you wanted if it has turned toxic. That's partly why I let you push me away. If I was toxic for you, I didn't want you to feel obligated to let me stay. I thought stability was something I should have at work, because it's what my parents always valued. But once I had it, it was strangling me."

"If anyone made things toxic between us, it was me bottling up my feelings and thinking I had to handle everything by myself…and then resenting you for my choice."

"Let's say mistakes were made on both sides, based on historical data, and we're going to do better this time."

She kisses me on the cheek, but pulls back before I can turn and take her lips with my own, ending the conversation. She's right. There's more to say. But I still want to kiss her.

"I like the sound of that. But back to your job, what are you going to do now?"

The giddy excitement rising in my chest says I should let her in on my secret project. "I'm not sure, but I started designing again. I had an idea and couldn't let it go. You inspired me. Can I show you?"

Penny climbs off my lap as I reach for my laptop, snuggling in close to me like she used to on the couch in her apartment. Her familiar weight tucked against my side gives me the courage to open the file.

CHAPTER 29

PENNY

"So I was thinking, relationships are hard. What if there was a way to gameplay with your partner through different situations in an arena where the stakes are fictional but the players are real?"

"I'm listening." I give him my full attention. He's coding again! I remember how broken up he'd been when he talked about losing that first job. This is huge!

Dash clicks a few keys, and a crude animation of a blonde woman pops up on-screen. I don't want to be presumptuous, but is that me?

"Before you say anything, the graphics are basic and not my forte, but I needed people to be able to move them around. Here's the cool part though." He clicks into the section for setting up an avatar. "I've added data points for appearance, sure, but I also added points for character traits, habits, quirks, sexual preferences, communication style, love language, and past traumas."

I scan the first item on each list—type A, needs to feel

in control, talks to her cat, blended orgasms, bottles up emotions, physical touch, difficult childhood.

"Oh my God! It *is* me!" I reach across him to the scroll pad and scan the rest of the very long list. Every observation, every characteristic is spot-on. I couldn't have filled this out so thoroughly myself. Had he really paid this close attention? He noted my favorite meals and how I take my coffee, my preferred number of orgasms, and my favorite sex toy.

"I couldn't get you out of my head. I started a spreadsheet as a way to calm my racing thoughts while we were together. Once we were apart it was torture, loving you and not being able to be with you. I thought if I coded you, I could get you out of my head long enough to sleep. It hasn't worked yet."

"Dash—"

He cuts off my words with a kiss I readily return. When I try to get closer, I knock his laptop, and he lunges to save it. The moment broken, he clears his throat and reverts to professor mode.

"So, the idea behind this game is that each player creates as detailed an avatar as possible alongside their partner, and then they play through common relationship challenges together as a way to get to know each other and foster communication. By playing it together, you create time and space to play while also learning about each other. I think this would have served us much better than playing *Call of Anarchy* by myself and wallowing in my sorrows. What do you think?"

My brain is going a mile a minute, trying to process.

In the professional tracks of my mind, I want this game for my portal. Wouldn't it be amazing if couples could input their own features and then play with toys virtually and in real life to explore and deepen their connection? This would also help model the communication and relationship strategies that people so often think they can skip over in favor of a new vibrator to spice things up.

My emotional center is on overload. He'd really seen me. All these months, he'd been watching and testing and remembering everything that makes me...me. Have I ever really been seen so fully by a partner? I don't think so. Even my parents only got to see what I wanted them to see. Dash was brutally honest in creating this character, and he still loves me. I sit silent and still as that revelation washes over my heart. He's seen every part of me and still wants to know more.

"Show me yours" is all I can think to say.

He opens up the generic male avatar. The list of characteristics isn't nearly as long. I scan it and see that he hasn't been anywhere near as precise with his own.

"I think you need to add some things to that list. It doesn't have 'dangerous cooking skills' or your gamer's thumb on it," I tease. "It's also missing that noise you make when I—" I slide my hand over the erection trapped in his pants. He lets loose a guttural groan that shakes me to my core. "Yep, that one." I reach over and close the laptop, setting it down on the coffee table behind me. "And it doesn't even mention that you hyperfocus on things that bring you pleasure, like new games or my tits."

So saying, I turn to face him, straddling his lap on my knees. I take his hands and place them on my breasts and moan with relief. I better say what I need to say before I lose the ability to talk entirely.

"And it's missing the part about you being a generous lover, a faithful friend, a partner in adventure, and a forgiving soul. I'm so sorry for all of it, Dash. Can you forgive me?"

"Penny, I've never wanted a second chance at anything more than this. Can you forgive *me*? What if the company fails?"

"Then I'll have my supportive boyfriend by my side to help me plan the next adventure."

"God, I've missed you." He pulls me close, burying his nose in the crook of my neck, inhaling deeply and sending a shiver down my spine.

"I've missed you, too."

"Liar. You've got a toy box a porn star would envy."

I grip his face and make him look me in the eye. "And yet, none of them love me like you."

I watch the slow grin dawn on his face and know that he feels the same way I did when he unveiled his prototype. I was an idiot to make him leave.

"Dash, I know we have a lot to talk about, and work to do around how we communicate, but there's one way we communicate that I have never doubted. And now that I'm touching you, I am too horny to think straight. Do you think we could…"

"Have sex on a couch in my mother's garage?"

I nod frantically. "I promise we'll keep doing the hard

work later, but I really need you. I've missed you so fucking much."

"It's like a reward." Dash grins and slides his hands under my shirt to cup and tease my sensitive breasts, pinching my nipples just a little, just enough to get them hard, just the way I like it.

Damn, he really has been paying attention. I gasp, my eyelids fluttering closed, and he stops. I open my eyes immediately to find him smugly watching me.

"If we're going to do this, you have to be quiet. I don't want my mom to hear."

"I feel like I'm some naughty teenager sneaking around."

"Does that turn you on?"

"Not as much as being your good girl who can be as loud as she wants does."

"We'll get back to that. I promise."

I kiss the promise from his lips. "Deal."

The only sounds that fill the garage are our panting gasps for oxygen and the subtle rustle of clothing being pushed aside and zippers gliding down. Dash slides his hands over my entire body, and it's a real struggle not to cry out in delight. I missed this man in so many ways, but the way he loves me, body and soul, tops the list.

He traces my neck down to my shoulder blades and beyond, deftly unhooking my bra so he can enjoy my breasts unimpeded. I'm still wearing my shirt rucked up around my neck, bra trapped inside, easy to drop back down if his mom interrupts. I try to touch him back in all the places he likes—his ears, the crook of his neck, his hip bones—but he keeps me at a distance.

"You first. If you touch me, I'm going to forget about everything but being inside you."

Him getting inside me right the fuck now sounds like a pretty good plan to me, so I fight against his hold to pull him closer, and he tumbles me, pinning me to the couch. His hard cock presses against my leg. I try to open my thigh wider, urging him into the cradle of my hips, but he resists and playfully slaps my ass as he tugs my jeans halfway down my thighs, just low enough to get his hand inside and keep my thighs firmly together.

"My, my, aren't we impatient. You've soaked through your panties, Ms. Maxwell. So eager."

He traces a finger along the elastic of my panties, edging ever closer to the lips they hide, but not quite giving me what I crave. I can't stifle my frustrated moan.

"Tell me. Say it," he whispers. "Tell me what you need."

"I need you. All I ever needed was you."

"Good girl."

He finally pushes my knees up, the scrap of soaked silk to the side, and two thick fingers inside my desperate channel. I cry out with pleasure as he caresses the spot I taught him to find, and then startle to silence as the rev of a car engine in the driveway freezes us both in place. We listen carefully as a vehicle backs out of the drive, and then…silence.

"Is there anyone else in the house?" I ask.

"No," Dash says harshly, resuming his internal

massage and adding his magic fucking thumb to my clit. "Be as loud as you want."

"Fuck, yes!" I yell as I ride his hand, my hips chasing the orgasm only he can provide. "Dash, I need more."

He lifts himself off me and I let him go, letting him lead. He can do whatever he pleases as long as he keeps pleasing me. With his free hand he roughly pulls down my panties and jeans to my ankles before returning his attentions to my G-spot. When he replaces his thumb with his curious tongue, I can only shout my encouragement. Words have deserted me.

The rasp of his tongue over my folds, the suction of his lush lips against my clit, and the insistent coaxing of his fingers inside my tight pussy combine to free my soul from my body in a shattering climax. My body shakes and trembles beneath him, but my mind floats free on the waves of pleasure he's created. Even when he sheds his own pants, dons a condom, and pushes inside me, I can't grasp the words of praise or encouragement. I simply open my arms and legs, welcoming him home.

He pushes my already overloaded body right back up and over my limit, a second orgasm crashing against the receding waves of the first. Helpless, I let the pleasure consume me. Before long he joins me over the edge, his boneless weight pinning me to the couch. We are a tangled mess of limp limbs, half-shed clothing, and heaving lungs.

It seems ridiculous to me, but tears gather at the outer corners of my eyes before spilling back across my temples to disappear in my hairline. I haul in a shaky breath, and Dash raises his head in alarm.

"Hey! Are you okay? Did I hurt you?"

I shake my head no and wrap my arms around him, pulling him back down to my chest and holding on tight. "No. These are tears of relief."

*D*ASH

After we recover and get dressed again, we move the conversation away from the too-tempting couch to the kitchen table. I make coffee, hers with cream and two sugars, and cut up an apple for a hasty snack plate with some cheese sticks and butter crackers to go with her brisket. Panini charcuterie. That would make for a good article, if I still had a job writing articles. While I putter in the kitchen, my mom comes home, and I introduce the two women in my life. Mom seems to take it in stride that I am dating a sex toy designer, and begins putting away the groceries while I sit across the table from Penny.

"So what are you going to do now that you've left the magazine?" Penny asks gently.

I rub my hand over the back of my neck and take another sip of my coffee. "If there's anything I've learned from this whole debacle, it's that I need to be doing something that keeps me interested. So I'll probably keep freelancing and gigging for a while, until I figure out another big project." I shrug, as if it doesn't bother me at all that my career is so unstable, but I can tell Penny isn't buying it.

"Dash, you need to work the way that works best for you. If that means hopping from gig to gig, I think that's great. You know, we've gotten a lot of positive feedback from the community portal you built into our website. I'm sure there are other companies out there who have specific community requirements who could use that kind of expertise. You are smart and curious, and you'll continue to find the things that motivate you to succeed."

"And if I don't succeed? If I'm happy but just getting by?"

"I believe in you, and I trust you to make the career decisions you need to. If you are happy, I am happy."

That's it. That simple statement unlocks a flood of barely contained stress and anxiety that I've been suppressing for months, feeling like I'm not good enough, that I can't compare to her level of success, and therefore she deserves better.

But she believes in me enough to give me the grace and space to figure my shit out.

"That's lucky, because I believe in you too, Madame CEO. I know this company is going to take off like a rocket once the products get into more…hands. I want to support you too."

I reach across the table and cover her hands with mine. Why did we decide sitting far apart was a good idea? I really need to touch her, like right now. My mom closes the fridge door with a snap, and suddenly I remember. This will have to do.

"I had an idea. The new game? I want you to take it and develop it. I think it could be a great tool to sell access to while you're ramping up your 2.0 prototypes. Clients can customize it to each partner's pleasure profile. You could even use it to suggest types of toys they might enjoy as well as giving them a safe space to play out their communication issues."

"We could enroll couples and have them complete detailed surveys, and code avatars for them individually? That would be incredible. One of the things people were asking for were videos to demonstrate techniques and toy usage. Could that be incorporated into the game?" I love that she immediately sees the vision and is excited.

"Absolutely. It's a long way from being ready for public consumption, but there are so many ways we could adapt it to work for your needs."

My mother turns from the counter and crosses to me. "Hold on," she says. "Are you saying you designed a game to help couples learn to talk to each other? This week? Out in my garage?" Mom leans her hip against my shoulder and bends to kiss my head when I nod. "My baby. That's remarkable. I'm so proud of you." Then she turns to Penny. "The door to the garage is thin. Don't toy with my son. He's been hurt too many times before."

"No, ma'am. I intend to love him as best I can."

"Good. If you need more alone time to fix things, just say so and I will go get my hair done."

Eyes wide, I turn back to Penny as my mom leaves the room, marveling under her breath about young love.

"Did...did that just happen or am I hallucinating? And if I dreamt that up, are you a dream too?" I ask, holding back laughter.

Penny chuckles as she sits in my lap and drapes her arms around my shoulders. "If this is a dream, I don't want to wake up."

When her lips connect with mine, the jolt of electricity is undeniable. No, this is very real, and I am very lucky to have a second chance to get it right.

"Mom, you should go get your hair done!"

CHAPTER 30

When I start the video conference call with Dash sitting next to me on camera, we are met with surprised silence. Of course it's Nicola who breaks the ice.

"Oh, thank fuck. Now that you two have kissed and made up, maybe we can get back to normal around here."

I smile and raise my hand to quiet the resulting cheers from my loyal crew. After taking a much needed staycation with Dash to reconnect and work on things, I called for an all-staff meeting on my first day back. The funding deadline is fast approaching, and I need updates.

"Thank you all for joining the call. I know it was last minute that I took time off, but it was necessary." I glance at Dash, seeing my love reflected back at me, feeling grateful for every minute we spent making up. "And appreciated. Let's start with updates. Where are we at?"

Zarah jumps into the fray first. "As of two days ago,

the last of our delayed inventory cleared the ports! We've been able to commit to filling all existing orders."

"I've already received the skids, and am getting things organized as we speak," Mike chimes in.

"That's amazing! How did you manage to get the containers unloaded, Zarah? Weren't we weeks behind?" I ask.

"Well, I took a day, wandered around by the docks, noticed which bar they all went to after their shift, and hung out for a few hours. I let several burly men buy me drinks before I found the one I was after and convinced him to 'accidentally' grab our container so we could unload early." Zarah examines her nails and rubs them against her shirt as if this isn't a big fucking deal.

"You are amazing. I will never underestimate you again."

"See to it, boss lady!" Zarah laughs, her dark curls bouncing. "Jen's got good news too."

"Jen? How is everything at the factory?"

"Things are good. They are starting to reopen the production lines at reduced capacity, but they are open, so we should be able to start getting fresh units made any day now. I've also done some research on starting a second factory line in Europe to diversify our suppliers."

"That's a relief. Do I want to know how many hours you've spent on the phone to China this week?"

"No. No, you do not. But better me than you. You just scare them, and they tell you lies to keep you happy. They still don't know I speak Mandarin and think I'm some lackey, so I get all the dirt when they talk in the background of the call."

"Brilliant. You are simply brilliant," I say before turning my attention to Emmie, who is frowning. "Emmie, how are we doing on design?"

"I'm still frustrated that there isn't enough room for a vibe next to the fingering mechanism, so I've been playing with prototypes for the next version to make more room. Based on feedback from the community portal and surveys, I also want to look at warming features. We should whiteboard together soon."

"It's a date. And Nicola? Where do we stand on funding? I'm sorry I kind of dropped that in your lap this week, but—"

"Don't be sorry. I fixed it."

"What do you mean *you fixed it?*"

"We needed money to float us through the launch. I got it."

My jaw drops. I know I must look like a gasping fish, but I am too surprised to care. "Elaborate. Please."

"Well, the article didn't really do us any favors. Thanks for that, by the way." She directs that jab at Dash, who takes it gracefully and drops his head.

"I'm truly sorry about that. It won't happen again."

"Oh, you could write about us again, just maybe run it by me first? It turns out that being called cowards pissed off a lot of the VC bro-dudes, but Veronica Lim took it as a challenge. She told her team at Greenlight Go to award their next five capital grants to underrepresented entre-preneurs. Starting with us."

"Oh my God! Really? How much?" I am bouncing in my chair.

"Not quite enough. I've got the funding offer right here." Nic taps a few buttons and a file appears in the chat.

I try to suppress a sigh, but it sneaks out anyway. "Damn. I know you did your best. At least it'll buy us a little time to figure out something else."

"I already did!"

I swear to God I'm going to kill her if she doesn't take me out with a heart attack first. I know she set that up on purpose to mess with me. "Wait, what? I swear I have only been gone a week!"

"Yes, but what a week it was. I talked to Hayley Prescott."

"I thought we weren't considering approaching her anymore after her negative review."

"Will you let me finish the story?"

I raise my hands and lean back, gesturing for Nicola to take the floor.

"So, no shit, there I was, scrolling through InstaSnap, when I saw her review. I watched it, and realized from the way she was holding it that she hadn't properly adjusted her MiO. I slid into her DMs and sent her the link to the portal and offered to give her some private coaching, and voila! She's a believer! She's been buzzing about it all week."

I groan at the pun, but inside I feel golden. Each and every member of my team went above and beyond in my absence to solve major problems. I am so freaking proud.

"So do you think she'd be interested in investing if I approached her?" I ask Nic.

"I already talked to her about it, and she is jazzed! We still need to work out the numbers, but between her social media platform and a buy-in for partial ownership, I think we're going to be okay."

I fight the tears of relief that spring to my eyes. CEOs don't cry.

Dash wraps an arm around me and I lose the battle. *Fuck it.* This CEO can cry if she wants to.

"You are all so amazing. I can't believe the way you've all stepped up this week. I am the luckiest CEO in the world to get to work with such talented and loyal people. I appreciate every one of you, but I don't want you to have to keep going above and beyond to make this work. I don't want my friends to burn out. I wasn't going to say anything if we were going under. But since we are funded through at least the end of the year, I want you all to start thinking about hiring some freelancers or contract help for some of our upcoming projects. Make a list of tasks that could be taken off your plate by someone new, especially anything that will tie you up for the busy holiday season."

Emmie snickers and mutes herself.

"We'll get some job postings up. I've invited Dash to join us, in a consulting role, to continue developing the community portal. He's also got a relationship-building game in the works. I think it will help our customers build healthier relationships *and* use our toys better."

"Actually, if we're hiring, there is a young indie

designer just getting started I think you should meet. Izzy Hayes's game inspired me to start the project, and I think she would really thrive here. I'll work on connecting you." Dash says his piece and sits back, giving me the floor.

I turn my attention back to my screen team. "So? What's next?"

They groan and fall out of their chairs, laughing and chasing away any lingering doubts. Will the next six months be perfect? No. But it doesn't have to be. It will be enough. And we will keep going, making products to help people connect with their bodies and each other.

I don't have to be perfect either. I took some time to relax with Dash, and my team rose to the challenge. I'm not a failure for resting. I'm not weak because I loosened my grip. I am still too controlling, but I'm working on it.

I am human, and that's divine.

DASH

Penny sits hunched over her computer, refreshing the browser and muttering. It has been six months since I moved back in, but she still has a tendency to get lost in her work. The new European production line is set to start running in Slovakia tonight, and she's watching for updates like a kid watching baby chicks hatch. I set the order of ramen on the counter, and with one gentle finger I slowly lower the screen of her laptop.

When she finally looks up at me, she's got a thousand-mile stare going.

"Take a break, babe. A watched pot and all that. Time to come up for sustenance. It's our prep night."

I make sure she eats some of her favorite ramen, and turn her phone to silent. I keep the conversation to the mundane to let her mind rest. I figure I have about half an hour before she succumbs to the pressure to check again, and I don't want to play my trump card yet.

"So, can we go through the schedule for the week?"

Ever since our reconciliation, we have been more deliberate about planning the times I need to do things and adding reminders to my phone. It's a system that works for hitting deadlines, but using it for chores is new. More importantly, it's the plan Penny and I settled on together to take the onus of persistent emotional labor off her and keep things balanced. Sitting down to fill out the schedule every week gives her a chance to talk about her needs, and me a chance to voice concerns. And we both put reminders in place to help us achieve our goals.

Am I perfect? No. But I am enough. Just as I am.

"This week we agreed to switch, so you've got dishes and I've got laundry, since I'll have late meetings all week. Do you have any dinner plans?"

"I've still got some free meal kits I could order in. Maybe we could look at them together this time, so I don't assault your taste buds?"

That earns me a laugh. I'll take it.

"Sounds good. Are there any motivational sound bites you need me to record?"

In the beginning of this experiment, I had asked her to record herself saying *Come on, Dash!* so I could program it to play as the alarm sound for my chores. That way she didn't have to be the one reminding me, but I'd still get the dopamine hit of her voice. Something about the way she says my name cuts through any other distractions. Now it's a running joke, and I ask her to record outlandish things.

"Could you record one that says, 'Wash the dishes, and I'll give you a blow job'?"

She laughs again and tosses a soy sauce packet at me. "Dash, stop it."

"No, that's counterproductive. But what about, 'Oh baby, just like that,' in that voice you use when I have my tongue on your clit."

She sets down her chopsticks, fully intrigued now.

I scoot my chair closer to whisper in her ear. "I still think you should let me record one for you that says, 'Good girl.'"

"I'd never get any work done."

"Or how about one that says, 'I love you and you don't have to be perfect to earn that.'"

When I pull back to look at her face, she has her eyes closed and her lips pursed. I might've pushed too far, and I try to scramble back into levity. But before I can find the words, she climbs into my lap, straddling my chair, and wraps her arms around my neck, hugging me tight. I hold her to my chest as quiet tears dampen my T-shirt.

"Thank you," she murmurs eventually. "I needed to hear that. Neither one of us is perfect, but we are enough in all the right ways. Thank you for giving me a second chance."

"Thank you for giving me that first chance. Who knew catching a vibe in a bar in Las Vegas would change my life?"

"Speaking of that first chance, I've got an idea for something to take my mind off work."

"Oh yeah?"

"Yeah. How's your thumb feeling after a full day of gaming?"

"Like that was a warm-up for the championship game. Put me in, Coach! I'm ready to play."

"Oh, I'll put you in," she teases as I rise to the task and from the chair, carrying her toward our bedroom.

This hasn't wavered. The sexual chemistry that drew us together hasn't lessened with repetition or familiarity, but rather the intimacy of the act continues to deepen each time we come together. Her inventions might bring her the pleasure of physical release, and I like it when we play. But I am the one holding her heart, and usually the toy, in the aftermath. It's a joy to know this creative and adventurous woman wants me as much as I want her. And if I can give her the release from anxiety she needs tonight, my thumbs, fingers, lips, and cock are at her service.

"Promises, promises," I tease back as I toss her on our bed.

CHAPTER 31

KEEP READING! CAUGHT A VIBE EPILOGUE

DASH

"Are you ready for this?" Penny asks as I straighten my collar and smooth back my curls.

Nerves are making me jittery, and I flex my hands open and closed several times to force out the tingles. *I can do this. Penny is counting on me.*

"Yes. I'm ready." I pick up the MiO 2.0 and step out from behind the curtain of the show booth, anxious but prepared to present her latest invention and unveil my game that links to it.

I really don't like being on this side of the table. The days when I wrote freelance articles and picked up hot chicks in bars in Las Vegas are looking real good right about now. Yes, it only happened that one time, but it felt a hell of a lot better than this. I'm used to asking the questions, not answering them.

I glance at Penny, marveling at how she went from

hot chick to love of my life, and how much farther we've gone together. I'm a lucky man indeed, and if I make it through this interminable day alive, maybe she'll let me pick her up in a bar again.

The first reporter approaches and immediately makes eye contact with me, not any of the three other people running the MiO booth at T-Con this year, who happen to be women. It's been two years since I blew open the controversy around the MiO, and the conference has only just come back in person after two years virtual.

"So, this is the famous sex toy, huh? Is it as good as they say?" the man asks with no introduction or manners. He deserves absolutely everything I'm about to unleash. Hearing Penny and Nic recount their most terrible encounters from the last con make me deter-mined to give as good as I get.

I lean in and with a conspiratorial whisper and say, "It's better."

"I don't get why it's so revolutionary. An orgasm is an orgasm. I mean, it's not natural. Woman shouldn't be getting off without a man. This is just a cheap substitute. Why are you promoting that?"

Penny snort laughs behind me, but I keep a straight face. These are the kinds of rude questions they face all day long at these events. I'm ready to do my part.

"First of all, I wouldn't call this cheap. It's an advanced piece of robotics engineering and worth every penny. It has twice as many moving parts as the average vibrator. Secondly, do some single women rely on these devices? Sure, but married couples enjoy them too. MiO gives women a tool to better understand their bodies and their pleasure responses. And if 'an orgasm is an orgasm' to you, you're part of the problem. When is the last time you thought about a new way to make your partner feel good? Are you experimenting? Is sex fun?"

The poor reporter in front me of glows redder and redder with embarrassment as I turn the obnoxious questions back on him. He splutters as he tries to formulate his rebuttal. I save him the trouble.

"Here is our latest innovation. We've developed a two-player game that allows couples to input a long list of personal characteristics to create a pleasure profile. Playing the game together creates a fun shared experience for learning about each other and makes playtime afterward better for you both. We're hoping to expand to three- and four-player versions in the next six months. Can I give you a brochure?"

I tuck the folded pamphlet into the reporter's hand.

"Feel free to give me a call if you have any questions. Bye now!"

As the man walks away, still reeling, a bevy of laughter floats over my shoulder.

"Did you see his face?" Nic cackles.

"An orgasm is an orgasm. This is what we're fighting, people. Take note!" Izzy Hayes says with vigor.

Hiring her onto the team to take over game development was stroke of genius. This game needed male and female perspectives to make it work, and she is brilliant. She took my prototype and turned it into a fully realized game in the space of a year and half, which freed me up to do the freelance work I'm drawn to. I am no longer an official employee of Penny's company, but I'm happy to keep a finger in. Even if that means getting tapped for trade shows to be the male shill. I'll do anything for the woman I love.

"My hero." Penny bumps her shoulder against mine and I grin. Speak of the devil.

"Was I that bad?"

She's got a mischievous glint in her eye as she replies. "No. You took the blindside hit and managed to follow up with coherent, non-insulting questions, proving once again I was right to take a chance on you at the bar."

"That is a really low bar."

"You were the only one to clear it that day. And many days since."

"Thank God I did."

I brush her fake red bangs back from her forehead to press a short kiss to her temple, and try to contain myself. I'd gotten a wild idea as we'd planned for this conference, and I am dying to act on it. But I have to get the timing just right so I don't spoil the surprise.

"Back to work, you." She elbows me playfully, but the joy in her eyes doesn't fade.

I put that there, and I'm going to do my damnedest to keep it there forever if she'll let me.

Download the rest of Penny and Dash's epilogue here: https://dl.bookfunnel.com/bwfuulyfnn

CHAPTER 32

OPENED UP

Have you read the Exposed Dreams Series yet? Start here with Opened Up.

If one more thing hits my desk today, I'm going to snap.

Sofia Valenti cradled her aching head in her hands and questioned the wisdom of working with family once again. Joining Valenti Brothers Construction had always been her dream. But since Gabe's death, that dream had become a nightmare.

She pushed aside the stack of time cards she needed to process for payroll to give the contracts her cousin Seth had dropped off a first read-through. Dropping her cheater glasses down from their perch atop her head, she squinted at the fine print. Seth and his best friend, Nick Gantry, were incorporating their custom woodworking business into the larger family firm, and the details of the deal fell, as usual, onto Sofia's desk. The thought of woodworking drew her mind to the purchase order for cabinets that had landed on her desk late in the day. Needing to get that done so it could be filled first thing, she pulled it from the stack and laid it on top of the thick folder of legalese. The contract could wait.

Perfect. The order form was only half filled out. She clicked her computer screen awake and opened the supplier's website, while she let a soothing stream of curse words flow through her mind. Now she'd waste precious minutes looking up part numbers that damn well should have been filled in.

This was not how she envisioned using her double degrees in Business Administration and Interior Design. Her thoughts drifted to the naïve but tempting dream she'd shoved into the back of her mind the day after Gabe died: the pretty, airy design studio, a waitlist of clients eager for her services, her father's respect. All of these goals had taken a back seat when her mother had lost her eldest son and fallen apart. She carefully tucked the dream away and turned her mind back to the pain-in-the-ass order.

Someone had needed to step in and keep the place running while her parents had dealt with their grief. Bills and contractors needed to be paid, and she'd needed a temporary job while she got her design business up and running. That had been three years ago. Truth be told, the mind-numbing work had gotten her through the worst of her grief after Gabe died, but now she needed more.

Basic cabinet package, bulk drawer pulls, the same

retractable faucet kit they put in every house. The list never varied much. Valenti Brothers stood for good work at affordable prices, and their orders reflected that ethos. Though it hurt her creative soul, at least the part numbers were easy to find bookmarked on the site. With a few clicks, the order was entered, approved, and in queue for payment. If she was going to be stuck doing the office work, at least she could do it well.

As her mother and father, Josephine and Domenico Valenti, argued over how to pull back from the company and retire, the bulk of the day-to-day responsibilities fell on Sofia's shoulders. It had been months since she'd played with a design. No one even knew that she was available for design consults, because Dad never told anyone. Frustration weighed heavily on her mind as she tucked the PO into the appropriate file and pulled the contract back in front of her.

The legalese began to blur, and her glasses fogged over. She pushed the glasses back into her hair and blinked away the tears. God, she needed a break. A week at the beach would do. Hell, even a weekend over in Monterey would work. The soothing waves and brisk sea air would clear out the cobwebs in her mind. Since that wouldn't be happening any time soon, she hauled in a deep breath and reached into her emergency drawer. Her stash of snack-sized candy bars was flush, and she chose one with care. Almond Joy. She could certainly use a little joy today. She unwrapped the candy and popped the whole thing in her mouth.

She wouldn't mind a little action involving nuts

either, but she'd have to get out of the office regularly for that to happen. What had seemed like a temporary drought of male interest was turning into full-on climate change. The Almond Joy disappeared before she had a chance to taste it, so she reached for a mini 100 Grand. This time she focused on the chocolaty, sugary goodness filling her mouth and soothing her scrambling mind.

A hundred grand would certainly be nice right about now. If she had some reserves, she could finally get out from under her father's thumb. When she'd started, having everything wrapped up with a neat little bow had seemed ideal. The plan was simple: work for the family business, live in a family property rent-free, pull a small salary to cover expenses but not drain their coffers, with the understanding that someday she'd have equity in the firm and would make commissions from her design work. Now that little bow was pulling tighter around her neck every day, and her father didn't understand that she was suffocating.

If she was ever going to make a name for herself, she needed capital to invest and time to design. Right now, her bank account was crying by the end of the month. As long as she was stuck at this desk, trudging through paperwork and indulging in pity parties, her account was going to keep weeping.

Enough. She slid the drawer closed and double-checked her planner. Two more hours before she could knock off for the family meeting her dad and Zio Tony had called. At least she knew she wouldn't have to rely on her freezer for dinner. Family meetings always took place around her mother's table, laden with food. She put her head down to focus on her remaining tasks, despite the images of her mom's lasagna triggering her salivary glands and tempting her to open the drawer just one more time.

Giving up on the contract until her brain was fresh, she rearranged her desk for the eighteenth time and began the rote task of entering payroll. In all her years of being the older sister, she had learned that she needed to leave on time. Enzo and Frankie would inhale more than their fair share if she was late. After the day she'd had, that was *not* happening.

Adrian Villanueva heard the muttered curses as he pushed open Sofia's office door. That didn't bode well for his request, but he didn't have a choice. The tile that had arrived at the Chu project wasn't right, and he needed Sofia to call the supplier and sort it out before the warehouse closed for the weekend. He couldn't fall behind on that job, or it'd set off a chain reaction of delays and angry customers as his other sites suffered. He protected the Valenti Brothers' reputation as if he'd earned it himself.

Taking his life in his hands, he strode up to the prickly office manager's desk with a grin on his face. It wasn't a hardship to smile at Sofia Valenti. For years, he'd had to remind himself that, no matter how touchable her soft blonde waves looked or how her blue eyes twinkled at his jokes, she was off-limits. When he'd started working for her father as a teenage dropout, she'd been a sixteen-year-old stunner, and she'd only improved with age. Despite the fact that she was now old enough to choose her own partners, she was still the boss's daughter. He wouldn't do anything to jeopardize his relationship with Dom Valenti, certainly not while he worked up the courage to ask for the keys to his future. But in this case, his smile was wasted. She hadn't even looked up. He tried a different tactic in his charm offensive.

"Hello, beautiful."

"Ugh." She rolled her eyes, her manic fingers still flying across her number pad. The stack of time cards rapidly moved from one pile to another, her rhythm unbroken.

"I need your help."

"Get in line." He knew the snark was meant to be sarcastic. That was the usual tone she took with him, but the furrow between her brows looked like it was carved in granite. He wanted to smooth it away with his thumb, but he had a firm no-touching rule. The last thing he needed was to lose his precious restraint around her, and giving in to his impulse would trigger exactly that.

Focus on the problem. Get in, get out.

"The tiles on the Chu project are wrong. I need you to straighten it out with the supplier."

She closed her eyes and let out an ear-piercing scream. It surprised him into stepping back.

"What was that for?"

"Long story." She finally looked up, her slate-blue eyes

brimming with anger and frustration. *Damn.* Nothing in his arsenal was going to smooth over whatever else was making her scream. His best option now was to muscle through the details and get out of her way.

"Here's the original order form and the packing slip. It looks like they switched the final numbers. We need to catch them before they leave, or we lose three days on this project, and I'll have to pull crews from scheduled work at other houses to finish."

"You've got to be kidding me! I need to be out the door in half an hour. I'm not a miracle worker."

"Could have fooled me."

"Yeah, yeah. Flattery will get you nowhere. Give me that." She snatched the paperwork from his hand and grimaced.

"So, got a hot date?"

Her head snapped up, eyes wide with surprise and...offense?

"Excuse me?"

"You said you had to leave. It's Friday night..."

"Screw you. When's the last time you saw me leave this office before eight p.m.?" She gestured to her small room, walls covered in mismatched sample cabinets and drawer pulls for the clients to see, and desk layered in papers.

"Just trying to make conversation. So why do you have to leave, then? It's well before eight, as you say."

"Dad called a family meeting. He's got something he wants to talk to us about."

Jealousy clenched briefly, even as he clenched his own

fist in response. It was always this way. Family first. He'd started working for Valenti Brothers in high school as a general laborer. After his father had been deported, he'd been forced to become the man of the house far sooner than intended, working any and all hours to keep his mother and sisters safe and sound.

Over the last twelve years, he'd worked his way up, learning, apprenticing, proving his worth. He now led his own construction team, with Dom and Frankie leading the other two since Tony had officially retired last month. He'd always expected to work alongside the old man until Gabe had finished college and was ready to step in. But Gabe had chosen a different path, one that led him to the army and Iraq. One that hadn't led him back home.

He could see the opportunities, his own potential to fill that role. He wanted it so bad he could taste it: the stability, the power over his destiny, the sense of finally belonging. But as long as business was decided over family dinners, he was stuck, always on the outside looking in. He needed to get his ass in gear and ask Dom the question he'd been choking on for months. As casually as he could, taking care to bury his frustrations deep, he asked, "Oh, yeah? Any idea what about?"

She raced a highlighter across the invoice and reached for her phone, already tackling his problem.

"None. And if you don't get out of here, I'll never finish so I can find out. Shoo! Hello? Yes, can I speak to Javier? Thank you."

She continued entering numbers while she calmly

reamed Javier a new one and wrangled a guarantee that the tiles would be delivered to the site by Saturday at ten a.m., no extra charge. He had no idea how she juggled it all, but better her than him. He backed out the door, wondering why that prim tone of voice turned him inside out.

~

Phone call done, payroll half entered, contracts still waiting, Sofia lowered her swirling head to her desk. *What nerve that guy has!* Calling her beautiful, asking if she had a date... She knew she wasn't beautiful, not by a long shot, but she didn't need to be teased about it at work. Once upon a time she'd dreamed she was a lovely princess in a beautiful castle just waiting for Prince Charming. But little girls' dreams often fade in the face of cold, hard reality, and hers was no different. Now, she was an overweight, underappreciated servant approaching thirty, trapped in a mismatched dungeon, and no one was coming to save her.

She hated that in spite of Adrian's insulting endearments and rude questions, the man still had the power to awaken the yearnings she kept carefully suppressed. There was no use getting turned on if there was no one to enjoy it with, so she tried to avoid it at all costs. But there was something about him...

His dark, chocolate brown hair, his peanut-butter-colored eyes, the perfect combination of sweet and nutty... She reached back into her drawer and pulled out the big guns, a double pack of Reese's cups. She slowly chewed the sugary treat and pretended that it filled the aching hole in her chest.

She'd watched him during her shy teen years, afraid to approach the boy who was already a man. He'd intimidated the hell out of her with his confident, cocky air. When she'd come back to the company after a few years of experience in college, she'd been ready to pursue the strong tug of attraction, but every minor advance crumbled against the firm wall of physical distance and relentless teasing he kept between them. If he'd pushed her away when she'd been young and beautiful, she could only imagine he'd run screaming if she approached him now. She'd packed on weight in the months following the funeral, and her sedentary job and borderline depression were keeping it there. She'd let herself go, and now she could barely find herself in the reflection in the mirror. She didn't have a chance in hell with a guy like him, so she did her best to keep her inappropriate longings well contained. Humor and sarcasm were her defensive weapons of choice.

She had to laugh or she'd cry. Adrian was a trusted employee and a minor jerk, no matter how attractive she found him. She could handle him and this pesky response he provoked. He probably had no idea that his words had wounded. Most men didn't. It likely didn't occur to him that words like "beautiful" or "gorgeous" *could* hurt. He would never imagine that his casual conversation rang like a condemnation in her mind. He had no clue, and that was why he could never know that his broad shoulders and strong arms made inner Sofia weak in the knees.

He would never know because she'd die sitting behind this desk, all alone. She was well and truly stuck. The futility of her situation weighed on her heart. It wasn't fair. This wasn't how her life was supposed to go. The anger she tried hard to keep hidden from the rest of the family flared hot in her chest, lashing out at the one person who couldn't defend himself.

Damn it, Gabe. Why did you have to go and change every-thing? I want the life we had planned. I wish you were here.

But wishing would not make it so.

She shut the chocolate drawer firmly on her feelings and grabbed her purse. Time to see what Dad was up to.

Read the rest of Sofia and Adrian's story here: Opened Up

ACKNOWLEDGMENTS

This book is the product of so many incredible minds lending me their strength and knowledge. Lora DiCarlo, designer of the revolutionary Osé, gave me incredible access to her and her team so I could understand the nuances of running a start-up through a pandemic. Anthony La Santa, Briony Deege, Dror Kogot, Mazie Star, and Mark Hazelton, thank you for helping me flesh out this world. If you are interested in learning more about the inspiration for the MiO, here you go: LORA DICARLO

Benjamin Luff, thank you for staying up until god knows what hour your time to give me a glimpse into the life of video game designers. Your notes were invaluable.

Stacey Hamel, Shannon Donahue, and Katie Skye thank you for the beta reads that helped me hone my ADHD rep and characterizations. I know ADHD presents on a spectrum and not everyone experiences the same challenges, so your eyes on the nuance was greatly appreciated.

As usual, many thanks to Jennifer Graybeal and Julia Ganis who helped me turn around edits on this beast on a ridiculously tight turn around.

Any remaining errors or inaccuracies are certainly my own because I couldn't stop tweaking.

Wicked Wallflowers, your Saturday night calls are directly responsible for my sanity and the naughtiest chapters in this book. #LateNightWritersClub on TikTok, because you continue to show up for your dreams, you got my butt in the chair for my own. I couldn't have written this without you. Any writers out there are welcome to join us. Check my website for the schedule and Discord link. Friends For Eva members, your cheerleading has been unparalleled. Thank you all!

I need to thank my parents for welcoming my children with open arms when I shoved them through the front door and bolted. Without Camp Nana & Daddad, I would never have made it through editing 100,000 words in a week. Also, many thanks to my Aunt Sue for letting me hide in her basement so I could focus. And to my three girls for getting it when Mommy says, "I'm going out to work now," so I could hit my deadlines and we could enjoy the adventures this summer together uninterrupted.

To my husband, who has supported this dream from the start and who fuels my belief in true love on the daily. I couldn't write these books without the hero in my life.

And a massive thank you to YOU, dear reader, who took a chance on an indie author hustling after a dream. I hope you caught a vibe with Penny and Dash and will come back for the rest of the Quarantimes Crew. Look for Emmie's story, Electric Love, next!

ABOUT THE AUTHOR

Eva Moore writes sexy contemporary romances featuring compelling characters finding love in the modern world. Pulling up her Chicagoland roots, she has chased adventures around the globe, with stints in France and Singapore. Eva now lives in California (at the wine end, not the movie end) with her college sweetheart and three gorgeous kiddos. She loves hearing from the outside world while she's hiding in her she-shed. Please visit her at www.4evamoore.com.

www.ingramcontent.com/pod-product-compliance
Lightning Source LLC
Chambersburg PA
CBHW030356200726
48286CB00014B/1461